Please feel free to send me an email. Just know that my publisher filters these emails. Good news is always welcome.

Ashley Winters – ashley_winters@awesomeauthors.org

Sign up for my blog for updates and freebies!
ashley-winters.awesomeauthors.org

Copyright © 2016 by Ashley Winters

All Rights reserved under International and Pan-American Copyright Conventions. By payment of required fees you have been granted the non-exclusive, non-transferable right to access and read the text of this book. No part of this text may be reproduced, transmitted, downloaded, decompiled, reverse-engineered or stored in or introduced into any information storage and retrieval system, in any form or by any means, whether electronic or mechanical, now known, hereinafter invented, without express written permission of BLVNP Inc. For more information contact BLVNP Inc. The publisher does not have any control over and does not assume any responsibility for author or third-party websites or their content. This book is a work of fiction. The characters, incidents and dialogue are drawn from the author's imagination and are not to be construed as real. While reference might be made to actual historical events or existing locations, the names, characters, places and incidents are either products of the author's imagination or are used fictitiously, and any resemblance to actual persons living or dead, business establishments, events or locales is entirely coincidental.

About the Publisher

BLVNP Incorporated, A Nevada Corporation, 340 S. Lemon #6200, Walnut CA 91789, info@blvnp.com / legal@blvnp.com

DISCLAIMER

This book is a work of FICTION. It is fiction and not to be confused with reality. Neither the author nor the publisher or its associates assume any responsibility for any loss, injury, death or legal consequences resulting from acting on the contents in this book. The author's opinions are not to be construed as the opinions of the publisher. The material in this book is for entertainment purposes ONLY. Enjoy.

Praise for Faking Delinquency

Faking Delinquency is definitely a breath of fresh air. From the basic plot line it seems like this book should be bogged down with the cliché. But Ashley writes in such an original and graceful way that the entire story reads like something new. The characters are fantastic, you can't help but be attached to them, and by the time camp is over you're desperate to still continue with them on further journeys.
-Ashley, Goodreads

Cliché story indeed! Good girl falls for bad guy. But Miss Goody pretending as delinquent and pull up some serious prank like bald a girl is makes this book to fun for read! Will and Falice are adorable with their pinky promises! And not to mention Ty who can perfectly suit as Louis.T. He is something else :)
- Vinodini Subaramaniam, Goodreads

I LOVE THIS BOOK SOOOOO MUCH!!!!! I have read this book at least 20 times. I hated waiting for the updates on wattpad. Congrats Ashley! I love you and you such an amazing writer :) I'm so happy for you that you are getting this book published you have no idea.
-Rumsha, Goodreads

Faking Delinquency is one of the best books I've ever read! The way Ashley portrays the characters sucks you right into the plot, making you feel as though you are attending Camp Sunshine Brooks right along with them. I have read and reread it at least five times and still can't get enough!
-Kristin, Amazon

Amazing first read this book when it was still on wattpad, and I had to retead it. This version is amazing, still got the feels wven after havung read it before. So READ IT, and get ready to fall in love with the characters and their stories.
-Victoria Faria, Amazon

Faking Delinquency

By: Ashley Winters

ISBN: 978-1-68030-841-9
©Ashley Winters 2016

Table of Contents

PHASE 1 1
PHASE 2 18
PHASE 3 32
PHASE 4 44
PHASE 5 51
PHASE 6 61
PHASE 7 74
PHASE 8 83
PHASE 9 93
PHASE 10 99
PHASE 11 112
PHASE 12 125
PHASE 13 135
PHASE 14 148
PHASE 15 163
PHASE 16 178
PHASE 17 187
PHASE 18 206
PHASE 19 225
PHASE 20 239
PHASE 21 249
PHASE 22 258
PHASE 23 269
PHASE 24 281

PHASE 25	*292*
PHASE 26	*301*
PHASE 27	*325*
PHASE 28	*341*
PHASE 29	*350*
PHASE 30	*359*
PHASE 31	*369*
Mission Accomplished	*385*
TWO YEARS LATER	***405***

*To Valarie,
an amazing friend and writer buddy, who has
claimed Will Dyer as her own*

FREE DOWNLOAD

Get these freebies and MORE when you sign up for the author's mailing list!

ashley-winters.awesomeauthors.org

PHASE 1

"Falice, can you do me a huge favor?"

My eyes didn't stray from *Cinder* as I held up my pointer finger, signaling to Caroline that her huge favor would have to wait until I finished the page I was on. Of course, I'd probably end up reading more than the rest of this page before looking up. I couldn't help it— it was *Cinder*. And besides, it wasn't my fault that Marissa Meyer made Prince Kai a ridiculously perfect character.

He was officially one of my book boyfriends.

Three pages later, I finally dragged my eyes away from the book to look at Caroline, who was wearing an amused smile as she sat across from me at our lunch table.

"Yes?" I asked as Caroline brought a hand through her curly blonde hair. She had it down this morning, but during second block, she pulled it into a messy bun, the humidity becoming too much for her. I couldn't say I blamed her. I, for one, seriously regretted throwing on a spaghetti-strap tank top this morning. The tank top would have been great if it didn't mean I had to wear a sweatshirt all day. Stupid two-fingers-to-a-strap rule. Having my wavy, brunette hair pulled back in a French braid kind of helped, but not really.

"Okay, let me just begin by telling you that I would never take you away from your reading unless it was important," Caroline said, giving me one of her teasing looks that was meant to be innocent but never really turned out that way. "This is, like, life or death. It is!" she added when she caught my expression.

I snorted. "Yeah, okay, sure it is. What's the favor then? And whose life am I saving?"

"You'll be saving... this drawing's life," Caroline said with a laugh as she held up her sketchpad for me to see. "Please tell me if this poor girl's arms are different in size."

"I don't see how having uneven arms is going to kill the girl," I replied. "I was told this was life or death, Caroline Baker. I'm feeling pretty cheated right now, like my opportunity to be the next Thor has been stolen from me."

"Um, hate to break it to you, but no one can replace Thor."

Fair point. Also, I would just like to take a moment to point out that Thor was also a fictional boyfriend of mine. I was a real player, fictionally speaking. "Yeah, but still," I whined.

"Whatever." Caroline rolled her eyes. "Just tell me if they're symmetrical."

I sighed, acting as though she was being a pain, but ended up grinning instead. *Whoops.* "Fine," I said, turning my attention to her drawing and giving it a closer look. So far, she had sketched the outline of a girl's body onto the page. "They look fine to me," I told her after a moment of glancing between the two arms, as though I could actually tell if there was a difference between them. "You, my friend, are too much of a perfectionist for your own good."

Caroline flipped the drawing toward her, seemingly scrutinizing it. "You're sure?" she asked.

"Of course, I'm sure." *Totally.*

"I agree with Falice," said someone from behind me. "Even though I have no idea what you guys are talking about."

I twisted around in my seat to greet Beth Robbins, my other best friend and partner in non-existent crime, as she stood before me with one of the cafeteria trays in her hands. She, like Caroline and I, had her hair tied back. However, her raven hair wasn't long enough to tie back into a bun or braid, so instead, it was in a tiny ponytail. "Thank you, Beth!" I turned back around and shot Caroline a triumphant look. "See, Beth agrees with me."

"Beth always agrees with you," Caroline said with a dismissive wave of the hand.

"That's because Falice is always right," Beth retorted as she slid into her designated seat at our lunch table.

I laughed. "Yeah, Care. *Duh.*"

When Caroline just snorted and went back to staring at her drawing, I added, "Stop worrying, Betty Crocker! The arms are perfectly symmetrical."

"That's what you're worried about?" Beth demanded. "Wait, why am I even surprised? This is Caroline we're talking about."

"Hey!" Caroline exclaimed, shooting Beth a half-joking exasperated look. "I just want to make sure the drawing is coming out the way it's supposed to."

"I don't see what the big deal is," Beth said, taking a scoop of her chocolate pudding and plopping it into her mouth.

She swallowed before continuing. "So what if the arms might not be symmetrical? If they look basically the same then…"

Caroline's eyes widened in horror. "So you're saying there's a possibility they aren't?" She held out her sketchpad for us to see. "Guys, seriously, are they symmetrical or not?"

I tossed Beth a pointed look. "Now look what you did," I said, fighting back a smile.

Beth snorted. "Whoops."

Caroline started to say something about how we were no help at all, but a sudden commotion cut her off before she could finish her sentence. My eyebrows rose as I shifted in my seat, turning to where the noise was coming from. While it could get pretty loud in Gardner High's cafeteria— especially when there was only about a week left of school, not including finals— it didn't usually get this loud.

"Isn't that Arabelle's table?" Caroline asked.

I could barely bring myself to nod as I stared down the steadily growing crowd of students that was beginning to surround a table— my sister's table, to be more precise— with their eyes seemingly glued on two girls as they shrieked and threw their fists at each other. Neither of the girls were facing me, and there were a bunch of people blocking my view so I couldn't see very much. I could tell, however, that one of the girls had brunette hair tied back in a not-so-messy messy bun, and the other had straight black hair that fell beyond her shoulders. Despite everything, my first thought was: *How can she have her hair down on a hot day like this?*

My eyebrows creased as the two lunch monitors struggled to wedge themselves between the curious teens, each of them getting jostled as they did so. I winced when one of the teachers got elbowed in the stomach. "Ouch," I muttered.

"That has gotta hurt," Beth said, finishing off my final thought. "Animals," Caroline fumed. I could just imagine her shaking her head, her blue eyes (that I was jealous of) narrowed in disappointment. "Seriously, what is wrong with people?"

"Maybe it's a riot about the cafeteria's food," Beth suggested, despite the fact that it was pretty obvious that only two girls were involved, and they were beating each other up in the middle of the cafeteria for who knew what reason. However, if the girls were who I thought they were, then I had a good idea.

I spared a fraction of a second to glance back at my friend and let out a spasm of a laugh. "The food here is good though," I said, my eyes straying back to the girls fighting and the students clustered around them.

"That is true," Beth said.

"Why am I not surprised you agree with her?" I laughed as I heard a slap and Caroline yelp.

The lunch monitors reached the middle of the crowd and tugged the girls apart. They struggled against the teachers momentarily before standing still, deciding to continue their fight with their eyes. I let out a long sigh as the monitors began to move them out of the throng of students. It was when they emerged from the crowd that my suspicions were confirmed. "Come on, Belle," I muttered.

As though she heard me, Arabelle glanced up, her brown eyes meeting my own from across the cafeteria. Was that a small smile showing on her face? It was. And just like that, I almost had to fight down a laugh. Of course, she'd be smiling at a time like this. I mean, of course, she would. She'd given the other girl, Sadie, a bloody nose. And to top it all off, some of Sadie's hair had blood in it, too. Arabelle was probably extremely proud of the fact that Sadie's face was contorted into a glower as she spewed angry words that were too low for me to hear.

A short moment later, Arabelle and Sadie were led out of the cafeteria and everyone went back to their normal lives. I believed a good chunk of the kids in the cafeteria should consider themselves lucky, seeing how people who stood up and encouraged this kind of behavior usually found themselves with a detention slip. But I had a feeling these lunch monitors had no interest in filling out that many slips right before summer vacation. I sure wouldn't if I were them.

When Arabelle and Sadie disappeared from sight, I nibbled on my lip, picked up *Cinder* again, and decided to pretend that my friends weren't staring at me and things hadn't just gotten really awkward, really fast.

"Falice…"

I looked up at Caroline. "Yeah, Betty Crocker?"

Caroline smiled, and I almost let out a sigh of relief. That smile made it clear she had no interest in forcing me to talk about what just happened. "Seeing how you're always right, can you please double check the arms?"

Before Caroline could turn her drawing toward me, Beth pulled it from her grasp, brown eyes narrowed with what I could tell was feigned concentration. "Hmm, you know," she said, "the left arm actually looks a little bigger than the right one."

Caroline gasped and ripped the sketchpad out of Beth's hands. "What?!" she exclaimed.

Beth burst into a fit of giggles. "I was kidding," she assured her. "Care, they're even, okay? If you want a professional opinion, why don't you go ask the art teacher?"

"The art teacher grades almost completely on participation, and never actually tells you when you've completely screwed up!" Caroline grimaced. "Guys, this isn't funny," she added when I couldn't help but join in on the laughter.

"The art teacher never tells you when you've screwed up because you don't suck at art," Beth pointed out, and I nodded in agreement. "I, for one, have been told many times how many lines I need to fix and how crappy I am at shading."

"Art is the place where your ego goes to die," I said with a grin.

Caroline didn't seem convinced, and a moment later she erased both of the arms. "I'm just going to start over," she muttered.

I glared playfully at Beth. "Look what you did," I said. Beth grinned. "Whoops."

"Dad's going to kill you."

Arabelle, who didn't seem as concerned about her impending death as she should have been, snorted. "He's not going to kill me," she said, picking at the strap of her black Racerback tank top. She, unlike me, had actually worn a tank top that followed the dress code. Oh, the irony. "Maim, maybe, but not kill. I suspect that after he screams me right into oblivion, he won't have enough energy to commit a felony."

I rolled my eyes, shifting my backpack on my shoulder and my sweatshirt in my arms. I could not put into words how freaking happy I was to take off the sweatshirt when the day ended. If I had it on much longer, I would have overheated. Let's just say that too much heat and I didn't mix very well.

"Yeah, okay," I replied. "And why did you come pick me up anyway? I thought you'd be spending your suspension playing *Mortal Kombat*."

Yup, Arabelle landed herself a three-day suspension. Our dad, who was on his lunch break at the time the fight went down, was forced to leave work and pick her up from school. He was apparently pretty pissed, and had promised to deal with her later before slamming the door behind him and heading back to the office. I couldn't say I was surprised. This was the last suspension before an expulsion.

"Because I missed your gorgeous face obviously," Arabelle said with a mischievous smile.

"Then look in the mirror," I retorted.

Arabelle nudged me playfully. "That's not the same and you know it."

That was true. Despite the fact we were identical, Arabelle and I never looked at ourselves that way. To us, we looked completely different. Maybe it was the way we did our hair differently or the fact that our facial expressions were entirely our own— I didn't know. I just knew that whenever I looked at Arabelle, I never felt like I was looking at someone who shared my face.

"Uh-huh," I said. "Now tell me why you decided to leave the house, walk all the way to the bus stop, and pick me up."

"Okay, so along with the whole missing-your-gorgeous-face thing— which is totally true, by the way— I also decided to get out of the house before I, you know, accidentally broke the TV by chucking the remote controller at it." Arabelle grinned. "You know, because I feel like if Dad came home to find a broken TV, he really would find the energy to kill me. And I don't really feel like dying today. It's been a good day. I mean, I got to break Sadie Valle's nose."

"Good call." I paused. "Wait, you didn't tell me you broke her nose!"

"Okay, so I might have exaggerated a bit there," Arabelle confessed with a shrug. "But whatever. I should have broken her nose. That little— *jerk*," she quickly amended as a mother pushing a stroller rounded the corner, "deserved it. She threatened my loved one's honor, so obviously I had to set her straight."

I snickered. "Your loved one's honor? Really?"

"Shut up," was Arabelle's fabulous reply. "Anyway, it's not my fault that in the name of defending honor, Sadie Valle found herself with a bloody nose. It was completely necessary."

I was suddenly in the mood to watch *Mulan*. "You do know that you don't have to say her last name every time she's mentioned," I pointed out. "I know who Sadie is. It's not like we know more than one."

"Yes, I do." Arabelle glanced at me for a moment before returning her gaze to the house across the street. "Sadie Valle is like her evildoer title. Saying just her first name would ruin the effect."

"Evildoer title? Oh my god, Arabelle." I was barely holding back a laugh at this point. "You're crazy, you know that?"

Arabelle chose to ignore my comment and went on about how Sadie Valle, the apparent evildoer of Gardner, Massachusetts, sucked and would always suck. I half-listened in almost complete silence, only opening my mouth to make a jab or two. Those, of course, were countered with a good-natured shove.

After crossing the street and walking by a few more houses, we reached our own house. My eyes barely glanced at the blue, two-story home as we hurried up the stone walkway and our feet pounded up the porch. I just wanted to get inside so I could flop on my recliner and read until sundown. Or you know, until my dad came home from work and proceeded to kill— ahem, maim— my sister.

"Do you know what time Dad is coming home?" I asked as Arabelle and I entered the house and headed to the living room. When we reached it, I tossed my backpack and sweatshirt onto the couch before flopping onto the recliner, *Cinder* in hand. The recliner was of an ugly color (mustard yellow), but so damn comfortable. I could sit in it for hours.

Arabelle collapsed on the living room floor and picked up the TV remote. "Like he'd tell me," she said.

"Well, if he plans on killing—" "Maiming."

"—you, then he might as well give you the time when he plans on doing so," I finished, ignoring Arabelle's interruption. "You're sure he didn't scream something along the lines of, 'When I get home at so-and-so time, you are in for a load of trouble'?"

"Oh, you know what?" Arabelle mused, twisting around long enough to shoot me a smirk before turning back to face the TV. "I do recall Dad saying, 'Arabelle Elisabeth McAtee, I am going to maim you at so- and-so time!' Those were his exact words. Totally serious."

"Okay, smartass," I replied, rolling my eyes.

Arabelle snickered. "My ass is so smart it's in advanced math."

"You're failing math."

"That's because my ass isn't doing the class for me."

I snorted. "Where do you even come up with this stuff?"

"My ass," Arabelle said as though the answer was obvious. "Duh. Now, why don't you stop distracting me and read your book? Prince Kay awaits, right?"

My gaze flattened. "Prince Kai," I corrected.

"Whatever!" Arabelle shook her head. "Just read already."

I immediately opened the book and started searching for my current page. If I were smart, I'd probably use a bookmark, but nope. "Fine," I grumbled. "But not because you told me to."

Arabelle laughed. "Whatever you say, Falice. Whatever you say."

At five o'clock, my dad arrived.

I was standing at the kitchen counter looking for food when the front door slammed, and I immediately cringed. From the harshness of the slam, I could already tell this fight was going to be bad. Like really, really bad. And loud. Really loud. It looked like I'd be hiding in my room for the next hour or so.

My dad appeared, looking absolutely livid. His usually pale face was beginning to turn red, his right hand was on the side of his head, and his gray-brown strands of hair were twisted into his fist. I was suddenly afraid he would mistake me for Arabelle and start screaming at me. It hadn't happened before, but hey, there was a first for everything.

"Hey, Dad," I said softly.

My dad nodded. "Hi," he replied. I could tell from the softness of his tone that he was struggling to keep calm. "Where is your sister?"

I didn't reply, just glanced toward the living room where I could hear the distant sounds of Arabelle's game and her cusses as she died... again. I really hated it when he asked me where Arabelle was right before their fights began. It felt like I was being tossed in the middle.

"Thank you," he said stiffly before dropping his work stuff on the island and leaving the room. I watched as he disappeared into the small hall that led to the living room, and a moment later I heard Arabelle's defiant cry. Here we go.

"Dad, what the hell?" Arabelle demanded. I had a feeling he'd turned off the TV.

"Don't use that language with me, Arabelle," my dad snapped. "Well, can you blame me? I've been trying to beat that guy for the past hour!"

"I don't care." His tone was final. "We need to talk about what happened at school today."

"I don't think we do," Arabelle said casually. I mentally face-palmed. It was like she was begging to get screamed at. Then again, she probably was. She just loved pushing our dad's metaphorical buttons.

"You beat up a girl at school, Arabelle!" my dad exclaimed. "How many times do I have to tell you that you can't resort to violence for everything?"

Arabelle replied with some witty comment about how our dad needed to take a chill pill, it wasn't like she'd broken Sadie's nose, and I took that as my cue to leave.

But first... peanut butter.

I tugged open one of the cabinets and pulled out the jar of peanut butter. And then, I plucked a spoon from the drawer next to the dishwasher. There. Now I had all the binging supplies I needed.

Studiously ignoring the escalating voices from the living room, I hurried toward the stairs and began my journey to my bedroom. I'd already unscrewed the cap and taken a scoop of peanut butter by the time I reached the landing. Peanut butter was such a beautiful thing. It was the food I went to whenever I was upset, stressed, uncomfortable, or just in the mood. That's why whenever Beth had me and Caroline watch a bunch of chick flicks that did not have happy endings (which should be a crime, in my opinion), I always had a jar with me.

I paused when I reached my bedroom door. It was closed. My eyes shot down to my full hands. Well then.

After a moment of deliberating and trying to block out the intensifying screams from below, I shoved my spoon into my mouth and twisted the doorknob, my bedroom greeting me from the other side. *Ha- ha, door, ha-ha*, I mused to myself as I shut my door with my foot. Falice, one. Door, zero.

I flopped onto my bed and let out a small sigh as my eyes glided over the items in my room. I didn't have much furniture— just my bed, bureau, and bookcase. My bookcase, as usual, caught my attention; not just because of the books and random items on the shelves, but because it was still decorated with Christmas lights from last year. Every time I looked at it, I was reminded of my laziness.

It was the same when I looked in my closet. My miniature Christmas tree was sitting on the floor, still decorated, the box shoved beside it in the corner.

Thoughts of my Christmas decorations drifted away as I fell back on my bed and stared up at the ceiling, peanut-butter-covered spoon in mouth. I could hear the distant shouts of my family members from downstairs, but it was a hell of a lot quieter up here than down there.

I really hoped my dad didn't expect to get anywhere with the whole "you can't resort to violence for everything" line. It was true, obviously, but with Arabelle it would go in one ear and out the other. Especially when Sadie was involved. And, seeing how Sadie had punched her first the last time, there was no way Arabelle felt guilty about what she did.

My eyes closed. At times like these, it was hard not to wonder if things might have been different if my mom hadn't died when Arabelle and I were two. If that car crash hadn't happened… would Arabelle and my dad get along? Would my mom be there to calm my dad down before he let his anger get the best of him? That was the problem with my dad and Arabelle, I thought. They both had tempers. And not to mention, they were both stubborn.

I pulled the spoon out of my mouth and twisted it between my fingers, lips pursed. I couldn't help but wish that for one day— just one— they could get along. Was that really too much to ask for? Really?

Well, apparently yes.

For a little while, I just sat there, not really sure what to do with myself. The fighting continued. I cursed myself for forgetting *Cinder* downstairs. I was at such a good part, too.

A couple scoops later, my door opened. My eyes shot in the opening door's direction, watching as Arabelle appeared in the gap. She looked positively pissed, which I couldn't say that was surprising, seeing how she'd just spent who knew how long screaming at our dad. Though, I had to say, this fight went by a lot quicker than usual. And her anger seemed to go deeper, like our dad had hit some sort of soft spot.

Arabelle spotted the peanut butter in my hand. "Are you done with that?"

I sat up, wordlessly handing over the peanut butter and spoon to

Arabelle as she collapsed beside me on the bed. She took it and murmured a small thanks. "He didn't kill you," I observed as she plopped her first scoop into her mouth.

Arabelle put on a smile. "Just maimed."

My eyebrows creased. Her tone and smile were... off. "What's wrong?"

Arabelle didn't respond, just stared at my bookcase with a blank gaze and finished her first scoop of peanut butter. I watched as her expression began to change. Her cheeks were reddening, and was it just me or were her eyes beginning to water?

Oh god, what had happened? "Belle?" I asked softly.

Arabelle stuck the spoon back inside the peanut butter jar. I expected her to move in for another spoonful, but when she twisted the cap back on and dropped the jar onto my bed, I realized she was done. This was more than a little shocking. We almost never settled for just one scoop. It just wasn't done. "So, apparently Dad has had enough of me and my 'attitude,'" Arabelle began, using air quotes.

"What do you mean?" I asked. I mean, it was pretty self- explanatory, obviously, but something in her tone and her body language told me there was more to it.

"Apparently, Dad doesn't know what to do with me anymore so he's bringing in 'help'." She sighed deeply when my expression remained blank. "He's going to ship me off to some damn delinquent camp over the summer."

I blinked. "What?" Arabelle groaned. "Yeah."

I didn't know how to answer that. It was just so unexpected. My dad wasn't the kind of person to actually enforce punishments. He handed them out, sure, but when it came down to it, he just didn't have the energy to continuously enforce the punishment he deemed fit. So for him to do something like this... I just couldn't believe it.

"You know, I think I would have preferred death," Arabelle grumbled.

"I'd rather you didn't die," I said, trying to sound light but failing. "So you're not allowed to die. That's an order."

Arabelle shoved me playfully. "You're telling a rule-breaker that dying is against the rules. Smart, Falice, really."

I was not going to admit she had a point.

"I just can't believe he's doing this to me this summer of all summers," Arabelle said, the semi-light tone of voice disappearing in an instant. She frowned. "You know what? I can believe it. He knew I had plans with Danny this summer. This is just like him."

I resisted the urge to scowl, which was my automatic reaction whenever Danny was mentioned or around. Danny, Arabelle's boyfriend, was probably one of the worst human beings to exist on this planet. Arabelle didn't agree. She thought he was this sexy, sweet, amazing guy that could do no wrong.

Ew.

I think I just puked a little in my mouth.

Anyway, Danny had an older brother who moved to London after graduating college. Said older brother offered to have Danny and a selected friend come to London to visit June through August— the entire summer. Danny decided to bring Arabelle, and she didn't hesitate for a second before accepting his invitation. I was surprised when my dad agreed to let her go in the first place. He didn't trust Arabelle in the comforts of our own home, let alone in another country. Maybe he wanted her out of his hair and having her off the continent seemed like a good way to go. I had no idea. Either way, her plans were foiled now.

"I'm sorry," I said softly.

Arabelle shook her head and stood up, crossing her arms over her chest. I watched as she began to pace around my room, her bare feet sinking lightly into the purple carpet. "No," she muttered to herself. "No. I'm going to London, no matter what Dad says. He will not stop me from going on this trip."

"How?" I asked.

She hesitated before shrugging. "I don't know yet. But I'll think of something." Her lips twisted as a determined expression took over her face. "I will."

And then she left, the door shutting softly behind her.

For a short moment, I just stared at the door, not really knowing what to do or how to think. And then I turned around, grabbed the jar of peanut butter, and twisted off the lid.

PHASE 2

    I would have you know that on a normal occasion I don't wake up cussing like a sailor who just had their leg lopped off. I mean, I was never one to shy away from swearing, especially in my head, but I still wasn't one who swore more often than not. This morning, however, was a different story. I mean, wouldn't you curse if you woke up to find your twin sister's face a few inches from yours, with a creepy smile on her lips? If you wouldn't, you're a stronger person than I am.
    "Arabelle, what the hell?" I seethed as I sat up, palms covering my eyes. I breathed deeply, trying to slow my heart rate. She was lucky I didn't have a heart attack. Or peed my pants, seeing how I hadn't peed in approximately seven hours. *Make that six and a half*, I thought as I spared a glance at my alarm clock. "It's not even six o'clock! I'm not supposed to be up for another half-hour!"
    I watched through slits as Arabelle fell back on my bed, way more energetic than she should have been at five-forty-five in the morning. Any other day it was a hassle getting her out of

bed before seven, the time we had to leave for the bus stop. And, on top of that, she was suspended and therefore had no need to get up early. She was up to something, and by the expression on her face, I knew I wasn't going to like it.

"Good morning," Arabelle said cheerily, flashing me another wide smile.

"Stop smiling at me like that, you creep." I threw my comforter away from me and stood up, running a hand through my bed-hair. As bed-hair went, today's wasn't too bad. Most of it was contained, seeing how I had it braided the day before. "Now, care to tell me why you felt the need to come in here at an obnoxious hour in the morning and try to give me a heart attack?"

"You and I look a lot alike," Arabelle said, beaming.

I stumbled over to my bureau, somehow managing to trip over my own feet as I headed across the room. Great. My balance ran away with my sleep. When I reached my bureau, I spun around to face Arabelle, eyebrows raised in disbelief. "No, really?"

If she woke me up this early just to remind me of our resemblance, I was going to have to kill her. Not maim. Kill.

Arabelle grinned. I turned back to my bureau and grabbed a pair of shorts, a pair of underwear, and a tank top at random. After a moment's thought, I checked to make sure this tank top actually followed the dress code. It did, which was great because I honestly was not in the mood to search for another shirt if it didn't.

"Have I ever told you how pretty you are?" Arabelle asked sweetly as I twisted around and headed back toward my bed. She put on another smile.

Faking Delinquency 20

"Yeah-huh," I said. "Now, can you do me a favor and get out? I need to change."

Arabelle snorted but complied, closing the door softly behind her. I stared after her for only a short moment before hurrying to get dressed. I didn't know what was going on with her, but the more she flashed me that freaky little smile, the surer I was that I did not want to find out.

I half-expected to find Arabelle right in front of my door when I opened it, but I was happily surprised to find my doorway empty. Maybe she'd realized how sleep-deprived she was and went back to bed. I doubted it, but it was a nice thought.

After brushing my teeth and haphazardly tossing school items into my backpack, I headed downstairs and into the kitchen. It was there I found Arabelle leaning against the counter while she waited for her waffles to pop from the toaster. My eyebrows rose as I entered. I just couldn't comprehend what was going on here. It was way too early for my brain to have to work this hard.

"Hello, my favorite twin in the entire world," Arabelle chirped as I plopped my bag on the island. She smiled again.

"You frighten me," I said. "And I'm pretty sure you told me the Olsen twins were your favorite twins in the entire world."

"Um, that was in second grade," Arabelle retorted, her overly cheerful façade fading for a moment as we fell into our usual banter. I almost let out a sigh of relief. *Thank God.*

"Then how come you said it two weeks ago while we were watching *Beastly*?" I asked as I headed toward one of the cabinets and pulled out a bowl. I actually wanted toast, but I wasn't in the mood to wait for her waffles to finish. Even if they were probably due to pop at any moment.

And, wouldn't you know it? A moment later, they popped, right when I began to pour Cocoa Puffs into the bowl. Huh. I didn't know whether to feel triumphant because I was right or dejected because I could have had toast after all.

"I was talking about Alex Pettyfer," Arabelle lied.

"That would be a little more believable if Alex Pettyfer was actually a twin," I said, pouring in the milk now. "Just saying."

After muttering something that sounded like "Well, he should be a twin," Arabelle decided it was time to resume her creep-Falice-out-to- death thing before saying out loud, "Anyway—"

"Yes, I'm aware we have a striking resemblance," I interrupted, grabbing a spoon. I tossed a glance in her direction. "Being identical twins does have that effect."

Arabelle tugged at a stray strand of my hair, tilting her head to the side. "No one would know the difference." She pulled away and took a huge bite of her waffle. "But would this work?" she mumbled through stuffed cheeks.

"Would what work?" I demanded. I had a feeling that if I weren't so sleep-deprived I'd be able to put the pieces of this ridiculous puzzle together. That, and if Arabelle actually told me what the hell was going on instead of muttering things and smiling her I'm-going-to-kill-you-in-your- sleep sort of smile.

Arabelle didn't answer for a moment, just chewed on her waffle, and continued mumbling to herself. I thought I heard something along the lines of, "No, it's absolutely crazy," but I wasn't sure enough to reply with, "*You're* absolutely crazy." I just stood there and ate my cereal, eyeing her warily while I waited for her to answer me properly.

Finally, she looked over at me again. "Please promise to keep an open mind," she said.

Now, I was scared. "I don't know if I want to," I said through a mouthful of Cocoa Puffs.

Arabelle gave me a pointed look.

"Fine," I relented. "I promise to keep an open mind. Now, what's up?"

Arabelle let out a deep breath. "I think I found a way for me to go to London with Danny over the summer."

This fact probably would have been more exciting if I didn't hate Danny and if she wasn't practically whispering (her tell-tale way of saying that what she was about to suggest would be a major infraction of the rules). So, instead of being immediately happy for her, I gave her a suspicious look and took another bite of my cereal. "Oh, really?" I asked after swallowing. "How?"

"I was thinking" —Arabelle flashed me a considerably less creepy smile— "that you could go to the camp in my place."

I blinked.

And then I burst out laughing, almost dropping my Cocoa Puffs onto the tiled floor. "You're hilarious," I breathed through guffaws. I had to set the bowl down on the island as another round of laughter threatened to have me curling in on my stomach. "Seriously, Belle, you should be a stand-up comedian."

When Arabelle just stood there, eyebrows raised and arms crossed over her chest, my laughter slowly died out. Oh, damn, she was serious.

"Look, Belle, I love you and all, but I don't want to *be* you, alright?" I shook my head. "That's nuts."

"Come on, Falice!" Arabelle pouted. "You used to love going to camp."

"Yeah, a normal camp."

"And," Arabelle continued as though I hadn't spoken, "you already have experience with acting! Remember that drama camp you went to one year?"

I reached for my bowl and ate some more of my cereal, using that short moment to think of a sensible reply. Or try to anyway. "I went to drama camp when I was twelve," I said. "And it was for a week. I seriously doubt that makes me Hollywood-worthy, Belle."

"You don't need to be Hollywood-worthy." Arabelle finished off her waffle. "You just need to fool Dad."

I gave her a look that I hoped conveyed how crazy I thought this entire situation was. "I'm sorry you're stuck going to a camp because Dad's moody, but—"

I cut off when I heard the sound of my dad coming down the stairs. A moment later, he appeared in the kitchen, clad in plaid pajama pants and a white T-shirt. "Morning, Dad," I greeted before stuffing another spoonful of cereal into my mouth. I could only pray my stance looked natural. Even if it didn't, though, he probably wouldn't notice. He looked as tired as I felt.

"Good morning," he replied, smiling a little. "Did you sleep...?"

His eyes landed on Arabelle and widened in surprise. "Oh, Arabelle! You're up?"

He'd meant the question good-naturedly, but Arabelle glared as though he'd insulted her. Then she dropped her plate in the sink, folded her arms over her chest, and stormed out of the room.

My dad shot me an incredulous look as Arabelle stomped up the stairs. "What did I say?" he asked.

"Nothing." I shrugged. "She's upset about last night, that's all."

While my dad muttered something unintelligible under his breath and moved to make his morning coffee, I leaned back against the island and finished off my Cocoa Puffs, thoughts jumbled. One minute I was having a perfectly nice dream about… well, now I couldn't remember what, but still… and the next I was being woken up and informed that Arabelle intended for me to go to Camp Delinquency— or whatever it was called— in her place.

Well, Arabelle would need to ask one of her other favorite twins to attend in her place because I wasn't going. No. I was going to stay home, read books, hang out with Beth and Caroline, and avoid my summer homework like it was the plague. Like every other summer I'd had since starting middle school.

I mean, it couldn't be that bad, could it? Maybe while Arabelle was at camp, she'd meet a nice delinquent boy, and they could marry and have nice delinquent babies. I wouldn't have to deal with Danny and his pig-headedness anymore. That would be great.

On the other hand, the nice delinquent boy could end up being… not so nice.

I scowled. No. I wouldn't give in. I wouldn't. I wasn't going to pretend to be my sister.

I wasn't.

Nope. Not a chance.

That being said, by the time lunch came around, my resolve had all but died.

It was amazing how much deliberating one could do during four blocks. Of course, my mind was already elsewhere because it was June, and no one wanted to be learning geometry when summer was right around the corner, but wishing for vacation only reminded me of Arabelle's request. And that made me ask questions that I was truly scared to answers. They repeated in my head, planting little doubts in my head until they grew too huge for me to take.

I still thought the idea of going to Camp Delinquency was ludicrous, laughable, insane, but what would happen if I said no? Would Arabelle ever forgive me? Or would she hate me forever because I'd ultimately been the one to keep her away from the summer she'd been anticipating? Arabelle and I had been best friends since birth. The thought of her hating me was unbearable.

But what if Arabelle's plan fell apart and we got caught? What would happen then? How did Arabelle expect to pull this off, anyway?

Had she even thought that far? And where would my dad think I was throughout the entire summer? Would my acting skills even be adequate enough to…?

"Falice?"

I blinked, and suddenly, I wasn't lost in the depths of my head but sitting at a table in the cafeteria. I blinked again when I realized Caroline and Beth were both staring at me with concerned expressions on their faces. Apparently, my troubled mind was obvious. Oops. "Yeah?"

"What's going on?" Caroline asked.

"My dad and Arabelle got into huge fight last night because of what happened yesterday," I explained, glancing toward Arabelle's table. "And my dad said he was sending Arabelle away for the summer."

"Sending her away?" Beth's eyebrows raised. "Where?"

"Some delinquent camp," I said, wiping a hand down the length of my face. "But Arabelle doesn't plan on going because she's supposed to go to London with Danny."

My friends' faces scrunched at the mention of Danny. They'd been around the house while he was there a couple of times, and had come to the same conclusion I had: He was a pig that didn't deserve my sister, or really any girl for that matter.

"Well, how does she expect to get out of it?" Caroline asked. "She doesn't actually think there's a way for her to go to London now, does she?"

I paused before answering. "She's already thought of a plan," I said finally, picking at the hem of my favorite white shorts.

"What plan is that?"

I bit my lip, preparing myself to answer, when my cell phone vibrated in my pocket. "Hold on," I murmured, tugging the cellular device out of my pocket and sliding it open. I wasn't surprised to find that it was a text from Arabelle. She was the only person besides my dad, Caroline, and Beth that had my cell phone number, and everyone else was either working or sitting at the lunch table with me.

I'm sorry about this morning. I know it's a lot to ask. Springing it on you like that was definitely not the way to go.

We'll talk about it later, I typed back before shutting my phone and pocketing it again. The phone vibrated a moment later, but this time I ignored it and returned my attention to my friends so I could tell them what they were waiting to hear. "She wants me to go in her place."

"She can't be serious." Caroline's face contorted into an expression of utter disbelief. When I just nodded, she folded her arms over her chest. "This is crazy, even for her."

"You can't go!" Beth exclaimed. "We're supposed to see that movie in July! And what about Caroline's back-to-school party?"

"That's the most concerning part about this to you? Besides, it's not like you have anything to worry about. Falice obviously said no." Caroline's eyes searched my face, and her confidence seemed to dwindle. "You did say no, right?"

I pursed my lips. "Not exactly..." "Falice!" my friends cried in unison.

"I didn't say yes," I said. "I just need to talk to her about it first."

"What is there to talk about?" Caroline uncrossed her arms just long enough to eat a piece of popcorn chicken. "Asking you to do this is selfish, to say the least."

She wasn't wrong, but I had this nagging feeling that said Arabelle's need to go to London went deeper than sightseeing and hanging out with her boyfriend. She'd seemed desperate this morning. At the time, I hadn't really noticed it, but now, when I was actually awake, it was obvious.

"I know," I replied. "I get that. I just... I want to hear her out."

Beth and Caroline looked like they wanted to argue, but instead they just glanced at each other, said okay, and then changed the subject.

"Belle?" I called as I shut the front door behind me. "I'm home!"

I slid off my Keds and dropped my bag on the island before heading to the stairs. Seeing how the TV in the living room was off, I had a feeling Arabelle wasn't on the main level. As to which room she'd be in upstairs was a matter of guessing. Even though we had our own bedrooms, Arabelle tended to flop wherever she felt like flopping.

She was in her bedroom today, sitting back on her bed with her laptop in her lap. She looked up as I entered, giving me a small smile in greeting. "Hey," she said. "Have fun at school?"

I leaned against the doorframe, folding my arms. "Oh, it was great. I mean, I got to learn about all these shapes. Did you know there's such thing as a triangle?"

Arabelle snickered. "No, I wasn't aware."

"That's what you get for skipping out on school," I teased.

We laughed. My grin dimmed, and I pushed off the frame to sit down beside Arabelle on the bed. She scooted over, so I had more room, her eyes locked on her computer screen. I didn't have to look over to know she was on Facebook, probably chatting with Danny about what was going on.

"About this morning..."

"I know it was stupid to ask you like I did," Arabelle said. "To ask you at all, really. I just didn't know what else to do."

I sighed. "I don't really think there's a good way to go about asking a question like that. Though I could have done without the creepy smiles. Just saying." My lips pricked upward as Arabelle let out a small laugh. "I'm going to give you a chance to plead your case."

Arabelle's eyes widened. "Really?" she breathed. I nodded. "Yeah."

That was what I decided at school today. I'd listen to Arabelle's reasoning, and if it was good enough, then I'd see where I'd go from there. If not... then I'd see where I'd go from there.

If this were almost anyone else, I'd probably be worried that she'd fabricate a story to get me on her side. But this was Arabelle. She might have done some irresponsible things, but she didn't lie— not to me, not about things this big. Besides, we'd long figured out each other's tells when it came to lying. There was no point.

"Okay, well, one reason is that it's freaking London," Arabelle began. "And I know that's not a good enough reason to ask this of you. Then there's Danny— but not for the reasons you probably think."

My eyebrows creased.

"Lately, it feels like he's always too busy for me, and that he's drifting away from our relationship. And that kills me,

Falice." Arabelle pursed her lips, and from the reddening of her cheeks, I knew she was tempted to cry. "We've been together for so long, and I'm afraid that if we go the summer without seeing each other, that'll be it. He'll have distanced himself so much that there will be nothing left for him. He'll leave me."

I leaned back against the pillows, my head falling on Arabelle's shoulder as she finished what she had to say. "I know you don't like him, Falice," she said. "But I do. I really, really do, and I don't want to lose him. If I can make it work, I want to try."

It was silent as I processed Arabelle's words. Even though I hated Danny, hearing how torn Arabelle was made me want to help her find a solution to this problem that clearly caused her a lot of pain.

But there was a solution.

A ludicrous, laughable, insane solution.

Before I could even think about stopping myself, I closed my eyes, let out a breath of air, and said, "I'll do it."

"What?"

My eyes opened and locked on one of the many posters hanging on Arabelle's bedroom walls. The members of Fall Out Boy stared back at me. "I'll do it," I repeated, sitting up and looking over at Arabelle. "I'll go."

For a moment, Arabelle just sat there, like she couldn't fully comprehend what was going on. Then she shoved her computer aside and threw her arms around me. "Oh my god, thank you so much!" she squealed. "I love you, I love you, I love you!"

I folded my lips before pulling away and placing my hands on her shoulders. "I'll go," I said, "under one condition."

Arabelle nodded, wide eyes searching my face. "Okay," she replied. "What condition?"

"If you promise to stay out of trouble— or at least try to— from now on." My grip tightened. "No more fist fights with Sadie. No more getting yourself suspended or thrown in detention. No putting yourself in a position to get yourself expelled."

Arabelle hesitated. "That won't be easy," she admitted.

"I know," I said. "But you really don't need to find yourself in this situation again, do you? Plus, what would Dad say if I came back from Camp Delinquency and you were still acting the same?" When Arabelle nodded her head from side to side, I added, "I don't believe that you need to be sent to this camp, but I do believe that you need to learn to control your temper. Please, just try."

Arabelle pursed her lips, thinking my demands over, before nodding. "Okay," she said. She smiled. "I promise."

I held out my little finger. "Do you pinky promise?"

Arabelle paused, eyeing my finger apprehensively. Going back on a pinky promise in this household was like breaking an unbreakable vow. It obviously wouldn't end well.

Finally, she gave me a small smile, nodded, and hooked our pinkies. "Yeah," she said.

"Okay then." I paused. "Now what?"

Arabelle's smile turned mischievous. "Now," she said, "we think of a plan."

PHASE 3

"Give me your best angry look," Arabelle said as she kicked back on my bed, her arms folded behind her head. I wrinkled my nose at her, and she grinned. "Oh geez, I hope that's not it."

I huffed and brought a hand through my hair. It was pulled back in a ponytail, Arabelle's go-to style besides a bun. I never really liked having my hair done like this, but seeing how I was supposed to be Arabelle at the moment, it didn't really matter. "Give me a second to prepare myself, would you?"

Arabelle sighed deeply but nodded, using my moment of preparation to play with her side-braid. That was our compromise. I'd pull my hair back in a ponytail so long as she braided her hair. I wasn't the only one that needed to get used to hairstyles that weren't my own. She had to pretend to be me until her flight took off after all.

After closing my eyes and letting out a deep breath, I contorted my face into the best furious facial expression I could muster. It wasn't exactly easy, seeing how when I was in a good mood, it was difficult to pull a serious expression, let alone pretend to be upset. Somehow, I managed... for about ten seconds anyway. Then a smile broke out before I could stop it, and the next thing I knew, I was giggling.

Arabelle laughed, shaking her head. "That was actually pretty convincing until you ruined it."

"Well, sorry." My hands went to my hips as I rolled my eyes. "This isn't exactly easy."

"I know." Arabelle's lips pricked upward. "But you're going to have to hold the glare eventually. At least, when Dad's looking."

I pursed my lips and twirled my hair with my pointer finger. The more I thought about it, the more worried I became. What if I couldn't convince our dad I was Arabelle? We had everything else figured out: where I'd pretend to be going for the summer, how Arabelle would get herself to and from the airport, how to handle my dad possibly checking on me while I was away. But if I couldn't pull off a simple glare and silent treatment, we were screwed.

"How did you convince Dad?" I asked.

I didn't want to lie to my dad more than I had to, and Arabelle needed to practice being me as much as I needed to practice being her, so I begged her to be the one to ask him if I could attend a summer camp we'd found in California. It, like the behavioral camp, lasted until about a week before school started. A perfect choice. And Arabelle had performed spectacularly. If I hadn't known better, *I* would have thought she was me.

"I just channeled my inner-Falice," Arabelle replied with a shrug.

"You and I know each other better than really anyone else. So I just thought about how you'd respond and what your facial expression is usually like when talking to Dad. And, besides, I'm not a terrible person. I can be nice when I really want to be."

My lips twisted as I thought over Arabelle's response. When she put it like that, it didn't sound too hard. I'd witnessed so many fights and silent treatments between my dad and Arabelle that I'd lost count. It shouldn't be difficult to conjure up the right facial expression and attitude. But that wasn't my problem. Keeping up the facial expression and attitude was my problem.

Ugh.

"I don't know if I'll be able to pull this off," I whispered in dismay, dragging my hands over my face. "Belle…"

Arabelle stood up and placed her hands on my shoulders. "You are going to do great," she assured me, giving my shoulders an encouraging squeeze.

"How do you know?"

Arabelle opened her mouth to answer, but the sound of our dad's scream cut her off before she could. Then she started laughing. Uh-oh.

I frowned. "What did you…?" "Arabelle Elisabeth McAtee!"

My dad's bellow didn't seem to discourage Arabelle in the slightest. Her laughter continued. Until she seemed to realize something anyway. Then her smile fell, and she cursed. "Put your hair down!" she hissed, waving her hands frantically. "Dad can't suspect anything."

Arabelle and I fumbled to undo our hair. As I tugged out the hair tie and fluffed my hair so it looked less like I'd just rolled out of bed, I shot Arabelle an accusing look. "What did you do?" I demanded.

With her hair pulled back into its standard ponytail, Arabelle rushed to my bedroom door. She opened it and stuck her head out. I sighed deeply. "I may or may not have shaved his head while he was sleeping," Arabelle admitted, pulling back and flashing me an impish grin.

My mouth dropped. "Seriously?"

"Wait and you'll see." Arabelle winked.

Unable to help myself, I scurried over to the doorway and poked my head out, too. And there was my dad, storming down the hall in all his bald-headed glory. I hadn't seen him this infuriated since Arabelle went to a party and came home at two o'clock in the morning, smelling like beer.

It took more self-control than I'd like to admit in order to hold back the laugh that threatened to sputter out. I should have known Arabelle would find a way to get back at our dad for trying to ship her off despite our agreement. I mean, she once traded the sugar for salt because he'd handed her pepper instead of salt at the dinner table.

I stepped out of the room and leaned back against the wall across from my room. Arabelle barely had time to spare me another wink before my dad was there. I just couldn't fathom how he could be such a deep sleeper that he wouldn't notice Arabelle shaving his hair off. It made me incredibly thankful I was a relatively light sleeper.

"Arabelle," my dad seethed.

"Nice hairdo, Dad!" Arabelle cooed. "It looks great on you."

"This isn't funny." "But, Dad, it really is!"

My attention was stolen away as my phone vibrated in my pocket.

It was a text from Caroline.

We're here!

With a small glance in my family members' direction, I pushed off the wall and headed downstairs. Even before I hit the main level, I could hear Beth's impatient raps on the front door. I didn't even have to see to know it was her. Out of all of us, she was the most impatient.

"I'm coming!" I called.

Beth's hand froze in mid-air when I opened the door. "Finally," she huffed before breaking into a smile. "How's 'Operation: Stupid' going?"

That was the nickname they'd given my plan to pose as Arabelle. I told them almost right away that I agreed to go, and as expected they attempted to talk me out of it. But I held my ground. I already made a promise to Arabelle, and I wasn't the kind of person to go back on my word, no matter how ridiculous. When they realized I had made up my mind, Beth and Caroline agreed to help me.

"Good," I replied. "If you don't count me laughing every time I try to pull a serious expression."

"You'll be fine," Beth chirped.

Caroline toyed with one of her low pigtails. "Yeah," she agreed. "You're determined enough to pull it off."

"Thanks," I said before stepping to the side and gesturing for them to come in. "Just a warning— Arabelle and my dad are having a bit of a... disagreement."

Caroline and Beth followed me into the kitchen, where we all plopped into our self-proclaimed seats at the table. "What are they fighting about now?" Caroline asked. "I thought Arabelle was giving your dad the silent treatment."

"She was until she shaved him bald."

"What?" Beth burst out laughing while Caroline gave me a blank look.

"Yeah." I scratched an itch in the depths of my hair and fought with another temptation to smile.

"All this because he plans on shipping her to... what was the name of the camp again?"

"Camp Sunshine Brooks," I replied. I still couldn't get over the fact that there was actually a behavioral camp with that name. I thought Camp Delinquency was so much more fitting. At least it made sense. Though, maybe there was a brook nearby. I didn't get the chance to look it up online.

"Right." Caroline nodded. "But I don't get it. Why punish him if she's not even going?"

"But he's having her sent there," Beth said. "Did you just meet Arabelle yesterday?"

I grinned. Caroline opened her mouth to answer, but then Arabelle bounded down the stairs and her retort was all forgotten. We all turned to face her as she ambled to the table and slid into one of the free chairs. She took her time getting comfortable, a thoroughly amused expression plastered on her face. Clearly, my dad had reacted exactly like she wanted him to.

"Dad's calling Pizza Hut," Arabelle said.

I blinked. "What?"

"Yeah, he's totally freaked out," Arabelle said, leaning back in her chair. "So he started calling random companies to try to get hair- regrowth products."

"And he thought Pizza Hut would be able to help him?" Caroline asked, confused.

"No, I think he misdialed." Arabelle grinned. "Last I heard, they thought he was prank calling him. Do you think there's a chance he'll order something? I could go for some breadsticks."

Camp Sunshine Brooks wasn't near a brook, but it was near a lake.

Because that wasn't confusing at all.

"God, this camp sucks," Arabelle said as she took a huge bite of her third breadstick. After our dad stormed out of the house with a baseball cap on his head, she'd picked up the phone and ordered a large cheese pizza and breadsticks from Pizza Hut. She then realized she only had five dollars, so I had to help pay for it.

"That's very encouraging," I drawled. "Seriously, it makes me look forward to this experience so much more now."

"Sorry." Arabelle finished off her breadstick. "Damn, these things are so good."

"What does the website say?" Caroline inquired from her spot on the living room floor. She took a big bite of her slice of pizza and then gasped when sauce dribbled down her chin.

I scanned Camp Sunshine Brooks' homepage. "Basically, that they're a behavioral camp in New Hampshire. Oh, apparently it's named Camp Sunshine Brooks because the founder's last name was Brooks."

"They still should have named it something else," Beth said. She was the only one who opted out of having pizza, and was currently curled up on the recliner, her arms wrapped around her legs. "Like Camp Sunshine Lake or something."

"Or maybe a name that doesn't include 'sunshine' in it," Arabelle suggested.

Beth let out a short laugh. "That, too."

I set my laptop on the cushion beside me and reached for another slice of pizza from the box on the end table. "All in all, the camp looks sucky but survivable."

"That's good to hear," Caroline said. "Wouldn't want you dying there, would we?"

"Preferably not." I dragged my computer back onto my lap with my free hand. Hopefully, I wouldn't drop any sauce on my laptop. That would suck. Not as much as this camp, but still. "Though, the etiquette classes might bore me to death. I guess we'll have to wait and see."

Arabelle patted me comfortingly on the shoulder before sitting up straight and putting on a serious expression. "We should probably double-check to make sure we've thought of everything," she said. "We are executing this plan on Monday after all."

Monday. That was so close. Scarily close, really. Especially when I still hadn't mastered my performance.

"Okay," I said, pulling up the document I'd created in order to keep track of our plans. While I usually didn't care much about staying organized, it was kind of necessary for this.

"So we have me going to a camp in California. Dad is going to drive you to the airport, and then Danny will pick you up there to bring you to the international airport when it's actually time for your flight."

I mentally congratulated myself for not making a sour face when mentioning Danny's name.

Arabelle nodded. "Yep."

"You'll be taking my phone and I'll be taking yours," I continued, "so that you'll have my phone on hand in case Dad tries to call. Your phone will probably be confiscated the second we get to Camp Sunshine Brooks, so you probably won't be able to get a hold of me."

"When you get back from London, Danny will drive you to Caroline's house and she'll drive you back here. That's what she gets for being the only one who knows how to drive." I wrinkled my nose playfully at Caroline, who reached forward and slapped my leg. "Ow!"

Caroline shrugged. "You asked for it."

"Anyway, Belle, you are not to use the money Dad gives you for the ticket. You'll sneak it back to him after this is all over. Somehow, we'll figure out how to pay him back for the camp in California." I took out a hunk of crust. "When time comes to leave on Monday, I'll use your duffel bag and you'll use mine, but we'll be packing our own clothes. But we'll be wearing each other's clothes when leaving the house." I paused. "Am I forgetting anything?"

"Yes," Beth said with a pout. I immediately knew she wasn't being serious. "You forgot to find a way to get back in time for the back-to- school pool party at Caroline's house."

I gave Beth an apologetic smile. "Sorry."

"I think that's everything," Arabelle said, her gaze thoughtful as she tried to come up with anything we could have possibly forgotten besides me not making it to Caroline's party. After a moment, she nodded and took another breadstick from the swiftly emptying box.

"Yeah." My lips twisted. "I just have to get my act together before—"

The door slammed, and we all looked in the front door's general direction. I think it was safe to say my dad didn't find the hair-regrowth product he was looking for. Then again, maybe he did, and he was just ticked because he had to buy some in the first place.

My dad appeared in the living room's doorway. I hurried to close any browser window Camp Sunshine Brooks related, despite the fact that it was highly unlikely my dad would see anything from across the room, and with the screen facing away from him. "Hey, Dad," I said, giving him a small wave. "We ordered some pizza. I hope that's okay."

"That's fine," he said. He avoided looking at Arabelle as he directed his attention to my friends. "Hi, Beth, Caroline. Sorry, I left in such a hurry earlier. I'm sure the girls have clued you in."

Beth and Caroline smiled sympathetically. "Hi," Caroline replied, while Beth said, "Hey."

My dad smiled back at them before glancing down at the leftover pizza and breadsticks— or, rather, breadstick. "Is it okay if I have some?"

Before Arabelle could snap at him and start up yet another argument, I nodded. "Sure! Take whatever you want."

Faking Delinquency 42

My dad thanked me before grabbing the last breadstick and dunking it in the sauce. "I'll see you girls later. If you need me, I'll be in my office."

And then he left the room.

"What an asshole," Arabelle huffed after he was gone. "Taking the last breadstick? Low blow."

"Yeah, well, you did shave off all his hair," Caroline reminded her. "True." Arabelle continued to pout for a moment before sitting up and clapping her hands together. "Okay! Let's get back to work!" She gestured for me to get up. "Come on, Falice. It's time to channel your inner-Arabelle."

I groaned, but did as I was told, standing up and crossing my arms over my chest. "Let's do this."

It was eight o'clock on a Sunday night, and that meant it was time for bed. I hadn't gone to bed this early since elementary school. But I had to wake up at four-thirty the next morning, thanks to the long drive to and early start at Camp Sunshine Brooks. Yay.

Zipping the duffel bag I borrowed from Arabelle, I hefted it from my bed and threw it over my shoulder, shuffling to Arabelle's room and opening the door. She jumped as I entered, but let out a relieved sigh when she saw it was just me. It took only a short glance her way to realize why she'd been anxious. She was still packing clothes into the duffel bag I lent to her.

"Sorry," I said softly, holding up my duffel bag. "Where do you want me to set this?"

"Anywhere is fine," Arabelle replied, gesturing to her room as a whole. "I'm almost done."

I set the duffel bag at the foot of her bed and sat down, watching silently as Arabelle finished packing her things. It was hard to believe that tomorrow, I'd be at Camp Sunshine Brooks and she'd be on her way to London. That we were actually going to do this. That I was actually going to do this.

"Thank you," Arabelle murmured as she tugged the zipper shut. She turned to face me, a small smile forming on her lips. "Again. I can never repay you for this."

I stood up and hugged her. Arabelle hugged me back. "You're welcome," I whispered before pulling away and taking Arabelle's packed duffel in my hand. "I hope this works out for you, Belle."

Arabelle folded her lips together. "Me, too," she said.

After a quick hug, I said good night and left Arabelle's room, heading back to my own. I dropped the bag on the floor and crawled into bed, staring blankly at the ceiling once I was comfortable. In nine hours, I'd be leaving for New Hampshire.

Nine hours.

PHASE 4

I stood in front of my mirror, wincing as I pulled on my hair too tightly while putting it into a ponytail. *Ouch.* And this was one of the reasons why I truly detested doing my hair this way. I always managed to hurt myself.

At least, it was only temporary. Once I was at the camp, I could wear my hair however I wanted. No one there knew Arabelle's preferences. I could be myself as long as I blended in properly.

Someone rapped briskly on my bedroom door. "Who is it?" I called, toying with the ponytail. I silently prayed it wasn't my dad. I did not want to have to undo and then redo my hair.

"It's me," Arabelle replied. "I need something to wear."

I hurried to let Arabelle in. She wasted no time, making her way to my bureau and selecting a plain yellow T-shirt and a pair of jean shorts. "I'm going to get clothes from your room," I told her. "Don't forget your duffel on the way out."

Arabelle nodded, and then I was gone, speed-walking to Arabelle's room and shutting the door behind me. I struggled not to think about what came after this while I plucked a red and white striped Racerback tank top and a pair of jean shorts from their respective drawers. I slipped them on and then eyed myself in her mirror. I almost smiled. So far, so good.

Now for the hard part.

After grabbing my duffel bag from where I'd left it, I started down the stairs. I barely made it three steps before Arabelle caught up to me, nudging me playfully in the back with her duffel bag. "Ready?" she whispered.

I nodded in spite of my aching stomach telling me that I wasn't ready. Or maybe I was just hungry. Or both.

My dad was sipping at a cup of coffee when we entered. I carefully avoided his gaze, attempting to look grumpy as I dropped the duffel bag on the floor and trudged toward the refrigerator. I grabbed the box of waffles, sparing a quick glance Arabelle's way. She smiled comfortingly at me.

Then she aimed her smile at our dad. "Morning, Dad," Arabelle said cheerfully, setting her duffel bag beside one of the island's stools.

"Good morning." My dad smiled at her and then glanced at me. I forced myself to meet his smile with a glare before busying myself with the waffles again. The less I looked at him, the better. "Good morning, Arabelle," my dad said with a resigned sigh. It was the sigh he usually gave when he knew Arabelle wouldn't reply, but felt the need to try anyway.

I ignored him, plopping my waffles into the toaster and grabbing a plate from one of the cabinets. It was easier to ignore him if I pretended he wasn't talking to me. He was talking to Arabelle, and I wasn't Arabelle. There was no need for me to reply.

From the corner of my eye, I watched as Arabelle took the box of Cocoa Puffs from the cereal cabinet. Not her first choice, but I wasn't a huge fan of waffles, either. This was what we got for not having the same taste in breakfast foods.

We ate in silence for the most part though Arabelle made a point of speaking to our dad every once in a while. She attempted to add me into the conversation, just like I would have if this was Arabelle pulling a silent treatment, but I just shook my head and stared at the wall, going over the plan in my mind. *Convince Dad. Get to camp. Live through camp. Come home.*

It seemed so easy, putting it in the simplest of terms. But I knew it wouldn't be.

"Are you girls ready to go?" my dad asked eventually, his voice raised over the sound of the faucet as he filled his empty coffee cup with water. "We should get going."

Resisting the urge to nod and say "yup", I dropped my empty plate in the sink and sauntered to the front door so I could grab Arabelle's Converse. *You've got this*, I told myself as I bent to tie the laces. *Dad doesn't suspect a thing. Just don't freak out for the next two hours and you'll be fine.*

A nervous laugh escaped. Two hours. Because that didn't sound impossible at all.

"Hey, Belle, can you toss me my shoes?"

The sound of Arabelle's voice made me jump. Damn. I hadn't even heard her walk in. "Yeah," I said softly, grabbing my Keds from the floor and tossing them to her. Arabelle caught them and grinned. "You scared the crap out of me, by the way."

"I noticed." She started putting her shoes on. "You're doing

I let out a deep breath before smiling. "Thanks."

Arabelle was about to reply, but then my dad emerged from the kitchen, our duffel bags in hand. "Here you go," he said, handing them to us. I made sure to snatch mine with more force than usual, scowling at the floor as I shrugged the strap over my shoulder. *Hold it*, I commanded. *Think of something that ticks you off.*

I proceeded to shove every irritating thought I could into my mind. Being forced to get up this early in the morning, pulling my hair on accident, the time Beth lost the book I let her borrow, when Danny came over and acted like he owned the place…

These thoughts helped me keep up my act long enough to throw open the door and stomp down the porch. I let the scowl fall after I'd thrown the duffel bag into the trunk and slammed the backseat door behind me, however. There was no point in pretending to be annoyed when no one was around to see it. Why waste the energy?

Soon enough, my family joined me in the car. As she collapsed into her seat, Arabelle gave me a discreet thumbs-up. I returned the sentiment, lips pricking upward ever so slightly.

My dad started the car and backed out of the driveway. And then we were on our way.

"If you didn't know any better, you'd think it was a regular camp." My fingers dug almost painfully into the strap of my duffel bag as

I stared down the campground. Arabelle was right— if I didn't know this was a behavioral camp, my first thought would be that this was just like any other summer camp. But I did know better, so I was certain that the obstacle course to my far right wasn't for fun. What was it for? Damn, I really should have read more into things.

"Yeah." I massaged my temple and closed my eyes. Even though I napped for most of our trip to New Hampshire, I still felt like I could collapse into bed and sleep for days. "I wonder what the sleeping areas are like."

"Dad will be back with your cabin number soon enough," Arabelle assured me, draping an arm over my shoulder and tugging me toward her. I glanced at the building to our left. It was divided into sections: the head office, the cafeteria, and the gym. Their titles were carved into wooden signs over the doorways, in all capital letters. The bathrooms were adjacent to this building.

My eyes locked on a boy with tan skin and dusty brown hair as he emerged from the bathroom. He met my stare almost immediately and glowered. It was the kind of glower that told me he would gladly kill my future children and me. I immediately dropped my gaze to the woodchips, stomach pinching. What did I do to him? Share the same air?

"Oh, do you see that guy by the bathrooms?" Arabelle asked, nudging me playfully. "He's hot."

I dragged my eyes toward him again, but looked away just as quickly. Sure, he was attractive but the glare he was still sending me kind of chucked my attraction for him out the window. "He'll eat me in my sleep," I said, casting an incredulous glance in her direction. "And enjoy it."

"True." Arabelle snickered. "But he's hot, so that's okay." I rolled my eyes.

The boy's presence was (almost) forgotten when our dad exited the head office, papers in hand. It was then that everything became very real for me. I was standing inside Camp Sunshine Brooks, and I was going to be a camper here. I wasn't going to leave with my dad and forget all about this boy that was probably still shooting me with a look that could kill. Nope, I was going to stay here, probably get murdered by this kid, and then somehow figure out how to report it to whoever was in charge. Maybe my roommate would take pity on me and report it herself.

Unless my roommate hated me as much as this guy appeared to. "I don't know if I can do this," I whispered in a panicked voice.

"Belle…"

Arabelle's arm tightened around me, but she didn't say anything.

Our dad was within earshot now.

"Arabelle," he said, holding out the papers for me to take. I took them, silently cursing myself for forgetting to snatch them roughly from his hand. I was too distracted by the fact that I was here. "This is your cabin number and schedule for the summer. Henry O'Brien, the head of the camp, will notify me about your progress throughout the summer." When I didn't answer, he sighed. "Please understand I'm doing this for you."

I turned my gaze away, eyes landing on the bathrooms again. The boy was gone. *Thank God.* Hopefully, that would be my last encounter with him.

"I love you, Arabelle. I know you don't believe it, but I do. And I think this could really be great for you." I forced myself not to look at him as he placed a hand on my shoulder. He wouldn't try to hug me. Arabelle would have just shoved him away, and he knew it.

Finally, he sighed and stepped away. "Falice, I'll give you a minute to say goodbye, and then it's time to go."

Arabelle nodded, and my dad sauntered away, toward the car that sat in the makeshift parking lot. She turned to me and smiled a smile so full of faith that I almost forgot how scared I was. *Almost.* "I'll see you in August," she murmured, tugging me into her arms. I hugged her back, squeezing my eyes shut. August. That seemed so far away. I could make it until August, right? Right?

"Yeah," I said. "I'll see you then."

We pulled away. As I crossed my arms uncomfortably across my chest, Arabelle let her hands fall to her sides. "I love you," she said.

"I love you, too." I punched her lightly on the shoulder. "Now get out of here."

Arabelle grinned and turned around, ambling back to the car. I watched as she hopped into the backseat and slammed the door behind her. A moment later my dad drove off, and then I was alone. Here at Camp Sunshine Brooks, which wasn't on a brook.

I twisted around and let out a deep sigh. Various campers were milling around, some in search for their cabins, others just standing there, like me. Workers were around, too, helping the campers find their cabins.

My grip on the duffel bag tightened. Thank God Arabelle sneaked me a full jar of peanut butter before leaving the house.

PHASE 5

The cabins were about a two-minute walk from the main area, so once I got directions from a nice worker named Joel, I began my trek, hands already moving to undo the ponytail and replace it with a messy bun. I paused when I reached Cabin 12, stomach in knots. It looked all right from the outside— nothing fancy, but not the rundown living quarters I was expecting. Taking a deep breath, I twisted the doorknob and pushed the door open.

A room that resembled something much like a college dorm greeted me from the other side. There were two twin beds, perfectly made and complete with a comforter and pillow, and two bureaus. From the utter emptiness of the room, I could only assume that my roommate hadn't arrived yet.

I'd just sat down on the bed farthest from the door when the cabin door swung open, revealing a tall girl with dark skin and wavy black hair. She didn't appear intimidating at all, not with the amused smile on her face and the *Big Bang Theory* T-shirt she was wearing that had "Bazinga!" printed on it.

"So you're my roommate, huh?" she mused as she strutted in, shoving her hands in her shorts' pockets.

"Hey," I said, giving her an awkward wave. "I'm Fal—Arabelle."

Shit. Seriously, Falice? Slipping up with the second person you saw? Smooth.

"Falarabelle?" The girl snickered, tossing her duffel bag onto the bed across from mine. "That's a lovely name."

I couldn't help but grin. I liked her already. "Yeah, the name has been passed down for generations. It's quite an honor, actually."

The girl snorted. "I like you, Falarabelle." She unzipped her duffel and began unloading the clothes she'd packed. "I'm Vanessa, by the way. Is this your first year here?"

"Yeah." I nodded, and stood to unpack my own duffel. My eyebrows creased as I grabbed a few shirts. People attended more than one year? "You?"

"Third year running," Vanessa replied. "They just can't get enough of me, you know?"

I finished with the shirts and moved on to an assortment of shorts and pants. "I guess not," I said, dropping the clothes carelessly into the drawer.

While Vanessa and I finished unpacking, we made small talk, learning a bit more about each other. We didn't go in depth, but I learned that she loved the *Big Bang Theory* and *Supernatural*, that she was also sixteen, and lived in Maryland with her mom. She didn't mention a dad or siblings, and I didn't ask.

"So what'd you do to land yourself here?" Vanessa asked, plopping onto my bed once she was finished unpacking.

I sat down next to her. The bed wasn't as comfortable as mine back home, but at least it didn't feel like I was sitting on a rock.

"Got into one too many fights at school," I said with a shrug. "How 'bout you?"

"Theft."

My eyebrows rose involuntarily as surprise flitted its way through me. I didn't know what I was expecting, exactly, but I did know that wasn't it. Why was I so shocked? It's not like I knew Vanessa all that well. We met maybe five minutes ago. Should I be worried? I mean, she seemed nice enough, but…

"Don't worry," Vanessa said. "I'm not going to take your stuff. I don't rob my new best friends, Falarabelle."

New best friend? A smile found its way to my lips. It felt good, knowing I had at least one friend here. At least, I wasn't completely alone now.

Vanessa's gaze drifted to the clock hanging on the wall. "Oh!" she exclaimed, standing up and absently patting her shorts. "We should get going."

My eyebrows rose. "Get going where?"

"To the lake," Vanessa replied with a knowing grin. "The head of the camp, Henry, always begins the year by going over the rules and whatnot." She made a face. "Boring as hell, but not nearly as bad as those damn etiquette classes."

I was about to ask Vanessa just how terrible the etiquette classes were when she grabbed onto my arm and dragged me toward the door. "Come on, Falarabelle!" she said cheerfully. "It's time to go be bored."

She sounded a little too excited to be bored.

With a shake of the head and a small laugh, I allowed Vanessa to tow me outside. She let me go after we left the cabin, and we walked side by side, chatting softly as we made our way back to the main area. We walked by a few campers on the way, and I found that none of them seemed nearly as happy to be there as Vanessa did.

"I firmly believe they made this hill is steeper than it originally was just to make our lives harder," Vanessa told me, pointing to the hill we'd need to go down in order to get to the lake as we approached. "I mean, it doesn't seem that bad on the way down, but coming back up? Ugh."

I opened my mouth to answer, but someone called Vanessa's name before I could get the words out.

"Yo, Vanessa!"

Vanessa and I turned. A boy sauntered toward us, dragging a hand through his short brown hair as a goofy smile showed on his face. As his hand fell, he tugged his white long-sleeve shirt into place. I glanced Vanessa's way and noted the way her expression brightened at the sight of him.

"Hey, babe!" She winked. "Glad to see you've landed your ass in Hell again."

"Burn, baby, burn!" the boy shouted, throwing his fist in the air. "Who is this?" he asked once he reached us, tipping his thumb toward me. He gave me the once over. "I'm going to call you Jessica. Because you look like a Jessica."

What?

"She's Falarabelle," Vanessa corrected. "Damn, Ty, how could you not know that?"

"Falarabelle?" Ty sucked in a breath. "Geez. I'm sorry to hear that.

I really am."

"It's just Arabelle," I said with a small smile.

"Yeah, well, I'm calling you Jessica," Ty informed me. "If you don't like it, well, sucks for you."

Vanessa rolled her eyes at him. "You are such a doofus. Why am I with you again?"

"Because you love me," Ty replied with a grin.

"No, I'm pretty sure it's something else," Vanessa teased. She brought her thumb and pointer finger to her mouth in mock thought.

Ty gasped in feigned horror. "You wound me, Vanessa Andrews."

"I know, Tyler Kadeth." Vanessa patted him comfortingly on the shoulder, a bright smile on her face. "But you love me anyway."

Ty sighed deeply, muttered something about Vanessa being mean, and then started down the hill. A moment later, he turned around, eyebrows raised. "You coming?"

Vanessa and I glanced each other and grinned. Then we nodded and caught up to him, walking side by side as we made our way down the hill.

"So you guys come here every year just to see each other?" I asked as we neared the edge of the hill. From where I was standing, I could see other campers hanging around by the lake, either on the grass or sand.

Vanessa nodded. "Yup. We met each other our first year here, and he lives too far away to see him any other time of the year."

I scrunched my face in thought. "But, couldn't you just go to a regular camp instead of coming back here?" I asked.

"No." Vanessa shook her head, glancing at Ty before looking back at me. "A lot has happened between my mom and me and let's just say that she'd never send me anywhere but here. Except maybe to an even more disciplined place."

Curiosity and sympathy spiked, but I didn't ask her any more on the subject, not wanting to pry. If she ever felt comfortable enough, she could tell me then. I wasn't going to force her now. Especially when I just met her. "Oh," I murmured.

Vanessa grinned. "Anyway, Ty and I come here every year, and so does our friend, Will, who you have yet to meet. He's a delight. You'll love him."

"Are you being sarcastic?" I asked.

"I'm not sure." Vanessa laughed at my confusion, but didn't explain as she looked at Ty. "Is he here yet?"

Ty shrugged. "He's not my roommate this year, but I'm guessing he is. He always gets here before us." He chuckled. "It's like he just can't wait to come back. Though, who can blame him, right, Jessica?"

For a moment I just stared at him in confusion until I remembered I was Jessica. Ugh, I had too many names now. Falice, Arabelle, Falarabelle, and now Jessica. Hopefully, this Will guy would call me by my actual name— or, rather, Arabelle's actual name.

"Sure," I drawled with a smile. "If you say so."

We reached the edge of the hill and headed for the grassy area. I didn't know about the others, but I was not in the mood to get sand in my shoes this early in the morning. Vanessa and Ty immediately began to search for Will, and Ty informed me that I had to be on the lookout for "the guy with hair." Because that was incredibly helpful.

"Don't ever witness a major crime," Vanessa said absently as she stood up on her tiptoes and searched through the crowd of maybe twenty teenagers.

"Psh," was Ty's fabulous reply. "I'd be an amazing witness."

"I found him!" Vanessa exclaimed, completely ignoring Ty's words as she grabbed onto our hands and tugged us forward. She released me from her grip almost immediately, but she and Tyen twined their fingers briefly before she let go. I wondered why they weren't able to hold hands, but I couldn't muster the energy to ask.

Vanessa led us toward a boy that stood away from the crowd, his hands shoved into his pockets. His back was turned, so I couldn't see his face, but I recognized the outfit. "So I see you decided to come again this year, huh?" Vanessa called teasingly.

The boy turned, and I swallowed what might have been a gasp of shock. It was the same guy that glared at me earlier. He wasn't scowling now, but he didn't look happy by any means. "Hey," he said. His gaze slid my way, but if he remembered me from earlier, he made no move to show it.

"This is Jessica," Ty said, gesturing to me. Vanessa rolled her eyes. "No, that's Falarabelle." "Arabelle," I amended.

Will's eyebrows lifted. "Huh," he said.

"Yeah, huh." Vanessa teetered back on her heels, the amusement clear on her face.

"Everyone, if you could please gather around!" a man called.

I followed Vanessa, Ty, and Will into the swarming group of teens. A moment later, the same man who'd asked for attention requested that we all sit, and that's what we did, staring up at the man as he stood before us. Though he was clad in jeans and a T-shirt, he reminded me of the soldiers in the movies. And, on top of that, he looked a lot like Bruce Willis, with a bald head and a dusting of facial hair on his chin and cheekbones. Maybe he was Bruce Willis, and this was secretly a movie where we were part of without knowing. But that was probably just my imagination.

"Welcome to Camp Sunshine Brooks," the man said. "I'm Henry O'Brien, and I'm in charge of this camp."

As Henry O'Brien went on to introduce the rest of the staff, I slid a glance in Will's direction. He was staring forward, looking incredibly bored as he listened— or pretended to listen— to what Henry had to say. All traces of his earlier anger were gone. For now, at least.

"If you keep staring, he's going to notice."

I jumped as Vanessa's whisper tickled my ear. "I'm not staring," I muttered.

Vanessa laughed, clearly not convinced. "Are you infatuated with my good man, Will, Falarabelle?"

I rolled my eyes. "Of course not."

Vanessa whispered something else, but I ignored her, attention returning to Henry as he continued on with his speech. "As you can tell, this is a co-ed camp, but this does not give you the invitation to take advantage of this fact. No romances. This place is to help campers reach their potential, not to encourage summer flings."

So that would explain why Vanessa and Ty kept their public displays of affection to the bare minimum.

"Later this week, we'll be taking a trip to the county jail, so you'll get a visual of the possible consequences of your actions. Along with this, if you commit a major infraction of our rules here, you will be sent to isolation, which is to be considered a miniature jail sentence."

My eyebrows rose. A visit to the county jail? Isolation? Wow.

"Every day, along with your etiquette class and hourly activities, you will participate in a community service of some sort," Henry said. "There will be seminars and guest speakers throughout the summer as well. Every night, you will do a set of exercises. I'm sure you all saw the obstacle course which we use to help keep you guys fit while you're here. There will be surprise drills. The goal is to complete the course within five minutes."

I tried imagining myself going through the course within five minutes and wound up visualizing myself collapsing after the first two sections. Well, I guess that showed how well that would work out.

Henry ran us through the basic rules of the camp— which basically came down to respecting and listening to those around us— and then went on to explain how the components of our schedules would work. I thought most of it was self-explanatory and probably didn't require the amount of detail he went into, but then again maybe it was different for some of the other kids here.

Finally, after what felt like forever, he let us go.

"I won't keep you any longer. If you could all head up to the cafeteria, you guys can eat breakfast before officially beginning your first day. Thank you."

"You are absolutely going to love breakfast!" Vanessa squealed in my ear, nudging me as we headed back up the hill. "Like really, really love it."

After almost tripping over a root, I wondered why Henry didn't just do this little pow-wow in the main area. "Oh, I will?" I asked.

I guess we'd see about that.

PHASE 6

"You are such a liar!"

I scowled playfully at Vanessa as we made our way down the food line, trays gripped tightly in our hands. You know how school meals are stereotyped as really shitty, barely edible even? Well, that was what food at Camp Sunshine Brooks appeared to be like. Worse, really, seeing how I couldn't even determine what was on my tray. It made me yearn for Gardner High's food.

"No," Vanessa drawled as one of the two cafeteria ladies slapped a pile of I-didn't-even-know-what onto her tray. "You're obviously going to love it. Isn't this food gorgeous?"

I snorted but didn't reply as I accepted a carton of chocolate milk from the other cafeteria lady and followed Vanessa to one of the free tables in the small cafeteria. Ty was already there, scarfing down the goo as though it wasn't one of the most repulsive things any of us had ever seen. When he saw us approaching, Ty broke into a wide grin. "Babe!" he called with a wave. He pulled out the chair next to his, and then his attention turned to me. "Why, hey there, Jessica."

"Hey, yourself," I replied, plopping next to Vanessa and dropping my tray on the table. Vanessa winked. I looked at my food suspiciously. Should I even dare to eat this? My brain said no, but my rumbling stomach said yes.

"I see you've been introduced to the wonderful food of Camp Sunshine Brooks," Ty said.

I poked at my second breakfast. At that moment, I wished I'd eaten more than two waffles. If I had, maybe I would have been full enough to not eat what was in front of me. "What is it?" I asked, nose scrunching with disgust.

"I'm pretty sure that it's oatmeal," Ty replied. He glanced at Vanessa. "What do you think?"

Vanessa bravely took a huge spoonful and swallowed. "Yup," she said, not even blinking. When she saw my expression, she laughed. "No, Falarabelle, it doesn't taste much better than it looks. We've just been attending a lot longer than you have."

That made me feel so much better.

"Come on, Jess," Ty said, wriggling his eyebrows. "Take a bite. I dare you."

"Well, since you dared me." I hesitantly took a small scoop of "oatmeal" and brought it to my mouth. I'd never had oatmeal before, so this experience was probably going to ruin all oatmeal for me, but whatever. If I was going to live off this stuff all summer long, then I might as well get used to it now.

However, when I tasted what was on my spoon, I changed my mind. Maybe I wasn't better off.

"Ew!" I cried, screwing up my face as I swallowed. "That's gross."

Vanessa and Ty burst into a fit of guffaws while I stuck out my tongue as though that was going to solve the problem.

Ew, ew, ew, ew.

"Then why are you eating it?"

I froze, eyes darting to the source of the voice. Will scowled before sitting down in the spare seat next to mine, opening his carton of chocolate milk, and taking a swig. Only Will, I couldn't help but think, could make drinking chocolate milk seem so intimidating.

It was when he gave me a look that said I was incredibly stupid that I realized I still had my tongue hanging out. My mouth snapped shut.

"Uh," I muttered after a moment of silence, wiping my mouth with the back of my hand. Will's eyebrows rose, and irritation sparked. Why was he picking on me? "Because you need to eat in order to survive?"

Vanessa and Ty snorted while Will rolled his eyes and took another gulp of his chocolate milk. I picked up my own chocolate milk and sipped at it, praying that it would take this awful taste out of my mouth. It kind of did, but not enough.

"Will, leave Falarabelle alone," Vanessa reprimanded, pointing at him with her spoon. "Or I'll throw the rest of my oatmeal at your face."

Will didn't seem fazed by Vanessa's threat. He just shrugged and finished off his chocolate milk.

"You might want to eat more of that," Vanessa said, pointing her spoon at me now. "If you take food, they expect you to eat it. At least, more than one bite."

Suddenly it became quite clear why Will had opted out of breakfast altogether. "Seriously?"

"Seriously."

Lips pursing, I forced down another scoop of oatmeal. It went down easier than the last but not much. I wondered if lunch and dinner were going to suck as much as breakfast, and how long it would take to get used to the meals like Vanessa and Ty clearly had. A long time, I decided as I barely suppressed a gag. A long, long time.

"When do you think the first surprise drill will be?" Vanessa asked. When I glanced her way, I noticed that she'd finished her oatmeal and was now toying absently with her spoon.

"Today," Ty said.

"Duh." Vanessa rolled her eyes. "When today?"

The thought of having to go through that dreaded obstacle course today made my stomach ache. Then again, that could have been my stomach rejecting the oatmeal, but whatever. Why did they have to put us through a surprise drill today? It was our first day here! I mean, I kind of understood. Doing surprise drills first thing would help all us first-years understand how things worked around here. But still. Today… really?

"Well, last year they had it in the afternoon, didn't they?" Ty asked.

"Yeah, I think so." Vanessa tilted her head to the side, her brown eyes narrowed with concentration. "What about the year before?"

Ty shrugged. "Who the hell knows?" He grinned my way. "When do you think the surprise drill will be, Jessica?"

"Never." I smiled cheekily. "Is that too much to hope for?"

As though to answer my question, an ear-splitting whistle sounded off. I quickly cover my ears and spun to face the cafeteria door where Henry stood with a whistle in his hand. He didn't seem apologetic at all as he folded his hands in front of him and called, "Girls and boys! Please report outside! Surprise drill!"

Vanessa snickered. "Well, I guess that answers my question."

I watched from the corner of my eye as Will pushed in the top of his milk carton and stood up. Without a word, he walked away toward one of the trashcans at the other end of the room.

I let out a yelp when Vanessa grabbed me by the wrist and tugged me from my seat. The next thing I knew I was being dragged outside with the other campers, back into the main area. The obstacle course seemed even more daunting now that I knew I'd have to work my way through it— and in five minutes, no less. My eyes landed on the rock wall at the end of it all, and I gulped. How did they expect us to go through all of this in such a short amount of time?

How was this going to work anyway? Were we going to go individually and endure our public humiliation by ourselves, or were we all going to be sent in at the same time? I wasn't quite sure which would be worse. While I didn't prefer going through this obstacle alone, going through the course with everyone else worried me. What if I got trampled to death?

Henry stood before us all, an amused expression on his face as he watched us all take in our surroundings. "You guys look so scared," he teased. "There's nothing to worry about, folks! Your life won't end if you don't make it through this thing."

While his words did ease some of my stress, I still eyed the obstacle course as though it was the SAT— or, you know, how I planned on eyeing the SAT when I entered junior year.

"Now, here's how this is going to work!" Henry continued, clapping his hands together. "I'm going to call two of you at a time, and you're going to race to the end. Don't feel bad if you don't make it before the timer goes off. It takes time to get used to the obstacle course's challenge. Just try your best, alright?"

Nobody answered, but something in our faces must have pleased him because he smiled and nodded. "Alright!" He clapped his hands again. "First up, Tyler Kadeth and William Dyer."

Vanessa and I watched as Will and Ty sauntered over to Henry. Henry smiled at them and clapped them on the backs before gesturing for them to get into their starting positions. They complied, moving to stand in front of the first obstacle in the course— two connected slides. I felt a faint smile curl on my lips as Ty grinned and gave Will a thumbs-up. Will nodded in return.

"Get ready," Henry called. "Get set. Go!"

And then they were off, running up the slide with an ease I was instantly jealous of. My eyes followed them through the course. They made it seem so easy. Like this wasn't much of a challenge at all. I could only hope my turn would go as smoothly as theirs. I knew it wouldn't but oh well. It was a nice thought.

They made it to the rock wall in what felt like no time, and two workers helped them into the proper gear so they wouldn't get hurt if they fell down. And then they were racing to the top.

"Come on, Will!" Ty called, hazel eyes looking down at Will as he grinned. "Is that the best you've got?"

Before I could stop myself, I snorted. Vanessa laughed freely and shook her head. "He's such a doofus," she said.

"But he's your doofus," I reminded her. She beamed. "That's true."

Our attention turned back to the boys as Will climbed up the wall with new fervor, a determined expression taking over as he scurried to get ahead of his friend. It paid off— soon enough, he was in the lead. He made it to the top of the wall seconds before Ty, plucked the small white flag from the top, and started his way back down.

The timer went off mere seconds after the boys were both on the ground, flags in hand. Will tossed Ty what might have been a smug look. It wasn't much different from the frown he'd given me earlier, but there was a spark in his eye that seemed to say "Ha-ha I win." I folded my lips to keep from smiling as Ty waggled his white flag in Will's face. Will's reaction was priceless.

"Well done," Henry congratulated with a smile. "Will wins!"

The crowd of teens clapped lamely. I joined them, silently praying that I wouldn't be called next, but that if I was, I'd be called with Vanessa. At least, I could trust that she wouldn't make fun of me for doing poorly.

"Next up," Henry said while Will and Ty handed the flags back to the workers and headed back toward us. "Arabelle McAtee and Tiffany Blake."

My stomach dropped. Why?

Vanessa patted me comfortingly on the back. "You'll do great," she murmured.

I eyed her skeptically but nodded and stepped forward. Taking a deep breath, I made my way out of the crowd and to Henry, glancing from side to side in an attempt to find Tiffany Blake. Was she as welcoming as Vanessa? Probably not. I knew better than to get my hopes up that everyone would be as friendly as my new friends were.

I found Tiffany as pushed her way through the crowd and strolled toward Henry, staring him down with a defiant expression and pushing a hand through her long brunette strands of hair. I folded my lips together nervously when her gaze shot over to me. Her face immediately contorted angrily, and she crossed her arms over her chest. "What the hell are you looking at?" she demanded. "You got something you wanna say to me?"

"Tiffany," Henry chided.

Tiffany rolled her eyes. "Whatever," she snapped. She scanned me up and down before rolling her eyes again. "Let's get this over with."

I glanced at Henry, and I'm sure my expression must have been pleading because he smiled encouragingly. "No need to worry," he assured me.

I didn't believe him, but didn't argue. I just followed Tiffany over to the slides, arms crossed loosely over my chest and stomach tightening with unease.

"Ready?"

My eyes sought out Vanessa. She gave me a thumbs-up. I tried to nod, but found I couldn't.

"Get set."

I swallowed and turned back to face the slide. *Please don't fall down, please don't fall down, please don't fall down.*

"Go!"

And then suddenly I was too overwhelmed to really feel anything as I scurried up the slide. Of course, I didn't make it very far. A curse escaped before I could stop it when I slid back down. Dammit!

"Loser." Tiffany sneered. I barely had time to look up at her before she disappeared down the other side.

I closed my eyes, let out a deep breath, and willed myself to forget everything— forget the pressure, forget Tiffany, forget how much I hated walking up slides. Just go with it.

My eyes opened, and I ran up the slide, this time making it to the top. I completely ignored the ladder as I hopped to the ground and sprinted over to the next obstacle— a ludicrous amount of tires set into two long lines. I tried my best to get a beat going while I raced through the tires, but at the last set I found myself tripping and falling face-first in the mud.

Well, shit.

I hoped Arabelle wasn't too attached to this outfit.

I stood up and made my way over to the wooden wall, which had a thick rope hanging down the middle. Grabbing onto the rope, I struggled to find a footing on the wall. How did one even go about climbing up this thing? I had no freaking idea.

"Shit!" I hissed as I lost my grip on the rope and tumbled to the ground. I groaned. *Ow.*

Wincing, I forced myself to get back up and grab hold of the rope again. How much time was left? I wanted this to be over, and I wanted it to be over now. I could only imagine the way everyone was looking at me. This was like the time I presented a science project and forgot everything

I was supposed to say right as I got up in front of the class. I'd had everything memorized, and then the second I turned to my classmates— nothing.

Somehow I made it to the top and over the other side. I'm not quite sure how, but I did.

I'd just made it to the bottom when the timer went off and Henry called for us to stop where we were. I glanced to my left and sighed when I saw Tiffany just before the rock wall, an irritated expression on her face. My gaze veered upward, to the top of the rock wall, and landed on the little white flags.

I wanted a little white flag, ugh.

"Good job, girls." Henry nodded. "Come on back."

Swallowing the oncoming mortification, I trudged back to Vanessa and the others, careful not to meet Tiffany's mocking gaze as I did.

"I'm serious, Belle," I whispered, balancing Vanessa's phone in the crook of my neck as I scooped out a spoonful of peanut butter from the jar and held it out in front of me. "I fell in the mud, and it was just so humiliating."

The path was so dark I almost couldn't see anything, but that didn't stop me from glancing around as I picked my way toward the main area. It was past nine, so everyone would be in their cabins by now. That meant I'd be less likely to be caught if I was as far away from the cabins as possible. I had no doubt that if someone caught me, they'd tell one of the workers. So, better safe than sorry.

Arabelle laughed softly, apparently not grasping just how upset about this I was. "Come on, Falice. It was your first try. It'll get easier over time."

I scowled into the darkness. "But what if it doesn't?"

"Well, then you'll call me over your friend's phone and complain about it again," Arabelle replied cheekily. "Why are you using your friend's phone by the way?"

"We had to turn in our phones earlier," I said softly. "Vanessa brought two. The one she gave them was her phone from three or four years ago."

"Smart."

"I know." I sighed. "But, Arabelle…"

"Falice, you're over-thinking this," Arabelle told me, her tone comforting. "You know you are. So you had a hard time with the obstacle course, but what about everything else? From what you've told me, you're doing amazing so far. You already have two friends. Maybe they can help you out. You know, give you tips on how to make it through the course without falling on your face again."

"I guess," I mumbled, despite the fact that I didn't really believe her. There was a nagging feeling inside me that told me I was going to fail, no matter how hard I tried. I knew it was just me clinging to my earlier embarrassment, but I couldn't help it. "But what if you're wrong? What if I can't do this? And what if someone finds out? I already slipped up once today."

"You will be fine," Arabelle assured me. "Stop worrying so much. It's going to take some time to get used to how things work around there, and you can't expect to be perfect on the first day. Especially when the most sport-related thing you do is walk up and down the stairs."

"Thanks," I deadpanned.

I could practically see Arabelle grinning. "You're welcome." "Okay, well, I have to go," I said, nudging the dirt with the bottom of my shoe. "I don't know when I'll be able to call again."

"Okay." Arabelle sighed. "It was nice hearing from you. I miss you already!"

"I miss you, too." I smiled faintly. "I love you." "I love you, too." Arabelle paused. "Bye." "Bye."

I hung up the phone, pocketed it, and then stuffed the scoop of peanut butter into my mouth. Between Arabelle's words and this scrumptious peanut butter, I was already starting to feel a little better. So I screwed up with the obstacle course today. So I embarrassed myself in front of, like, thirty people. Things would get better. Probably. Hopefully.

"Hey."

I jumped, nearly dropping everything in my hands as I spun in the direction of the voice. It was Will. At first, I didn't really comprehend what Will's presence meant. I couldn't get past the fact that he'd just scared the crap out of me. But after a moment, I caught on, and I froze. Oh god. Did he overhear my conversation with Arabelle? I couldn't tell from the expression on his face, but I had a feeling he did. Why else would he let me know he was there? There was a small chance he'd just wanted to frighten me, but I doubted it.

"Hi," I said dumbly, dropping my spoon into the jar and twisting the cap back on. "What... what are you doing out here?"

"I could ask you the same question," Will said. His brown eyes bored into me, like he was trying to solve something in his mind. Because that didn't make me uncomfortable or anything. "Though I'm pretty sure I already know."

I teetered back and forth on my heels. "Oh, really?" I asked. I shot an anxious glance at my surroundings. If Will was out here, who else could be lurking in the shadows, listening to our every word? "And why do you think I'm out here?"

Will folded his arms over his chest. "You're pretending to be someone you're not."

My stomach plummeted. "What?" I squeaked.

"That's why you were talking to a girl named Arabelle on the phone, right? She's the one who's supposed to be here, but you came instead." Will's eyebrows lifted again. "So who the hell are you?"

"That's a lot to assume from a single conversation." I scrambled to think of an excuse. I had to get him off my tail *now*. "I'm pretty sure there's more than one Arabelle in the world, Will. Just because I was talking to someone named Arabelle, doesn't mean—"

"Then why are you afraid of getting caught?" Will demanded. "And how did you slip up today, *Falarabelle*?"

I cringed as Vanessa's new nickname for me slid from his mouth.

Something in the way he said it was so wrong. "I—"

"Don't bother pretending." Will's eyes met mine, and I resisted the urge to take a step back. "We both know you'd be lying."

I gulped. Well, this was most definitely not part of the plan.

Oops.

PHASE 7

"So who the hell are you?" Will repeated when it appeared that my voice box had officially died. When I continued to stare at him with a mixture of fear and exasperation, he sighed. "You have a name, don't you?"

"Yes," I muttered, fingers gripping the peanut butter jar so tightly they hurt. His condescending attitude was pissing me off. I guess I had his unpleasant attitude to thank. At least, now I had my voice back. "I have a name."

"What is it?"

I looked him in the eye and said, "Arabelle." Will glowered. "You're not fooling anyone." "Yeah, well, you have no proof, so…"

Will held up his cell phone. I blanched. Dammit. Was I the only one who hadn't thought of bringing a second phone? But then again, why would I? I was new to this whole breaking-the-rules thing. "You wanna bet?" he asked. When I fidgeted uncomfortably, Will's eyebrows quirked upward. "Well?"

"Fine," I hissed. "My name is Falice, okay? Why do you care anyway?"

Will nodded as though my answer satisfied him, which I guess it should have, seeing how he got what he wanted. Why he wanted to know my name? I'd probably never know. He didn't appear to plan on telling me anytime soon.

"Are we done?" I snapped. "Can I go to bed now?"

Besides Danny, I'd never really disliked anyone. I mean, there were people that irked me to no end, yeah. But with Will, it was different. Everything about him— his constant dirty looks, his way of talking down to me, his general attitude— made me want to hit him. Hard. In the face. With a tree. Because I could totally pick up a tree, let alone slap someone with it.

"Not quite."

I sighed. "What?"

Will didn't answer for a moment, just looked me up and down like he was sizing me up. Checking to see if I was worthy of his time. "Here's the deal," he said. "If you don't want to find yourself packing your bags, you're going to do what I want, when I want."

I blinked. "What?" I asked blankly.

Will rolled his eyes. I guess I earned that one. "When I need you to do something for me, you do it. No questions asked. If you can handle that, I won't report you. If not, then—" He shrugged. "—not my problem."

For a moment, I had the absurd urge to burst out laughing, not unlike when Arabelle informed me she planned on shipping me here in her stead. I just couldn't believe it. Blackmail. He was blackmailing me. This was so typical that it was almost comical. Why hadn't I seen this coming? I should have. I really, really should have.

The want to laugh died out as my mind sifted through the possible things Will could have had in mind. Whatever he wanted me to do wouldn't be good. Why did I have a feeling he'd ask me to do something dangerous or life-threatening? "What kind of things are you talking about?" I demanded. "You're not going to make me do things that'll get me killed, are you?"

That earned me another eye-roll. Apparently, I'd asked an outrageous question. I didn't see what was so ridiculous about it. It seemed perfectly valid to me. "Of course not. Don't be stupid. So, do we have a deal or not?"

Will outstretched his hand. My eyes darted between him and his hand as I hesitated. I didn't want to agree to his deal for obvious reasons. But what choice did I have? I'd been found out on the first freaking day of camp. If he turned me in now... well, for starters, Arabelle would be screwed.

What was I supposed to do?

This was usually the time when I'd call Arabelle for help. But I couldn't. Not only because I just hung up with her, but also because I didn't want to give Will the satisfaction. No, I had to make this decision on my own.

Finally, after Will shot me an exasperated look that told me I was running out of time, I sighed deeply and held out my hand. We shook on it. "It's a deal," I mumbled.

Was it weird that I was a little excited to go to prison?

Not that I would be imprisoned, but I would be visiting one for a few hours while I learned about how choices had consequences. Vanessa informed me that the trip wouldn't be all that interesting— in fact, it would be the opposite— but I didn't care. I'd always wondered what the inside of a prison looked like, and now I was going to find out.

"Falarabelle," Vanessa said as she and I ventured over to where Henry was dividing people into groups, "your enthusiasm about visiting jail frightens me."

"What? I'm curious!" I shook my head and laughed. "This is like a once in a lifetime opportunity."

"Yeah, unless you get your ass arrested later on in life," Vanessa pointed out.

I could feel Will's eyes on me even before I glanced his way. In the past few days, I'd almost grown used to his knowing looks, though they became no less irritating. It was like he was daring me to tell Vanessa the truth. "Come on, Falice," his eyes seemed to say. "Just spit it out already. I dare you."

I looked away from him, back toward Henry and the vans that would drive us to the local jail. "That's true," I said. "But highly unlikely."

"Yeah, Jessica doesn't seem like the type of person to get herself thrown in jail," Ty said, shrugging his shoulders and tossing me a goofy grin.

"Neither do you, and you came pretty close, remember?"

My eyebrows rose. Ty had almost landed himself behind bars? What did he do? I wanted to ask, but I refrained from doing so. Now wasn't the time, and besides, I didn't want to pry.

"Vanessa, Tiffany, Peter, Will, Seth, Lydia, Kenna, Ty, and Arabelle, you guys will be riding in Van Three," Henry announced, eyes on his clipboard. He looked up long enough to gesture to one of the workers, Joel, I realized. "Joel will drive you guys."

"Hell yeah," Ty said with a grin.

Vanessa, Ty, Will, and I sauntered over to Joel, who stood apart from the group with his hands tucked in his pant pockets. He wasn't much older than we were— maybe in his early twenties. He had short brown hair and a stubble. While facial hair didn't work for a lot of guys, it worked for Joel. I smiled faintly as we reached him. He was just as friendly as when I'd met him.

"Hey, guys," he said with a bright smile on his face.

"Cousin," Ty replied, nodding. He tried to keep a serious expression for about half a second before letting it fall.

"Cousin." Joel rolled his eyes and grinned. What?

"Joel and Ty are cousins," Vanessa whispered to me. "In case you haven't caught on yet."

"So how's Delaney?" Ty asked.

I didn't even have time to wonder who Delaney was before Vanessa told me. "Joel and Delaney have been dating for a few years now. They met in college."

I nodded. "Oh," I whispered.

"Delaney is great," Joel replied with a laugh. His eyes veered to Vanessa and I. "Hello, Arabelle. I'm glad you found your cabin all right."

I smiled. "Hey."

A moment later, Tiffany and the other kids riding with us arrived, and we all headed to the van. Ty tried to call shotgun, but Joel just chuckled and told him to get his butt in the back where it belonged. After pouting and trying to use the family card, Ty followed us into the back of the van. I was just thankful that Tiffany and her friends ended up sitting in first row. Tiffany and I hadn't spoken since the obstacle course, and I wanted to keep it that way. She made me uncomfortable. Not just because she reminded me of what happened, but because she just gave off that vibe that said to stay away from her or there'd be hell to pay.

I buckled up, glancing at Will from the corner of my eye as I did so. Seeing how there were only three seats to a row, he was stuck sitting with the other boys riding with us. He didn't seem to care all that much. He just turned his gaze toward the window and ignored everyone.

I faced my window, thinking about Will's pointed look from earlier. While I wished he would quit looking at me like that, I couldn't help but think: why not tell Vanessa the truth? She'd proved to be a great friend over the past few days, and, despite the fact we'd just met, I felt like I could tell her almost anything. Besides, if I didn't tell her, and she found out, she would be pissed.

With that thought in mind, I decided that if one person already knew, what would another hurt?

"No way!"

I resisted the urge to slap a hand to Vanessa's mouth as I perched on her bed, legs crossed. Instead, I stared her down, willing her with my eyes to quiet down. If she didn't, someone was bound to hear, and while I wasn't opposed to Vanessa finding out my secret, I was against the rest of the camp finding out, too. That would kind of defeat the purpose.

My telepathic message didn't seem to transmit, however. It appeared I wasn't telepathic. That was mighty disappointing. "Shh," I whispered finally, shooting a concerned look between her and the door. "Someone's going to hear you."

"So when you said your name was Falarabelle, it was because you slipped up?" Vanessa practically shrieked. Apparently, when I said, "be quiet," she took it as "I must speak louder."

"Vanessa," I said slowly, "I love you and all, but shh!"

Vanessa clamped her mouth shut, and I let out a sigh of relief. At least, now, we could continue this conversation without risking the whole world finding out that I was, in fact, not Arabelle McAtee. "Yeah," I answered, "I accidentally started to say my real name earlier. My name is Falice."

She didn't answer for a moment, just sat there and stared at me with wide eyes. At first, I thought she was in shock but then I realized she was just trying to calm herself down enough to have this conversation at a relatively appropriate decibel. "And Arabelle is… where?"

"She's in London," I replied. "With her boyfriend."

"And you came here for her."

I nodded.

"But why?" Vanessa caught herself before yelling again. "Why would you do this for her? In case you didn't notice, this place kinda sucks."

I nodded my head, not able to disagree with her. Over the past week, I'd learned this place was bearable, but unpleasant. Not that Henry, Joel, and the other workers didn't make this place better. They did. But the etiquette classes, the exercises, the pep-talks... they sucked. There was no other way to put it.

"She was really torn up about it," I said, scratching an itch on my nose. "And I don't know, I just felt like I needed to help her."

Vanessa grinned. Then she kicked back on her bed, eyes on the ceiling as she probably thought over my confession. She was surprisingly hyper for someone who'd complained all day about being bored out of her mind. Though, I didn't blame her for complaining. The jail visit wasn't nearly as interesting as I hoped it would be. We spent most of our time in a conference room at the police station, where we were warned to think what we were doing before we did it. The tour of the jail was just as monotonous, but at least, I could say I knew what the inside of a prison actually looked like now, and not just from seeing it in the movies.

"This is so awesome," Vanessa breathed. She winked at me. "Does anyone else know?"

I nodded, lips pursing. "Will does."

Vanessa laughed. "Ah, I bet that went over well. He's totally using it against you, isn't he?" When she saw my expression, her laughter faltered. "Oh god, he is? I was just kidding."

"Apparently," I drawled, untangling my legs and sprawling out next to my friend. "If I don't do what he wants, when he wants, he'll report me."

Vanessa cocked an eyebrow. "Wow." "You can say that again."

"Wow," Vanessa repeated with a laugh. "Ah, Falarabelle, it won't be that hard. Will's not that bad of a guy. He's not going to get you killed or anything."

I stared at her. Sure, she thought that, and Will had told me the same thing, but it still didn't make me feel any better. He could make me do anything. *Anything.* And I'd have to do it because this wasn't just about me. If I got caught, Arabelle would be caught, too.

"Yeah, but what will he make me do?" I wondered aloud. "That's the problem. I have no idea what he's capable of."

Vanessa blinked and thought about it for a second before sighing deeply. "That, my friend, is a dilemma."

"You can say that again."

Vanessa smiled. "That, my friend, is a dilemma."

PHASE 8

"Are you ready to learn some manners, Falarabelle?"

I let out a small laugh. Even from the gym's doorway, I could see the chairs positioned in a wide circle, the usual setup for this time of day. At the end of the class, we'd be expected to fold up the chairs and place them against the back wall, so we'd have room to do our nightly exercises. At this point, I wasn't sure which was worse— the etiquette classes or the nightly exercises. They were pretty much tied when it came to sucking.

"Oh, yeah," I said sarcastically. "Learning manners is my favorite thing to do."

Vanessa snorted. "Definitely."

"Jess, Vanessa!" Ty called from behind us. "Wait up!"

Vanessa and I stopped and turned, waiting patiently as Ty and Will caught up to us. I forced myself not to look at Will as they approached and concentrated on Ty, a small smile appearing on my lips. These days, seeing Will made me uneasy. Every time he opened his mouth, I'd tense up, just waiting for him to make good on his blackmail. But it had been over a week, and he still hadn't forced me to do anything. With anyone else, really, this would have been comforting. But with Will? Not so much.

"Slowpokes," Vanessa teased, placing her hands on her hips. Ty rolled his eyes. "You wound me."

"Um, excuse me."

My attention veered from my friends as Tiffany shoved me to the side and shot me a quick glare before storming inside. I blinked. "Um, okay," I muttered.

"Well, at least, Tiffany said 'excuse me'," Vanessa said, eyeing Tiffany's distant figure with a mix of irritation and amusement. "That's an improvement."

I didn't answer, just smiled and entered the gym, selecting the closest available chair and plopping down. Vanessa, Ty, and Will followed my lead. After I sat, I looked over at Tiffany and her friends. Tiffany was still glowering at me like Will had the first day of camp. I frowned. Why did people keep glaring at me like that? Was I a glare magnet?

"Ah, shit," Vanessa said. When I looked her way, I saw that her eyebrows had knitted with alarm. Her eyes flicked between me and Tiffany. "It appears you've gotten on Tiffany's bad side."

"What?" I asked blankly. How the hell had I managed that? "Kids here obviously aren't angels, but Tiffany is on a whole 'nother level," Vanessa explained. "I wouldn't put it past her to be Satan in disguise."

I shifted uneasily. "And I got on her bad side… how?"

"I'm guessing it's because you happened to be creating a roadblock in front of the gym." Vanessa sighed. "You don't really have to do anything major."

"So what exactly should I be expecting?" I asked, casting a nervous glance in Tiffany's direction. I really didn't want to deal with this right now. It was bad enough that I had Will to deal with. Adding Tiffany to the list of things I had to worry about didn't exactly sound appealing. But I didn't really have a choice.

"Well, you got in her way, so I'm guessing she's either going to push you, throw something at you, or tie your hair to your bed," Ty said.

My eyebrows rose. "Tie my hair to the bed? Are you serious?"

Vanessa shrugged. "One year, someone wound up with their hair tied to the bed, and we just assumed Tiffany was the one to blame. No other kid here seems to be that vindictive."

"Great," I muttered. "This is just great."

Without meaning to, my gaze nudged itself toward Will. He was staring at the opposite wall, a thoughtful expression on his face. A moment later, his eyes flicked over to me and I looked away, staring at the floor and crossing one leg over the other. If I thought I was screwed when Will found out my secret, what was I now?

I didn't have a chance to ponder more on the subject, because a moment later the etiquette instructor, Penny, arrived and claimed her spot in the middle of the circle. "Hey, guys!" she greeted. She clapped her hands together and smiled brightly. "Are you guys ready?"

The circle of campers mumbled in response. Penny grinned. "Glad to hear it. Let's begin!"

"You guys are doing great!"

Even though Henry's words were meant to be encouraging, I inwardly flipped him off as I struggled to do another push-up. Twenty push-ups ago, his reassurance was uplifting. Now, the sound of his voice made me grit my teeth. Unless he was telling me that we were done with exercises, I didn't want to hear his voice. At all.

The exercises here were ridiculous. We were supposed to try for one hundred push-ups and crunches, and then there were other exercises we were expected to do. And, seeing how I could barely make it to ten push-ups without my arms giving up on me, I wasn't having the easiest time meeting the goals. I think it was safe to say that I wasn't going to be able to move properly tomorrow, which sucked because I obviously had to move tomorrow.

I groaned as my arms buckled and I fell to the floor, breathing hard. From beside me, Vanessa grimaced sympathetically. She'd only stopped once or twice since we started. How she'd managed that, I didn't know. I could only hope that over the duration of my time here I'd learn her ways.

"Come on, guys," Henry said. "Just a few more and then you'll be done!"

"You can do it," Ty whispered from my other side. He had a pained expression on his face, but his pace was steady. When I replied to him with a frown, he put on a smile. "You got this, Jess."

I forced myself off the floor and started again. Even as I began, I could feel my arms wearing out, and I knew I'd probably fall back down in a push-up or two. I think it was time I faced reality: I sucked at push-ups.

"Okay!" Henry said. "You guys can stop. Ten-minute break until crunch time. Just a reminder that if you'd like a popsicle, you can head to the cafeteria."

I whimpered and picked myself off the floor. While Vanessa, Ty, and Will stood up, too, I stretched out my arms and winced. "I freaking hate push-ups."

Vanessa threw an arm over my shoulders. "It gets easier, I promise," she assured me.

"I have no upper-body strength," I told her as the four of us exited the gym and headed for the cafeteria. I hoped there would be orange popsicles this time. They were my favorite.

"Not yet, but I'm sure you will soon enough." Vanessa smiled. "Damn, you should have seen Ty during our first year. It was hilarious, really."

"I don't think it was hilarious," Ty replied, shooting a mock-annoyed glance in Vanessa's direction. "In fact, I think it was opposite of hilarious."

My eyes darted between the lovebirds. "What's hilarious but not hilarious?" I asked.

"Ty couldn't do a single push-up."

"I could, too!" Ty exclaimed, waving his arms in the air. I watched his arms with a tinge of jealousy. I had a feeling that if I attempted to do that, my arms would snap off.

"Don't lie," Vanessa said as she pointed an accusing finger at him. "You and I both know it's the truth. So does Will. Right, Will?"

All eyes turned to Will. He glanced between Ty and Vanessa before shrugging. "I'm pretty sure he did half a push-up before collapsing," he said.

Ty's mouth fell open while Vanessa guffawed triumphantly. "Dude!" Ty cried. "Whose side are you on?"

"It's okay, Ty," I said. I lifted a hand to pat his shoulder, but then I realized that hurt, so I let it fall back to my side. "Last year, in gym, I could only do four."

"That's more than zero," Vanessa pointed out.

"Um, excuse you, it was half a push-up," Ty retorted with a shake of the head. He tossed Vanessa a playfully exasperated look. "Why do I date you?"

"Because you love me obviously," Vanessa teased. "Don't worry, I love you, too."

"Good. If you didn't, I'd have to reconsider coming back next year."

"Empty threat!" Vanessa exclaimed. "You'd come here just to stare at my ass."

As though to prove Vanessa's point, Ty's eyes swerved down to Vanessa's butt.

Vanessa and Ty continued to bicker as we reached the cafeteria and fell into the back of the line. The two cafeteria ladies were handing out popsicles of different flavors. After receiving their popsicles, some kids found seats in the cafeteria, while others left the building, probably to get something from their cabins.

My eyes latched onto Tiffany as she and her friends left the line, popsicles in hand. She gave me a cold glare and sneered. Vanessa's earlier words flitted through my mind, and I recoiled before I could stop myself, leaning away from her as she exited the cafeteria. My back brushed fabric, and I jumped. Who...?

I twisted around and swallowed. Will lifted an eyebrow at me, but didn't say anything. "Sorry," I muttered, facing forward again.

I was silent the rest of the way through the line, listening to Vanessa and Ty tease each other and casting an occasional fleeting look Will's way. We arrived to the front of the line swiftly enough, and I was lucky enough to get an orange popsicle before they ran out. My eyes widened slightly when Will requested an orange popsicle too. I wasn't sure why, exactly, but it was surprising to realize I had anything in common with him.

As we ambled over to our table, someone grabbed me by the wrist and tugged me to a stop. I let out a small squeak, but then calmed down when I realized it was Will, not Tiffany. Then I remembered Will also made me uneasy, and my discomfort level rose again. "What?" I asked.

"Meet me outside at ten," he said simply.

Before I could ask for more details, he released his grip on my wrist and followed Vanessa and Ty to our table without looking back.

"Will?" I called, fingers curling in my pullover as I crept down the path that lead to the main area. I'd never really been afraid of the dark, but now I couldn't help but nervously scan the area around me and jump whenever I heard a twig snap. I think my growing paranoia about Tiffany was getting to me. "Are you out here?"

No reply. I teetered back on my heels, arms crossing protectively over my chest. Of course, then I remembered my arms were sore, and I had to go back to curling my hands into fists. My eyes skimmed the trees and then the cabins in the distance. Was I even in the right place? When Will said "outside," did he mean where he caught me making the phone call, or did he mean right outside the cabins? Or did he mean somewhere else entirely?

    I was going to have to teach him how to be more specific. Or maybe not since I didn't feel like receiving another death glare.

    "Falice."

    I jumped, heart ramming itself into my throat as I twisted around. Will stood before me, looking not the least bit apologetic about the fact that he'd nearly given me a heart attack. He and Arabelle would get along in that respect, I thought. They both enjoyed freaking me out for no apparent reason. "You scared the hell out of me," I said with a glare.

    "Sorry," Will replied, not sounding very sorry at all.

    I pursed my lips. "No, you're not," I snapped. Trudging closer to him, I resisted the urge to wrap my arms around myself. Instead, I kept my arms at my sides and forced myself to meet his gaze. "Why did you call me out here?"

    Will didn't answer, scanning my face. I fidgeted uncomfortably while he did so, not really sure what he was searching for, but not wanting to ask. I just wanted to get back to my cabin so I could go to bed. We had to wake up early in the morning, and I really didn't feel like being sore and sleep-deprived. "I need you to do something for me," he said finally.

    The hair on the back of my neck rose. It was the moment of truth— the time when I could stop imagining the worst and actually find out if my assumptions were actually what Will had in mind. I prayed that he wasn't about to ask me to commit a felony. "What do you need me to do?" I asked softly.

Will raked a hand through his hair, and I felt another pang of jealousy. Dammit, I wished I could do that without my arm screaming at me.

I nibbled on my lip while I waited for him to answer my question. He took his time about it, too. At this point, I think it was pretty clear he just enjoyed watching me squirm.

Finally, after what felt like forever, Will let his hand fall and he told me what he had planned for me: "I want you to make Tiffany's life a living hell."

My eyebrows shot upward. "What?"

He didn't answer, just watched as I processed his request— or rather demand. I took a step backward and placed a hand on my forehead, eyes shooting toward the night sky. He wanted me to make Tiffany's life a living hell? *Why?* What reason did he have to ask this of me? "Why?" I demanded, voicing my question out loud as I returned my wide eyes to him.

"I have my reasons," Will said with a shrug. "Would you rather have me go to Henry? I could always wake him up and—"

"Just shut up for a minute," I snapped, dragging my hand down the front of my face. It seemed my utter disbelief made me forget my arms were sore. What the hell kind of task was this? I wouldn't know how to do this even if I wanted to— which I didn't. I wasn't that kind of person.

But if I didn't agree, then the entire plan would be destroyed. "How would I even accomplish this?" I asked. "I would have no idea how to go about it."

"I'll help you," Will offered. "And I'm sure Vanessa and Ty would jump at the chance of doing this."

My eyebrows rose. "You really don't like Tiffany, do you?" "No one likes Tiffany." Will shrugged. "So are you in or not?"

I paused before answering. I didn't want to do this, obviously, but did I really have any other choice? Well, I could let Will report me to Henry and have myself shipped home. But that wasn't much of a choice, was it? *What would Arabelle do?* Well, if she was in my position, I seriously doubted she'd let anything stand in her way of reaching her goal, no matter what she had to do.

I gulped. "Fine," I said. "I'm in."

Will nodded, and I could tell he wasn't surprised by my answer. "Good," he said.

"What exactly does making Tiffany's life a living hell entail?" I asked. The longer we talked, the more I realized I wasn't exactly afraid of Will anymore. He still made me uncomfortable, sure, but for the most part he just irritated me.

"We'll talk about it tomorrow at breakfast." He glanced in our cabins' directions and then back at me. "You can go back to bed now."

I scowled. "Oh, thank you." "You're welcome."

Without another word, I side-stepped him and began my journey back to my cabin, hands tucked under my armpits despite the soreness as I shivered. I'd imagined Will forcing me to do various things, but not once had I imagined this. It was just so... I didn't even know.

I had to make Tiffany's life a living hell. Yeah, this definitely wasn't going to go well.

PHASE 9

"So what did Will want?" Vanessa asked the moment I pushed open the cabin's door and stepped inside.

I leaned back against the door and closed my eyes. When my eyes opened, I found Vanessa sitting up in her bed, her knees pulled up to her chest with her arms wrapped around them. Her eyes were alight with excitement. "He's asking me to do the impossible," I grumbled.

"Ooh, sounds fun!" she squealed.

Fun? Nope, I didn't think so. For me, "fun" consisted of watching movies or TV shows, reading books until my eyes couldn't keep themselves open anymore, and going to the beach with my friends. This was nowhere near my category of "fun."

I hurried over to Vanessa's bed and collapsed onto it. After I fell back on her comforter and re-closed my eyes, I muttered, "Yeah-huh, sure."

"So tell me about Mission Impossible," she said, nudging my arm with her foot. "I'm sure it's not that bad."

I looked at Vanessa. "Will wants me to make Tiffany's life a living hell."

She burst out laughing, her head falling back on the wall as she did. I couldn't tell if she thought I was kidding. Either way, she seemed incredibly amused.

"Oh my god," Vanessa breathed as her guffaws came to a gradual halt. "That's brilliant. I have the sudden urge to hug him."

I almost shuddered. Will just didn't seem huggable. "So, when do we start?"

I smiled faintly. "I guess that means you're helping me then." "Of course!" Vanessa shook her head. "Like you could do this alone. Besides, I've been waiting a long time for that jerk to get what she deserves."

I paused. "I just… I don't know what he expects me to do. He said we'll go over things during breakfast tomorrow, but…"

"I guess you'll have to wait until tomorrow to find out then, won't you?" Vanessa said.

She was right, but that didn't make this situation any less exasperating. I wanted to understand what Will wanted me to do now, not tomorrow morning.

Ugh. Why did Will have to be so difficult?

After staring blankly at the ceiling for a little while, I got up and walked over to my side of the room. I kicked off my shoes and got down on my knees so I could grab my duffel from underneath my bed. It was peanut butter time. *Yum.*

"Are you ever going to share that?"

I sat up and twisted off the lid. "Nope." "Rude."

I snorted, stood up, and sat down on my bed. Then I took a scoop of peanut butter and plopped it into my mouth. "Mm. So good."

Vanessa scrunched her face at me. "Get a room, would you?" "I am in a room."

With a shake of the head, Vanessa stood up and flicked off the light switch. "If you're not going to share," she drawled, "then you can eat in the dark."

I pouted. "Ouch." "Mm-hmm."

"Hey, you!"

I barely had time to turn around before food flew into my face. For a moment I just stood there with my eyes squeezed shut, too shocked to really comprehend what had just happened, but then I wiped it away, grimacing at the feel of it on my fingers. Apparently, the oatmeal here felt as nasty as it tasted.

"I think she looks better this way, don't you, ladies?"

My eyes opened and locked on Tiffany and her minions while they guffawed as though they were the funniest human beings to have graced planet Earth. When I continued to stand there, Tiffany sneered. "What's wrong? Are you mute?"

I glanced at my table, where Vanessa was currently preparing to stand up, anger flashing across her face. Ty held her back and gently tugged her into her seat. Good, I thought. Having Vanessa and Tiffany get into a fight in the middle of the cafeteria wasn't something I wanted.

Tiffany scoffed and shook her head. "That's what you get for getting in my way," she spat. "Stay out of it, okay, dipshit?"

One more brief look at my table. Will raised his eyebrows and gestured at me, as though to say, "Well, do something." When I frowned at him, he rolled his eyes. Because his random gestures were supposed to hold all the answers. Yeah, right.

After silently cursing Will for making me do this and struggling to think of a smart response, I forced a smile on my face and said, "Sure thing." Then I grabbed some remaining oatmeal from my face and flicked it at her.

Tiffany screeched and swiped at her face, and I hurried away from her while she was still distracted, over to my table where my friends waited. My heart beat fast, and for a moment I thought I was going to be sick. I couldn't believe I'd just done that.

"Nicely done!" Vanessa congratulated as I placed my tray on the table and sat down. She clapped her hands. "Oh my god, that was so great."

I smiled a small smile. "Thanks," I said.

"I'm going to kill her," I heard Tiffany snarling. "I'm going to *kill* her."

Resisting the urge to turn around and watch Tiffany storm back to her table, I looked over at Will. "Did I do it right?" I asked.

Will shrugged and sipped at his chocolate milk. Like almost every other day since arriving here, he'd decided to skip breakfast. I'd followed his lead once or twice, but for the most part I suffered with the oatmeal. It was easier than waiting until lunch to have a somewhat decent meal (and by decent, I mean not pleasant, but not gag-worthy either).

"I think that's the closest to 'good job' you're ever going to get with him," Vanessa said.

Will rolled his eyes but didn't argue.

"So, Vanessa tells me that you're expected to make Maleficent's life a living hell," Ty said, resting his chin on his hands and grinning at me.

"Speaking of." I grimaced as I swallowed some oatmeal. "You said we'd discuss what I had to do during breakfast. It's breakfast."

"Great observation," Will said sarcastically. "Don't be a smartass, Will," Vanessa said.

Will scowled at her. "For now, you just need to be ready for when she retaliates," he told me. "Even the smallest things make her miserable."

That was easier said than done. Unlike Arabelle, I'd never been put in a situation to get even when someone did something callous towards me. I mean, I'd slapped back when someone slapped me first, but I'm pretty sure this wasn't the same thing.

"So what about when she does retaliate?" Vanessa took a huge bite of oatmeal. "What do we do then?"

"Then we show her that she didn't win like she thought she did." Will chugged down the rest of his milk and crushed in the top of the carton. He was always doing that. "Are you up for it?" he asked me.

I shrugged. "Do I really have a choice?"

"Yes," Will stated. "They're just not the choices you'd probably prefer."

He could say that again.

"Yeah, I'm up for it," I said stiffly, taking another bite of my oatmeal.

I'd just have to channel my inner-Arabelle. Arabelle did this kind of stuff all the time— like my dad's newly acquired baldness. I'd have to push past my fear of consequences and go with the flow. Besides, it wasn't like the temptation wasn't there. I'd always wondered what it would be like to get even with others, or to just prank in general. Now, I supposed, I'd be able to find out.

PHASE 10

I wasn't able to tell Arabelle what happened with Will and Tiffany until a few days after the food-in-the-face incident, and she didn't take it very well.

"You have got to be kidding me."

I bit my lip before nibbling on a small spoonful of peanut butter. I was careful not to take too much, and I silently reminded myself that one scoop was all I could have for now. Finding a way to ration this was harder than I thought it would be. "I'm not kidding you," I said after swallowing. "Belle—"

"Falice, oh my god." I could visualize Arabelle bringing a hand frantically through her hair. "Someone found out? Why didn't you call me right away?"

"I'm sorry," I said. I leaned back on my bed and stared up at the ceiling. "But don't worry. I'm handling it."

"Handling it how?"

I chewed on my cheek for a moment before replying. While I knew I needed to divulge sooner or later, the stress in her voice didn't make me keen on doing so. "We made a deal,"

I said finally. "If I keep up my end of the bargain, then he won't go to Henry."

"What kind of deal?" Arabelle demanded. "Dammit, Falice, if he made some kind of creepy, perverted—"

"Get your head out of the gutter, you freak," I said with a roll of the eyes. "You really think I'd go that far to keep your secret? I love you, Belle, but no. Seriously. The deal isn't anything like that."

"Then what is it?"

"I have to do what he wants me to do, when he wants me to do it," I replied.

"How is that not anything like what I was thinking?" Arabelle sighed. "He could ask you to do some pretty perverted things. What did he ask you to do?"

"I have to make this girl's life a living hell." "What?" Arabelle's tone was blank.

"This girl, Tiffany," I elaborated. "I have to make her life a living hell. I don't know, she bumped into me on our way into the gym and then blamed it on me. Vanessa and Ty were telling me how I'd managed to get on her bad side, which isn't a good thing. And then that same night, Will said I have to make her miserable."

"I'd think that was adorable if it weren't for the circumstances," Arabelle muttered.

"Adorable?" I asked, incredulous. "How the hell would that be considered adorable?"

"He's obviously having you do this because she was a jerk to you." She sighed again. "How could you even agree to this? You're not a violent person."

I blinked. Arabelle thought Will was doing this because Tiffany was a jerk to me? Yeah, right. Will wouldn't do that.

That would require him to care about me first, and he didn't. We weren't even friends.

After hearing an exasperated sigh on the other end of the line, I was ripped out of my reverie. "Sorry," I said. "I don't plan on being violent. I'm just going to retaliate when she does something to me. Which I'm sure she will, seeing how I flicked food in her face in the cafeteria."

"You what?"

"Well, she threw food at me in the cafeteria the other day, and I knew I had to react, so I just flicked it back at—"

My words cut off as the cabin door flew open and Ty and Vanessa piled in. I grinned and waved at them as they shut the door behind them.

They waved back before pulling each other close and kissing each other. I rolled my eyes and turned away, my attention returning to my sister. Ty and Vanessa weren't being gross about it, but it was still awkward to watch PDA.

"What?" Arabelle demanded. "You cut off suddenly. You okay?" "Yeah, sorry," I said with a small smile. "My roommate just came in. I'm going to have to let you go."

"Okay!" Somehow I knew she had a mischievous smile on her face. "If Will makes a move on you, kick him in the balls."

With those last inspiring words, she proceeded to hang up on me. She was going to do great things someday. Great things!

"Who was that, Jessica?" Ty asked, plopping next to me on my bed and stealing my spoon from my hand. I made a small cry of protest when he scooped out some peanut butter and brought it to his mouth. My poor beloved...

"You've probably just traumatized her," Vanessa said, snatching the spoon out of Ty's hand and giving him a slight shove. "Geezum, Ty. Don't steal the poor girl's peanut butter. You're aware she lives off the stuff, right?"

"Oh, sorry, Jess." Ty pouted apologetically. "Will you ever forgive me?"

"You're now on probation," I said, seizing my peanut butter from him and twisting the cap back on. "Ugh, if I run out because of this, I'll have to kill you."

"It was one scoop. You'll live." Ty smiled. "Now, who was that on the phone? Secret boyfriend none of us know about?"

"No," I replied, shooting Ty with a look that told him he was incredibly stupid for even making that suggestion. "That was my sister."

Ty grinned. "Oh, nice. Older or younger?"

"Older." I tossed a glance in Vanessa's direction. She shrugged and sat down beside me, looking at her nails. I didn't have to ask to know she hadn't informed Ty of who I really was. She'd promised me the day I confessed that she wouldn't tell a soul. It seemed pointless now. Ty was the only one in our group that didn't know I wasn't Arabelle. It felt wrong keeping him out of the loop.

"Oh, sucks for you, man. I'm the younger one too. Though, I'm not the only younger one." Ty paused. "How much older? A year? Three?"

I laughed, shaking my head. "She's five minutes older than me."

Ty blinked once, twice, three times. "Oh," he said blankly. Then he was all grins again. "Well, that's not too bad then! You lucky little asshole. What's her name? Are you identical or fraternal?"

"You're so awkward, you know that?" Vanessa pointed out, rolling her eyes.

"It's my awkwardness you find so adorable," Ty retorted with a wink. His eyes traveled to me. "So how 'bout it, Jessica? What's your twin's name?"

After hesitating a moment and sharing a meaningful look with Vanessa, I let out a long breath of air and said, "Her name is Arabelle."

There. Now everyone in my circle knew.

"Wow." Ty blew air through his teeth. "Your parents weren't creative enough to think of two names?"

Well, maybe not.

"I'm in a relationship with an idiot," Vanessa muttered. I could see the disbelief on her face as though she couldn't fathom how someone could be so stupid. "I need to raise my standards. This is just sad."

Ty's eyebrows knit with confusion. "Vanessa, what is your problem? Upset that you don't have a twin named Arabelle?" He grinned at me. "I'm sure one of those Arabelles would agree to be your twin."

"My name isn't Arabelle," I said before Vanessa could slap the poor boy.

"Oh my god, how many names do you have?" Ty exclaimed. "Are you like CIA? I bet you're CIA."

"Again, idiot." Vanessa threw her hands up in exasperation. She was probably going to throttle him if he didn't catch on soon.

"I have three names," I informed him as I reached over the side of my bed and tugged out my duffel bag. I dropped the peanut butter jar inside before sitting back up and dropping my hands carelessly on my lap. "My first, middle, and last. My name is Falice Alison McAtee."

"I thought your first name was Arabelle."

"Yeah, I may have fibbed about that," I admitted. "As I said, my sister's name is Arabelle. She's supposed to be here, but I'm here instead."

Ty blinked. "You chose to be here? There has to be something wrong with you, Jessica. Something seriously wrong with you."

"You choose to be here!"

"Yeah, but that's because I love her," Ty said, pointing blindly in Vanessa's direction. "Unless you're in love with your sister— which would be pretty weird, Jessica, but whatever— then I don't see a good enough reason to come here willingly."

It was during moments like these when Arabelle was lucky I loved her. Did she not understand how incredibly awkward it was to explain this situation multiple times? Well, then again, I wasn't supposed to be explaining this situation at all. Oh well. I was glad I told them. It was better than them finding out later on and feeling hurt that I didn't confide in them sooner.

"My dad and my sister don't get along," I explained. "She got into one too many fights at school, and I guess it was the final straw. So my dad sent her here, but Arabelle had plans with her boyfriend. She asked me to come here instead. After a bit of convincing, I agreed to come here for her." I shrugged.

"So, basically, you agreed to enter Hell while she gets to suck face with her boyfriend?" Ty shook his head. "I'd love to have you as a sister, Jessica."

"Aw, thank you," I cooed. "Anyway, Will found out, and he blackmailed me, hence the 'Operation Destroy Tiffany' thing."

Ty didn't seem at all surprised that his friend would blackmail me. "Ah," he said.

"Mm-hmm."

Ty stood up and stretched out his arms, and his shirt rode up, his stomach area becoming visible. When I looked at Vanessa, I found that she was ogling at him. If it weren't for the fact that I was here, she'd probably throw herself at him.

Ty opened his mouth to say something, but then Will threw open the door, stepped inside, and kicked it shut in one swift motion.

He cocked an eyebrow at all of us, an unimpressed expression on his face. "It's almost time for exercises," he said when none of us moved. His eyes reached mine. "Do you think you'll be able to do them without falling a hundred times?"

"Always nice to see you, Will," I said. "Did you come here solely to mock my lack of coordination, or did you actually have something to contribute to society?"

Will stared at me. "I overheard Tiffany and her minions," he said.

My eyes narrowed. "And?"

"It appears that Tiffany is ready to get back at you for what you did in the cafeteria," he finished, crossing his arms over his chest. He frowned. "And I'm pretty sure it's going to be worse than throwing food in your face, Falice."

"How much worse?" I asked. His tone was making me nervous. Not that I wasn't already anxious enough as it was.

Will shrugged. "I don't know. I couldn't exactly stand there and listen in on their conversation. They would have known something was up, but I do know that she's capable of really anything."

"Oh, that's lovely," I snapped, standing up and wrapping my arms tightly around myself. My nails dug in painfully as I glared at the boy in front of me. I wasn't mad at him, exactly, just scared about what Tiffany was about to do. "Tell me again why I'm supposed to make this girl's life a living hell when her revenge could, you know, kill me."

"You're really dramatic," Will told me. "Like I'd let her kill you.

Besides, I thought you said you could handle it?"

"I can," I said with a deep exhale. "But still. This was your brilliant idea in the first place."

For a moment I just glowered at him, boiling in the aggravation of this entire situation, but then my thoughts cut off suddenly when I realized what Will had said. "Did you just say you wouldn't let her kill me?"

"Aw," Vanessa cooed playfully. "Does Will care about someone?

That's new."

Will shot a glower in Vanessa's direction. "I did say that, and no, it doesn't imply that I care. I just came here to warn you, and that's it."

With that, Will stormed out of the cabin, the door slamming shut behind him.

Vanessa snorted. "Yeah, Will so doesn't care."

Ty winked at me. "Don't worry, Jessica. Will caring about you isn't the worst thing in the world."

I blinked and stared unseeingly at the door for a short moment before shaking my head and falling back on my bed.

"Will and I aren't even friends," I mumbled. "Just because he doesn't want to see me dead, doesn't mean he cares."

Vanessa grinned, flicking me on the nose. "Considering that Will wouldn't mind seeing a good number of the population dead, I think it does."

I bit the inside of my cheek to keep from crying as I closed my eyes and felt them burn beneath my eyelids. I'd been so worried about Tiffany retaliating during exercises that I'd forgotten about what she could do after Vanessa and I went to sleep. How could I have been so stupid?

"Vanessa," I called into the darkness. "Vanessa, wake up!"

No one answered. I brought a shaky hand to my head and winced. *Ouch, ouch, ouch.* I'd believed Vanessa wholeheartedly when she told me about someone having their hair tied to their bed, but part of me was hoping it wasn't Tiffany who was behind it. But now here I lay, "basking" in the proof that Tiffany was the culprit.

"Vanessa!" I cried in dismay. "Wake up, please!" Tiffany had tied my hair to my bed.

Somehow she'd managed to sneak into our locked-up cabin and knot my hair along my bedpost without waking me up. She'd also managed to do it in a way that made it impossible to move without pulling my hair. Even just lying there was painful. So much for being a relatively light sleeper, huh?

"Vanessa!"

I heard a groan, and from the corner of my eye I saw Vanessa roll over. I silently prayed this wasn't just her moving around in her sleep. She did that a lot. And she snored. Loudly.

"Ugh, what time is it?" Vanessa mumbled groggily, much to my relief. "Why are you yelling?"

"Help me!" I grimaced. "Tiffany snuck in— oh my god, ow—"

Vanessa cursed under her breath and tumbled out of bed, stumbling over to the light switch and flipping it on. I blinked at the sudden light. Vanessa edged over to me, her eyes wide as she processed what Tiffany had done to me. "Oh, shit," she whispered.

"How bad is it?" I asked, lips trembling. "Are we going to be able to get me out without cutting my hair?"

Vanessa was silent for a moment. "I think we need help if there's any hope of getting you out with all your hair," she admitted. "I'm not even going to touch it. We need an expert."

"And that expert is?"

Vanessa didn't reply. She just scurried over to her bed and pulled out her cell phone, quickly dialing a number and pressing her phone to her ear. I could hear her telling someone what happened, but I couldn't bring myself to concentrate on her exact words. My head hurt so damn badly.

Vanessa hung up and rushed back to me, her hands hovering over my hair. I pressed my lips into a tight line as I fought to hide my pain. "I'm going to kill her," Vanessa muttered darkly.

"You and me both," I replied.

Vanessa smiled weakly at me, like she knew I didn't really mean it, but couldn't bring herself to make a joke. I could tell she was itching to free me from my hair prison, but I also knew she was too afraid that she'd completely ruin my hair by doing so. And I was glad she refrained herself. If she were Arabelle, she wouldn't have hesitated and would have butchered my hair in the process.

I watched as the cabin door opened and Ty and Will stepped in. I wasn't at all surprised that they were the ones she'd called, but I didn't see how they were the experts either.

"Jesus," Ty whispered.

Will didn't say anything as he knelt beside me and began working on my tangled hair, a look if intense concentration on his face as his fingers moved through the strands. I was astonished by his gentleness. I had many adjectives for Will, but gentle wasn't one of them.

I gritted my teeth but kept quiet as Will worked. Slowly but surely, strands of hair returned to where they belonged, and the pain began to ease. I watched Will from the corner of my eye while he untangled my hair. It was amazing how he could find a way to salvage this. I would have reacted like Vanessa— completely overwhelmed and too scared that I'd ruin everything to actually do anything about it.

When my eyes began to hurt from looking to the side for too long, I faced Vanessa and Ty. They were watching the scene in silence, hands clasped together. I could still see the anger on Vanessa's face for what Tiffany did, but also the awe that Will was managing to untangle my hair. Ty looked horrified and impressed.

More hair fell down the side of my face. "Thank you," I said.

Will's hands stilled, his eyes reaching for mine. His eyebrows raised like he wasn't sure who I was talking to. When my eyebrows lifted in return, he seemed to catch on. "What for?" he asked, his fingers moving through my hair again.

"For untangling my hair," I replied slowly. Wasn't it obvious what I was thanking him for?

"Oh." Will paused. "No problem."

I was distantly shocked by the lack of hostility in his voice, but I didn't say anything, just stared straight forward and waited for Will to finish.

"Aw, Will is making friends," Ty said, bringing a hand to his heart. He had on the expression of a proud father. I couldn't help but smile at that. Leave it to Ty to lighten the mood. "They grow up so fast."

"Shut up, Ty," Will grumbled.

"You do know it's okay to have more than two friends," Vanessa pointed out. "Besides, it's not like you two aren't friends already. I mean, you actually sacrificed sleep to help her out of this mess."

I blinked. In all honesty, I didn't consider Will a friend. When he didn't make me uncomfortable, he ticked me off. However, Vanessa was right— Will had gotten up in the middle of the night to help me out. But, still. He was blackmailing me. Friends didn't blackmail friends.

"You guys are ridiculous." I could hear the exasperation in Will's voice, but the tenderness of his fingers didn't change.

"It's not that hard, you asshat." Vanessa rolled her eyes. "Just ask Falice if she'll be your friend. Come on."

Will sighed deeply. And then he was hovering over me with a thoroughly annoyed expression on his face. "Falice, be my friend so they'll shut up."

I cocked an eyebrow. "Fine."

Will shot a look in Vanessa's and Ty's direction. "There," he said. "Now I have three friends. Happy?"

"I'm not unhappy," Vanessa answered smugly. "Though you could have actually asked her."

"I did."

We went quiet again as Will went back to work. I found myself almost dozing off while Will's fingers slid through my hair. By this time, over half of my hair had been freed, and the pain had dulled considerably. In the back of my mind, I struggled to find a way to get back at Tiffany for this, but nothing useful came to mind.

"There," Will finally whispered. "All done."

I sat up, raking a hand through my hair and wincing. My head still ached. "Ow," I mumbled. I looked up at Will, who was now standing straight with his hands stuffed in his sweatshirt's pockets. "Thanks, Will."

"You said that already," was Will's fabulous reply. "Now, how about we talk about getting even?"

His expression was unreadable as Vanessa and Ty flopped onto the bed beside me. I didn't answer at first, biting down on my lip as I struggled to think of something— and failing, again.

"Okay." I paused, eyes gliding over to Vanessa and Ty before returning to Will. "Do you have any ideas?"

Will thought my question over for a moment before nodding. "Yeah," he said. "I do."

PHASE 11

"No."

"Why not? You were perfectly fine doing it an hour ago." "Well, I've changed my mind."

"You're not allowed to change your mind." "Sucks for you, because I just did."

Will and I locked glares. I think it was safe to say that our "friendship" wasn't getting off to a great start. In the week we'd been "friends," we'd done absolutely nothing but bicker. Will had proved himself to be a truly infuriating human being, and I'm sure he would say the same for me.

"Falice," Will drawled, his eyes boring into mine. If he thought he was going to glare me to death, he was sadly mistaken. Let's just say, I'd grown less afraid of him turning me in, and more aggravated with him in general. "You don't have the privilege of changing your mind. It's in the job description."

"No, the job description is me making her life a living hell," I corrected. "I'm allowed to change my mind if the plan is completely idiotic."

When Will first explained his plan, I was all for it— at least, the most I could be in this situation. It seemed like an okay plan at the time. But now that we were actually standing (well, we were actually crouching, but whatever) here, ready to put the plan into motion? Yeah, I could see the holes. Lots and lots of holes. For one, we had no idea she was even going to be there. Two, we were taking a huge risk of being caught. It was the middle of the day.

"Are you sure she's even going to be here?" I demanded. "For all you know, she's doing sports today."

"I have swimming with her," he said. "So yes, I'm sure."

I glanced at Will from the corner of my eye. He had his sweatshirt on, but his pants had been replaced with swimming trunks. Proof that he, in fact, had swimming at the same time Tiffany did.

"Falice, you came here to act like Arabelle, didn't you?" Will asked, his tone betraying his irritation. "Would your sister do something like this?"

"I'm supposed to say yes," I said, "but I'm going to say no because I'm Arabelle at the moment, and I wouldn't do this."

Will let out an exasperated breath of air. I wondered if he was resisting the urge to throttle me. "Look," he said. "If you do this, I'll help you complete the course in five minutes."

My eyes narrowed. "You're lying," I told him. "No, I'm not."

I stared at him hard, like that was going to force him to tell the truth if he wasn't already telling it. I found it difficult to believe that Will would seriously offer me something like this. Especially when I technically had to pull this off if I didn't want to find myself booted from camp. It just didn't make any sense.

But, even so, it was tempting. Did I really want to spend the entire summer fumbling— quite literally— with the ropes? If there was a chance he would actually help me, would I want to take it?

I pursed my lips. I guess there was one way to find out if he was telling the truth.

I held out my hand, pinky outstretched. "Pinky promise."

Will flicked his eyes between me and my finger twice before scoffing. "You've got to be kidding me."

"Pinky promises are legit," I said, eyes narrowing again. "If you're really going to help me, this will make it final. There's no going back."

"Is your pinky going to cut off my head in my sleep if I don't?" "Don't doubt the power of my pinky, Dyer."

Will raised his eyebrows before rolling his eyes. He hooked his pinky around mine and shook our fingers.

"There," he said, letting his hand fall. I could see the annoyance and disbelief on his face. I'm pretty sure he thought I was crazy. "It's official. Now, take the damn container to the locker room."

I sighed and accepted the container from Will's hands. Inside were spiders— lots and lots of them. How many, exactly, I wasn't sure, but I wasn't about to sit down and count them all. I may not have minded spiders by themselves, but a horde? I'd pass.

On the bright side, they weren't snakes. Snakes and I had a rocky relationship. And by "rocky relationship" I meant they made me want to pee myself.

My eyes dragged themselves to the building we were hiding behind. It was pretty much a huge wooden box, divided into two sides, one for the girls and one for the guys. The locker room was rather pathetic looking on the outside— faded red with peeling paint everywhere— but it wasn't that bad on the inside. Not like the locker rooms at school, but not terrible. Tiffany and her minions were supposed to be inside there now. And I was about to unleash a throng of spiders inside and then lock the door.

Genius plan, Will. Really.

"We don't have all day, Falice," Will hissed. "You're supposed to be hiking, remember?"

"No, I forgot," I said.

After glaring at Will, I rolled my eyes and crept to the door. I looked around nervously in search for someone who could potentially witness my misdemeanor, but there was no one. And why would there be? Right now, everyone was off doing their own hour of physical activity before we were all taken to our various community service assignments for the rest of the afternoon.

I shook my head to dispel all of my anxious thoughts and slunk the rest of the way to the girls' locker room. For a moment I paused, ear against the door as I listened for Tiffany's voice. She was in there, along with her friends. Was anyone else in there? I hoped not. But I couldn't exactly wait for them to leave, so even if there was anyone else in there, they'd have to be stuck with the spiders, too.

Sorry, I mentally whispered to any potential innocent bystanders. Then I pulled open the door.

I only left a small gap, so they'd be less likely to notice if they weren't in the stalls. After listening hard for any sense of alarm, I lifted the lid on the container, tilted the container forward, and dumped the contents on the floor.

"Do you guys hear that?" Tiffany asked abruptly.

The lock to one of the stalls unlatched, and in a panic I dropped the container, locked the locker room shut, and took a step back. I let out a long, shaky breath of air and then watched as Will emerged from our hiding spot and shoved his hands into his sweatshirt pockets. "I hope you didn't want that container back," I said stupidly.

Will lifted his eyebrows, but if he had a witty response in mind, it was cut off by a high-pitched screech.

Shit. I stumbled backwards and fell, letting out a small, embarrassed laugh. Only me. Well, and Beth. She always managed to trip over nothing, too. When we were younger, Caroline used to call us the Clumsies.

"You're talented," Will said, holding out his hand. I didn't hesitate before allowing him to help me up. "Nice going."

"Shut up," was my genius reply.

The shrieks grew louder. Will grabbed onto my wrist and tugged. "Come on," he said.

He didn't have to tell me twice. In an instant, I spun on my heels and sprinted for the woods with Will right behind me. The farther away we got from the locker room, the more my stomach, which had been tight with anxiety since Will and I headed for the locker rooms, began to lighten. And instead of feeling uneasy, I felt a distinct sense of triumph, like I'd accomplished something major. I still hated this entire thing, but…

"I did it," I breathed, lifting a hand to push my hair back. I shook my head, a disbelieving smile curling on my lips. "I did it!"

"You did." A small smile of his own was pricking Will's lips upward. "Congrats, McAtee. I didn't think you had it in you."

For a moment, I just stared. Will was smiling. He was *smiling*. Yeah, the smile was near non-existent, but it was still there. It transformed his entire face, making him seem less intimidating and look more like an approachable teenager.

Will noticed the smile a few seconds after I did, and it immediately slipped off his face, the frown returning.

"Way to be," I said finally, rolling my eyes. "Make me do it while thinking I couldn't?"

Will shrugged. "I was seeing if you'd prove me wrong."

My head twisted in the direction of the locker room, where I could still hear the distant screams of Tiffany and her minions. "Do I even want to know where you got all those spiders?" I asked.

"Probably not."

It wasn't long before Henry found out what we'd done to Tiffany and called a camp-wide meeting. I was back with my hiking group for ten minutes before the worker in charge of our group, Dennis, told us we had to go back down for an emergency meeting at the lake. I walked beside Vanessa on the way there, careful not to mention anything about the locker room in fear that some kid would hear and tattle on me. Vanessa did the same.

"Today is Friday," Vanessa said, ecstatic as we made our way down the hill. "You know what that means?"

"Ice cream instead of popsicles!" I cheered. "The only truly glorious food to enter this camp."

"That's because the cafeteria ladies didn't make it," Vanessa pointed out.

"True."

"Does anyone know why we're being called down here?" a boy asked. When I looked his way, I recognized him as Seth from the van. "It must be some serious shit, right?"

Vanessa and I shrugged along with everyone else though we obviously knew perfectly well why we were being taken away from our activities. "I have no idea," Vanessa added, pursing her lips in mock-thought. "Maybe they finally realized the food here sucks ass and wanted to apologize."

Seth snorted along with a couple other kids who'd been listening in.

"Language," Dennis warned.

Vanessa folded her lips together and gave me a look that said,

"Whoops." I smiled.

We made it to the lake area and sat down with the other gathered kids. Vanessa and I found spare spots next to Will and Ty, who were sitting at the back of the crowd. After I sat, I looked up at Henry. He had a grim expression on his face, his hands folded in front of him.

"There's Tiffany," Vanessa whispered.

I followed Vanessa's gaze and found Tiffany and her friends huddled a few feet behind Henry, their arms crossed over their chests. When she caught me looking, Tiffany glowered.

"I'm sorry to interrupt your daily activities," Henry said after everyone arrived. Oh god, he sounded stiff. He was pissed. He hid it incredibly well, but I could tell. It wasn't unlike how my dad hid his anger, though Henry was much better at doing so. "But it has come to my attention that one or more campers here have committed multiple infractions of our rules."

We were silent though many curious glances flicked around.

"Today, someone released spiders in the girls' locker room. Now, I don't know if this was a silly prank or something else, but either way, it's inexcusable. You are expected to treat everyone with respect. This is not respectful— it's cruel. The girls in the locker room could have fallen and hurt themselves, had a panic attack, or had some other potentially dangerous reaction.

"If you have a problem with another camper, come to me or another worker you trust. Don't participate in these childish antics."

I was careful not to let any of my nervous energy show. Knowing Tiffany, she was watching my every move, just waiting to pounce. If I showed any guilty signs, she'd take me down. There was no question about it.

"If you are responsible for what happened today, I'm giving you this chance to come forward and admit your wrongdoings. If you choose not to, a harsher consequence will be dealt out to you. As for everyone else, if you have any information about what happened, please inform us. You are not better off keeping this information to yourself."

Everyone remained silent. I resisted the sudden urge to look over at Will and glanced around at everyone else, nibbling my lip.

Henry waited patiently for the culprit to turn themselves in, but when it became clear that no one was about to fess up, he let out a soft sigh. "Okay then. Until the person behind this is found, there will be no more Ice Cream Fridays. I'm sorry to everyone who had nothing to do with this. It is not your fault, but I'm afraid this is how it has to be. Hopefully, this will give one of your fellow campers the incentive to do the right thing."

A few stifled groans, but other than that, nothing. I swallowed down my bubbling disappointment. Damn. I'd really been looking forward to Ice Cream Friday. But there wasn't really much I could do about it— well, besides turn myself in, which I wasn't about to do.

"You may go," Henry said, releasing us. I almost let out a sigh of relief. Finally.

I followed my group back up the hill. As I passed by, I caught Tiffany's gaze and resisted the urge to look hastily away. Her glower was still there, but I recognized from the expression on her face that she knew it was me who was behind this. "It was you," her death-glare told me. "I know it was. And you're not going to get away with it."

Because that wasn't scary or anything.

The night after I dumped the spiders in the locker room, I woke up to something tickling my nose.

I scrunched my face and groggily brought a hand up to scratch the place that itched. However, as my hand made contact with my face, I discovered what a huge mistake I'd just made.

"Shit!" I hissed, pulling my hand away. There was something there— something gooey and gross. And after staggering over to the light and turning it on, I found that it was leftover oatmeal. Great.

"Who turned on the sun?" Vanessa demanded blearily. She groaned, pulling her pillow out from under her head and throwing it over her face.

I would have laughed at her if it wasn't for the situation. Instead, I grimaced and waggled my hand over the nearby trashcan. "Tiffany was here," I announced.

That caught Vanessa's attention. She sat up, blinking. "What?" she mumbled with a yawn.

"Yep."

One more hard flick, and then it became clear that the rest of this oatmeal wasn't coming off willingly. It was times like these when I really wished I'd packed napkins or paper towels. Luckily, Vanessa had the foresight to pack a box of tissues, so I just grabbed one of those and wiped away any excess oatmeal. While the tissue helped get the oatmeal off my hand, it didn't take the stickiness away. Well, it appeared I'd be taking an early morning trip to the bathroom.

"What did she do?" Vanessa asked.

"She oatmeal-ed my hand," I replied, chucking the used napkin into the trashcan. As I began my search for my shoes, I added, "Which isn't that bad considering…"

I trailed off, and my lips tugged into a frown. Where the hell were my shoes?

"What?"

I didn't answer, just got on my knees and dragged my duffel bag from underneath the bed. Tiffany had stolen my shoes? Seriously? What was the point in that? Maybe she'd get a kick out of me having to trudge to the bathroom barefoot. But, luckily, I had Arabelle's Converse in my... I cursed when I unzipped my duffel bag and found it filled to the rim with oatmeal. "What the hell?" I breathed.

Well, Arabelle wasn't going to be happy. Those were her favorite shoes.

"Falarabelle?" The bed creaked, and a few moments later Vanessa was crouched beside me, eyeing the contents of my bag. "Ah, shit."

"Couldn't have said it better myself." "Was your peanut butter in there?"

I froze. I hadn't even thought of that. "Damn—" My curse cut off as I spun around to face my bureau and spotted my peanut butter and *Cinder* on top. Thank God. "No," I said, letting out a long breath of air. "That's a plus, I guess."

After pushing my bag back under my bed, hiding it until I figured out what to do with it, I stood up straight and headed over to my bureau. It was too cold outside to walk around with just a tank top on, so I was just going to grab my pullover and then—

Or maybe not.

"What the hell?" I hissed, gaping at my empty drawer. "She took my clothes too?"

"Seriously?" Vanessa appeared by my side and gawked along with me. "Was she envious of your style or something?"

"I doubt it." I sighed. "I guess it was too much to hope for that she'd settle with putting oatmeal on my hand."

"I guess so." Vanessa paused. "So where the hell are they?" I shrugged. "I have no idea."

Vanessa and I spent another moment or two staring blankly at my empty drawer before deciding we had better things to do with our time. I slammed the drawer shut. "Can I borrow your shoes?" I asked with a yawn. "I need to go wash my hands."

"Yeah," Vanessa replied. "You can borrow my flip flops. I'll go with you."

I smiled. Having Vanessa with me would make me feel a lot less paranoid. At least, I wouldn't be by myself if Tiffany attacked. "Thank you," I said.

"No problem."

Vanessa grabbed her flip flops from underneath her bed and tossed them to me. While I threw them on, she sauntered over to her bureau and tugged open one of the drawers. "She left me my clothes," she said. "I half expected her to take mine, too, just because she sucks like that."

"You must be her favorite," I teased. When Vanessa tossed me a disturbed look, I grinned. "You're so lucky."

"Shut up." Vanessa threw me her maroon Aeropostale zip-up sweatshirt. "Now let's go, you shit-face."

"It's oatmeal-face to you, buddy," I said, following Vanessa out of the cabin. Her flip flops were too big, but they would do for now. I curled my toes into them as we headed out, scanning our surroundings. All I could see was Tiffany jumping out at any moment, a sneer on her face.

As we walked, my eyes latched onto something odd in the trees.

Was that…?

"No way," I breathed, coming to a stop and squinting up at the trees. "Did she seriously…?"

"Falarabelle, what's going on?" Vanessa asked. She followed my gaze and sucked in a breath. "She did not."

I spun around on my heels, gaze devouring the trees around me. All around me, my clothes were draped from tree branches— most of them high up, but some of them low enough for me to grab if I jumped high enough. My jaw dropped. "She did."

Vanessa didn't answer for a moment, just gaped along with me at my clothing display all around the woods. How many trees were now decorated with my clothes? Did she stick to this section or spread out all around? I prayed it was the first option. At least, then we'd have a small chance of gathering my clothes before it was time to wake up.

"I'll go get the guys," Vanessa said blankly. I nodded. "Yeah, okay."

Vanessa dashed back to the cabins, and I stayed put, clean hand going to my hip as I continued to stare up at the trees. The pullover I'd been searching for flapped lightly in the wind.

I pursed my lips. Well, this was going to be interesting.

PHASE 12

I ran to the bathroom to wash my hands, and when I returned, I found Vanessa standing where we'd just separated, Will and Ty at her sides. We set to work. At first, I was nervous about Will or Ty— mostly Will, not going to lie— seeing my underwear, but I didn't have the time to be worried. Tiffany spread my clothes throughout the woods. Luckily, she didn't spread them out so far that it would be impossible to find everything in time. At least, that's what Will said when I gave him a panicked look.

So we split up and started climbing trees. It was long, hard work, but somehow we managed to pull it off. By the time the wake-up call started, we were finished. It was an accomplishment I'd undoubtedly be proud of for the rest of my life.

And now, as a reward for our hard work, we were cutting tree branches.

It was kind of ironic that today's community service would be to clear out a path in the local high school. I spent my early morning climbing trees and plucking my clothes from their branches, and now I was cutting branches down. *Ha.*

I was actually kind of having fun. The work itself was tedious, but Vanessa and Ty managed to make it worthwhile. Will's moodiness could be amusing at times as well. And Tiffany's obvious dissatisfaction with the way her prank went down helped, too. It was oddly satisfying knowing that she lost this battle.

"Falice, are you even listening to me?"

I blinked, turning my attention to Will, who had an annoyed expression on his face as he snapped off another branch. It fell into the trash bag he held in his other hand. This was his second trash bag so far. "Of course, I'm listening," I lied.

Will scoffed. "Sure you were." "I was."

"Sure."

I took my pruner to the tree in front of me and cut off a branch. It fell to the ground, more than an inch from my bag's opening. "Uh, so what were you saying?" I asked as I bent to pick up the fallen limb. I tossed Will a cheeky grin.

Will rolled his eyes. "Listening my ass." I stuck my tongue out at him.

Will gave me a look that said I was incredibly stupid before saying, "I was asking if you came up with a plan yet."

I straightened and tossed the branch into my bag. "It's been less than ten hours," I replied. He was expecting a newbie pranker like me to come up with an amazing prank in less than a day? That was hilarious.

"So?"

"Dude, give her a minute to revel in the fact that Tiffany failed to humiliate her," Vanessa said, appearing out of what felt like nowhere. She left a couple of minutes ago to deposit her filled trash bag at the path's opening. She had an empty bag in her hand now and an amused smile on her face. "Patience, my friend. Patience."

"Since when are you patient?" Ty teased.

Vanessa swatted at him. "Besides," she continued, ignoring her boyfriend completely. "Falarabelle needs to figure out how to clean her duffel bag before she can do anything else."

"What?"

"Tiffany filled my duffel bag with oatmeal," I explained. With a grimace, I cut yet another branch. This time it fell straight into the trash bag. *Go Falice!* I silently cheered. "And my sister's shoes were in there, too."

"Aw, that sucks, Jessica," Ty said with a pat on my shoulder. "On the bright side, they weren't your shoes."

"True." I smiled. I glanced at Will. "I'll try to think of a plan as soon as possible, okay?"

Will shrugged. "Whatever."

I mentally rolled my eyes before going back to trimming trees. Vanessa and Ty chatted while we filled our bags, and I joined in every so often, but for the most part stayed quiet, struggling to come up with a prank that would reach Will's expectations. However, I couldn't keep my mind from trailing back to Tiffany's past revenge scheme. Where did she get the oatmeal from? Last time I knew, they didn't keep leftovers.

When I asked my question out loud, Vanessa, Ty, and Will paused. "Uh..." Vanessa's gaze turned sympathetic. "I'm pretty sure Lynn and Gina throw out the leftover oatmeal." Will frowned. "Yeah, they do."

Well, shit. "So are you saying I wiped my face with oatmeal from the trash?" I asked, knowing full well what the answer was, but still not comprehending.

"Yeah."

I nodded, lips pursed. "Lovely."

Excuse me for a moment while I go vomit.

"You could always take the leftover oatmeal in your bag and dump it on her head," Ty suggested. "Bet she'd love that."

Vanessa and I laughed. "That sounds like a perfect idea, Ty," I agreed. "I'll definitely keep that in mind."

Ty beamed. "Thank you, Jessica. Glad to be of service."

I thought of an idea one day later. Will loved it.

Just kidding.

"I'm sorry, what?"

I hesitated before answering, using my trash picker to pluck a Subway cup from the ground. Today, a small group of us was cleaning a stretch of road, while other groups were off doing other community service. I definitely would have preferred clearing out another path, but I guess this was better than some of the other tasks they had us do. Definitely, less energy-consuming.

After putting the cup in the trash bag, I looked at Will. He was staring at me with an incredulous expression on his face as though he couldn't fathom how senseless I was. That's probably exactly what he was thinking, too, knowing him. But I didn't care because it was my turn to have a stupid plan now.

"You heard me," I told him, picking up the napkin now.

"Yeah, I did." Will shot me a glare. Ooh, scary. I was happy to report that Will's glares officially had no effect on me. "You are aware how incredibly idiotic your plan is, right?"

"If two eleven-year-olds can pull it off, I'm sure we can," I retorted, pushing a few stray strands of hair out of my face. From behind me, I could hear Vanessa and Ty snickering.

"Oh my..." Will shook his head. "You've got to be kidding me.

Your idea revolves around *The Parent Trap*? Tell me you're kidding."

I snorted down a laugh, eyes flicking toward Vanessa. "Vanessa," I said. "Which is better? Having a prank inspired by *The Parent Trap,* or Will having seen it?"

Will glowered. "Whoever hasn't seen *The Parent Trap* hasn't had a childhood."

"I bet you had a crush on Lindsay Lohan," I teased.

"Back to the discussion at hand," Will muttered, evading my comment. I wasn't sure if it was because he really had a crush on Lindsay Lohan, or if he was just annoyed with me. Maybe it was both. "That was Hollywood, Falice. Please explain to me how you expect to pull this off."

"Yeah, Jessica," Ty said. I glanced at him and smiled when I saw the playful grin on his face. "I can't wait to hear this."

"Oh, come on, guys." Vanessa laughed. "Falarabelle has obviously thought this through." She winked at me. "Right, Falarabelle?"

I rolled my eyes at my friends as I sauntered over to the next piece of trash. It was astounding how much garbage was out here. Honestly, did people not care about the world anymore? By the amount of wrappers, cans, and other trash strewn about, I would say no. "Isn't it obvious?" I asked. "We just drag her mattress out to the lake, that's all."

"Oh, that's all." Will scoffed. "You are aware mattresses sink, right?"

"Really? Well, I am now." I sighed. "What else can we use?"

No one answered for a moment. Then Vanessa asked, "Aren't there inflatable floats somewhere in Henry's office? For the last week of camp?"

Will looked like he didn't want to answer for fear that I'd get my hopes up and continue insisting we do this ridiculous plan. "Yes," he said slowly.

Vanessa shrugged. "Those obviously float. And they're big enough to fit a person."

Will frowned. He clearly wasn't happy with Vanessa for encouraging this. "Okay," he said. "So how are we going to get into Henry's office, grab the float, get into Tiffany's cabin, get her onto the float, and get her into the water without waking her or anyone else in the process?"

He had a point, but I still had to fight the sudden urge to slap him. "I'm sure you'll figure it out, right, Dyer?"

"How come she calls him by his last name?" Ty asked suddenly. "Are we not cool enough to be referred to by our last names?"

"Um, maybe that's because your last name is Kadeth," Vanessa replied. "Tyler Kadeth, like what is that?"

Ty snorted. "Okay, Andrews. You're just jealous you don't have a cool last name like the rest of us."

Will let out a long, exasperated sigh. I watched as he grabbed a soda can from the ground and chucked it into his bag, not even bothering to use his trash grabber. "No, I won't, because this idea is stupid," he told me, ignoring Ty and Vanessa as they continued bickering about surnames.

"Your spider idea was stupid." "This is stupid*er*."

I was about to point out the irony of him calling me stupid when he just used the word "stupider," but before I could, a worker I distantly recognized but never spoke to suddenly stood in front of us and the words died in my throat. I turned to look at him, eyes wide. He, unlike the majority of his coworkers, appeared to be a grouch. He had his arms crossed over his rotund belly. My eyes shot to his balding head and then back to his face. The man glared at me, like he thought I was silently judging him for losing his hair.

"Is there a problem here?" he demanded, tone stiff as he regarded me and Will with suspicious eyes. For a moment, I panicked. Had he heard what we were talking about? No, I doubted it. He'd be dragging us back to camp if that were the case.

"N-no," I said quickly. "There's no problem."

The worker's eyes narrowed. "You sure about that?"

"Yes," Will said, bringing the attention— thankfully— away from me.

The worker tossed Will an annoyed look before relenting. "Okay," he said, not sounding convinced. "Less talk, more work."

With that, the man stomped off, back to where he'd been conversing with Penny.

"That's Gilbert for ya," Vanessa said as we watched him leave. "He's such a grump."

"That's because he still lives with his mother," Ty said.

"And you know this how?"

"A hunch."

Vanessa snorted. "Okay."

For about thirty seconds, Will and I were quiet as we listened to Ty and Vanessa discuss Gilbert's hypothetical home life. I looked around for another piece of trash, not fully concentrating on Ty's theory that no one except his mother would ever love him. Will just stood there, staring at them with a blank gaze. Then he decided to resume our argument. "We're not doing your idea," he said.

I huffed and shook my head. "Yes, we are. Come on, Will, we did yours!"

"If I were you, I'd clean and whine at the same time," Vanessa suggested, gesturing at Gilbert with a small wave of her hand. I almost shivered. He was staring at us. Because that wasn't creepy or anything. "We don't want him coming back here, do we?"

"No, we do not," I mumbled in agreement. Then I shot a glare Will's way and picked up trash. Did I really care that he didn't agree with me? No. Did it matter that I didn't care? No, not really. His muscle was definitely required. Still, I managed to tell him indignantly, "Will, if you don't help me, I'm going to do it anyway."

Will stared at me for a long time before replying. "You know, when I first met you, I knew you were stupid, but I underestimated just how stupid you really are."

My free hand sought out my hip. "You are such an ass."

Ty sputtered out a laugh. "Oh my god, 'ass' seems like such a huge insult when Jessica says it. Am I right, or am I right?"

I feel like Will would have slapped Ty upside the head if we weren't still under Gilbert's scrutinizing gaze. But we were, so he had to settle with discreetly flipping Ty off while adjusting his trash bag. I couldn't help but laugh at that. He'd done it in such a creative way that it was impossible not to be a little impressed.

"Like you'd be able to pull this off by yourself," Will retorted, his attention swerving back to me. "You can't even do exercises without collapsing."

I shot him an unimpressed look as I plucked yet another Subway item from the ground. People in New Hampshire, I determined, must really love Subway.

"Well, she collapses a lot less often than she used to," Vanessa said. "So that's a start."

I sent her a smile. She winked.

Will wasn't swayed. "Are you seriously encouraging this?" "Come on, Will." Vanessa nudged a piece of garbage into her bag.

"Let the poor girl have a stupid idea. With your brains, we'll probably be able to pull it off."

Will stared at her for a moment, jaw clenched, as he let his gaze fall and got back to work. I could tell from the set of his shoulders that he was fully aware he'd manage to pull this off— he just didn't want to. *Ugh.* Why did he have to be so stubborn? Sure, my idea was a re-enactment of a favorite childhood movie, but it was still a prank, wasn't it?

"Will," I said softly. "You said I have to make her life a living hell.

Shouldn't my ideas count for something? Come on, please?"

I could feel Vanessa's and Ty's eyes on us as Will picked up trash like he didn't hear me. He was thinking over my words though. I could tell. I bit my lip and waited for his verdict. In all honesty, I'd wanted to pull this prank since I first watched the movie when I was little. Arabelle and I always talked about doing it to someone, but whenever the opportunity arose, I backed out for fear of getting in trouble. But since I had to pull a prank anyway, I wanted to at least give it a shot.

Finally, after what felt like forever, Will sighed. "If this ends badly, it's all on you," he warned. "Do we understand each other, Falice?"

I suppressed a smile. "Yes," I said. "We do."

PHASE 13

Despite Will's constant we'll-never-pull-this-off attitude, the plan was actually quite simple when put in the barest of terms. Vanessa, our personal thief, offered to sneak into Henry's office and steal the float. Ty, who resided in the cabin next to Tiffany's, agreed to do reconnaissance for a couple days so we'd have an idea when the girls fell asleep. After that was done, all we had to do was sneak into Tiffany's cabin (which was made easy with Vanessa's lock-picking experience), place Tiffany on the float, and then walk her down the hill.

Of course, getting her on the float and down the hill was easier said than done, but I remained optimistic.

"Carefully, roll her onto the float," Will whispered to Ty as we all stood around Tiffany's bed.

Ty shot an incredulous look Will's way. "Why do I have to do it?" he hissed. "I don't wanna touch it!"

It took a lot of self-control not to laugh at him.

I fidgeted uncomfortably while Will rolled his eyes at his friend. Tiffany was motionless in her bed, her breaths long and even. I squinted at her, wondering not for the first time if she was a deep sleeper. I hoped she was. It would really suck if she was a light sleeper. Like, a lot. But, as Ty continued to defend his right not to be the one to roll Tiffany onto the float, I decided Tiffany was probably a deep sleeper. Ty wasn't exactly being quiet.

"Shh!" Vanessa slapped Ty on the shoulder. "Do you want to wake up the she-devil?"

Ty grumbled under his breath, but stopped arguing.

"Falice," Will said, his gaze traveling over to me now. "You do it."

I opened my mouth to object, but then shut it, knowing that I really had no right to argue. This was my idea. I should be the one to do the parts everyone else was unwilling to do. So instead of complaining, I just nodded, let go of my end of the float, and shuffled over to the other side of Tiffany's bed. I lifted my arms and then hesitated, lips twisting uncertainly. How exactly did one go about this sort of thing?

When Will let out an impatient sigh, I snapped into action, gingerly lifting the blanket and pulling it to the end of the bed, just under her feet. Tiffany moved then, and I froze, heart beating quickly in my chest. *Oh shit, oh shit, oh—*

Tiffany sighed, and my panic came to an immediate halt. She was still asleep.

I let out a slow breath of relief. Thank God.

Rolling her onto the float was slow, painful work. I couldn't push her too hard or else she'd wake up, so I had to nudge her carefully. It was both tedious and nerve-wracking—not a good combo. While I repositioned Tiffany, Will and Vanessa held onto the ends of the float. Ty kept watch on the minions, making sure neither of them woke up during the process.

Finally, Tiffany rolled onto the float, and I was done. Boo-yeah!

"Hell, yes," Ty whispered. "Great job, Jess." I grinned. "Thanks," I said.

As Ty grabbed onto the third side of the float, I plucked Tiffany's comforter from her bed and draped it over her. Everyone's eyebrows shot upward. "What?" I asked with a shrug. "If she gets cold, she'll wake up. We want to at least make it back up the hill before that happens, don't we?"

"True." Vanessa winked. "Smart thinking, Falarabelle."

I smiled before shimmying between the float and Tiffany's bed, grasping onto the last free side. We all shared a glance, and then we were off, carrying Tiffany as quietly as we could out of her cabin. It was extremely difficult getting her out the door, but somehow we managed. I had no idea how, but we did. After that, lugging her to the main area felt relatively easy.

"If she wakes up," Ty said as we approached the main area, "I'm going to drop her and run. Just so you all know."

"If she wakes up, we're screwed," Will replied. "Especially Falice, since this was her brilliant idea."

"You suck," I informed him. It just seemed like something he should know.

Vanessa let out a breath of air that sounded something like a laugh. "Falarabelle, you give the best comebacks ever. Remind me never to get in a fight with you."

Our conversation fell away as we approached the hill. Traveling down the hill proved much harder than I anticipated, and if it weren't for the fact that the float would pop (and not to mention the look Will would give me), I'd suggest setting the float on the ground and just pushing her the rest of the way. On the bright side, Tiffany was a relatively immobile sleeper, so there a low risk of her rolling off the float.

"Oh, gross, she's drooling," Ty complained. "Guys, her saliva is gonna get on my hand. I'm so grossed out right now."

"Suck it up," Will snapped. "We're almost there anyway."

And we were. After countless stumbles, curses, and complaints, we were finally almost at the bottom of the hill. *Finally*, I thought. We were almost there. Just a little longer and then we'd have officially pulled this off!

"You know, you don't sympathize well," Ty said.

"I'm sympathizing with Scar from *The Lion King* right now." "What? Why?"

"He was surrounded by idiots."

I rolled my eyes and decided it would be best to ignore Will the rest of the way to the water. Vanessa appeared to have come to the same conclusion, her face scrunched with concentration as she stared down at the ground. My eyes scraped the hill's floor too. *Please don't trip. Please don't trip.*

"Careful, we're at the bottom," Will warned a few moments later. "Remember the small ledge."

Ah, yes. The small ledge. It was the portion of the hill that gave me many scrapes and bruises over the course of my time here. I always forgot about it, so I kept losing my footing. And, of course, I always managed to land on a really sharp rock because why not?

Luckily, though, this time I didn't slip. I remained cautious and aware of the stupid ledge. Everyone else did the same, and soon enough we were on the sand, the water greeting us from the other side. My lips tugged upward. We did it!

"Um, did anyone think about the fact that we had to get into the water so we could push her in?"

It was Vanessa who spoke. As we paused at the miniature beach's edge, I glanced at her, teeth digging into my lip. The thought had occurred to me, but for some reason I thought we'd figured this part out already, which we obviously hadn't. The fact that we came down here in sweatpants only made that point clearer.

Will gestured for us to put Tiffany down, and we complied, setting her as gently as we could onto the sand. Vanessa and I watched as she adjusted her sleeping position, completely oblivious to what was happening to her. Somehow, Tiffany managed to look unfriendly even while unconscious. Didn't people usually look innocent while they were sleeping? Or maybe that was only in novels.

"We could always go in our sweatpants," Ty suggested.

"My pajama shorts are dirty, and unless I want to sleep in jeans until the next round of laundry, I can't," Vanessa replied, raking a hand through her hair.

"That, and if Henry decides to check all the cabins, the soaked clothes are incriminating evidence," Will added.

"Damn. I didn't even think about that. But would Henry really do that?"

"I wouldn't put it past him."

I pursed my lips. What would Arabelle do?

Suddenly, I knew what I had to do. I didn't like it— I really, really didn't like it. But I didn't see any other options.

"Falarabelle, what are you doing?" Vanessa whispered, her tone colored with disbelief as I kicked off my shoes and pulled off my socks. I went to tug off my pants, but she grabbed onto my arm before I could. "Girl, stripping is for the clubs!"

"We need to get her into the water." I shrugged out of her grip and resumed pulling down my pants. At first, I was going to take off my shirt, too, just to be safe, but I settled with gathering most of my shirt and tucking it into the neck hole, sort of like a belly dance gypsy top. I could feel the eyes of everyone on me, and I swallowed uncomfortably. Just like a bikini, I mentally chanted. Just like a bikini.

"Boys, stop ogling," Vanessa teased as I edged toward the float. I flushed and cast a self-conscious look behind me. Though Vanessa had used "boys" plural, she didn't appear to be talking to Ty. I forced my gaze away, blush deepening.

With a deep breath, I stepped into the water, resisting the urge to squeal as the icy water curled around my toes. I thought the water was cold during the day, but it was nothing on the current temperature. My teeth began to chatter as I bent over and grasped the float in my hands. "Can one of you push from the other side?" I asked softly.

Will nodded and positioned himself at the front of the float. Together, we brought Tiffany into the water. When the float was too far out for Will to push anymore, I dragged her by myself, only stopping when the water reached my chest area. I gave her one last shove for good measure and then waded back to my friends, a small, victorious smile curling on my lips. Not just because we'd pulled this off, but also because I could finally say I'd reenacted my favorite prank from *The Parent Trap*. Arabelle would be so proud.

"We did it!" I whispered as I emerged from the water.

Vanessa cheered as softly as she could, waving her hands in the air. Ty joined in a moment later, letting out a short, "Whoop, whoop!"

I grinned while I hurried back into my sweatpants and stuffed my sandy feet into my shoes. When I straightened, socks in hand, I cast a short look in Will's direction. Something like a smile hinted on his lips. My smile grew.

Then his barely-even-a-smile disappeared, so quickly I thought I imagined it. "Come on," he said. "We should get back up the hill before she falls in the lake and wakes up."

Vanessa nodded. "Yeah, I'd rather not be here when that happens.

Well, I would, but then I'd get caught. Not preferable."

"Right," I agreed as I untangled my shirt. "Let's go."

We barely made it ten minutes into breakfast before a scream cut through the air.

Everyone froze, bewildered expressions taking over their faces. Some people held their spoons mere inches from their mouths, while others gripped their trays tightly in their hands, frozen where they stood. I was in the first group, spoon hovering as I cast a glance in Vanessa's direction. She shared my side-glance before dropping her spoon back into her bowl and faking an appalled expression.

"Nothing like the screams of the living to brighten up my morning," Ty mused. "I bet the water is positively delightful, don't you?"

Vanessa jabbed him in the ribs. "Shut up," she whispered.

"Someone will hear you."

"You cut me deep, Vanessa Andrews," Ty said woefully. He visibly struggled not to laugh.

I shot a quick look at Will before twisting around in my seat and watching the scene unfold with forced wide eyes. Gilbert, Joel, Penny, and Dennis were congregated in the corner, just as baffled as everyone else. "Everyone stay calm!" Gilbert yelled. "We're going to find out what's going on."

While all the workers left, the campers filed out after them, breakfasts abandoned. Will, Ty, Vanessa, and I followed everyone outside, to where they'd gathered in the main area. Teens were huddled in their separate social groups, chatting amongst themselves and glancing in the lake's general direction. The guys, Vanessa, and I chose a spot next to the rock wall.

"What do you think she's going to do this time?" I asked softly. "You know, as pay back."

Will shrugged. "I guess we'll find out." He was very comforting, really.

My attention averted to the left, and my eyes widened. Tiffany was storming up the hill, her face contorted with so much rage that I almost flinched. She was drenched, and her pajamas clung to her body as she clenched her hands into fists and spat out a string of curses, clearly not caring that workers could hear everything she was saying.

She was coming straight toward me.

I cast a frightened glance at Will without really meaning to. His eyes flicked between me and Tiffany, and something not unlike concern flashed across his face.

"Arabelle, I'm going to kill you!" Tiffany bellowed.

"Oh, shit," I whispered. I had the sudden urge to cling to someone, or maybe pee my pants. No one had ever really been angry at me before. I mean, irritated, sure. But enraged to the point where I wouldn't be surprised if they intended to murder me? No. "Oh shit! Oh shit, oh shit, oh—"

Will was just about to step in front of me when Tiffany was suddenly there, her claws digging into my shoulders as she shook me with so much force it made me nauseous. "You did this to me, didn't you?" she screeched. "Didn't you?"

I opened my mouth to answer, but then she shoved me, hard, and I fell to the ground, response forgotten. I groaned. *Ow*. But I refused to concentrate on how much it hurt, and willed the pain to fade into the background as I started to get back to my feet. Tiffany grabbed me before I could situate myself, her nearly black eyes glinting dangerously. She brought her fist up, and in a flash it began its descent…

And then she was gone.

"Fal—Arabelle!" Vanessa cried. She held out her hand, and I grabbed at it. Vanessa pulled me from the ground and into her arms. "Damn, girl. For a second, I really thought she was going to kill you."

"Me, too," I muttered with arms like limp noodles at my sides. "But where did she—?"

My head whipped to the side, and I let out a small gasp. Will and Tiffany were fighting— really fighting, with fists flying and legs kicking. I witnessed fights before, but this somehow felt worse. I wriggled out of Vanessa's grip and brought a hand to my mouth. "What is he doing?" I demanded. "He could get hurt!"

This was where Vanessa usually made a witty retort to make me laugh. But now all she could do was say, "She was going to hurt you."

My mouth snapped shut, and I gaped at the brawl before me, wishing I could do something about it but knowing I couldn't. It was like I was back at Gardner High, watching as Arabelle got herself into yet another fight and not being able to stop her. But here, it felt different. Here, I was in the middle of it all.

"Don't worry, he'll be fine," Ty assured me.

I nodded, though his words didn't put me at ease. "Hey, hey!" someone barked.

Gilbert appeared and grabbed both Tiffany and Will by the collars of their shirts, prying them apart. He looked irritated, like this was all just a huge inconvenience to him. "Who started this?" he demanded as he released his grip on their shirts and took a step back.

I stared at Will, hand still covering my mouth. His gaze found mine and stayed there, not straying even as Gilbert repeated his question. "Will did!" Tiffany shrieked, theatrical tears springing to her eyes.

My hand fell from my mouth, and my arms crossed over my chest. "He just came at me!"

"Is that true, William?" Gilbert asked.

I wanted Will to tell Gilbert the truth, to explain that Tiffany came after me and he defended me. But he kept his mouth shut.

"William?"

Will glanced at Gilbert before nodding.

"Looks like you've earned yourself a ticket to isolation," Gilbert announced, looking more excited about this than I thought he should have. It was so wrong of him to enjoy something like this.

"What?" It was Vanessa. "You can't—"

"I can, Miss Andrews, and if you don't want to join him, I'd shut your mouth."

I alternated quick looks between Will and Gilbert for a few seconds and then took a step forward, arms tightening, jaw setting with indignation. "If you're going to send him to isolation, you're gonna have to take me, too."

I honestly had no idea what I was doing. All I knew was that I couldn't let Will take the whole fall for something that wasn't his fault.

Gilbert looked me up and down. "What's your name?"
"Arabelle McAtee."

"And why, Miss McAtee, should I send you to isolation too?" Gilbert challenged, his expression telling me that he thought no more of me than he would a rodent.

I thought fast. "Because I started it." "What?"

I shrugged my shoulders and forced myself not to break my gaze. It was like the morning I performed as Arabelle. I called my inner-Arabelle out to play and held it. *Don't back down,* I told myself. *Arabelle wouldn't back down. Don't you dare.* "I started it," I repeated. "I came at Tiffany. Will thought Tiffany hurt me, so he pulled her off. He was just being a protective friend. So if you're going to send anyone to isolation, it's me."

Gilbert stared at me hard while he processed my words. Then he cocked an eyebrow. "Fine, you want isolation? You can join William there." He nudged me and Will forward, his hands resting on our backs. "Come on, you two."

I felt everyone's gazes on us as Gilbert led us away from the crowd, toward Henry's office. I slid my eyes toward Vanessa and Ty, where they stood with their arms crossed securely over their chests. I smiled slightly. Vanessa cracked a small smile in return.

Gilbert brought us through Henry's office so fast I didn't have a chance to get a good look at it. We walked down a short hallway and turned into another, smaller room. I looked around, nibbling on my lip.

The room was a replica of a cell, complete with bars and a bunk bed.

"Here you go," Gilbert said. "This will be your home for a week." I blinked. A week? Seriously?

Gilbert caught my look and lifted his eyebrows. "Oh, a week too long for you? Should have thought about that before you demanded to be locked up with your boyfriend." He looked between the two of us. "No sex in the cell, got it? Camp rules still apply."

Gilbert pushed us inside and locked the door. "Someone will bring you meals, and you'll get one hour of activity a day," he said. "Use this time to think about what you've done."

And then he was gone.

I did a quick scan of the room, careful to keep my eyes off Will as I moved around the cell. There wasn't much to look at, so the whole I- can't-see-you thing didn't work for very long. I wasn't quite sure why I was avoiding looking at him. Maybe it was because I knew I was about to get an earful for getting myself thrown in here along with him.

When it became clear that there was nothing else to pretend to find interest in, I sauntered over to the bunks and sat on the bottom bed. I bounced up and down a couple times before twisting my lips. Well, it seemed this bed was the equivalent of a rock. With a small sigh, I finally turned my gaze to Will and forced on a smile. "So," I drew out, "looks like we're bunk buddies, huh?"

Will didn't answer. Yep, this week was going to be great.

PHASE 14

"I bet Ty and Vanessa are bored out of their minds right now," I said, arms folded behind my head as I kicked back on my not-so- comfortable bed. *Like me,* I thought, but I didn't say this out loud.

Will didn't reply, but at this point that didn't surprise me. I'd long stopped expecting him to answer me. For the past two hours, I rambled about random crap in hopes he'd actually talk, but no luck so far. Apparently, I'd earned myself the silent treatment. My bad.

"Oh, come on, Will!" I whined, scooting off my bed and grabbing hold of the bunk's ladder. Will was lying on the top bunk while he stared blankly at the ceiling, jaw set in a way that informed me he wouldn't be acknowledging my existence anytime soon. Ugh. He was being such a baby about this. "Can't you just say, like, one word? Or not even that. A glare would suffice."

Nothing. Not even a twitch.

I sighed deeply, releasing my grip on one side of the ladder just long enough to drag a hand down my face. "Look," I said, "I'm sorry I got myself thrown in here, too, all right? It just felt wrong, you getting in trouble when you were only trying to keep Tiffany from hurting me."

Will looked over at me. If I was expecting some heartwarming reply about how this wasn't my fault, I was sadly mistaken. No, Will just glowered at me as if he was secretly plotting my death. Well, better than nothing I supposed.

"There," I mused with a grin. "Was that so hard?"

Was that grumbling under Will's breath I heard, or was that just my imagination?

"Ugh, you're being such a baby," I mumbled. Louder now, I said, "Stop throwing a temper tantrum. We're stuck in here for a week, and, unless you want me to talk your ear off, you might as well drop the act now."

It was Will's turn to drag a hand down his face. His resolve was dying, I observed with a small smile. His expression made it obvious. Apparently, two hours without telling me to shut up was his limit. *Ha.* "You're annoying," he said finally, flicking an exasperated glance in my direction before returning his gaze back to the oh-so-interesting ceiling.

I clapped my hands. "Yay! Falice, one. Will, zero. Boo-yeah!"

Will sat up then, raking a hand through his hair. Though his glower had downgraded to a scowl, I knew better than to hope he was any less irritated with me. "You are aware that you getting yourself thrown in here didn't get me in any less trouble," he pointed out, eyeing me crossly. "So what you did was pointless."

I shrugged. "At least, you didn't take the entire fall."

Will wasn't impressed.

For a fleeting moment, neither of us spoke. "Why didn't you just tell Gilbert that Tiffany was lying?" I asked.

Will didn't answer as he fell back in his bed and let out a long, agitated sigh. For a second I thought he'd resumed his silent treatment, but then he spoke. "Because then she would've explained why she was lying, and that would only result in her telling them you put her in the lake. And then that would most likely lead to them linking you to the spiders. It just seemed like the best option." He paused and looked over at me. "Why didn't you tell them she was lying?"

My eyebrows creased as I mulled over his question. Why didn't I tell them the whole truth? "I don't really know," I admitted. "I guess I figured that if explaining what really happened was a smart decision, you would have done it yourself."

Will lifted an eyebrow.

I wriggled uncomfortably under his gaze. "What?" I asked, suddenly self-conscious.

Will's other eyebrow rose at my reaction, and then he shook his head. "That's stupid."

He was unbelievable. "What?" I demanded. "Why?"

"Because you shouldn't rely on other people's decisions to make your own." Will's gaze lifted to the ceiling. "You need to follow your own gut feeling, not somebody else's."

I huffed. "I just can't win with you, can I? Now say that I had told them the truth. Would you be any less pissed off?"

Will couldn't seem to reply to that.

"God, Will. I did rely on my gut. It said you probably knew what the hell you were doing so I should probably keep my mouth shut. I'm not an idiot. No matter how stupid you think

I am, I do have a brain." I stepped off the ladder and folded my arms over my abdomen, an irritated expression crossing my face. "So why don't you stop sulking. Okay?"

Will gave me a hard stare before he finally let out a long sigh and said, "Fine."

Not the enthusiasm I was hoping for, but it was still more than I expected. "Okay," I replied, scratching an itch on the back of my neck. "So, are we good?"

Will nodded. "Yeah." I smiled. "Great!"

We fell silent again as I fell back on my bed and stared up at the bed above me. Even though we were doing the exact same thing as before I forced Will to talk to me, I felt better, like a weight had been lifted from my chest. At least, now, I knew I wouldn't be facing a week-long silent treatment. Unless, of course, I managed to piss him off again, which I guess wouldn't be difficult to do. Will got annoyed easily.

My thoughts traveled from Will and his short temper, to Tiffany, to the pranks we pulled on her so far, and then made an abrupt stop at Will's promise. Had he meant what he said? Well, even if he hadn't, he had no choice now. He pinky promised. And pinky promises were legit.

"Hey, Will?" I murmured.

"Mmm?"

"About your promise to help me through the course…"

"Kind of hard to do that when we're stuck here, Falice."

My gaze flattened. "I know that. But when we get out of here, when can we start? Because I really don't want to make a fool of myself again."

Will deliberated for a moment or two before answering. "We could probably start the night you get out if you wanted.

We'll have to do it after lights-out. That'll make it harder, but if you can run through the obstacle course in the dark, then you'll definitely be able to go through it in the daytime."

My lips folded together as I suppressed a smile. So Will hadn't been lying after all. "Thank you."

No answer. I was just going to pretend he'd nodded in response.

Yup. Definitely.

"Do you have a seven?"

I giggled as Will sighed deeply and tossed me a seven of hearts. I took my seven of clubs and put them together before placing them beside me on the floor. We were using the pack of cards Joel had been kind enough to sneak us on the first day of isolation when he delivered our dinner. Joel was swiftly becoming one of my favorite people on the planet.

"How about a four?" I asked.

Will's eyebrows arched as he relinquished his four. "I think you cheat," he said.

"Oh, yeah, Will, because I totally spend all my time plotting how to cheat at Go Fish."

Will rolled his eyes. "Why can't we play a good card game? You know, the ones we haven't been playing since we were five?"

"Because, when we were five, life didn't suck," I said with a grin as I organized my pairs. "That, and I don't really know any card games. And you're probably a sucky teacher with your lack of patience. So we're going to play Go Fish and Old Maid like the cool people we are."

"I didn't realize how incredibly bossy you are." Will shot me a look that made me snort out a laugh. When I didn't answer, he said, "Are you gonna take another one of my cards or what?"

Concealing a smile, I asked, "Do you have a two?"

Will took a dramatic scan of his cards. I let out a breath of laughter as his eyes darted between the cards and me. Will, I realized, wasn't all that hard to be around when he wasn't out there with everyone's eyes on him. He was like a different person in here. Kind of, anyway.

"Go fish!" Will exclaimed smugly, a small smile on the tip of his lips. That was another thing. In here, he was always cracking those small smiles that barely made their way to his lips, like he was resisting them but couldn't help himself.

I did not think it was cute. Most definitely not.

"Oh, way to be," I teased with a grin as I plucked a card from the deck. I bit my lip to keep from laughing when I saw what card I'd chosen. "I got my wish!"

Will scrunched his face in a way I could only describe as playful. I never thought I'd attach the word playful to Will Dyer, but there it was. "You suck," he told me.

"You suck more." I stuck out my tongue. "Now, do you have an eight?"

Will was in the middle of handing me his eight when Joel appeared behind— or, rather, in front of— the cell's bars with his hands behind his back. He chuckled when he saw us sprawled on the floor, cards between us. Will and I turned to face him, me with a smile on my face, Will with his usual impassive expression.

"Henry says you can have your hour of activity now," Joel said. "But remember you're not allowed to socialize with any of the campers, and you have to be productive."

I glanced at Will. "The course?" I asked. Will nodded. "Sure."

Will was a surprisingly good teacher.

Even though he seemed more laidback in isolation, I still expected him to get frustrated and yell at me as I struggled through the course. But he didn't. Instead, he showed me the best methods of how to get through it the fastest way possible, and how to push past the distractions around me. He brought me through the course over and over again, excluding the rock wall. According to Will, I should try to save three minutes for the wall, and complete the rest of the course in two minutes. That was a pretty daunting task, but challenge accepted.

Joel stood a few feet away, keeping time, and cheering us on as we went through the course. "You're doing awesome, guys!" he called. "Ten minutes until you have to go inside, okay?"

"'Kay!" I replied, face pinched as I climbed up the dreaded wooden wall, my grip tight on the rope. Will was waiting patiently behind me while I attempted not to fall for the thousandth time.

I reached the top and hopped over, landing hard on my feet. I winced as sharp needles stung my feet. *Ow.*

"You landed hard on your feet again, didn't you?"

I glanced up at Will, who was now perched on top of the wooden wall. How had he gotten up there so fast? "Yeah," I muttered. "How did you get up there so fast? And how is that comfortable?"

Will shrugged and dropped to the ground. I felt a sting of jealousy as he stood up with ease, clearly not in any pain. Or maybe it wasn't a sting of jealousy. Maybe it was a leftover needle in my foot.

"Show-off," I teased with a playful shove.

"Hey, hey, no violence," Will joked. "I could report you for that."

"Oh, and what are they going to do to me? Put me in a smaller cell?"

"If you guys are done, we can just head back now," Joel offered before Will could come up with a retort.

Will and I glanced at each other, shrugged, and then headed back to where Joel was still standing. Joel met us halfway, and then together we went back to Henry's office.

"Hey, can you bring us a board game or something?" I asked as we approached the office. The request slipped out of my mouth before I even really thought it, but after I asked I realized how great Chutes and Ladders sounded right now. Then again, anything sounded better than a one-hundred-forty-fifth round of Go Fish. Not that I was keeping count.

"I'm sure that could be arranged." Joel smiled. "Anything else?" "Good food?" I suggested.

"Ah." Joel grinned. "That'd probably be a bit more difficult." Will snorted while I laughed.

We reached the office and headed inside, back to the cell. I'd be lying if I said I minded all that much. Isolation felt more like a vacation than punishment.

"I'll see about getting you that board game," Joel said. "But hide it when people come around, okay? Having fun in isolation is like breaking the law."

"Isn't having more than one person in isolation already like breaking the rules?" I asked. "We're not exactly isolated."

"Don't give them any ideas, Arabelle," Joel teased.

After locking the door behind us, Joel disappeared down the hall. I collapsed on my bed and stared up at Will's mattress. My arms and legs were a little sore from the amount of effort I'd put into going through the course, but I didn't care. I was feeling much better about the course than I had before, even if I did still need a lot of work.

"Thanks," I said, letting out a content sigh. "For helping me with this."

"No problem." Will sat on the edge of my bed. "I'm sure you'll be fine anyway."

I laughed shortly. "Maybe I'll manage to only fall once next time." "Maybe."

"Ah, Arabelle would be so proud." I smiled.

"She should be, seeing how she's the one who got herself tossed in here," Will said.

I sat up, dodging the bottom of Will's bed. "What are you in here for?" I inquired, head tilting slightly to the side. "If you don't mind me asking. What did you do?"

Something in Will seemed to deflate. Any hint of a smile disappeared, and his eyes darkened. I immediately regretted asking, and my stomach turned in on itself guiltily. "I'm sorry," I muttered hurriedly. "That was so inconsiderate. You don't have to answer."

Will shook his head. "No, it's fine." He cleared his throat. "I just don't like talking about it."

I nodded. "Yeah, I get it," I replied. My eyes shot to the door. The sudden weight in the air was suffocating, and all I wanted was for it to lift. "So, uh, what do you like to do? You know, outside of here?"

A smile hinted on his lips again. I almost let out a relieved sigh. I didn't push the smiling Will too far away. That was good. "You're trying to make small talk?" he asked.

I shrugged, a hint of a blush coloring my cheeks. "Well, we're in here for a week. Might as well become best friends."

Will scoffed. "Best friends? Are we going to braid each other's hair and make friendship bracelets now?"

In answer, I grabbed his arm and pulled him closer to me. Will toppled over with a small oomph, almost landing in my lap. I brought my hands to his hair, a grin taking over my face as I attempted to braid the strands. "Dammit, Dyer," I said, pushing him away from me. "You get me all excited about hair-braiding, and then you have the audacity not to have long enough hair. How dare you?"

Will blinked. "I can't believe you just tried to braid my hair," he said blankly.

As he blinked again and shook his head, I laughed. "Will, I should have warned you," I said, shooting him a mischievous smile. "When I become comfortable with someone, I let my true, crazy self shine."

Will's expression became dry. "Oh, great."

I shoved him good-naturedly. "You jerk." I gestured to the cards from their spot on the floor. "You ready for another stupendous game of Go Fish?"

"Nuh-uh." Will shook his head. "I'm done losing at Go Fish.

We're playing Rummy." "What?"

"You heard me." Will smirked. "Rummy." "No!" I whined. "I don't wanna play Rummy."

"Sucks for you."

The next thing I knew I was being dragged to the floor and dropped in front of the discarded cards. I groaned as Will shuffled the cards. What even was Rummy? "Don't cheat," I warned, tossing him a pointed look. I could see him rigging it so he'd win, and I'd lose, just because he sucked at Go Fish and I didn't.

"I'm not going to cheat."

I grumbled under my breath as Will started dealing out the cards. "How do you play this anyway?"

"The rules are simple, really," he began. "First off…"

Over the course of the next few days, Will and I became more like friends instead of partners in crime while playing card games, board games, and other games, like rock-paper-scissors. We practiced the course pretty much every time we were let outside though once we opted to swim instead. Sometimes, when we couldn't think of anything better to do, we just sat and talked. It felt so strange connecting to Will like this. Even weirder because I knew that when we rejoined the Camp Sunshine Brooks community he'd revert back to the Will he was before— always glaring, always moody, always irritable. I was really dreading it. That Will didn't seem so real to me anymore. I wasn't sure why.

At least, I had the chance to see this side of him. Even if it was only for a week.

"I'm bored," I complained.

There was only so much time one could spend staring at the bottom of Will's bed without losing interest. But what else was there to do? I mean, we'd already played Chutes and Ladders, Go Fish, Old Maid, Rummy, and the other card games he'd taught me. A few minutes ago, we even made a card house. Of course that got ruined when Will decided to knock it over because apparently he was Godzilla, and there was nothing I could do about it.

I'd been ignoring him, but now I was bored. And, like I said, we usually talked when we were bored.

"Oh, so you're talking to me now?" Will asked.

"How many days are left?" I asked instead of answering his question.

Will sighed as though I was annoying him. I probably was, but whatever. I was still irked at him for knocking over the card house. It was turning out so great, and then bam. "Like, two. Maybe three. I don't know."

"Well, you should know," I scolded. "One of us has to be keeping track."

"And that one has to be me?" Will countered.

I scowled. "I was just starting to like you, Will," I said. "Don't ruin it."

"Flattering."

I grumbled under my breath and shut my eyes. I didn't want to be annoyed with him during our last days here. Not when he was going to revert the second we left.

"You should smile more often," I blurted. "What?"

And then he was leaning over side of his bed, astonishment coloring his face as it had his tone.

I shrugged. "You know, smile. Be nice. Like you are in here. You'd be a lot happier."

Will scowled, though it was pale in comparison to his past dirty looks. "Who says I'm not happy?"

"It's obvious, Will." A smile hinted on my lips. "Out there, it's like you're permanently miserable."

Will rolled his eyes. "That's because it sucks here."

I shrugged again. Sure, he said that, but I had a feeling it was something more. Whether it had to do with the reason why he came here, I didn't know. All I knew was that there was a different reason for why he was so unhappy. "Okay, Will," I relented with a sigh.

"Why do you care anyway?" Will asked. He was still leaning over the edge of the bed. It was a wonder the blood hadn't rushed to his head yet. I'd be dizzy by now.

"Like I said: I've started to like you, Will. Is it wrong for me to consider you a friend?"

I raised my eyebrows at him while I waited for a response. I'd be lying if I said I wasn't nervous for his answer. While he'd already said we were friends, I had to remind myself that Vanessa forced him to. I had no idea if Will actually considered me more than a pesky girl he was blackmailing. I hoped he thought more of me than that.

"I guess not," Will finally muttered.

My stomach loosened, and I smiled. "Is that your awkward way of saying we're friends now, Dyer?"

Will gave me a flat look. "I'm done talking sentimentally with you," he said, disappearing back into his bunk's area. "I'm a man, Falice. I do not talk about feelings."

"Men can talk about their feelings!" I objected. "Not talking about them makes you an ass, not a man."

Will was saved from answering by Joel. "Sorry to interrupt," he called from the doorway. "I come bearing gifts."

I glanced over at him. "Oh my god, did you buy me *Scarlet*?" I asked, referring to the sequel of *Cinder*. I was almost finished with the book, and I really didn't want to wait until the end of the summer to find out what happened next. That was going to suck.

"Not quite," Joel replied, chuckling. He held up his hands, emphasizing on the two trays. "Food sufficient enough for now?"

I sighed theatrically. "I suppose."

I slid off the bed and ambled over to the door. Joel opened it as I approached, and I accepted the trays from his outstretched hands before returning to the beds. After setting my own tray on the mattress, I handed Will his. "Thanks, Joel!" I said with a smile.

"No problem, Arabelle." Joel returned my smile. "Just two more days, and you guys are good to go. Oh, and Gilbert wanted me to remind you not to have sex in the cell? I have no idea."

Oh, Gilbert. You are so damn creepy.

Joel left, and I turned to Will. "Hey, Will," I said.

Will stabbed a piece of potato with his fork. "What?" he asked.

"Joel keeps track of the days."

Will gave me a flat stare. "Screw you, Falice."

"Uh, uh, uh." I waggled my finger at him. "No sex in the cell." "I take it back," Will said. "We're not friends anymore."

"Of course not!" I exclaimed, grinning when Will's eyebrows lifted. "We're best friends. Duh."

"I worry about your sanity."

"Well, sucks for you. You'll have to visit me in the asylum because that's what best friends do."

Will shook his head and continued eating his dinner. I was going to pretend that meant I won the banter. With a small fist-pump, I plopped on my bed and put my tray on my lap. Tonight was meatloaf, potato, and corn. While the potato didn't taste that bad, the meatloaf was definitely not to be desired.

"Hey, Will," I said through a mouthful of potato. "What?"

"We're best friends now."

"Oh my god, you suck. Just shut up."

I grinned. Oh, what a wonderful friendship indeed.

PHASE 15

"And she's alive!"

I fist-pumped and let out a soft, "Woo!" as I closed the cabin's door behind me and faced Vanessa. She was sitting with her legs crossed on her bed, a huge smile plastered on her face. It seemed she was as happy to see me as I was to see her.

My eyes drifted to my bed, and a satisfied shiver ran down my spine. Oh, how I missed this bed. While this was a downgrade from my bed at home, this bed was still a lot better than the one in isolation. *Hello, beautiful,* I thought happily. *May we never be parted ever again.*

"Isolation couldn't possibly kill me," I joked, facing my friend again. "I'm invincible!"

"It wasn't isolation I thought was going to kill you." Vanessa hopped from her bed and walked over to me, wrapping her arms around me. She gave me a tight squeeze before letting go. "I didn't think Will was going to let you live to see the end of the week. I mean, not only because he probably didn't appreciate what you did, but also because I was sure you guys would irritate the shit out of each other. It was bound to get bloody."

I shrugged. "He wasn't happy, but I told him to get over it, and he did. We're all good now."

Vanessa's eyes went wide. "He got over it? Just like that?" "Um, yeah," I said.

"Wow."

"I didn't think it was that big of a deal," I said.

Vanessa shook her head disbelievingly. "Not a big deal? Have you seen Will lately?"

Her lately and my lately were completely different things. My lately consisted of small smiles and easy banters. Her lately consisted of moodiness, glares, and cold, sarcastic remarks. Maybe that was why I didn't find it so hard to believe he'd given in so easily. My view of Will had been altered over this past week.

"Yeah," I said with another shrug.

Vanessa eyed me skeptically for a moment before her mouth dropped. "Oh my god," she whispered. "You two hit it off in isolation, didn't you?"

My eyebrows skyrocketed. "What?"

"Did you guys kiss? Are you guys, like, a thing now?" Vanessa grabbed me by the shoulders and gave me a slight shake. "Falarabelle, I need details."

I removed her hands from my shoulders and returned her wide-eyed look with one I hoped conveyed how crazy I felt she was in that moment. "Um, why would we kiss?" I asked after a few seconds. "Nothing happened in isolation, Vanessa, honestly." I paused, head tilting thoughtfully to the side. "Though I did kick his ass at Go Fish."

Vanessa continued to stare at me, her eyes narrowed like she was searching for a hint that I was lying to her. It was like she wanted something to have happened between us. I couldn't fathom why. I mean, yeah, Will and I became friends, but that didn't mean I had romantic feelings for the guy. The thought almost made me laugh out loud. One week in isolation wasn't going to change everything.

"You're sure?" she asked eventually, listing her head. She squinted at me some more.

"Yeah, I'm sure."

Vanessa finally relented. "Okay."

"It's like you want us to be dating or something," I said, voicing my inner thoughts as I walked over to my beloved. The peanut butter was waiting for me where I'd left it, and I smiled.

"What? Oh my god— no— what? Most definitely not."

Peanut butter now in hand, I spun around to face Vanessa. "Dude," I said, unscrewing the cap. "We just became friends."

"I know, I know!" Vanessa waved her hands at me. "It's just... I don't know. I wouldn't object to you guys dating." She grinned.

I gaped at her. Where was this all coming from? One week I was gone, and now she was envisioning me dating Will? "I'm never getting thrown in isolation again," I announced with a shake of the head. I laughed. "You've been driven to madness."

"Girl, it's not my fault you don't see the chemistry," Vanessa defended herself with a broad smile. "You didn't see Will before you got here. He was so much worse than he is this year." She winked. "Someone had to do something to change that."

I rolled my eyes at her implication and fell onto my bed. Ugh, this bed felt so damn comfortable. It was beyond amazing. I wished I could just sleep here for a week. But of course, I couldn't. Unlike in isolation, I had a daily schedule to abide by. "Ugh," I mumbled, eyes slipping shut. "I am so not looking forward to exercises. My arms are so out of practice."

"Oh, yeah, change the subject," Vanessa teased. I opened my eyes and peeked over to see her grinning at me. "But yeah, you're pretty much screwed. I think that's the true punishment of isolation. The torture afterward."

"And you know this how?"

"Whatever." Vanessa stuck her tongue out at me. "But still, it only makes sense. I mean, it seems like you didn't have a hard time in isolation at all." She paused. "How did isolation work anyway?"

I dragged my fingers through my hair. "We had to share a cell. It had a bunk bed, so we didn't have to share a bed, thank God. Whenever we had to go to the bathroom, we had to ask an available worker to bring us to Henry's office's bathroom. Same for showering."

"What did you do when it was time to change?"

When she wriggled her eyebrows, I rolled my eyes. "Whenever Joel was there, he let me go to the bathroom to change. When he wasn't, I made sure Will had his head covered with a pillow. And the same went for me when he was changing."

"You didn't peek?" When Vanessa saw the expression on my face, she held up her hands. "Hey, hey! I wouldn't have blamed you if you did— you two seeming perfect for each other or not. The guy's hot."

"Don't you have a boyfriend?" I asked.

"Yes, and he's hot, too," Vanessa said. "I'm allowed to acknowledge other boys' hotness. Ty doesn't care as long as he's the only one I want— which he is."

My lips pricked upward. "You guys are so cute." "Aw, thank you—"

A high-pitched whistle cut off whatever Vanessa was about to say next. We both looked out the window, toward the main area. Another surprise drill. Great.

"Dammit!" Vanessa complained as we hurried for the cabin door. "I'm so not in the mood for this."

I grimaced. I wasn't either. "Gotta love surprise drills."

"No, we don't. We can hate them if we want. It's a free country." "Oh. Well, then I'm all set on hating them."

As we scuttled down the path and to the main area, I felt a distant sense of anticipation course through me. Yes, this was a surprise drill. Yes, I hated the idea of going through this again, especially if there was a chance I'd be paired with Tiffany. But this time, I was prepared. It was time to put Will's lesson into action.

You're going down, I told the obstacle course as we approached the group of teens waiting for everyone else to arrive. *It's on like Donkey Kong.*

"I didn't fall this time!" I squealed for what was probably the fifth time, ecstatically clapping my hands together.

From beside me, Vanessa snorted and clapped along with me, an amused smile tugging at her lips. I wondered how long it would take for my enthusiasm to get annoying.

Thanks to Will's lessons, I managed to make it through without collapsing once. I didn't make it further, but I didn't publicly humiliate myself. It also helped that I didn't get paired with Tiffany this time. I had a feeling that if I did, she would have knocked me down on purpose. After all, she didn't get a chance to get back at me for putting her in the lake.

"Congrats!" Vanessa threw an arm over my shoulder and grinned. "Maybe you can use this gusto to make this etiquette class a little less boring."

Normally, the mention of etiquette class would make me pout, but today, I was in too good of a mood to care. Etiquette class had nothing on me. I'd survived the obstacle course. Obviously, this made me untouchable. *Obviously.*

"Are etiquette classes even salvageable?" Ty wondered aloud. "Probably not," Vanessa admitted. "I mean, Penny is awesome and all, but the classes suck."

Ty and I nodded in agreement.

When we reached the gym, I spared a glance in Will's direction. He had his gaze focused straight ahead, his mouth kept in a straight line. I willed his lips to lift upward, even if just a tiny bit, but nothing happened.

We entered the gym and found seats on the far right. I sat in the chair between Vanessa and Will, a small smile itching its way to the surface as I thought about my earlier triumph. It probably seemed stupid that I was this happy about something so small, but I couldn't help it. "Thank you," I said, looking over at Will. I sent him a grateful smile.

Will's eyebrows creased. "For what?"

I was about to answer, but then someone tapped me painfully on the back and my response was forgotten. I turned around and was greeted by Tiffany, who retracted her hand, crossed her arms over her chest, and glowered with such intensity I couldn't help but wonder if she believed looks could kill. Part of me wanted to shrink away— mostly the part that traveled back to the morning Will and I were sent to isolation— but another part, the defiant part, refused to give her that satisfaction. "Hello, Tiffany," I said.

Tiffany's glower deepened. "I know it was you."

"I'm afraid I don't know what you're referring to," I lied.

Was Tiffany growling under her breath, or was I just imagining things? "I know you were the one who put me in the lake," she hissed. "You and your stupid friends."

Tiffany spared a disdain-filled glance at Will. Even without looking, I knew Will wasn't giving her the reaction she would have wanted.

"But Tiffany," I said, and her eyes snapped back to me, "I can barely get through exercises."

Tiffany's jaw locked. "I don't know how you did it, but you did." Her eyes were bright with hatred. "And don't think I'm going to let you get away with it. You're not going to win."

I forced my lips into a smile. "Okay. Have a nice day, Tiffany."

After glaring at me for another moment or two, Tiffany flipped me off and stormed over to where her friends were waiting. I watched her leave, my stomach in knots— a mixture of nervous energy and a small sense of victory. It felt... good to stand up to her like this. Nerve-wracking, but good.

When Tiffany was seated, I looked over at Will and smiled. His lips twitched in return.

"I feel like Tiffany's going to explode someday," Ty said. He used his hands as a representation of an explosion. "All that anger is going to overpower her and then boom." He made a fake explosion with his hands again. Then he grinned his goofy grin.

"You're talking about someone exploding, and you're laughing," Vanessa said. "You are aware of that, aren't you?"

"Yeah, but it's Maleficent." "True."

"She's planning something," Will murmured.

I cast a fleeting look in Tiffany's direction— just long enough to see her seethe some more— before returning my attention to Will. He had a frown on his face, his expression both thoughtful and distantly concerned.

"Way to ruin the cheerful atmosphere," Vanessa rebuked. "Geez, you couldn't let the poor girl have five minutes of happiness, could you?"

"Well, he's right," I said with a shrug. "It's obvious."

"Yeah, but he didn't have to bring it up right now." Vanessa reached behind my back and whacked Will on the shoulder. "Ugh, you're such a mood killer, you know that?"

I pressed my lips together to suppress a smile as Will rolled his eyes at her. Despite the fact that I knew an attack was coming, I couldn't help but feel lighthearted. My good mood was here to stay, it seemed, and I was all set not worrying about Tiffany until she retaliated.

Will's gaze returned to me, and I knew he didn't share the same sentiment. "Just be careful," he said.

I nodded. "I will."

Okay, so maybe I was lying when I said I'd be careful.

I didn't mean to lie— really, I didn't. I just wasn't as paranoid as I probably should have been, considering the situation. I guess now I knew not to be in an overpoweringly good mood because it would bite you in the ass.

My lips trembled as I pressed my back against the locker room's far wall, my eyes fastened on the floor. If only there was a chair or, I don't know, something that I could stand on to avoid them. Maybe then I wouldn't be as terrified as I was. It would still be terrible, maybe even unbearable, but at least, I would know they probably couldn't touch me.

Snakes. That's what I was staring at. Friggin' snakes.

They were scattered all over the floor, slithering toward me with their beady little eyes and long, disgusting bodies. In the back of my mind, I wondered where the hell she'd gotten them all, but for the most part, I couldn't think of anything further than my fear, which was threatening to suffocate me. Already, my breathing had become shallow. Was I going to faint? Oh god, please no. The thought of being unconscious with these things crawling all over me... no.

I forced my breathing to steady, letting out long, deep breaths. These snakes weren't poisonous, I told myself. They weren't large enough to eat me whole. I would be okay.

But I wasn't convinced, not really. Ever since I watched that documentary on Animal Planet when I was five, I had been terrified of snakes. No pitiful optimistic chants were going to erase that fact.

How did Tiffany figure it out?

Probably luck. It didn't matter, anyway. She'd pulled it off. I wanted to bang on the walls, to scream for someone to help me, but something held me back. If I screamed, if I cried, Tiffany would win. I'd give her exactly what she wanted. And somehow that seemed worse than dealing with the snakes on the floor.

So I kept my mouth shut.

Someone was bound to realize I was missing. I was late for my hour of swimming. Vanessa had swimming with me, so she would know something was up when I didn't show. But even if she did figure out what happened, I found it hard to believe they'd let her leave the area. While this camp wasn't jail, the workers kept a firm eye on us while we participated in our activities. She could probably ask to go to the bathroom, but I doubt she would be able to get up here without a worker by her side.

A snake touched the edge of my shoe. My eyes slipped shut, and

I let out a long, shaky breath of air. *It's not actually touching you.* I tried to remind myself. *It's touching your shoe; not your skin, your shoe.*

Once again, the chants were not enough. I still cringed because felt like the snake was touching me.

I wouldn't scream, I wouldn't scream, I wouldn't scream.

However, I would kick at the snakes as they neared me. "Shoo!" I hissed. "Go away!"

The snakes didn't seem to understand me. I cursed under my breath. Damn, I would have killed to be Harry Potter right now. He had that cool ability to talk to snakes. What was it called again? Parseltongue? Maybe if he were here, he could convince them to leave, or just kill the dang things with his wand.

Sometimes, it really sucked not being a wizard.

My eyes flew open, and I covered my mouth with my hand to keep from screaming as a snake wrapped itself around my ankle. *Shit, shit, shit.* I shook my leg viciously, my eyes burning with panicked tears. Honestly, if I was in here for much longer, I had no doubt that I was going to burst into tears or faint. And neither would be very pleasant.

How long had I been trapped in here anyway? How much time had passed since all the other girls finished changing and left?

If I hadn't been running late, this wouldn't have happened. If I hadn't misplaced my stupid bathing suit, I would have been able to leave with the other girls. And then I wouldn't be stuck here while they got to swim laps and not have snakes wrap themselves around their ankles.

On the bright side, my mind whispered feebly, *your arms won't be sore for evening exercises.*

Thank you, mind, for attempting to cheer me up, but the fact that there were over a dozen snakes in here kind of dampened my optimism.

"Falice?"

My gaze shot to the other side of the locker room, toward the door.

"Will?"

I can't begin to express how relieved I felt to hear the latch unlock and see Will step inside the locker room. His brown eyes were wide, and he was breathing hard, like he'd been running.

"S-snakes," I whimpered. "Why did it have to be snakes?"

Will pursed his lips and held out his hand. "You'll have to come through them," he told me, his tone gentle. "I know you're afraid, but you can do it, all right?"

I blinked back tears and nodded. I could do this. These snakes had nothing on me. Psh, no. I could do this, I could—

Okay, I so couldn't do this. "Falice, you'll be fine. I promise."

My eyes, which had fallen to the snakes, snapped up to Will again. His hand was still outstretched, his face almost impassive. However, there was something in his expression that told me he understood just how frightened I was. And, unlike the last time we'd dealt with creatures in locker rooms, he wasn't agitated at all. He was patient. Like he'd been in isolation.

I really liked this side of Will.

Taking a deep breath, I grabbed onto Will's hand. It was soft and cool in mine. I bit my lip when he gestured for me to walk toward him and lightly tugged my hand. "It's okay, Falice," he said softly. He gave me a small, comforting smile. "I won't let the mean snakes eat you, alright?"

I tried to snort, but failed. "Usually, I'd either find that incredibly funny or irritating," I said, "but since I'm deathly afraid of snakes, I don't."

Will's smile grew. "Just step in-between them. You'll be fine. I promise."

"Pinky promise?" "Pinky promise."

I took another deep breath and edged toward him, flinching when my feet brushed against the snakes' bodies. "Ew, ew, ew," I squeaked with a grimace.

Suddenly the snakes were behind me, and I was standing in front of Will. I looked up at him, eyes wide. And then, before I could really think about what I was doing, I threw my arms around him and squeezed. "Thank you," I whispered. "Thank you, thank you, thank you."

Will stood completely still for a moment, but then his arms wrapped around me and pulled me closer. I dug my face into his chest as I struggled to slow my rapidly beating heart. Instead of concentrating on the fact that there were snakes right behind me, I focused on Will and the fact that he was actually hugging me back. I've never really hugged a boy (unless you counted my elementary school friends and my dad), so this was a first. And I wasn't gonna lie— it felt pretty good.

I blinked and pulled away. "Thanks," I mumbled again, awkwardly rubbing my arms. I'd just admitted that hugging Will felt good. Something about that made me uneasy. It seemed too… I didn't even know.

"Are you okay?" Will asked.

I nodded. "Yeah, I'm fine. Can we get out of here? Please?"

Will nodded and moved aside so I could get through. I rushed out of the locker room, my arms wrapped protectively around myself. In that moment, I could honestly say I wasn't thinking about the snakes at all. I couldn't stop thinking about me hugging Will, and Will hugging me. My stomach tumbled, and my eyebrows creased. What the hell?

Will came to stand beside me. He was silent as he stared ahead, his jaw working angrily.

"Do you have any idea where she got the snakes?" I asked after a few moments of silence.

Will nodded. "The same place I got the spiders. There's this guy down the road who collects them."

Huh. "So you guys actually snuck out of camp to pull off pranks?" "Yeah." Will shrugged. "It's not hard to sneak out, if you do it at night. That must have been when she got the snakes; which means she most likely planned this while we were in isolation."

That didn't surprise me. "She's such an asshole."

Will absently nodded his head, his jaw still working. "I'm going to kill her," he muttered.

The sudden venom in his voice caught me off guard. This wasn't the first prank Tiffany had pulled on me, and it certainly wouldn't be the last. Why was this the one to tick him off? I put a hand on his arm, and he turned toward me. "Don't lose your head, Will," I said softly. "We'll get back at her for this, but we have to play it smart, alright?"

Will sighed. "Yeah," he agreed with a nod. "Yeah, okay."

I grinned. "I'm flattered you're this mad for my sake. Best friends for life, right, Dyer?"

Will's expression flattened. "We're not having this conversation again."

I nudged him playfully. "Tomorrow we'll make friendship bracelets, okay? I expect mine to be pink."

"Go swim," Will said, pointing at the hill. "I have some hiking to do."

I smiled and then sighed. "Thanks, Will. Seriously." Will glanced at me. "No problem," he said.

And with that we went our separate ways. I headed for the hill and Will started for the trails. I paused before I got too far and cast a fleeting look back at him. My stomach was twisting again, and for a moment, I wondered if I was coming down with something. Had I somehow frightened myself into becoming ill?

I shook my head and ambled down the hill. Mysterious stomach twisting aside, there was one thing I knew for sure: I was done feeling conflicted about this whole making-Tiffany's-life-a-living-hell thing. I was done feeling simultaneously guilty and triumphant. Tiffany had crossed a line when she placed me in a room with snakes. This was personal now.

From here on out, I was all in. Tiffany was going down.

PHASE 16

I was about ten minutes late for swimming. And, because Gilbert was the one on duty today, I got an earful for it.

Apparently, if I kept waltzing around like I owned the place I was going to find myself back in isolation "without my boyfriend around to keep me company." While Gilbert spewed his threats and dealt out his punishment (no popsicles for me during this week's exercises), I listened in an irritated silence. Vanessa was right: He was such a grump.

When Gilbert finally released me from his rant, I headed into the water, ignoring the stares of everyone around me as I did. Vanessa gave me a worried look, but she didn't ask me about what happened. It was kind of difficult to hold a conversation while doing laps. She just mouthed "Are you okay?" and when I nodded, she continued her laps in silence.

However, when swim time was over, Vanessa didn't waste any time before saying what she wanted to say. "What did she do to you?" she demanded.

"She locked me in the locker room," I replied. "Speaking of which, we should sneak to the cabin and change because the snakes are still in there."

Vanessa shot me an appalled look. "Snakes?"

I nodded, biting down on my lip as I turned my gaze to the hill. When I let my mind wander back to those moments in the locker room, I could still feel the fear slithering like the snakes through my veins. "If Will hadn't—" I paused, my eyes returning to my friend. "How did you get him anyway? He was hiking, wasn't he?"

"Well, Will had a huge feeling Tiffany was going to do something to you today, so he had me bring my phone with me." Vanessa pulled her cell phone out of her shorts' pocket and waggled it at me. "When you were running late, I quickly sent Will a text before getting in the water. He must have found a way to sneak away from his hiking group so he could get you."

I blinked. "Oh. Well, thanks." I dragged a hand through my damp hair. "If he hadn't shown up, I probably would have fainted. Snakes are like the only things that terrify me. You know, besides death and public speaking."

"You'll touch a spider, but you won't touch a snake." Vanessa snickered and shook her head. "You are unique, Falarabelle. Very unique indeed."

"That's what they tell me!" I grinned. "Either way, I am so getting back at her for this. Tying my hair to my bed is one thing, but snakes? Nuh-uh."

"Look at Falarabelle being all badass," Vanessa mused with a smile. She nodded though, and I knew she agreed with me. "I'm all in, girl. If I were you, my final straw would have been either when she tied my hair to the bed or when she stole all my clothes."

I thought about that for a second. "If my peanut butter or book had gotten involved, the second prank probably would have been."

Vanessa snorted. "You're so weird. Do you have a plan?" I shook my head. "Not yet. But I'll think of something."

For the next week or so, I plotted. Will, Ty, and Vanessa pitched some ideas, but nothing sounded quite right. Tiffany had hit me hard, and the only way for her not to win was for us to hit harder. Not just any prank would do.

"Have you thought of anything yet?"

I glanced up from the table and spotted Will as he pulled out the chair next to me and sat down. Neither of us had opted for lunch today. They were serving sloppy joes, which included less beef and more surprise meat. And, seeing how I was full enough to survive until dinner, I decided I wasn't in the mood to deal with the crappy food. "No," I said, shaking my head. "Not yet."

Will's hands fell lazily onto the table, palms facing upward. "Sooner the better," he muttered.

"I know—" My sentence cut off suddenly as my eyes landed on his right palm. "What's that?"

Will let out a small noise of surprise as I took his hand and pulled it toward me. "What the hell, Falice?"

I pointed at the scar on his hand. "How'd you get this?" I asked, eyes wide. It was a jagged scar— so jagged that something squirmed nervously inside me. What happened to him? Did he get into a fight? Or did he pull a "me" and trip, fall, and then land on a branch? I doubted it was the latter. Will wasn't the kind of guy that stumbled. He wasn't clumsy.

"It's nothing," Will said. He tried to tug his hand from my grip, but he didn't succeed. I was holding on too tightly. I wasn't quite sure why I was this concerned, but I was. I guess there was something inside me that knew this wasn't the result of some innocent accident. Someone hurt him.

What the hell was going on with me?

"This isn't nothing," I argued. Without even really thinking about it, I trailed my fingers over the scar with my free hand. "Someone hurt you, Will."

Will tensed as my fingers grazed his scar. It was then that I realized what I was doing and abruptly let his hand fall, pulling mine back toward me. What the hell was I doing? Freaking out over a scar? A lot of people had scars. I had one from falling off my bike when I was six. Arabelle had them all over the place from various things. So why did I care so much? And why did my fingers feel weird, like they were still in contact with his hand?

My gaze averted to the tabletop, and I felt my cheeks redden. *Get ahold of yourself, Falice*, I thought. *Come on!*

"What happened here?"

I looked up as Vanessa and Ty set their trays on the table and sat down. Vanessa glanced between the two of us, eyeing us suspiciously while she plopped into the seat on my other side. I wondered what tipped her off: my flushed face or Will's sudden obsession with the non-existent spot on the table.

"Nothing," I said quickly. "We were just discussing whether I had a plan or not. Which I don't."

Vanessa gave me a look that said I was stupid if I thought she believed that. If we were alone, she probably would have made another comment about how Will and I were perfect for each other. She'd been doing that a lot lately. However, right now she just nodded. "You gotta hurry it up, girl. I'm getting impatient. I wanna beat that girl's ass already!"

"I should be concerned that I'm in a relationship with someone so violent," Ty mused, "but Vanessa's right, Jessica. When can we kick the ass' ass?"

"I don't know, go ask Jack."

When Ty just stared at me blankly, I sighed. "Jack, jackass? Get it? No? Fine, okay, whatever."

It took Ty a second, but then he caught on and broke into a fit of guffaws, slapping his hand on the table. "Damn, Jessica, you're hilarious!" When he caught Vanessa staring at him like he was insane, his laughter died out, and he sighed. "What? She made a pun, and I found it punny."

"Punny?" Vanessa cocked an eyebrow. "That's not even a word." "Well, not in the boring dictionary."

"There's another kind?"

"Of course! It's called 'Ty's Dictionary of Awesome Words'."

"If it's a dictionary, why do the words have to be awesome? That's going to make the other words feel left out."

"I didn't make the title." "Could have fooled me."

As the lovebirds continued to bicker, I glanced at Will. He was staring at his scarred palm. It was like he was far away from here, back at the place and time he'd received the injury. And, from the growing frown on his face, I guessed it wasn't a very pleasant memory.

I folded my lips together to keep myself from asking him any more questions about it. He'd already made it clear he didn't want to answer. Besides, maybe he really did fall and just hated remembering the pain it caused.

Yeah, I didn't believe that for a second.

Will looked up suddenly, his eyes flicking over to me. He blinked and slowly shook his head, curling his hand into a fist. "What?" he asked even though he obviously knew what.

"Nothing," I replied. As curious and concerned I was about this, I wasn't going to force him to divulge. If he didn't want to talk about it, we wouldn't.

Will opened his mouth to say something but stopped when hissing noises erupted from behind me.

I jumped before spinning around in surprise. Tiffany and her minions were there, making snake impressions with their hands. My gaze flattened as I watched them. Seriously? "Aw," I cooed, "I always knew you were a conniving snake, but I didn't realize you knew it, too."

Tiffany stopped hissing, and in an instant so did the two girls behind her. "I heard that you like snakes," she replied with a malicious smile. She reminded me of a cat preparing to pounce. "In fact, I heard you like hanging out with them while you're supposed to be swimming."

I was suddenly reminded of my wish to speak Parseltongue. "I'm talking to you, aren't I?" I asked, smiling right back.

"Did you know that the camp directors think that the person who pulled the prank with the spiders is the same as the person who put the snakes in the locker room?" Tiffany asked.

"What happened with the snakes?" I asked, eyebrows rising. I was actually a better actress than I gave myself credit for. I sounded believable at least.

"You know what happened with the snakes." "No, I really don't."

I smiled cheekily. It was amazing, I couldn't help but think, how once I decided that I was all-in on the plan, the backtalk came to me so much more easily. It was like with Danny or with Will before we became friends.

"Tiffany," Will drawled, "if you have nothing smart to say, then leave. Your idiocy is killing valuable brain cells."

Tiffany's eyes snapped over to Will just long enough to glower at him. "You two are perfect for each other," she snarled, her glare alternating between Will and me now. "Both of you are ugly, vile, disgusting creatures that shouldn't even be allowed—"

"Do yourself a favor and pick up a dictionary on your way back to your table," Vanessa piped in, a cool smile taking over her face. "You obviously have no idea what the definition of ugly is." She paused. "Nor do you know the definitions of vile or disgusting. Honestly, honey, just read the whole damn thing. You need a serious lesson in vocabulary."

I watched as Tiffany's nails dug into her hips. Her menacing stare continued to move between us, like she was trying to figure out which one of us she'd attack first. "Just leave, Tiffany," I said. "You'll gain nothing by standing there."

"Except, the longer you stand there, the stupider you look," Ty added. I could tell he only joined in because he felt left out, but it worked.

With an eye-roll, Tiffany stormed away, her minions scurrying to catch up with her as she did.

I stared after her as she left, jaw set. Just because the camp blamed the snakes on the person who pulled the prank with the spiders, it didn't mean she'd won. Sure, no one suspected her. But who cared? No one suspected us either.

"Falarabelle, are you okay?"

I twisted back around in my seat, facing my friends. "Yeah," I told her. "I just… I want to give her back everything she's done to me. Everything. The snakes, the hair, the—"

I cut off suddenly as an idea sparked. That was it!

"I've got it!" I shrieked, clapping my hands together. "I've got an idea!"

"Oh, do tell!" Vanessa squealed.

I grinned. "We're going to give it back to her. Everything that she's done to me. A collage of pranks. We'll tie her hair to her bed, we'll set snakes loose in her cabin, and we'll steal her clothes and hang them out on the trees. And, if we have time, maybe we'll add something else for good measure."

Will, Ty, and Vanessa shared a glance. For a moment, I was nervous, thinking they were going to say the plan wasn't plausible, that we should do something else. But then Vanessa beamed, and I knew this wasn't the case. "Ooh, I like it," she said excitedly.

I looked over at Will. "Does your lack of argument mean you're in?"

Will's eyebrows rose. He looked like he wanted to make a retort but couldn't quite find one, so he settled with a short, "Yeah, I'm in." "Me, too!" Ty chuckled. "This is genius, Jess."

"I'm obviously in," Vanessa said. "I'm so ready to give this girl what she deserves."

"We need to figure out how we're going to pull it off, though," Will said, sitting back in his seat and folding his hands behind his head. He was staring thoughtfully at the back wall, like he was trying to put the puzzle pieces together.

"You're right." I nodded. "So how 'bout it, Dyer? Up for braiding hair now?"

Will's eyes drifted lazily over to me. "You're not braiding hair, Falice. You're knotting it to the bed. There's a difference."

"It was a joke," I told him, enunciating my words more clearly than I probably had to. I laughed. "Whatever, I'm going to need a knotting lesson. I was never in Girl Scouts, so I didn't get the chance to learn."

Will rolled his eyes, and I knew that if we were in isolation he would have continued the banter. But we weren't in isolation. We were in the cafeteria. "I'll handle the hair knotting and getting the snakes."

"Can Vanessa and I free the snakes?" Ty asked.

Will shrugged. "Sure, whatever."

Ty grinned. "Yay!"

"And then after, we'll all pitch in to get all of her clothes in the trees," I said.

Vanessa took a huge bite of her sloppy joe. "I'm so excited," she said through a mouthful of mystery meat.

I smiled. "Me too. So we all understand what we're doing?" Three nods. "Sounds like a plan to me," Vanessa said.

PHASE 17

"Do you think we'd be able to get our hands on some oatmeal?" I asked, my grip tight on the rake in my hands as I leaned against it, eyes swerving in Will's direction. He, unlike me, was actually raking the leaves around us. My pile was pitiful compared to his. I was going to blame that fact on the non-existent wind.

"Why would you want their oatmeal?" Ty asked. He shoved some more leaves into his pile and then turned to face me, a weirded out expression on his face. "I mean, it's understandable to be tolerant to the stuff, but to actually request—"

"I don't want to eat it," I explained, brushing some more leaves into my slowly growing pile. "I want it for the prank. I was thinking that I could put some in her hand like she did to me."

"Oh. Well, okay, that makes more sense."

I smiled. "So, Will, do you think we'd be able to?"

While Will thought over my answer, I looked around, watching as other kids attacked the leaves on the ground.

Today's community service was at a camp for wounded veterans. Henry had separated us into clusters and assigned us to different jobs. Some (like Will, Vanessa, Ty, and I) were raking while others were painting, washing cars, or... well, I couldn't remember what else. I wanted to be in the painting cluster (ironic, considering the fact that I abhorred art class), but at least, I didn't get separated from the others. And Tiffany wasn't around, so that was great.

However, the blisters I could already feel forming on my hands were not so great.

"I don't see why not," Will replied with a shrug. "Whatever happened to the oatmeal Tiffany put in your duffel?"

"I chucked it. I would have kept it to use against her, but it was nasty, and I didn't need it stinking up the cabin."

"And I thank you for that," Vanessa said. I grinned. "You are so very welcome."

Vanessa sent me a thumbs-up. I returned the sentiment before deciding it was time to push past my hate for raking and blisters and actually work. Though, I thought as I wielded my rake with new fervor, I couldn't fathom why there were all these leaves on the ground anyway. It was summer, not autumn.

From the corner of my eye, I watched Ty do a little dance while he worked. He reminded me of Beth when she cleaned her house— music blasting, hips swaying, smile beaming. "Guys," he said with an exaggerated slowness, "I am so excited."

"Stop dancing," Vanessa said. "For the sake of the world. Just stop."

"You hinder my potential." Ty huffed, but complied, the grin not leaving his lips. "Just so you know."

Vanessa replied, but I didn't hear her, because at that moment my rake decided it would be a great time to jab a rock and fly out of my hand. I groaned. *Stupid rake. You betrayed me.* I attempted, yet again, to use my telepathic powers to convince the rake to levitate, but it didn't answer my message. When that didn't work, I muttered a quick "Up!" but that didn't work either. Clearly, I was still a muggle. An incredibly lazy muggle.

"Falarabelle, I'm sorry, but you do not have the force," Vanessa teased.

I let out another groan. "Life! What is it?"

Will rolled his eyes and bent down, scooping my rake from the ground and holding it out to me. My eyes darted between him and the rake for a moment as I stood there, uncomprehending. Did he just...?

"Oh my god," Vanessa whispered, albeit loudly, to Ty. "Will just helped someone. Someone call Hell. I think it just froze over."

I would have pointed out that if Hell had actually frozen over, their lines would be down, but I was too shocked to open my mouth. I didn't know why I was so surprised. Will was already helping me with two other things: the pranks and the course. But when it came to stuff like this, he usually said something along the lines of: "Don't be lazy, Falice. Just pick up the damn thing."

Will's eyebrows rose, and I snapped out of it. Then I reached for the rake, my hand brushed his, and I froze. The same feeling I got when I grabbed Will's hand sparked through me. *What the...?*

I blinked and took the rake from his hands. "Thank you," I said softly, letting the bottom half of the rake fall to the ground and resuming what I'd been doing before I hit the rock. I avoided Will's gaze. I had no idea what was going on, but it freaked me out.

"No problem," Will replied. He cleared his throat.

"Oh god," Ty whispered to Vanessa. "What is happening right now? Are we in a different universe or something?"

"I don't know," Vanessa replied. "But I'm pretty damn uncomfortable in this universe. All the sexual tension."

I rolled my eyes. "Sexual tension? Seriously?"

Vanessa and Ty snickered. I cast a glance Will's way before quickly averting my eyes to Vanessa's ridiculously large pile of leaves. After letting out a small breath of air, I nudged some leaves into my pile, struggling to ignore the tumbling in my stomach. Though it didn't escape my knowledge that I couldn't blame it on the snakes this time.

It didn't take very long for me to at least partially figure out what was going on, and when I did, it took all the self-control I had not to pull Vanessa's phone from under her pillow and call Arabelle. I wanted to—really, really wanted to. But I couldn't. Not only had I used up enough of Vanessa's minutes, but it was too early in London for me to call, and if I attempted to take Vanessa's phone, I'd risk waking her up. And, I didn't want to wake her up, not before talking about this with Arabelle.

Vanessa let out a loud snore, completely oblivious to my sudden inner turmoil. Homesickness hit me like a tidal wave, and I brought a hand over my face as though that would push back the tears that were threatening to give way. A tear still escaped however.

Whatever was going on with Will, I wasn't certain. I had an idea, but it was crazy. Even just thinking about it made me want to shake my head. Me, have a crush on Will? Yeah, right.

But I couldn't deny the fact that things had obviously changed. How else was I supposed to explain what happened whenever Will and I made physical contact? Physical contact wasn't even required if I was being honest. Sometimes, I'd just glance at Will and butterflies would flutter around in my stomach. I'd chalked it up to the food, but—

These thoughts had been circling through my head ever since the veterans' camp. I wanted them to stop, but they wouldn't. They just reeled over and over again, begging for me to stop denying the obvious. I wasn't an idiot. I knew what was going on. It just scared me too much to admit it. I'd never had to deal with this before. No one at my school had really caught my eye. There were attractive guys, sure, but I never had romantic feelings for any of them. This was so out of my comfort zone.

I jumped, fingers pressing painfully into my forehead when someone knocked softly on the door. Wiping my eyes to catch a couple of tears that fell, I sat up and peered at the clock on the wall. It was past midnight.

I threw off my comforter and crept toward the door, eyes narrowed. The idea of opening it wasn't exactly thrilling. I mean, what if it was Tiffany? Yeah, the odds of that were near non-existent. She'd already retaliated, and she wouldn't knock before entering. But, then again, maybe she was trying a new tactic.

I grasped the door handle, hesitated, then unlocked the door and pulled it open. When I saw who was standing there, I paused, face slack with surprise. "Will?" I asked. "What are you doing here?"

Will removed one of his hands from his pockets to scratch his cheek. He shrugged his shoulders.

Did you know how difficult it was not to blush when I thought about what I was just thinking? Pretty damn hard. I wasn't even sure I was managing it. On the other hand, it was dark, so he probably wouldn't be able to see anyway.

Will's eyebrows creased. "Have you been crying?"

I blinked. How could he tell? Unless I bawled my eyes out, it was usually near impossible to tell I shed tears at all after wiping my eyes. Maybe he could detect the blush after all, but thought it was caused by tears, not my being flustered. "Uh, no," I lied lamely, totally helping my case by grabbing awkwardly onto my arm. Smooth move, Falice. Smooth.

Will frowned. "Yes, you have."

I sagged against the doorframe, teeth digging into my lip. "I was just homesick, that's all," I explained. "It's not like I bawled my eyes out or anything."

An expression crossed Will's face that I couldn't define. His eyes dropped slightly as he replied, "We all get homesick."

"Yeah." I shrugged. "So why are you at my cabin at twelve in the morning? Or is it at night? Ugh. Midnight is so confusing." I sighed. "Whatever. You know what I mean."

Will's eyebrows rose, and I'm pretty sure he was amused by my rambling, but he didn't comment on it. "Do you want to practice the course?" he asked.

I shrugged, nodded, and hurried to put on my shoes. Then I followed Will outside, listening to the sound of our footsteps as we traveled to the main area. They seemed especially loud this late at night— or early in the morning. This was the first time we'd been out this late to run through the course. Usually, he came to the cabin just after ten-thirty. So why did he choose to come at midnight tonight?

"Couldn't sleep?" I guessed, eyeing him thoughtfully. My stomach flipped, and I looked away.

Will shrugged. "I guess not." I sighed. "I couldn't either."

"Because you were homesick?"

I paused. "Yeah, because I was homesick."

I could tell from the expression on Will's face that he knew I was only telling the partial truth, and I was glad that he didn't question me further on the subject. Attempting to dodge explaining that I was having romantic feelings for the guy would be beyond awkward.

We reached the obstacle course, and I leaned back against the rock wall. The fake rocks dug into my back, but I ignored them. "I miss my sister, you know? I mean, I miss my dad too, but..." I shrugged. "I don't know. I guess it just hits harder with her."

Will claimed the spot beside me. His gaze was distant, thoughtful as he leaned his head back to face the night sky. "I wouldn't know how you're feeling," he said. "So I'd be lying if I said I understood."

"You don't have any brothers or sisters?" Will shook his head. "Nope."

I thought of my life without Arabelle and frowned. A life without my sister just wasn't right. At all. "I can't imagine that," I said. "Arabelle's like my best friend."

"I can tell." Will smiled. "Otherwise, you wouldn't have come here for her."

"I'm glad I did though."

"You are?"

I smiled. "Yeah, I am. If I hadn't, I wouldn't have learned to stop worrying about the rules so much." I paused. "I guess I have you to thank for that."

Will shook his head. "I didn't make the decision for you to come here. You did that on your own."

"Yeah, but I didn't really stop worrying so much until your blackmail." I grinned, nudging him with my elbow. "Just take the damn thank you, Dyer."

Will rolled his eyes, but he smiled a little bit again. "Let's do what we came out here to do, yeah? Go through the course. I'll time you."

As Will pulled out his cell phone and sought out the timer, I snickered and pushed off the wall, beginning my way to the starting point of the course. I took the stance Will taught me to take and waited for his signal to begin. Maybe this time I'd actually make it in two minutes. I've been getting better (almost) every time, but I've yet to meet the requirement to "unlock" the rock wall.

"Go!"

And I was off, throwing myself up the slide and over the other side in no time. I rushed through the tires, my head bent in concentration. I made it through in record time and ran to the wooden wall, my grip tight on the rope as I raced upward. I was over the top and onto the next obstacle in what felt like no time at all. The next part of the obstacle course was a set of monkey bars, which I could complete with no problem at all. Despite my lack of upper body strength, I was great at the monkey bars. Arabelle and I had races all the time when we were younger, so these weren't an issue.

I focused on keeping a steady pace while I rushed through the rest of the course. And when my stamina ran out, I forced myself to push past the weariness. I wouldn't call it quits and lie down. No. I could do this!

By the time I finally made it to the end, I was panting. I wiped a hand across my forehead and looked up, my eyes connecting with Will's. My breath caught, and suddenly my heart was in my throat. Yeah, I think there was no question about my feelings for Will. "How'd I do?" I asked, swallowing and averting my gaze to his forehead. Dammit, why did he have to be so attractive? Even his forehead was hard to look at without my stomach flipping.

"Falice McAtee," Will drawled, and the flipping in my stomach was forgotten as my eyes sought his again, "it looks like you've earned yourself a ticket to the rock wall."

I blinked. "What?"

Will grinned, twisting his phone around so I could see the time. "One minute and forty-five seconds. Good job."

My exhaustion was forgotten as I squealed and clapped my hands. "Oh my god!" I shrieked, jumping up and down. I probably should have kept my voice down— campers were sleeping, after all— but I was too ecstatic to care. "I did it, I did it!"

Will nodded. "Congrats."

I grinned. "Thank you, thank you, thank you!" With another small squeal, I threw my arms around him. "You're the best, Will. Seriously."

Will hugged me back for a moment before letting go. I backed away, lips folded as I realized what I'd just done—again. It was hard to feel embarrassed though when I was this happy. I'd completed the freaking course. Most of it anyway.

"We should probably head back," Will said, clearing his throat. "Early start tomorrow."

"Yeah." I nodded. I glanced around at our surroundings before turning back to face him. "Hey, can I go with you to get the snakes?"

Will blinked, shocked. I couldn't say I blamed him. I honestly didn't know why I asked, but now that I had, I realized just how badly I wanted to go. Sure, it was a trip to pick up freaking snakes, but it wasn't like I'd be the one touching them. I could stay outside if I couldn't deal. I just kinda really wanted to see what it felt like to sneak out.

"You do know what happened the last time you were in the same room with snakes, don't you?"

"Yeah." I shrugged. "But you'll be touching them, not me. It just seems fun sneaking out, and I want to give it a try." I pouted theatrically. "Please?"

Will cocked an eyebrow at me. "Sure," he said slowly. "But if we get caught, it's all on you."

I grinned. "I'm a ninja. If anyone gets caught, it's gonna be you."

With that, I snickered and turned away from him, practically skipping back to my cabin.

"Vanessa?"

"Hmm?" Vanessa hummed, barely casting me a glance as she rifled through her bureau in search of a shirt to wear. Though it didn't seem like she was paying attention, I knew she was. Vanessa was a spectacular multi-tasker.

I wrung my hands nervously. "Um, I realized something," I said, picking at my shirt now. Despite my serious sleep deprivation, I felt wide awake. I'd expected some serious yawning and eye watering, but so far, so good.

"What did you realize?" Vanessa asked, holding a *Supernatural* shirt in front of her. A moment later she switched off, trading it with a *Big Bang Theory* shirt.

"I realized," I began, then paused. I swallowed. Why was this so hard to get out? I already knew Vanessa would be excited about this, so why was I so apprehensive? Because it felt wrong to tell someone else before I told Arabelle? Because this was the first time I would say the words out loud? "Uh…"

"Uh?" Vanessa looked over at me then, her eyebrows raised. When she saw the expression on my face, she tensed as though sensing trouble. "Falice, what's going on?"

I sighed deeply and collapsed onto my bed, staring blankly at the ceiling. Great, now she was looking at me. That made this so much easier. Not. "I figured out that I like Will," I muttered.

"You like shrimp? Gross, girl. I'm sorry, but I cannot support your taste in—"

"Will, Vanessa! I like Will!"

I sat back up and eyed Vanessa warily as I waited for her reaction. She was frozen where she stood, eyes wide as she stared at me. Was that a good sign? A bad sign? I couldn't tell. However, when she continued to just stand there, I began to worry.

"What?" Vanessa asked finally.

"Don't make me say it again," I groaned, covering my face with my hands. "It's so embarrassing."

I peeked through the spaces between my fingers, watching as Vanessa suddenly squealed, jumped in place, and clapped her hands. Her reaction wasn't unlike mine when I completed the course. That, of course, only reminded me of how I hugged Will and only reminded me how much I would love to hug him again.

"Aw, that's so cute!" Vanessa said. "I love it!"

I couldn't help but grin. "It's not that exciting but okay."

"It is, though!" Vanessa flopped beside me. "And once you tell Will—"

"Whoa, hold up." I held a hand to stop her. Vanessa's mouth snapped shut, but her eyes continued to speak for her. "I'm not telling, Will. And neither are you— or Ty."

Vanessa frowned. "But how do you expect to kiss the damn guy if you don't tell him how you feel?"

I shook off sprouting thoughts about kissing Will. Had I ever thought about doing that? More than I'd like to admit. "Not a word," I said sternly, giving my friend a pointed look. "Seriously, Vanessa."

Vanessa sighed deeply as though I was truly exasperating and was making this way more difficult than it had to be. And maybe I was. But that didn't change the fact that the thought of her or Ty telling Will how I felt mortified me— even more than making a fool out of myself the first time I tried the course had.

"Don't judge me," I said, sticking my tongue out at her and squinting. "You're judging me. I can feel it."

Vanessa snorted. "I'm not judging you, girl. I was the exact same way with Ty. I mean, I had a few boyfriends in the past, but I never actually liked them. I just dated them because they asked. But, with Ty, I actually felt something, you know?" She sighed. "It's just… I know what it feels like to sit there and torture yourself with wanting to kiss the damn guy, but not being able to because you refuse to tell him how you feel out of fear of being rejected. And then you find out he liked you for a long time and was afraid to tell you because he was scared he'd get rejected."

My lips twitched. "How did you and Ty end up together?" Vanessa gave me a suspicious glance out of the corner of her eye, like she thought I was just trying to steer her away from the topic at hand. But I wasn't. I actually wanted to know. "He came to my cabin late at night— like past midnight," Vanessa began when she saw I was serious. "He was like, 'Will's right. I need to stop screwing with my head and just go for it.' And then he kissed me. My roommate, luckily, didn't wake up. She totally would have snitched if she had. She sucked like that." She smiled faintly at the memory. "That was my first summer here. And that was when we realized there was no going back, and we had no way to see each other except for here. So we made a pact to come back every year."

"Aw, that's so cute!"

"Yeah, and if Ty hadn't grown a pair, we probably would've left camp that year and never returned." She shot me a pointed look. "So either you or Will is going to have to grow a pair."

"Well, Will is the one who told Ty to grow a pair in the first place, so it should be him," I said. "Besides, he probably doesn't even—"

"Don't you dare say that he probably doesn't like you," Vanessa warned with a roll of the eyes. "He so does."

"How do you know?" I asked.

"Remember me making that comment about sexual tension earlier?" Vanessa stuck her tongue out at me. "I wasn't just joking around, Falarabelle. I mean, I was definitely fooling around, but that doesn't mean the tension wasn't there. You should have seen your guys' faces when your hands touched. It was priceless."

I rolled my eyes. Before talking to Vanessa, I was practically bursting with the urge to talk to someone about this. I thought if I waited one more moment I'd explode. Or worse, manage to slip up while Will was in the room. But now? I just wanted the conversation to be over. "Which shirt are you going to choose?" I asked, pointing at her discarded shirts from their spots on Vanessa's bed. "I'd personally go with the *Supernatural* one. I mean, Dean and Sam are too sexy to pass up."

Vanessa stood up and headed back to her bed where she took the *Supernatural* shirt in her hands. "That is true," she said with a laugh. "Okay, Sammy and Dean, I'm wearing you today!"

I left the cabin before she could begin stripping in front of me and made my way to the main area with my arms crossed lightly over my chest. There were about fifteen minutes until breakfast, so anyone outside was just milling around, killing time until they were forced to eat the dreaded oatmeal. *Yuck.*

"Hey."

I jumped. And then, after twisting around and spotting Will, I smiled. "Hey!" I grinned. "What's up, best friend?"

Will gave me a flat look, but it was ruined by the small smile that appeared. He glanced around and then moved in close, and my stomach went nuts. I was pretty sure I stopped breathing by the time he leaned toward my ear and whispered, "We're going to get the snakes tonight."

I fought down a shiver and nodded. "Yeah, okay," I said. "Make sure Vanessa and Ty know."

"Yeah." Will took a step back and brought a hand through his hair. "Meet me out here after lights-out, okay? After we get them, we'll stop to get some of the oatmeal."

I nodded again and smiled. "Sure thing, Dyer. Sounds like a plan." As our conversation fell, I slid a glance his way in search for what Vanessa referred to. According to her, it was obvious that he liked me back.

Ha, yeah right. I couldn't see it.

"Falarabelle!" Vanessa called. "There you are!"

Will and I watched as Vanessa and Ty meandered over to us. I could tell from the way their hands swayed that they were itching to hold hands. I felt bad for them. This was the worst place to have a romance— seriously, the worst.

Vanessa smiled broadly, her hands seeking her hips. "Do you feel that, babe?" she asked, eyes turning toward Ty.

"Feel what, my dear Vanessa?" "The sexual tension in the air."

Ty chuckled. "You know, that kind of reminds me of that song from *The Lion King*." Before any of us could begin to prepare, he belted out (and completely off-key, might I add), "Can you feel the sexual tension tonight?"

"Yeah, you failed majorly." Vanessa patted him teasingly on the shoulder. "But I appreciate the effort."

Will's and my gaze were blank as they laughed at our expenses. I wasn't quite sure why I didn't find this awkward. They were talking about sexual tension between Will and I, and I happened to have just figured out that I was crushing on him. However, all I could do was be amused. Something about the way Ty and Vanessa teased made it too funny to make me uncomfortable. And I was extremely thankful for that.

Their conversation about sexual tension drifted to Simba and Nala as we ventured into the cafeteria. From the corner of my eye, I saw Will roll his eyes. "Don't like *The Lion King*?" I asked.

We came to a stop at the back of the line, which was pretty much two people at this point, and waited for them to receive their food before moving forward.

"Who wouldn't appreciate a movie where the father is brutally murdered by his brother and said brother blames the death on the kid? It's demented."

"It's tragic." "And demented." "And tragic."

"I never said it wasn't tragic. I just think it's more demented than anything else."

I grabbed a tray with one hand, using the other to flick a stray strand of hair out of my face. "Did you even watch the rest of the movie?" I let out a horrified gasp. "Oh my god, have you not met Timon and Pumbaa?"

Will accepted the oatmeal from one of the lunch ladies, thanked her, and then shrugged at me. "I chucked the remote at the TV once Mufasa died and then left the room. I refused to come back."

Though I was incredibly upset by the fact that Will hadn't even finished the freaking *Lion King*, I couldn't help but laugh. "Aw, who knew you were so emotional?" I paused to thank the cafeteria lady as she served me some oatmeal. "You are aware that Timon and Pumbaa are so funny that you semi move on, right? I mean, there are a bunch of other sad parts, but—"

"Yeah, yeah." Will stopped as we requested chocolate milks and then resumed as we headed to our table. "I haven't watched it, but people talk about it enough for me to know. Simba apparently becomes a dipshit, so I wouldn't want to finish it anyway."

"Well, I'm going to make you watch it someday," I said with a smile. "You're going to watch the whole thing whether you like it or not." We took our seats at our table and set our trays down. "But don't worry, you can cover your eyes when Mufasa dies. I won't judge you. I do that sometimes when I'm not in the mood to watch him die again."

"That implies that sometimes you're in the mood," Will pointed out. "And how could you even make me watch it? It's not like we live anywhere near each other."

I paused, thinking over his words as Vanessa and Ty plopped into their seats and started eating their breakfasts. Where did Will live? What was it like there? What did he do there? Hang out with friends? Chill at the house by himself?

"Where do you live?" I asked after deciding that was probably the best question to start with.

Will swallowed down some oatmeal. "Washington," he said. "You?"

"Wow." I blinked. "That's so far away. I live in driving distance.

In Massachusetts."

"So it looks like I get out of watching it." Will eyed me smugly.

"Ha."

I smiled cheekily. "Don't worry, Dyer. I'll find a way."

"I'll make a deal with you," Will said, pointing his spoon at me.

"If you touch a snake without screaming, I'll watch *The Lion King* in full— without looking away when Mufasa dies."

Hmm, tempting. However, that would involve me touching a freaking snake. Was that really worth it? He lived in Washington, so it wasn't like I could just walk over to his house and make sure he followed through with his end of the deal. After this summer, we'd probably never see each other again.

My stomach clenched. I did not like the sound of that, not just with Will, but with Ty and Vanessa, too. Not seeing them ever again was an incredibly painful thought. They were my best friends.

"Deal," I said quickly. For some reason, having this deal comforted me, like I subconsciously thought it would keep our connection even after the summer was over. I held out my pinky. "Pinky promise."

Will glanced at me and my pinky for a moment before folding down all fingers except for his pinky. I let out a small laugh as I hooked our pinkies together and shook them. Then I let our fingers fall, careful not to display any emotion except for amusement.

"Okay, Dyer. It's a deal. Just don't judge me if I wet my pants while touching the snake."

Will sent me a discreet smile. "Okay, Falice. Whatever you say."

PHASE 18

I waited about fifteen minutes after lights-out before I slipped out of bed and pulled on my shoes. By then, Vanessa was even antsier than I was. She hopped up and down on her bed while I got ready to go. "Dude," she hissed as I slipped on my second shoe. "Could you put your shoes on any slower?"

"I could," I replied, and slowed my pace just to prove it. I grinned when she huffed. "Dude, chill yourself. We'll be back soon. It's not like you're going to have to wait all night to pull the prank off."

"That's not what I'm excited about," Vanessa said, and I glanced at her, eyebrows raised. She winked at my confused expression.

Oh.

"You are aware that we're going to pick up snakes, which I hate, right?" I finished tying my shoe and stood up, hands on my hips. "So, nothing romantic is going to be happening."

"This is the equivalent of going to see a horror movie." The next thing I knew, Vanessa jumped off her bed, grabbed me by the arm, and pushed me outside. "Go get 'em, tiger!" she squealed.

I turned to give her an unimpressed glance, but found a closed door in her place. So I gave the door a flat look instead before twisting on my heel and venturing down the path that led to the main area. I was just going to assume we were meeting there. One of these days, Will would actually tell me where he wanted to meet instead of settling with "outside." Or maybe he wouldn't. Oh, well. Until then, I was stuck guessing.

It seemed I guessed correctly. As I entered the main area, I spotted Will leaning against the rock wall, his gaze cast absently ahead of him. When he saw me approaching, he pushed off the wall and sauntered over to me, one hand gripping a duffel bag. "You ready?" he asked.

I nodded. "Yeah."

Will's lips pricked upward. "Okay then. Let's go."

As Will grabbed onto my elbow and steered me toward the camp's entrance, I glanced at Henry's office. Was he still up, or did he go to bed the same time we did? And if he was still awake, what if he looked out the window of his cabin and caught us walking down the road? This was why I didn't sneak out. The thought of getting caught threatened to send me into a panic.

As though he sensed my sudden anxiety, Will said, "He's in bed." "You're sure?"

Will nodded. "He goes to bed at the same time we do." My eyebrows rose. "And you know this how?"

"I'm madly in love with him and watching him while he sleeps gives me great pleasure." Will couldn't conceal his smile when I burst into laughter. I had to cover my mouth to keep my amusement from alerting the apparent love of Will's life. Vanessa was going to be mighty disappointed when she found out. "No. May I remind you that I had to sneak out to get the spiders?"

Oh, yeah. "Right," I said, scratching an itch on my temple and tossing him a smile. "Though, I have to say, I think you and Henry would make a cute couple."

Will returned my cheeky grin with a sour look. I don't think he appreciated how much effort it took to make that joke with a straight face. In fact, I was mentally patting myself on the back for not stumbling over the word "couple."

We exited Camp Sunshine Brooks and headed up the road. I forced myself to let my anxiety go away as we travelled further and further from camp. This was my first— and probably only— time sneaking out. Might as well enjoy the experience.

"It's going to be about a fifteen-minute walk to the shack," Will told me, swinging the duffel bag aimlessly in his hand. He glanced at me with teasing eyes. "Are you going to be able to handle a fifteen-minute walk with snakes right beside you?"

I scowled playfully at him. "Yes." Maybe.

"Because if you can't, you should probably just go back…" "No!" I exclaimed with a firm shake of the head. "Sheesh, I'm not going to miss my first time sneaking out just because snakes scare the crap out of me. Doing that would give them way too much power."

Will's lips were lifting again, like he just couldn't help himself. I was so relieved that he hadn't completely reverted to his previous attitude after leaving isolation. He still never smiled in front of Vanessa and Ty, but he wasn't as grumpy and broody as he was when I first met him. And while I wished he'd smile in front of the others, I was happy the Will I considered as *more than* a friend hadn't disappeared.

"This is your first time sneaking out?" Will asked, not sounding surprised. I mean, we were both well aware of the fact that I didn't usually break the rules.

"Yeah." I shrugged. "Where would I sneak out to? Anywhere I'd want to go, my dad would let me if I asked. Arabelle, on the other hand, has snuck out plenty of times usually to go to parties with her friends or to concerts my dad wouldn't let her go to. I think one time she snuck out to go to a midnight premiere at the movie theater."

Will chuckled. "I'm not surprised."

My lips twitched. "I'm guessing you've snuck out then," I said, crossing my arms over my chest. "At home, I mean. Not just here."

Will tensed at my words. It was barely noticeable, but his arms definitely tightened. I looked at him, eyebrows drawing with concern. Was he okay? What did I say? "Yeah," he murmured. "I sneak out all the time at home."

I hesitated before answering. "Why do you sneak out then?" I asked. When Will seemed to tense even further, my concern grew. "Are you okay, Will?"

"I'm fine," Will said sharply. I frowned. Though his tone wasn't as harsh as it used to be, it was nearing that zone. "And I sneak out because I feel like it. Places to go, people to see."

I knew he was lying, but I didn't call him on it. "People?" I laughed. "Didn't take you as a people person."

Will rolled his eyes, but didn't argue.

We fell quiet then, and for a few minutes, the only noises around us were the sound of our footsteps and the occasional rustle in the woods. But then I grew tired of being stuck with my own thoughts and decided to break the silence. "So," I drew out, "where in Washington do you live?"

"Seattle," Will said.

"Oh, really? I've always wanted to go there." I smiled. "Do you like living there?"

He shrugged. "It's fine." He paused. "So what about you? Where in Massachusetts do you live?"

"Gardner." I sighed. "I love it there, but Arabelle hates it. She's always telling me how she and Danny are going to move to New York City when they're older."

Something in my tone and expression must have tipped Will off. "You don't like this Danny guy, do you?" he asked.

I snorted. That was an understatement. "He's a complete jackass." "How so?" Will scratched his cheek. "I'm sure he is, but you know."

Oh, where to start? Already, I could feel all of the things I hated about Danny clawing their way to the surface. I forced myself to pick one item in particular before everything could spew out at once. "Well, for one, he treats Arabelle like crap. Whenever he's not making lame excuses about standing her up— and he stands her up a lot, by the way— he's always making derogatory comments or getting on her case." I let out an agitated sigh. "One time, I heard him call her ugly. She is not ugly. She's freaking beautiful."

"Yeah, I know," Will murmured, his voice distant as though he didn't realize he was saying the words out loud.

My head snapped in his direction. "What?" I asked. At first, I didn't register what he meant, just because I knew Will saw Arabelle our first day at camp, and Arabelle and I always considered our appearances to be different, but then I caught on, and my cheeks immediately reddened. *Did he...?*

Will blinked and then shook his head as though to dispel his trance. "I mean, uh... you're identical. So I obviously know she's not ugly."

Will Dyer actually struggled to find words to say. Never thought I'd see that happen. And I so didn't find that adorable. Nope. Not at all.

Okay, I so did.

"Did you just call me pretty, Will Dyer?" I asked, a bright smile on my face. I prayed to God my blush wasn't noticeable.

"Uh..." Will swallowed. "So, I totally agree with you. She should dump his sorry ass."

Despite the fact that he didn't outright say it, his body language screamed that he admitted to calling me pretty, and was embarrassed about it. My flush deepened, and I had to turn away to keep him from seeing. Damn, this was awkward. Freaking amazing, but awkward.

"I know she should," I said, discreetly pressing a hand to my cheek to see if it had cooled. "But she's hell bent on making this relationship work."

"So, if you hate this guy, why would you do this for her?" Will asked.

I sighed. "I may hate Danny, but the way Arabelle ripped herself apart because she couldn't go to London with him was terrible to watch. I wanted to help her. Though, I'm not gonna lie, part of me is hoping she'll realize what garbage he is over this trip and end it with him." I shrugged. "Besides, Arabelle's done a lot of things, but she doesn't need to come here. She acts rude and all that, but she's a good person. She's nice to me, anyway."

"That's because she has a soft spot for you," Will replied with a faint smile. "We all have a soft spot for someone."

"Oh, really? Who do you have a soft spot for, Will? I bet it's your cat."

Will rolled his eyes. "I don't even have a cat."

"Do they remind you too much of Simba?" I grinned. "Aw, that's cute."

"Don't flatter the lions. My mom's allergic to cats."

"Ah," I said with a nod. "So you would have a cat if you have the choice. I bet you'd name it Fluffy. And it would be one of those white cats with the pushed in faces. You know, like that cat in *Cats and Dogs*."

Will snorted. "I'd rather have a dog. They're so much nicer than cats."

"I want a husky." I sighed dreamily. "I've always wanted o n e .

They're gorgeous."

"I've always wanted a husky, too," Will said. "Not sure why. I just have."

A smile sprang to my lips. So it seemed we both wanted the same dog. *Cue the butterflies, please. Wait, no. Don't cue them. I don't like them. I don't—*

Too late.

It was silent for a moment as I struggled to force my stomach to settle. It didn't. Will didn't seem to notice because he just looked straight ahead with a content expression on his face. I had to turn away to keep myself from staring for too long. Damn, crushes were crazy. At least, I realized how I felt so I could keep myself from ogling at him. This was getting so ridiculous.

"We're here," Will said suddenly.

My head shot up. At first, I couldn't tell what Will was talking about, but when I glanced to the right, I saw it. It was a dilapidated, ugly thing, and I wasn't surprised that I didn't see it when arriving to camp. It blended in well with the trees. "Ah," I said. "It's... lovely."

Will scoffed. "Yeah, it's delightful. And remember that you have to touch a snake without screaming. Unless, of course, you want to forfeit."

I groaned, but nodded and followed Will across the road, to the shack. This was going to be fun. Please note the sarcasm.

Ugh. I hated snakes.

"I hate you."

I grimaced and rubbed my hands vigorously on my shorts, unable to help but gag. Oh god, that was awful. I was going to puke. And then cry. And then maybe puke some more. And then, after that, I was going to smack Will. Crush or not, I was irritated with him. Very, very irritated.

"You love me." Will grinned, his eyes alight with amusement. The jerk. "And you know it."

For a moment, his words threatened to send me into a panic. *He knows! Shit, shit, shit!* But then I glanced his way, remembered that this was nothing but a banter, and rolled my eyes. "I so do not," I grumbled. I shot him a glare. "You just had to pick the biggest snake."

According to Will, since I was the one who chose which movie he had to watch, he should be able to choose which snake I had to touch. So what did he do? He went and selected the largest snake in the entire shack. It was also the most intimidating. And the ugliest. And the evilest. I'm pretty sure it was Voldemort's sidekick, Nagini. Okay, so maybe that was a slight exaggeration. But whatever. You get my point.

When I hesitated in front of the snake, not wanting to touch it, but not wanting to back out of the deal, either, Will smiled smugly and said something along the lines of, "Fine by me, I didn't want to watch a demented Disney movie anyway." So, I sucked it up and petted the damn thing.

And now I was regretting it immensely.

"Because I knew that one would be the one to scare you shitless," Will replied as though that fact should have been obvious, which I guess it should have been.

"You know what?" I demanded, crossing my arms over my chest and scowling. "I think you're out to get me, Dyer. Yup. I think you secretly can't handle the fact that I kicked your ass at Go Fish, and this is your way of getting back at me."

"Or," Will said, "I just chose the snake that would most likely make you scream and therefore lose."

"You really don't want to watch *The Lion King*, do you?" I asked. "Damn, boy. It's so good."

Will sighed deeply. "Well, now, I have no choice in the matter." "Serves you right for choosing the biggest snake, you jerk," I said with a grin.

"I don't even know where I'm going to get it," Will admitted. "I don't own it."

"Could you buy it?"

Will shrugged. "Probably not. I mean, my mom would be willing, but Rick—"

He cut off suddenly, his jaw working as anger spiked in his eyes. I glanced at him, concerned. What was going on? Who was Rick? And why did I feel like if I had the answers to my questions, I'd want to kick Rick in the ass?

When Will's expression didn't change, I stopped walking and placed a comforting hand on his shoulder. His feet went still, but he didn't turn to look at me. He just stared straight ahead, his grip tight on the duffel.

"Will," I said softly. "What's wrong? Who's Rick?"

His teeth dug into his lower lip. "Nothing's wrong. And Rick… he's no one."

My eyebrows creased, and I stepped in front of him, trying to grab a hold of his gaze. But Will looked away. I watched silently as Will attempted to calm himself down. He didn't seem to be able to though. As the seconds ticked by, his expression remained the same.

What did Rick do to make Will react this way? Did he hurt him? At the beginning of the summer, I might have been tempted to believe this reaction was just Will's way— he hated everything, right? But now, I could see that this went deeper than any of that.

"Will?" I whispered. When Will continued to pretend I wasn't there, I put my hands on his cheeks and forced his eyes to meet mine. "Will, it's okay. Rick isn't here, okay? He's not here. He can't touch you."

My breath hitched as Will grabbed onto one of my hands and closed his eyes. He let out a long sigh and opened his eyes again, an apologetic smile on his lips. And then he drew his hand away from mine.

I kept my hands in place while I searched his face for further signs of distress. When it appeared Will was okay now, I let my hands fall.

"Thank you," Will said softly.

I smiled, resisting the urge to ask any questions about what just happened. "No problem, best friend," I said instead, bumping him playfully with my shoulder. Will returned the sentiment. "Let's go get the oatmeal and put this plan into action, yeah?"

Will nodded. "Yeah."

For the most part, Will and I were silent as we traveled back and snuck into the back of the cafeteria. I wanted to start up a conversation, but Will seemed so lost in his thoughts that it felt wrong to intrude. However, when he started to get a troubled expression on his face, I'd ask him questions about the plan, even though he'd answered them all twice over. He didn't seem to mind having to repeat himself anyhow.

While I went to grab the trash bag with today's leftover oatmeal, Will found some disposable kitchen gloves and a plastic bag for us to use. I untied the bag, accepted the gloves from Will's outstretched hand, and then went in, nose scrunching. Will joined in a moment later.

"Fun fact," I said as I dumped my second scoop into the plastic bag. "This is almost as gross as when I had to clean the litter box when I was younger. And my cat's poop was disgusting."

"You used to have a cat?" Will asked.

"Yes. Her name was Mary-Kate. She was adorable, and then she ran away and never returned. She must have run into Scar."

Will gave me an unimpressed look, but that was the only response I got for the reference. "Mary-Kate? Like the Olsen twin?"

"Yup." I shrugged. "Arabelle named her. She wanted to get another, identical cat and name it Ashley, but my dad said no."

Will snorted but didn't reply as he stepped back into his thoughts. He was quiet the rest of our time in the cafeteria, and by the time we reached my cabin, the frown was returning to his face. I opened my mouth to distract him again, but Vanessa threw open the door before I could say anything.

"Finally!" she whispered, her tone exasperated as she grabbed me by the wrist and tugged me inside. "We thought you got lost or something."

I waved to Ty before sending Vanessa a smile. "Nope. Will just made me touch this big ass snake. It was awful."

Ty chuckled. "Oh, Jessica." He gave me two slow claps before turning to Will. His eyebrows crinkled. "You okay, man?"

All eyes went to Will. I folded my lips together, scratching absently at my arm. Will glanced at all of us before rolling his eyes. "I'm fine," he said. "Let's just do the prank, all right?"

"Yes!" I said, flashing a grin. "Let's go. You were the ones getting antsy, remember?"

Vanessa scrunched her face at me, but nodded. "Let's do it!" Will subtly tossed me a grateful look before heading back outside, the door shutting softly behind him. I moved to follow, but Ty grabbed me gently by the arm before I could take a step. "Is he actually okay?" he asked. "I mean, I know grumpy is his norm, but this seems different."

I forced myself to shrug off Ty's question. "He said he was fine."

Ty squinted at me for about thirty seconds before releasing his grip on my arm. "Okay," he said. Then he beamed. "Let's go, woo!"

I followed my friends outside. There, we found Will standing a foot from the cabin, an impatient expression on his face. "Could you take any longer?" he demanded.

"If you were a girl, I'd be asking if you're PMS-ing," Vanessa said instead of answering his question. "Keep that in mind."

Will was clearly unimpressed with Vanessa's retort but didn't reply with one of his own. I battled with another wave of concern. It was official: I hated Rick. Whoever he was, he was such a…

"Are you coming?"

My eyes, which had drifted to the ground, snapped up, latching onto Will's. His irritation seemed to dissipate when he saw how worried I was. "Sorry," I muttered, hurrying to catch up with the others. While I was lost in thought, they'd managed to get a few feet ahead. "Got distracted."

Will bit his lip and nodded. I gave him a smile as I fell into step beside him. "Let's just get through this prank without letting our irritation get the best of us, shall we?" I suggested, my smile growing as I faced him. Not going to lie, I kind of felt like I was trying to smile him back into a good mood.

Ty and Vanessa were the only ones who spoke during our journey to Tiffany's cabin. As they chatted, they held hands. I eyed their hands with a tinge of jealousy. I wished I could hold someone's— meaning Will's— hand. I wanted to know what it felt like to have someone love me and call me theirs.

I glanced at Will again. He seemed to have calmed down again, all signs of exasperation gone. I could only hope this Rick guy wouldn't ruin Will's night completely.

"Here we are!" Vanessa whispered suddenly.

It's time, I thought.

Vanessa picked the lock and led us inside, stepping as quietly as she could through the threshold. It hadn't changed at all since the last time we were here, except for the fact that there were more clothes on the floor.

"Dude, we should tie the other girls' hair to their beds too," Ty whispered. "Am I right, or am I right?" Will shrugged. "Fine."

After handing Vanessa the duffel full of snakes, Will went straight to work on Tiffany's hair. Vanessa gave Ty and me a thumbs-up before heading to the back of the cabin while eyeing the snakes from the gap Will left in the duffel.

"Jessica." "Ty."

Ty grinned at me. "Are you ready to oatmeal this shit?"

It was incredibly hard to suppress a laugh. I don't know how I managed, to be honest. "Of course." I wriggled my eyebrows. "Let's do this."

Ty held out his hand, and I handed over the spare disposable gloves. I silently congratulated myself for having the hindsight to stuff two pairs into my pockets before leaving the cafeteria. Otherwise, our hands would have paid the price.

I grabbed a handful of oatmeal from the plastic bag and handed it to Ty before creeping to Tiffany's bed, where Will was still knotting her hair to the bedpost. "Excuse me," I murmured, shimmying my way between him and the bed. "I'll just be a moment."

Will raised his eyebrows at me, but otherwise had no reaction. With a small smile sent his way, I set the oatmeal on Tiffany's hand. She didn't even twitch. Good. It would really suck if she wiped her nose while Will was working. It would ruin everything.

I retreated from the bed, ready to help Ty— though he looked like he was having enough fun by himself— but then spotted a permanent marker on Tiffany's bureau and paused. Suddenly, and idea sparked. *Perfect*, my mind whispered.

I grabbed the permanent marker and held it loosely in my hand. "I've got an idea!" I exclaimed softly. When everyone glanced my way, I held it up for them to see.

"What are you going to do, make a mustache on her face?" Will asked. Ty and Vanessa laughed.

"That would be so awesome," Ty said. "Do it, Jessica. I dare you."

"While your idea is tempting," I said, a sweet smile spreading on my lips, "I've got something better in mind."

I pulled the cap from the marker and sauntered over to one of Tiffany's friends. What was her name again? As I brought the marker toward her forehead, I strained my mind in an attempt to remember, but it was futile. So I shrugged it off.

After finishing off Minion One, I moved on to Minion Two, whose name I also couldn't remember. I wrote the same word on her forehead as I had on Minion One, folding my lips together to keep from laughing out loud.

"Will," I whispered as I stepped away from Tiffany's friends. "Are you okay if I write on Tiffany, or do you want me to wait until you're done?"

Will spared a glance my way. "Go ahead," he said softly.

I nodded and hurried over. I leaned over Tiffany and struggled to write what I wanted to write without bumping into Will. Of course, bumping into Will wouldn't be a tragedy by any means, but knowing me it would totally mess up my handwriting.

"What did you write?" Ty inquired as I pressed the cap back on the marker. He ambled over to us and looked over my shoulder. When he saw what I'd jotted down, he burst out laughing, covering his mouth with his hand to muffle the sound.

"What did she write?" Vanessa demanded, curious now, too, as she ditched the duffel and rushed over to us. "I wanna see!"

She, too, snickered when she saw what I wrote.

I beamed, staring down at the single word I'd written. What word was that you ask? Satan.

"Girl, that is so great." Vanessa wiped her forehead with the back of her hand. "What did you write on the other two?"

"I wrote 'hellhound'," I replied.

"Because they're like her dogs." Ty held out his hand, and I slapped it. "Shit, bro, you are so clever."

"You're a freaking genius, Falarabelle," Vanessa said. "Honestly, a freaking genius."

I smiled. "Thanks, guys."

Our conversation died out as we all turned to watch Will work. He ignored us completely, his fingers at ease as he continued to wrap and knot Tiffany's hair around her bedpost. And then, when he finished with Tiffany's hair, he went to work on the minions. Their hair was shorter than Tiffany's, so it didn't take him as long. "Done," he said in what felt like no time at all. He glanced at Vanessa. "You can release the snakes now."

Vanessa gave Will a mock salute before rushing back to the duffel. Ty grinned, copied Vanessa's salute, and then sauntered after her. After they left, Will moved over to me, standing so close that his hand brushed mine.

"I'm sorry," he said.

I blinked. "What?"

"For snapping."

I turned my head slightly, watching as he shoved his hands into his pockets. "Will Dyer just apologized to me," I said. "I must be pretty damn special."

Will didn't answer, but I could see a small smile begin to form on his face.

"The snakes have been released!" Vanessa called suddenly, ripping my attention away from Will and to the snakes as they slithered their way across the floor. I grimaced. *Ew, ew, ew.*

To get my mind off the snakes, I glanced behind me, eyeing the post-it notes from their spot on Tiffany's bureau. My eyes narrowed as I was hit with another idea. Then I uncapped the marker again and, using the bureau as a desk, jotted a message onto the small piece of paper.

"What are you doing?" Will whispered.

"Giving Tiffany a little warning," I replied. I flashed the final product at him. *Next time, you'll wake up with no hair*, the note read. "You like?"

Will failed to suppress a grin. "Oh, most definitely."

I smiled before trotting over to Tiffany and placing the note into her free palm. "There," I said with a sigh. I glanced over at Vanessa and Ty, watching with a distant sense of amusement as they dodged the snakes on the floor. And then it clicked that they were avoiding snakes, and my amusement dissipated. "Let's get out of here," I said, rubbing the rising goose bumps on my arms. "You know, before I end up touching one of them. I've reached my quota for the day."

Will opened his mouth to answer, but Vanessa and Ty scurried over to us before he could.

"Are you ready for phase two?" Vanessa whispered, eyes alight with excitement.

"I'm pretty sure we're past phase two," Will pointed out. Vanessa rolled her eyes. "Whatever. You get what I mean. Are you?"

I answered by tugging open one of the drawers in Tiffany's bureau. "Hell yes," I whispered with a smile.

Vanessa and Ty laughed at me before grabbing some clothes out of the drawers. Will grabbed the duffel from the opposite side of the room, and he and I stuffed it to the rim, packing it with as much clothing as we could. And then, when it was full, we piled the remaining clothes in our arms. After we had packed all Tiffany's clothes, we sneaked out of the cabin as quietly as possible. Vanessa shut the door, and we were off, heading for the trees surrounding the area.

For a moment, we all just stood there, staring up at the trees as they towered over us.

"Whoever throws the highest wins?" Ty suggested. We all shared a glance.

"It's on," Vanessa and I said with a grin.

"Falarabelle should get the first throw," Vanessa said. "This was her idea after all."

"Why thank you, Vanessa." I dropped Tiffany's clothes on the ground and then plucked a shirt from the heap. It probably wouldn't get very far. Like Arabelle so kindly pointed out, I wasn't a sporty kind of person.

Eyes narrowed, I reached my arm back, preparing to launch the shirt at the trees. And then, after a moment's hesitation, I flung it as hard as I could.

PHASE 19

The scream that erupted the next morning was probably loud enough to wake up the entire state of New Hampshire.

Vanessa and I sat up in bed, slapping our hands to our eyes in an attempt to wake ourselves up. What was going on? I dropped my hands and squinted out the window, eyeing the early morning light with more than a little distaste and confusion. Was someone dying? Because it sounded like someone was dying.

"What's going on?" I mumbled, my gaze traveling to Vanessa as she threw her comforter away from her and stepped out of bed. She teetered on her feet for a moment before standing steady.

Vanessa groaned, the heels of her palms pressing into her eyes again. "Ugh, this is so not—"

She cut off as another screech cut through the morning air.

For a moment I just sat there, eyes blank and thoughts muddled. Then I followed Vanessa's lead, kicking my blanket off of me, standing up, and wiping a hand across my face in one distracted motion. "We should go see…"

And then it hit me.

"Oh my god," I breathed, an incredulous giggle escaping before I could stop it. I could not believe that in our half-asleep state we'd forgotten! "Satan and her hellhounds are awake!"

It took Vanessa a second, but then she burst out laughing, her exhaustion fading away as amusement took over. "I have to see this," she said, slipping on her flip flops and starting for the door. She paused before exiting and tossed an impatient glance over her shoulder. "You coming or what?"

I nodded and shoved my feet into my shoes before following Vanessa out the door. Groups of campers were outside already, baffled and tired expressions on their faces. Vanessa and I stopped in front of our cabin, arms folding over our abdomens as we observed our surroundings. I'm sure Vanessa wanted to get closer to the scene of the crime, but we really didn't need Tiffany starting another fist fight and making more accusations. So we stayed where we were.

"Babe!"

Vanessa and I looked to the left, where we found Ty and Will strolling toward us. They, like everyone else outside at the moment, were still in their pajamas. However, unlike most of the guys milling around, they'd thrown on shirts before leaving their respective cabins. Ty was clad in a plain white tee while Will was in a white undershirt. Will in an undershirt was so unhealthy for me, honestly.

"Babe, who knew you looked so damn attractive in the morning?" Vanessa asked when Ty and Will came to a stop beside us. "Don't they look absolutely yummy, Falarabelle?"

I studiously averted my eyes to a group of girls, who were glaring in Tiffany's general direction.

"Falarabelle," Vanessa drawled teasingly, nudging my arm. "Don't they look scrumptious?"

My gaze drifted from the irritated girls and back to Vanessa. She had a broad smile on her face and a knowing look in her eye. I resisted the urge to scrunch my nose at her. "Yeah," I replied, flicking my eyes back to Will for a moment before turning away again. "You know, if you're into cannibalism."

Ty chuckled. "Well, you look mighty fine yourself. Bed hair looks brilliant on you."

Vanessa playfully propped her hair. "Oh, I try."

Ty's eyes scanned her from head to toe, a distant smile appearing on his lips. Vanessa wasn't wearing anything overly revealing, just a T-shirt and a pair of pajama shorts, but that didn't seem to matter to Ty. He was having a grand time checking her out.

"What's going on?" someone demanded. "Does anyone know?" "Are those clothes in the trees?"

My gaze involuntarily slid toward Will. However, when he glanced in my direction, I averted my eyes.

"Everyone calm down!"

We all watched as Gilbert, Joel, and a few other camp workers appeared from the main area's path. None of them seemed really all that pleased, which was understandable given the circumstances. I felt bad for the workers, being thrown in the middle of this without a say in the matter. Well, except for Gilbert. I found it incredibly hard to sympathize with him. "Why don't you guys get ready for the day?" Joel suggested, his tone significantly kinder than Gilbert's had been. He smiled. "I know it's a bit early, but there's no point in going back to sleep now."

"Yes." Gilbert nodded. "And while you get ready, we're going to figure out what's going on here."

Though he didn't say it, I knew there was an underlying message in his words. *And to the guilty party, whoever you are, don't for one second think you're going to get away with this.* I willed my expression to stay blank as he scanned the groups of kids with narrowed, suspicious eyes. No need to give him ammunition.

Finally, Gilbert released us from his stare and bustled in the direction of the screams. All but one worker followed.

"Go get ready for the day, guys," the worker said. I had no doubt he was staying with us so there wouldn't be a repeat of the time Will and I got sent to isolation. "Everything's fine."

No one moved for a moment, but then campers began grudgingly heading back inside their cabins. Vanessa and I hesitated before doing the same.

"See you ladies at breakfast," Ty said with a wink. "And, babe, I seriously suggest keeping your hair like that. You look so hot."

Vanessa winked right back. "Will do, babe. Will do."

"You know, your penmanship looked great in the dark, but in the light… not so much," Ty said. He glanced at me with his "pizza" inches from his mouth. "No offense."

I spared a glance at Tiffany's table, where Tiffany and her friends were all holding their silverware with death grips and glowering at our table. The disdain was clear on all of their faces. It didn't affect me like it used to though. While it used to take all of my power not to cower under Tiffany's gaze, now, I just met it with a carefully blank expression and then looked away, mentally shrugging it off.

Ty was right. My handwriting was awful. It didn't help that they'd clearly attempted to wipe it off, so the writing was smudged. But, either way, that didn't stop me from saying and acting like I thought otherwise. "You meant that entirely with offense," I replied with a laugh. "And I take it to heart, Kadeth."

"Was I the only one who caught the fact that she just called me by my last name?" Ty fist-pumped and let out a small whoop. "Does that mean I'm as cool as Will now? Am I in this special club of those referred to by their last names?"

I glanced at Will, feeling a small smile make its way onto my face. His eyes met mine, and the corner of his lips started to tug upward before falling back down again. I deflated a little at that. Why couldn't he just smile in front of Vanessa and Ty? Why hide that side of himself? I didn't ask him though. I just turned back to Ty and stuck out my tongue. "Who says I think Will is cool?" I asked. "How do you know that I'm not insulting you by referring to you by your last name? Maybe I think Vanessa is the only cool one at the table."

Vanessa stretched out her hand and I slapped it.

"You don't need to lie for Vanessa's benefit," Ty assured me. He smiled sweetly at his girlfriend. "She knows she's not cool."

As Vanessa whacked Ty on the shoulder and proclaimed that she was never returning to this hellhole, I twisted around and faced Tiffany's table again. Yep. Still scowling. Though, I was happy to report that she was no longer gripping her fork like she'd enjoy nothing more but to stab me with it repeatedly. She was picking at her food now although with more force than I thought was really necessary.

Then again, it had taken over four hours for Henry and the other workers to free Tiffany and her friends from their hair prisons and retrieve their clothes. And this was Tiffany we were talking about.

Her eyes met mine again, and I swear she attempted to murder me with them.

I took that as a sign that it would be wise to stop looking at her table and turned back around, attention on my friends. Vanessa and Ty were still bantering while Will was poking at the applesauce on his tray. My gaze settled on Will as I took a bite out of my pizza. How was he? He seemed fine, and quite content with acting like yesterday's sudden shift in attitude never happened, but I was still worried.

"Why are you staring at me?" Will asked without looking up from his food.

"I'm not," I lied. My eyes shot down to my tray. "Uh-huh. Sure."

"I'm not."

"Mm-hm."

"You can even check, dude."

"Well, of course you're not now," Will said with a scoff. "I'm not stupid."

I laughed softly, taking another bite of my pizza. "Hey," I said with a grimace. I swallowed my food before continuing. "Can we practice the course tonight? I really want to get started on the rock wall."

Will didn't answer as he dared to scoop some applesauce into his spoon and take a bite. His face didn't show any reaction, but I knew it didn't taste good. "Yeah," he said finally, his lips twitching. "We can do that."

"Yay!" I squealed, dropping my pizza back on my tray so I could clap my hands. "Thank you, Will."

Will nodded. "No problem."

The rest of the day went by smoothly enough. I went through my daily activities with my friends, and occasionally, I'd feel Tiffany's I'm- going-to-murder-you-in-your-sleep glare on my back. Sometimes, I'd turn around just to see if she was actually there, but most of the time, I just ignored it and went on with my day as usual.

And then, after dinner, I accidentally spilled meatloaf on the table while getting up to return my tray, so I had to stay back to clean up my mess while everyone else left. Awesome, right? The cafeteria ladies handed me a paper towel and a wet wipe before disappearing out back to wash the dishes. I half-walked and half-ran back to my table and fixed my meatloaf's wrongdoing (It was the one that jumped off my tray. I had nothing to do with it). Then I threw the used paper towel and wet wipe in the trash and headed outside.

Or tried to head outside anyway.

Before I could even take one step out the door, Tiffany was there, shoving me back inside and slamming me face-first against the wall. "Don't you dare call for your boyfriend, Arabelle," she hissed. "Wouldn't want to look like a baby, would we?"

I grimaced as she added more pressure. *Ow.* And, despite the fact that I knew it was stupid not to call for help, I kept my mouth shut. I'm not sure why exactly. I just did.

"You made a fool out of me, Arabelle McAtee, and that is not something I will tolerate."

When do you tolerate anything? I was tempted to snap, but she continued before I could get the words out.

"You may think you're smart and that you can get away with these little pranks you pull, but I'm promising you this: I will make you pay for what you did."

I kept staring at the wall as I struggled to come up with a retort. Tiffany continued to shove me painfully into the wall while she waited (oh-so-patiently). "Careful, Tiffany," I drawled finally. "Wouldn't want all of your hair to suddenly vanish, would we?"

I groaned before I could stop myself when Tiffany hauled me away from the wall just to slam me into it again. Fear sparked. What was I thinking, egging her on like this? She could hurt me. Yeah, Will made it clear that I was supposed to make her life a living hell, but I think it was also pretty obvious this had gone far beyond that as the weeks went by. The comment I just made, while somewhat satisfying, was incredibly stupid. I silently cursed myself.

"Don't you dare threaten me," she barked in my ear. Her hair brushed my cheek. "I will be the death of you, Arabelle. You think I'm Satan? Well, Satan's got nothing on me."

With that, she tugged me away from the wall. I thought that meant she was done with me, but I was wrong. Instead, she twisted me around, rammed me into the wall, and then drew her arm back, her hand curling into a fist. I barely had time to close my eyes and brace myself for impact before she punched me—hard. I let out a cry, tears burning in my eyes as Tiffany pulled away completely. My fingers flew to my cheek. This was the first time I'd ever been punched, and I couldn't say it was an enjoyable experience.

"Consider that a first taste for what's coming. I'll come after you when you least expect it. You better sleep with one eye open because you're dead."

And then she was gone, stomping back outside.

I watched as she left, fingers continuing to trail lightly over my cheek. I winced. Dammit, my cheek hurt. This was so going to bruise.

I closed my eyes, took a deep breath, and then left the cafeteria.

I really didn't have the energy to deal with the questions that would inevitably arise with the red mark, which was swiftly turning black and purple on my cheek. So instead of attending the seminar scheduled for this evening, I told Joel I wasn't feeling well and asked if I could sit out this one pep talk. Joel frowned concernedly for a moment before steering me to Henry's office to get me some Tylenol. When he spotted the growing bruise on my face, I told him I'd managed to whack myself in the face— clumsy, right? I wasn't sure he really believed me, but he didn't question me more on the subject. He just handed me a couple capsules of Tylenol and an ice pack, telling me to go rest and that he hoped I felt better soon.

So I spent the rest of my evening alone in my cabin. Well, not alone. I had my book, peanut butter, and incredibly annoying thoughts for company. They helped for a while until I finished my book and stopped eating my peanut butter. My thoughts made me want to punch them even though that would hurt me more than them. And I'd already been punched today, so I really didn't want to go through that again.

How I managed to hide the bruise from Vanessa when she came back to the cabin was beyond me. I wasn't sure why I didn't just tell her. I mean, she was my friend after all. Even if I wasn't in the mood, I should have at least said, "Hey, guess what? Tiffany punched me. I'm fine though. No need to worry." But I didn't. She didn't notice, and I didn't point it out to her.

And now I was lying in bed, fingers absently brushing my cheek and ears tuned on Vanessa's snores. I wasn't at all tired. Not only did my cheek still ache terribly, but also I was paranoid that Tiffany would waltz in at any moment, ready to enact her revenge. And, on top of that, the way *Cinder* ended was just— ugh. I needed the next book now.

I jumped, fingers digging into my bruise when there came a soft knock on the door. *Dammit. Shit. Ow!* Wincing, I forced myself out of bed. "I'm coming!" I called softly as I shuffled toward the door. As though in protest, Vanessa let out an especially loud snore. If I were to compare it to anything, it would be to a chainsaw.

"Will," I breathed after I pulled open the door. "What are you— oh, sorry, I totally forgot!"

Will, who'd been leaning lazily against the doorframe, stood abruptly upright, his eyes wide. "What the hell happened to you?" he demanded. His tone was rich with alarm.

"I need to get my shoes," I said, blatantly ignoring his words as I stepped back and shoved my feet into my shoes. "Okay, I'm ready to…"

Will stepped into the cabin and took a hold of my shoulder, gripping it in his hand with a gentle sort of firmness. My breath hitched.

Why did he have to affect me this way? Why now of all times? "Falice," he whispered. "What happened? Did Tiffany hurt you?"

"I'm fine," I muttered quickly. "Can we just…"

Will's thumb went under my chin, and he tilted my face upward and to the side as he observed my bruise. I grimaced. This was exactly what I didn't want to deal with. Though, I had to say, I did enjoy him showing so much concern for my well-being. "You're not fine," he said. "Falice, what happened?"

I shivered. "Tiffany punched me in the face," I admitted. Will tensed. "What?"

My lips twisted as my eyes met his. "Tiffany, she cornered me after dinner when I stayed back to clean up my mess. She shoved me into a wall, promised she'd be the death of me, and then she punched me."

Will's hand moved from my chin to cup my uninjured cheek. He stared at me intently while he searched my face for any hints of pain. "Are you okay?" he asked softly.

I nodded. "Yeah, I'm fine."

"Is that why you didn't show up to the seminar or exercises?" Will asked. "Vanessa said you wouldn't take your nose out of a book. You were hiding your face, weren't you?"

Nodding, I glanced sideways in Vanessa's direction. "I told Joel I wasn't feeling well. And I wasn't exactly hiding my face behind the book though that was definitely a plus. I was actually reading it. I finished it, too." I sighed.

Will frowned, eyeing my bruise again. "Why didn't you just tell us what happened?" he asked.

I shrugged. "I just didn't feel like talking about it." I stared up at him. "I'm sorry for not telling you right away."

Will nodded his head before sighing and letting his hand fall. I thought he was going to head outside or maybe gesture for me to lead the way, but instead, he pulled me to him and enfolded me in his arms. I almost gasped. Will was hugging me. *Will was hugging me.* It was one thing for me to hug him, but this... this was just so, well, it was kind of, sort of perfect.

After about two seconds of standing there, frozen with surprise, I wrapped my arms around him as well. I wasn't going to waste this time standing there in shock. *Sheesh, Falice.*

"Next time," he said softly, his breath tickling my ear, "tell me instead of hiding it. Got it?"

I nodded. "I will."

Will pulled away, took a step back, and let his hands fall to his sides. "Good."

I crossed my arms over my chest and grinned. "Hey, Will." "What?"

"You totally just hugged me."

Will's expression flattened. "So? You've hugged me before." "Yeah, but that's different." I smiled. "You hugged me!"

"You suck so much. I'm never hugging you again." Will rolled his eyes. "Now, let's go."

I followed him outside, my smile stuck on my lips. I wasn't quite sure why I was teasing him about hugging me. Honestly, the fact that he'd initiated the embrace sent my stomach fluttering. However, the embarrassed expression on his face was too adorable to ignore. If I had my— or, rather, Arabelle's— phone, I'd so take a picture of him. "Aw, come on, Dyer." I flashed him my pearly whites. "Don't be that way."

"It's not my fault that you suck," Will replied.

"It's not my fault that you make it so easy to embarrass you," I retorted.

"I'm not embarrassed." "You so are."

"Am not."

"Are."

"Not."

"Are."

"Not."

"Are!"

"This is becoming repetitive," Will said with a sigh as we came to a stop in front of the rock wall. "So I'm going to end the conversation now, and you're going to climb the wall. You okay with that or do you want to stand here talking about absolutely nothing?"

I beamed at Will as he averted his eyes to the rock wall. Though it was hard to tell in the darkness, I could faintly see a tint in his cheeks. "Oh my god," I murmured. "Will Dyer, are you blushing?"

Will glared at me. "Climb the damn wall," he snapped, jabbing his finger upward. "Go. Now. Shoo."

I bit my lip to keep myself from laughing at him. He was so damn adorable right now. Shooing me, really? "You're so cute when you're embarrassed," I teased. "Did you know that?"

Will gave me an unimpressed look. "Wall," he said. "Now."

With a playful roll of the eyes, I decided to stop torturing Will and situated myself in front of the wall, grabbing hold of one of the makeshift rocks. And then, without another word, I began my ascent up the rock wall.

PHASE 20

"Falarabelle, I understand being worried," Vanessa said, "but you can't keep letting her ruin your days like this."

I swallowed, flicking my gaze from the trees and to Vanessa as we made our way up the hill. I was soaked. Pine needles and dirt were sticking to the bottom of my feet, but I couldn't bring myself to care. Over the past few days, I'd gradually grown more and more paranoid. This was so much worse than waiting for Will to enforce his blackmail. I mean, I'd thought at the time that Will was capable of anything, but I also didn't feel deep down that he loathed me so much that he'd get me killed.

But with Tiffany? Yeah, not so much.

"I guess you're right," I said, not believing my words as I said them. I just couldn't help it. Tiffany was just waiting for me to let down my guard, and then she would attack. I knew she would. And I had a feeling this wasn't going to be like the pranks we'd been pulling back and forth over the course of the summer. Tiffany was done playing games.

"Ugh, look what's she's done to you." Vanessa threw a hand in the air, the other curled around her towel. "We're supposed to be making her summer hellish. Not the other way around."

My lips pursed. "Yeah, I know," I said. "I just wish she'd do whatever she has planned already. I wish she'd stop making me squirm like this."

"That's probably the best part for her." Vanessa huffed. "The Little—"

She cut off suddenly as we passed by a worker. She'd already had enough warnings about swearing. The next complaint would probably warrant a punishment.

Vanessa and I followed the other girls into the locker room. There were still three stalls open when we entered, and we dashed to claim the last two before someone else stole them from us. It happened before. One time, in the beginning of the summer, two girls got in a fist fight over a stall. Though, I had to say, their attitudes had improved since then.

After locking the door behind me, I threw off my bathing suit. To think that it was almost August, I thought as I switched the top of my bikini for my bra. I couldn't believe it. My time here was more than halfway over. I suppose I should have been happy about that. That meant I could go back home, back to my own bed and to my friends and family. But what about Vanessa, Ty, and Will? I didn't want to part with any of them. At all.

I swiftly changed into the rest of my clothes and then stepped out of the stall, edging out of the way as the girl waiting in line hurried to claim it as her own. Vanessa wasn't far behind, and soon we were exiting the locker room, heading back to our cabin to drop off our swim stuff.

"You know what you and Ty should do?" I asked Vanessa.

She glanced at me from the corner of her eye, lips twitching.

"What should we do, my dear Falarabelle?"

"You guys should just come to my house during the summer instead of here." I sighed. "Will, too."

Vanessa threw an arm over my shoulder. "Ah, that would be so great, wouldn't it? If only."

If only.

"I am going to pee my pants." I informed everyone. It just seemed like something they all needed to know. They were stuck in the van with me for the next five-ish minutes.

Vanessa, Will, Ty, and a girl named Kate glanced at me as I wriggled uncomfortably in my seat. I crossed one leg tightly over the other and met all of their gazes. At this point, I didn't care who heard. I'd been holding it all afternoon. Granted that it probably would have been a lot easier if I didn't keep drinking water, but, hey, I was thirsty.

"We'll be there in a couple minutes," Dennis assured me from his spot in the driver's seat.

"Okay," I said. "Thanks, Dennis!" "No problem."

"Please don't pee in the van." Vanessa scooted as far away from me as she could, pushing herself into Ty. He didn't seem to mind. In fact, from the wide smile on his face, I was guessing he was incredibly amused. "Seriously, please don't."

"Oh, I will," I joked. "And I'm gonna pee on you just to spite you."

Vanessa pretended to gape.

"Rude, much?" I smiled sweetly.

I spent the rest of the ride back to camp dancing in my seat and attempting to distract myself— unsuccessfully, of course. By the time we arrived at camp, I was afraid I actually would pee my pants whether I'd exaggerated earlier or not. Luckily, Dennis pulled in and let us out just in time, and I scurried to the bathroom without looking back.

The girl's bathroom here wasn't the worst of the public bathrooms I'd used over the course of my lifetime, but it definitely wasn't the best. The walls were cemented and covered in graffiti. The stalls were no better. The entire room stank of urine, too, which didn't help.

After relieving myself, I flushed, unlocked and kicked open the door, and then hurried over to the sink to wash my hands. My eyes glided to the mirror hanging over the sink as I turned on the faucet. Wow. The exercises and lack of junk food were really beginning to show.

Something moved in the right side of the mirror, and when I glanced up, I spotted Tiffany in the reflection, a wicked smile curling on her lips. I jumped and spun around to face her, eyes wide. Oh no. *Oh no, no, no, no.*

"Hello, Arabelle," Tiffany drawled, her smile growing. I fought the urge to recoil from her. She was so damn freaky when she smiled like that. "Did you miss me? How's that bruise doing?"

The bruise had actually faded to the point where you could barely see it anymore, but it was still sore to the touch. But I didn't tell her that. I kept my mouth shut as I glanced toward the door, calculating the odds of me being able to get to it before she grabbed at me. Which was none, seeing how she was blocking my way to the exit.

I was so screwed.

"Hi, Tiffany," I said, returning my gaze to hers. "How hard was it to get the permanent marker off your head? Oh, wait, I think it's still there."

And it was. Like my bruise, it had faded to the point where it was impossible to see unless you really looked, but it was still there. Triumph sparked at that. Having permanent marker stuck on her head with no proper way to clean it off must have been beyond aggravating.

The smile vanished from Tiffany's face. And then she was right in front of me, fingers digging painfully into my skin as she rammed me into the sink. I chomped down on my cheek to keep from crying out when the sink dug painfully into my back. "How does that feel, Arabelle?" Tiffany tilted her head to the side, menacing smirk returning. "Does it hurt?" she cooed. She added more pressure, and I bit my cheek so hard I tasted blood. "It does, doesn't it?"

Say something, my mind hissed.

"Nah," I gasped out. "Can't feel a thing."

Tiffany's eyes narrowed, and then she hauled me away from the sink and shoved me into one of the stall's walls. My head banged against it, and I grimaced. *Ow.* "Giving me attitude isn't going to get you anywhere," she snapped. "I'll just hurt you more."

"Why do you do stuff like this?" I demanded. "Do you enjoy seeing people in pain or something?"

I expected that remark to earn me another shove against the wall, but it didn't. Tiffany just dragged me away from the sink area and into one of the stalls. I didn't bother asking her what she was going to do to me.

She wouldn't answer, and I'd probably only end up getting punched in the face again.

And I really didn't want to be punched in the face again.

My thoughts flung themselves back to how concerned Will had been when he noticed the bruise on my face. If only Will were here now, then maybe my mind wouldn't have to make a desperate attempt to distract me from my fear.

I returned to the present just as Tiffany lifted the toilet seat. Suddenly, her plan became startlingly clear. "No," I whispered. "Oh god, please no."

Tiffany snickered at my sudden loss of bravado and then proceeded to slam me to the floor and force me face-first into the toilet. I squeezed my eyes shut and resisted the urge to scream as toilet water blocked my airways. *Please don't let me drown. Please.*

Tiffany flushed the toilet.

I fought down a terrified cry. Before this, the most experience I had with swirlies were those I'd seen in the movies. They weren't as funny as the movies sometimes made them seem. It wasn't funny, or even a little embarrassing. No. It was friggin' terrifying. My hair was yanked downward with the rest of the water, pulling so tightly that my head ached. I couldn't breathe, I couldn't see.

And then suddenly it was all over, and Tiffany was hauling me out of the toilet. I coughed and sputtered, shaking hands pushing hair away from my face.

"How'd that feel, Arabelle?" Tiffany asked sweetly. "Did you like that?"

I answered by coughing in her face. Tiffany growled, muttered something along the lines of, "Oh, you wanna play it that way, huh?" and then shoved me back into the toilet. The same emotions jolted through me as Tiffany repeated the process. Fear, pain, relief.

"Just so you know," Tiffany drawled as she yanked me back again. "I do enjoy seeing others in pain. Especially you. Your boyfriend's not here to save you this time, is he?"

I tried to wriggle out of Tiffany's grip, but it was no use. She had too tight a hold on me.

"Aw, you want to leave?" Tiffany asked. "But, honey, we're just getting started."

"Let me go," I whispered, thrashing again. Tiffany's grip loosened, but only temporarily.

"No, I don't think I will." I couldn't see Tiffany's smile, but I could feel it. "In fact, I think I'm going to do this."

She pressed my head forward, and no matter how hard I resisted, I still found my face enveloped by water. She reached to flush the toilet.

And then she was gone, letting out an enraged cry as she was yanked away from me.

I sputtered out a cough, lifting my head out of the toilet and twisting around before collapsing onto the floor in a heap. My eyes darted upward. Will had Tiffany pinned to the wall, his arm over her neck to keep her from attacking me again. "What the hell is wrong with you?" he barked. "What the *hell* is wrong with you?"

"Fal—Arabelle!"

My gaze shifted to the right as Vanessa and Ty halted in front of the stall. Vanessa made a noise in the back of her throat before helping me up, pulling me into her arms despite the fact that I was drenched with toilet water. I hugged her back, eyes burning.

"Are you okay?" Ty asked softly.

I nodded once. "Yeah," I rasped.

Vanessa held me out at arm's length for a short moment before letting me go completely, and we all silently turned to watch Will as he gave Tiffany a hard shove.

"Stay the hell away from her," Will spat. "Do you understand that? Touch one hair on her head, and I'll make you regret it."

Tiffany didn't answer, just glowered.

"Do you understand me?" Will demanded. When Tiffany just wriggled in his grip, he pushed her harder into the wall. I couldn't see his eyes, but I bet they were filled with the same loathing Tiffany's eyes always held for me. "Do you understand me?"

"Yes," Tiffany snapped. "Now let me go, asshole."

Will held her there for another moment, staring her down before shoving away from her. Tiffany barely spared me a glare before rushing out of the bathroom, probably to go complain to her minions about how insufferable we all were. I kept my gaze on Will as she left. He turned to me almost immediately, his eyes wide. The rage was gone, replaced solely with concern. "Are you okay?" he asked.

"Yeah." I nodded again. I gave him a small, reassuring smile. "I'm gonna need a shower though. Toilet water is so disgusting."

Will's eyes searched my face. "Are you sure?"

I folded my lips together. Honestly? I wasn't okay. I'd just received swirlies from some bully that thought it was cool to torture people. My head and back hurt, and right now, all I wanted to do was crawl into bed and sleep until I was thirty. But I couldn't tell him that. Not right now anyway. "Yeah, I'm sure," I said softly.

Will nodded, but I could tell he didn't believe me; not that I expected him to. He frowned and turned to Vanessa. "Vanessa," he said. Vanessa stepped closer to me, her expression carefully blank. "Can you make sure Tiffany doesn't attack her on her way back to your cabin?"

Vanessa nodded. "Yeah," she murmured. "Okay."

With that, Vanessa grabbed me gently by the arm and tugged me out of the bathroom, back toward our cabin. "He doesn't like you, my ass," Vanessa muttered playfully. I think she understood that I really didn't want to talk about what happened and was making an effort to steer clear of the subject. And I was grateful for that.

"What?" I asked. "He was just getting Tiffany off my back. That's all."

"You didn't see his face, Falice." Vanessa shook her head. "When we realized that you were taking way too long in the bathroom, it was like he just knew. And the expression on his face— holy shit."

I sighed. "It would be awesome if he returned my feelings— it would. But just because he was concerned about my well-being, it doesn't mean that he likes me that way.

Besides, I have other things to worry about right now. I don't need to think whether or not Will has a crush on me, too."

Vanessa gave me a strange look. "Like?"

I met Vanessa's gaze. "Like how I'm going to shave that asshole's hair right off her head.

PHASE 21

"I need to get my hands on a razor or something," I muttered as I raked a hand through my hair.

"You chose the wrong place for that," Ty said unhelpfully as he munched happily on his food. "At least, this is the wrong place for the type of razor you want."

That was true. Henry had everything but the simple reusable razors confiscated on the first day of camp. It was understandable but incredibly inconvenient at this moment in time.

"Well, then what can we use?" I asked. "I'm going to shave off all her hair. It's gonna happen no matter what."

I let one of my hands fall beside me in the small spot left on my seat, resting in the space between Will and me. He was in his usual spot on my left while Vanessa was on my right. Though, it felt like Will had been sitting closer to me lately. Or maybe that was just my hormones noticing the close proximity.

"We could use scissors," Vanessa suggested.

"Knowing me, I'd probably end up cutting her head open." I paused. "Then again…"

Will gave me a pointed look. "You know you don't want to cut her head open."

"Might be tempted if she keeps giving me bruises," I muttered.

The area on my back where she shoved me into the sink was bruised— badly. It still hurt like hell, but I was doing my best to ignore it.

There was no point in dwelling on it though. I had more important things to concentrate on, like how I was going to shave every last hair off Tiffany Blake's head.

"Couldn't we just cut her hair with scissors and then use a razor to shave the rest off?" Vanessa asked.

"That might work," I replied though I honestly had no idea if it would. I wasn't exactly an expert on the subject, but it was nice to have something to go on. Sitting here while Tiffany thought she had won wasn't okay with me. At all. "What do you think, Will?"

Will shrugged. "Maybe," he said. I could tell from his tone that he didn't think we should put our faith in the idea. "Not sure though."

I groaned and threw my head back with exasperation. "This sucks," I complained.

Will scratched the bridge of his nose before letting his hand fall, too. I almost jumped as our hands brushed. What should I do? Move my hand? Keep it there? Well, I probably should have moved my hand, but I couldn't bring myself to. Will wasn't moving his hand either, so why bother, right?

Yes, that was my logic, and I was sticking to it.

"Yeah, it does suck, Falarabelle," Vanessa agreed, tossing a glance in Tiffany's direction. I refused to follow her gaze. I wasn't acknowledging Tiffany's existence until I had a plan. It just wasn't worth it. "But don't give up, okay? Her hair is going buh-bye if I have anything to say about it, which I do."

I started to open my mouth to answer, but then Will's hand wrapped around mine, and any thought of a response shriveled and died. Holy crap, I was going to die. I was going to explode, and then I was going to die. Will was holding my hand. He was holding my hand!

And why? Well, I had no freaking idea. But I couldn't bring myself to care, for obvious reasons.

I cleared my throat. "Yeah, definitely," I said, clearing my throat again.

I glanced at Will. He was staring straight ahead and acting like he wasn't participating in this conversation. I squeezed his hand back, and his gaze turned over to me. I raised my eyebrows at him, and he shrugged, turning away again.

Okay, so he was going to randomly hold my hand and then not talk. Okay. Cool.

I'd be lying if I said I wasn't okay with this. How could I not be? I always wondered what it felt like to hold a guy's hand just because, and now, I knew. This wasn't like when Will saved me from the locker room with the snakes. He only held my hand so he could keep me steady as I traveled through the valley of death. Right now, he was holding my hand because he wanted to.

Let the butterflies fly.

My concentration went haywire through the rest of lunch. I could barely keep up with the conversation because my thoughts were so scattered. Was that Will's plan? To distract me from my anger so I wouldn't work myself up?

If so, it was definitely working.

I actually found myself dreading the end of lunch. Holding Will's hand was like the best thing ever— better than cake, really.

Yeah, I just said better than cake. Chocolate cake to be specific. Oh, yeah.

When lunch period ended, Will let go of my hand. I stood up with the others, staring blankly at my hand as we ambled over to the area where we deposited our trays. I just couldn't believe Will actually held my hand. "Dude, why are you staring at your hand?" Vanessa asked as we began our way to the exit.

I put down my hand as I looked up at Vanessa. She was staring at me as if she was questioning my sanity. "Uh," I mumbled. "I thought I saw a dot?"

Vanessa snorted. "Yeah, okay."

And then she disappeared outside with the others. I sighed deeply, shook my head, and hurried after them. Saw a dot? Really?

Damn, I was so stupid sometimes.

"So," I drew out, clutching on the rock wall tightly as I struggled to find my footing, "are we going to talk about what happened at lunch today or not?"

"I'm sure I don't know what you're talking about."

I scoffed, and if I thought I wouldn't fall, I would have shot Will a skeptical look and rolled my eyes at him. Didn't know what I was talking about? Seriously? "So your hand just moved by itself and held onto mine for the rest of lunch?"

Will didn't answer. I sighed and shook my head. I wasn't quite sure why I brought this up in the first place. I guess it tugged and prodded at me all afternoon, and by the time I got out here, it just kind of spilled out. I probably should have talked about this with Vanessa, but oh well. There was no going back now.

"You know, if I minded, I would have pulled away," I called, leaning back a bit and taking the chance to glance down at him. "If that's what you're worried about."

"I'm not worried," Will said. There was an undertone in his voice, one that I couldn't place. Why did he have to be so complicated and confusing?

"Ah," I replied so softly that I was sure Will couldn't hear me. My eyes shot upward as I searched for a rock to grab onto. It was long past my time-limit to get up the wall, but I didn't really care. I'd just improve the next time. First, I had to memorize which rocks would be best for me, and only then I could concentrate on speed. "So did Simba catch your tongue or something?"

"If that dipshit thinks he's getting that close to me, he has another thing coming."

I laughed so hard I almost lost my balance. "Dammit, Dyer!" I shouted playfully. "Don't make me fall."

"I'll make you fall if I want to," Will teased.

I rolled my eyes and continued towards the top of the wall. It got tougher the higher I went, but I knew that the real challenge would be getting back down. Will and I couldn't figure out how to set up the harness, so I decided to climb the wall without one. Will tried to stop me, but I wanted to climb the wall and I wouldn't let the lack of a harness deter me.

Yes, I was aware how stupid I was. Especially when I realized how high up the wall actually went.

"If the height scares you, come back down," Will said, the light bantering gone. "Better to be safe than to get a broken arm."

"Nuh-uh. I'm determined to make it to the top of this wall."

Will sighed but didn't comment more on the subject. "Just so you know, you were supposed to be down here already," he said instead.

"Well, sorry for not mastering the craft Mr. I-come-here-every- year," I retorted.

"That is a terrible last name," Will said.

"Yeah, might be a deal breaker for the ladies." Though I grinned, I felt my stomach pinch. Um, what ladies? Were there ladies? Oh god, please don't let there be any ladies.

"They'd be pretty sucky ladies if they ditched me because of my last name," Will pointed out. "I think that would be a deal breaker for me." "Oh, geez." I grabbed for another rock. "We're having girl talk.

Dammit, Dyer, where is my friendship bracelet?" Will scoffed. "You'll get it when you get it."

"You say that like you're actually planning on making me one," I said with a laugh. I finally reached the top of the wall and began my descent. "Glad to know you won't let girls walk all over you though. Shows you're not an idiot."

"You say that like at one point you thought I was an idiot," Will retorted, his tone light.

"I wasn't…"

I let out a curse and then a small cry when I lost my footing and tumbled from the wall. Fear flashed through me. Only I would manage to lose my footing because I was too distracted having a conversation. How damaging could a fall from this height be? Will mentioned something about a broken arm...

My thoughts of whatever was to come were cut short as I landed heavily in Will's arms. My weight brought us both to the ground, and somehow we ended up rolling once before coming to a stop. I squeezed my eyes shut, breaths quick and unsteady. I could feel Will on top of me, but I forced myself— or tried to force myself— not to concentrate on that. Hormones were pests at the moment. I was in pain here.

"Ow," I mumbled, bringing a hand to my head. Will groaned, and I opened my eyes. "Dammit, Dyer. I told you not to make me fall."

Will propped himself up on his elbows, but it didn't matter. His close proximity made my stomach go haywire. "I didn't make you fall," he said. "You fell completely on your own. You have two left feet, don't you?"

"Actually," I corrected, "I have two right feet. There's a difference."

Will laughed. As he did, his breath blew into my face and I felt myself shiver. Why wasn't he rolling off me? I didn't mind, but why? "Still your fault."

"No," I said, sure of myself. "You most definitely made me fall."

I didn't think I was referring to my fall from the rock wall anymore, and I think Will knew it. Something seemed to change in his eyes, and I felt another shiver run down my spine.

"I don't know why I held your hand today," he suddenly confessed. "I just did."

I smiled. I could tell that he was embarrassed by his confession, and in that moment, I think my feelings for him grew. It had nothing to do with the fact that he was practically lying on top of me, or that all I had to do was grab hold of his neck and tug him down an inch or two and then we'd be kissing. It was the fact that out here, when we were alone, Will felt completely free to be himself, to let himself be embarrassed, and to confess things.

God, I'd fallen for him. He'd made me fall. And I didn't mind it one bit.

"Well, if you ever randomly decide to hold my hand again," I told him, "I won't object."

Will smiled. "I'll keep that in mind," he said softly.

For a few moments, all Will did was stare, and for a split second, I thought he was going to close the distance between us and kiss me. I hoped he would, maybe even prayed, but he didn't. Instead, he got up and held out his hand. I accepted it and stood up, too. I took a moment to swallow my disappointment before smiling at him. I'm pretty sure I was blushing, but if he noticed, he didn't say anything.

"Next time," I drawled good-humoredly, "don't make me fall." "Not my fault God didn't grant you a left foot and a right foot."

Will glanced at the cabins' direction. "We should probably go to bed."

I nodded, and together, we strolled back to the cabin area. We didn't speak during our short walk, but the silence was a peaceful one. When it was time to part ways, Will turned to me, eyes scanning my face. "Are you okay?" he asked.

I blinked. "What?" "The fall."

"Oh, yeah. I'm fine," I assured him. "How about you?"

Will nodded. "In hindsight, we probably should have asked those questions first."

"Probably." I grinned.

His lips twitched. "I'll see you in the morning," he said.

"Okay," I replied. "And remember, my friendship bracelet needs to be pink. And if at all possible, I'd like my name to be on it. Yours can be on it, too, seeing how we're best friends and all, but that's completely up to you."

"You're the dictator of friendship bracelets." Will grinned. "Good night, Falice."

I took a step in my cabin's direction. And then, walking backwards now, I gave him a wide smile. "Good night, Will."

PHASE 22

I stepped back into the cabin to find Vanessa sitting on her bed with her legs crossed, excited and expectant. "So, Falarabelle," she said as I tugged off my shoes. "How's that dot looking?"

I let out a short laugh. Not what I was expecting her to say, but at the same time, not at all surprising. "Oh, shut up," was my fabulous reply. I grinned and fell back on her bed. Was she sitting there the entire time? I mean, she'd been in the same position when I left with Will over an hour ago.

"Hey, you're the one with the diseased dot on your hand, not me." Vanessa held up her hands as if to proclaim her innocence, but her mischievous grin betrayed her.

"Hey! Why is it diseased?"

"Well, it's obviously not healthy." Her smile grew. "I mean, unless you know of any healthy dots."

Freckles, I wanted to say. But instead, I said, "Oh, it's definitely not healthy. Probably gonna give me a heart attack."

Vanessa gave me a strange look, and I laughed. "Uh," she drew out, "how is a dot going to give you a heart attack?"

I held up my hand, which was dot-free except for a freckle, or two, and twisted it back and forth. My eyes traveled over it without much interest. My thoughts were back in the cafeteria. When Vanessa cleared her throat impatiently, however, my mind wandered back to the present. "Because the dot isn't a dot," I admitted.

"Then what is it?" "A boy's hand."

Vanessa's eyebrows quirked. "What?" she asked blankly.

I sat up then and let my hands fall carelessly on my lap. "Will held my hand at lunch today," I told her.

Vanessa's mouth dropped. "He what? Oh my god!"

I nodded, and a giddy smile curled on my lips. "Yeah," I replied. "While we were talking, he randomly grabbed onto my hand and… he held my hand for the rest of lunch."

"Did he tell you why?" Vanessa looked like she was about to explode with excitement. "Are you guys a thing now? Is that why you took so long to get back?"

"He doesn't know why." I shrugged. "And no, we're not a thing now. I only took so long to get back because I suck at the rock wall. I climbed it a good ten times. And, because I'm me, I managed to fall off on my way down."

Vanessa blinked, and for a moment her enthusiasm all but died. It appeared that my stumble from the wall was mildly concerning. "You fell? Dude, are you okay?"

I nodded and folded my lips together to prevent myself from smiling that stupid giddy smile again. "Will kind of caught me."

"Kind of?" Vanessa asked. "What do you mean kind of?"

"Well," I said, curling a stray strand of hair with my finger, "when he caught me, we fell, and we… rolled a bit"

Vanessa wriggled her eyebrows. "Oh, you rolled, eh? Who ended up on top?"

I snorted. Just the expression on her face almost made me not want to answer. Her tone wasn't helping either. "He did."

"And you assholes didn't kiss?" Vanessa exclaimed. "Dammit, Falarabelle! You could have just pulled him down a little bit— seriously, just a little bit— and voila!"

I couldn't help but laugh at her. Even though I was still dissatisfied with the fact that Will and I didn't end up kissing, the passion Vanessa had about this situation amused me more than really anything else. "Sorry to disappoint you," I said.

Vanessa huffed. "You should be."

"Would it make you feel better if I said that I actually thought we were going to?" I asked, nibbling on my cheek.

"What?" Vanessa froze for a moment before narrowing her eyes. "What do you mean?"

"I don't know." I shrugged my shoulders and twisted my lips. "For a split second, I thought he was going to kiss me. But he didn't."

Vanessa's expression turned sympathetic. "Oh, damn, girl. That happened with Ty and me before we started dating. It sucked major ass. You get all excited, and then *bam*— nothing happens. Left you feeling really deflated, didn't it?"

I paused before nodding. "Yeah," I admitted softly.

"Well, at least, he started making a move," Vanessa said. "I was about to hit him upside the head. I mean, it's so obvious that he has feelings for you—"

"Okay, I'm going to bed," I interceded, standing up and patting my sweatpants. I wasn't quite sure why but talking about the chance of Will having feelings for me just made the entire conversation awkward. I was okay talking to her about my feelings for Will but discussing his supposed feelings just brought things to a whole new level.

Vanessa laughed and fell back on her bed, legs still crossed. A moment later, though, she untangled them and sprawled freely. "God, I love you," she told me as I threw my comforter to the side and collapsed on my bed. "You're so funny."

"Hardy-har," I said, eyes rolling playfully while Vanessa forced herself out of bed to shut off the light. I draped my blanket over me and snuggled into it, getting comfortable. "Hey, Vanessa?"

"Yeah?"

I bit my lip. I knew it made me uncomfortable, but I had to ask. "How do you know?" I asked. "How do you know when he likes you back?"

Vanessa laughed softly. "That's the fun part, Falarabelle. You don't. You get to sit there wondering while everyone else around you knows, and you're stuck going, 'Dammit, how can they tell? He doesn't seem any different to me.' And then suddenly he's kissing you and everything finally makes sense."

Even though it wasn't very helpful, I couldn't help but smile. "Thank you."

I could feel more than see Vanessa's grin in the darkness. "No problem, Falarabelle. No problem at all."

Do you remember how I said heat and I didn't mix very well? Yeah, well, I meant it.

I wiped yet another bead of sweat from my brow with more force than what was probably necessary. I grumbled under my breath and jabbed at a piece of trash with my trash grabber. It was over one hundred freaking degrees outside, and I was out here picking up other people's trash. There should be a rule that children shouldn't be forced to go outside when it was over one hundred freaking degrees. And it would be because of people like me, who turned into the devil's spawns when they overheated.

My irritation levels were at an ultimate high, sparked by the incessant nausea and a headache. Vanessa, Ty, and Will were quite aware of this fact, and were careful not to provoke me as we continued doing our service for the community. At first, Ty tried to ask me about my upcoming plans with Tiffany— which were still pretty much non-existent by the way— but when he received my death glare, he decided it might be a good idea to ask me later.

"Damn, heat makes Jessica scary," Ty whispered loudly to Vanessa as he watched me aggressively swipe at more sweat. He grabbed a soda can and dropped it into his trash bag. "It's like she's turning into Will— you know, before Will went and got happy."

"I didn't go and get happy," Will muttered halfheartedly. I spared a glance his way and saw that he had his head down as he picked up trash. Even he couldn't pretend that his attitude hadn't definitely changed over the course of the summer. He was obviously struggling to contain his smiles whenever Vanessa and Ty were around, and his moodiness was at an all-time low.

I scowled at the ground. Why did he feel the need to keep up with this stupid façade? Why not let the others know that he had the ability to smile, joke, and have a good time?

Calm down, Falice, my mind warned. *You're aggravated with the fact that you're lightheaded and have a headache. You're not angry with Will or the others.*

"Ugh," I said with a sigh, wiping my head halfheartedly with the back of my hand. "Guys, I'm gonna puke."

"She speaks," Ty whispered, like I wasn't going to hear him.

Thanks, Ty. Thanks.

"Shut up, Ty," Will snapped. He turned to me, expression filled with concern. Even through my sudden need to vomit, I found him so damn attractive right now. "Falice, are you going to be okay? We could go get Joel, Penny, or Dennis."

I answered by slapping a hand over my mouth and giving my head a slight shake. I would have answered, but I was afraid that if I opened my mouth, I'd get puke all over the place— and no one wanted that.

Will gave me a knowing look before dropping his stuff and taking the trash bag from my hands. As he opened the bag, he nodded and said a soft, "It's okay." I hesitated for only a moment before vomiting into the bag. Behind me, Vanessa made a noise of disgust and sympathy. It was hard to care though. It's hard to care about anything while you were throwing up.

I hated puking. Everything about it felt so wrong. I just couldn't fathom how some animals regurgitate their food. How could they possibly enjoy bringing their food back up? It was just so wrong. So, so wrong.

And then, as soon as it began, it ended. I grimaced, pulled away from the trash bag, and wiped my mouth with a shaky hand. It was only when I looked up and saw Will standing in front of me that I realized what I'd done.

I just puked in front of Will.

I just puked in front of the guy I had romantic feelings for.

Oh god, just kill me now.

Will didn't seem to notice how absolutely humiliated I was, because he smiled a small, comforting smile. "Better?" he asked.

I nodded. I did feel better, actually, if you didn't count the emotional turmoil inside me. Even though I was still lightheaded, the fact that I vomited kind of eased my physical discomfort. "Yeah," I murmured. "Thank you."

Will nodded and handed me his trash bag. "Here," he said.

What? I gave my head a vigorous shake though that did absolutely nothing to help my lightheadedness, and gestured to my bag. "No. That has my barf in it, Will. I can't…"

"So what?" Will shrugged. "Just take my bag, Falice. It's not a big deal."

I side glanced at Vanessa and saw her grab for Ty's arm with an awed expression on her face. She appeared to be trying extremely hard not to hop up and down in a fit of squeals. I didn't understand why. Will suggested that he carry around my vomit for the rest of the afternoon. That was not something to squeal about. That was absolutely mortifying. "Will…"

"I'm taking your bag, Falice. Get over it." Will smiled at me. "It's okay."

"Oh my god!" Vanessa exclaimed. "Will just smiled. Did you see it, Ty? Did you see it?!"

Ty nodded slowly. His eyes looked like they were about to pop out of his skull. "I did."

The smile immediately slipped from Will's face, and he rolled his eyes. "Whatever. I'll be over there."

With that, Will picked up his trash grabber and walked away, toward a spot a yard or two away with my bag in hand. I swiped at my forehead again and sighed. The thought of Will lugging around my barf made me so uncomfortable. There were many ways to impress a guy, and that wasn't one of them. No. Just no.

"Holy shit," Vanessa breathed. I blinked. "What?"

"He just smiled."

It took me a second to remember that this was supposed to be a surprising fact. "Uh, yeah," I said, scratching an itch on the back of my head.

"Why are you not more pumped about this?" Vanessa demanded, staring at me with wide eyes. "This is… this is huge."

"Yeah, I know." I brought a hand to my head and closed my eyes. Ugh, I was too overheated to fake surprise. "I just really don't feel good right now."

"You don't look too hot either," Vanessa said. Her surprise dimmed as she eyed my face.

"Ironic, seeing as how I'm overheating," I said.

"Aw, even in such a shitty state you still have your sense of humor." Vanessa grinned. "Will was right, girly. You should really go get Joel or someone else. Maybe they'll let you cool off in the van for a little while."

I nodded. "Yeah, you're right. Okay."

Vanessa smiled. "And when you come back, we can talk about the fact that Will friggin' smiled, and that's friggin' amazing."

"O-friggin'-kay," I said. With a small smile, I gave my friends a wave and then trudged over to Joel, who didn't hesitate to let me head back to the van so I could cool down.

The embarrassment I felt about puking in front of Will dissipated the second dinner came around and he held my hand again. And while my bad mood sort of went away when Joel let me sit in the van, I could honestly say that my mood didn't fully recover until that moment. Will managed to turn things around without even really trying.

God, I was falling in love with him.

"Guys, I've got an idea!" Vanessa clapped her hands to get our attention. She grinned at me and then wriggled her eyebrows suggestively when she noticed how close Will and I were sitting. "You know, for how to shave Tiffany's hair off," she elaborated.

Everyone was suddenly all ears. "What's that?" Will asked, clearing his throat.

Vanessa took a huge swig of her milk. "Well, my dear Will. You know how I initially got sent to this place, right?"

"Because my babe's a hot thief?" Ty suggested before Will could answer.

"Yes, sweetie, thank you." Vanessa winked at him and nodded.

"And I think with my thievery skills, I could totally pull this off. Not to brag or anything."

Will cocked an eyebrow. "Pull what off exactly?"

Vanessa's smile turned mischievous. "I could steal Henry's razor. You know how I had a really bad headache last year and got taken to his office? Well, I saw him put his razor in his desk drawer. And it should be sharp enough for what we want to do."

Ty gave her a dubious look. "Hon, I have all the faith in the world in you, but…"

"If I get caught, what are they going to do? Put me in isolation?" Vanessa shrugged. "From what Falarabelle said, it's a dream."

Ty nodded his head from side to side before shrugging. "That's true," he said. "But you expect me to live through this place without you for a week? That's just mean!"

"Dude, we go through the entire school year without seeing each other. I think you can survive a week." Vanessa rolled her eyes. "And that's only if I get caught. Which I won't. So, what do you think, Will? We all know you get the final say."

I looked at Will, teeth digging into my lip. Part of me wanted him to say no. Vanessa might be right about the fact that the worst thing that could happen to her was to be thrown in isolation, but there was still a chance that they might also link her to all the other pranks. However, if I was being honest, most of me was mentally begging him to say yes. This was the best plan we had, and it was the only one that sounded like it would actually work. I knew Vanessa would be able to pull this off— she was Vanessa.

Will deliberated for a little while before shrugging. "Whatever," he said. He shot Vanessa a pointed look. "If you screw up, it's all on you."

"Always so comforting and inspiring, Will," Vanessa teased. "Don't worry. I won't screw it up. That asshat's hair is coming off."

"So when are we doing this?" I asked, nibbling on some meatloaf.

At least, they said it was meatloaf.

Vanessa shrugged. "I'm good to go whenever."

"You don't need to figure out how you're going to get the razor without getting caught?" Will asked.

Vanessa snorted. "It's not like there's max security here. It should be easy enough."

Will looked tempted to argue, but nodded. "Okay then," he said. "How about tomorrow tonight?"

I folded my lips to hide my growing smile as Vanessa and Ty grinned freely. "Sounds perfect," Vanessa said.

PHASE 23

Of all the activities we did at Camp Sunshine Brooks, I think hiking was my favorite; not only because all we had to do was walk around in the woods for an hour, but also because Seth always managed to trip over something and land in the most amusing positions.

Like right now, for example.

"Ow!" he hissed, face scrunched with pain as he struggled to untangle himself. How he managed to get in such an uncomfortable position by stumbling over a log, I had no idea. But I was having a hard time not laughing at him. "Dammit, I friggin' hate hiking. Dude, it's not funny!"

"Seth, language," Dennis called from a few yards ahead. He had his back turned, so he didn't know that Seth managed to trip. Again.

"I will watch my language when nature learns not to attack me whenever it feels like it!" Seth seethed. He groaned as he wiped his hands on his basketball shorts. "I hate trees."

While everyone else sidestepped Seth and continued with their hike, Vanessa and I sauntered over to him. It was when we reached him and I held out my hand that I could no longer hold my laughter. "Trees are amazing, Seth," I said. "Just so you know."

"Yeah, well, they're jerks to me." Seth accepted my hand and struggled to stand. He grimaced as he removed some more pine needles from his clothes. "Why is it always me?"

"Because you're clumsy?" Vanessa suggested. He glared. "What? You are! If Ty can get through these woods without tripping over a stick, I think anyone should."

That was so true.

Seth opened his mouth to argue, paused, and then snapped it shut. "Shut up," he retorted oh-so-fabulously before flicking off a stray pine needle and stepping around us. I gave it ten minutes tops before he found himself in another awkward position.

"That boy is gonna find himself stuck in a ditch someday," Vanessa said. "And it won't even be something big that causes it. No, the dude is gonna trip over a twig. Just watch."

I smiled. "Probably."

As we fell back into step with the others and continued our hike, Vanessa and I discussed tonight's plan as softly as we could. Normally, we'd keep our mouths shut while around everyone else, but we were at the back of the group today. I think it was impossible not to talk about this. I found myself strangely excited for what we were about to do, and because of that, it was all I really wanted to talk about.

"You're heading out about an hour and a half after lights-out, right?" I said softly, hopping over a rock and twisting around to face my friend. She gave me an expression that was meant to simultaneously compliment and make fun of my twirl. "I mean, I know we talked about this at lunch, but I just want to make sure."

"Yeah." Vanessa nodded. "That's when I'm going unless Will suddenly changes his mind and forces me to go later."

"He better not." I grabbed a branch from the ground and dragged it through the dirt before using it as a makeshift walking stick because I totally needed one of those. "I'm not waiting until one o'clock in the morning to do this. He couldn't possibly expect us to wait that long."

"He doesn't," Vanessa said, smiling as she shook her head. "Not you anyway. I'm pretty sure if he wanted us to wait, and you asked to do it at the time you wanted, he'd eventually agree to switch times. Having the guy in charge be in love with you sure does have its perks."

"In love with me?" My eyebrows shot upward. "I thought you said he had a crush on me."

"Well, now his feelings have obviously grown into love. Duh. And I bet you're in love with the guy, too."

I bit my lip and averted my gaze. I couldn't deny the possibility, even if I wanted to. Which I kind of did. It sucked not because of Will, but because I, unlike the others, wouldn't be returning to Camp Sunshine Brooks. My dad wouldn't send Arabelle back. If her attitude didn't improve, he would just assume the camp hadn't worked and would try to find some alternative. And I wasn't a hundred percent positive, but I think begging to be sent here would look a little suspicious. Just a little.

"I just wish this wasn't a one summer thing," I said. "I mean, I don't mind not spending my summer taking boring classes, doing various community service projects, and exercising like crazy, but I just wish…"

"I know what you mean." Vanessa threw an arm over my shoulders and squeezed. "We'll see each other again though, Falarabelle. You're too good of a friend to let go. And I seriously doubt Will is gonna just let you go either. You made him smile, dude. And trust me. That's not easy."

I attempted to draw a smiley face in the ground, but we left before I could finish. The smile ended up jagged and weird and had only one eye. Oh, well. It had character. Yeah. Totally.

"Seriously, you guys should just come to my house for the summer," I said. The more I thought about it, the more I wanted it. "We'll call it Camp Falarabelle. That way you guys can still see each other and you won't have to come here."

Vanessa laughed. "If I could, I so would. If only my mom would allow it."

I pursed my lips. Vanessa had explained her situation to me a few weeks ago. Apparently, after Vanessa got caught shoplifting, her mom stopped trusting her and their relationship was ruined. She didn't go into much more detail than that, but I got the gist of it. And from the information she gave me, I knew that her mom would never let her go to a camp just for the hell of it. A behavioral camp was the only option.

"Well, why not pretend that Camp Falarabelle is a behavioral camp too?" I asked, speaking the words as I thought them. I paused, eyebrows creasing as I continued to brainstorm. "I could make a website and everything. Except, you know, using a different name. Falarabelle doesn't sound very professional."

Vanessa started to answer, but at that moment someone let out a loud cry. Crunching branches followed.

Vanessa and I shared a side-glance. Seth.

We rushed to where the rest of our group had gathered, staring down at Seth, who was now in one of the mini ditches located in the area. As he groaned and untangled his limbs, Vanessa turned to me and smiled triumphantly. "See?" she said. "What'd I tell ya?"

"You called it," I replied. I didn't doubt Vanessa's prediction, but I never expected it to come true so soon. I just... Wow. Seth was so talented.

"You all right, Seth?" Dennis asked. Though his tone was concerned, his expression showed his amusement.

"Just peachy." Seth stood up and dusted his clothes. "I've said it once, and I'll say it again. I hate trees!"

Everyone laughed. I dug my branch into the ground and watched as Seth began his trek back up the ditch. Yep. Hiking was definitely my favorite activity.

"You would think that the popsicles in-between exercises would've been the second thing to go," I said to Will as we stood at the back of the line in the cafeteria. Ty and Vanessa weren't with us due to the fact that they "had to pee so freaking bad." Before they left, they asked us to save their spots, but I doubted if we'd be able to. Cutting here was as huge an offense as it was in kindergarten. Which was ridiculous because who wanted to get this place's food first?

Will shook his head at me, lips twitching. "Don't give them any ideas."

"I'm not." I shrugged. "I just think that would've made more sense than sending us to bed an hour earlier, you know?"

It was Will's turn to shrug. "I don't really care. My roommate and I never talk, so it's not like I don't go to bed at that time anyway."

"Unless we're out doing the course," I pointed out.

"Yeah, except for that."

We stepped forward, and I spared a glance behind me to check for any sign of Vanessa and Ty. They weren't anywhere to be found, but on the bright side, Will and I were still last in line.

My thoughts strayed from my friends and back to our plan— or, rather, its aftermath— as I faced forward again. Don't get me wrong, I was still excited, but I couldn't stop thinking about what brought us to this moment in the first place. "I wonder how she'll react this time," I murmured, looking at Will from the corner of my eye.

"Well, she's obviously not going to be happy." Will pursed his lips. "But if she touches you, I'll kick her ass."

"I know," I said. I folded my arms loosely over my chest. "Don't get yourself hurt because of her, okay? She's so not worth it."

"She could have drowned you in that toilet."

As serious as that sounded, I had to fight the urge to laugh. "Well, that would've been depressing, wouldn't it?" I asked.

Will gave me a look that said he thought I should be taking this more seriously. "Falice."

"Ugh, Will." I shook my head and finally released some of the laughter I'd been containing. "Lighten up! I understand what happened was dangerous, but aren't we at the point where we can joke and laugh about it? Because, you know, I didn't die, and that's pretty awesome."

I didn't bother telling him that the reason this conversation began was because I was worried about what Tiffany did, and how her reaction might be even worse this time. But he didn't need to know that.

Will's expression didn't change. "But it's not funny."

"It's a little funny." I paused when Will gave me a pointed look. "Okay, so it's not funny. But—"

"Exactly."

I wanted to make some witty retort, but as we continued our way through the line, I decided there wasn't one to be found. He didn't give me much to go on. How did one find a perfect retort for the word "exactly"? If you know, you are a far wittier person than I am.

We eventually reached the cafeteria ladies and asked for our usual flavor. I didn't think there would be enough for the both of us, but apparently kids weren't in the mood for orange popsicles today, which was pretty freaking awesome for us, seeing as how neither of us preferred the other flavors. The cafeteria ladies each handed us an orange popsicle, and after we thanked them, we headed off to our table and sat down.

As I unwrapped the popsicle, I spotted Vanessa and Ty entering the cafeteria. Finally.

"So, on a scale of one to death, how awful do you think her reaction is going to be?" I asked, tone casual as I plopped my popsicle into my mouth. I twirled the popsicle stick absently with my fingers while I waited for Will's response.

Will's eyebrows rose. "Death isn't a number."

I gave him a dry stare. "Ha-ha." When Will's expression turned smug, I rolled my eyes. "Fine. On a scale of forever happiness to death, how awful do you think her reaction will be?"

Will speculated this for a moment before sighing. "I'd rather work with numbers."

"Sucks for you." I smiled.

Will gave me an unimpressed look. "Okay. Uh…" He pulled the popsicle from his mouth and twisted his lips. Finally, after what felt like forever but what was probably thirty seconds, he said, "I guess, on a scale of forever happiness to death, it would be in the range of being petrified by the basilisk."

It was official: Will Dyer was my soulmate.

Will's eyebrows quirked— probably due to my slack-jawed, holy-crap-Will-knows-about-the-wizarding-world expression taking over my face— and brought the popsicle back to his mouth. "Anyway," he said, "if she does anything to you, you'll just let me know, and I'll handle her. It's as simple as that."

I mentally shook off the stupid expression on my face— I didn't have to see it to know I looked like an idiot— and smiled. "Well, unless she kills me," I pointed out. "Then I can't come get you."

"Didn't we just determine the range on the stupid, non-numerical scale you created?" Will asked.

"True." I nodded my head from side to side. "But, by those standards, I still wouldn't be able to come get you. Being petrified and all."

"Whatever." Will waved his hand dismissively. "Either way, I won't let her."

I patted his shoulder, ignoring the feeling that shot up my hand. "Glad to see you care so much, Dyer."

Will shrugged. "Why wouldn't I?"

I bit my lip to force back a giddy smile fighting its way to the surface. It was getting so damn hard to hide my feelings from him. "I dunno. Maybe because I'm the dictator of friendship bracelets?" I grinned. "Which, by the way, I expect to receive soon. Summer's coming to an end, you know."

The smile that started to form on Will's lips fell a little, and I felt mine do the same. The end of summer loomed over us like an oncoming storm. "Yep," Will said after a moment's pause. "It is."

I twirled the popsicle and then pulled it out of my mouth. "I never thought I'd dread the end of this summer," I admitted. "But I am."

Will's eyes, which had drifted to the tabletop, snapped up to me. "You are?"

I nodded. "Yeah. You guys are… well, I just don't want to leave and never see you guys again. You know?"

Something in Will's eyes changed, just like the night I fell off the rock wall. My breath caught. I wanted to kiss him so badly right now, but I couldn't not only because I still wasn't a hundred percent sure he liked me back, but because this wasn't after lights-out. Kids and workers were scattered around. We'd get in trouble.

Will blinked. "Yeah," he mumbled, sitting back in his seat and taking a bite out of his popsicle. "But I come back here every year, so…"

I copied Will's movements and sighed. "If only my dad would send Arabelle back. Then maybe I'd come again."

"You'd do that?" Will's eyes widened. "Seriously?"

I nodded, and, in that moment, I realized that I meant it. I wanted to. Despite the exhausting and constantly boring schedule, I was enjoying myself here. I never thought I would, but I really was. Even without the pranking, I'd probably still be having fun. Will, Ty, and Vanessa made this summer what it was. "Yeah," I said. "I would."

Will smiled. I had a feeling he wanted to say something— something meaningful that would make my cheeks heat up— but all he did was nod and say, "Cool."

Well. That worked, too.

"Yes, cool." I stuck my tongue out at him. "What's cool?"

Vanessa and Ty appeared, pulled out their seats, and flopped carelessly into them. I gave them a wave as they unwrapped their popsicles.

"That I'd come back if I could," I replied with a shrug. "Apparently, that's cool."

"Stupid more like." Ty grinned. "Jessica, I think you love this place too much. I definitely wouldn't come back here if it weren't for Vanessa. No offense, Will."

Will rolled his eyes while Vanessa gave me a knowing smile. "Well, maybe Falarabelle has someone she wants to come back for," she drawled, wriggling her eyebrows at me.

I glared. Really?

When Vanessa just shrugged and beamed in a way that said, "I love you!" I sneaked a glance in Will's direction. Oh god, he was staring at me. And why did he suddenly look irritated? Okay, so maybe irritated wasn't the right word, but he didn't look happy. That was so not a good sign.

Well, that did great things for my stomach really.

"Ooh, does Jessica have a crush on someone?" Ty waggled his popsicle at me. "I think I know who it is!"

Of course, he did. Vanessa probably told him the day I admitted I had feelings for Will. She didn't tell me that she'd confided in Ty, but she didn't have to. It would've been more surprising if she hadn't. "Oh my god, Ty, shut up," I muttered, bringing a hand through my hair. Then I stuck my popsicle into my mouth so I wouldn't have to talk.

"So you do have a crush on someone." Ty winked. "It's Gilbert, isn't it? I knew you had the hots for him."

I was going to kill him. Not maim. Kill. "I'm not talking about guys with you," I snapped, popsicle still in mouth. I guess that showed how well that plan panned out. "Now, just drop it, okay?"

Another fleeting look Will's way. He had his jaw set, and even though he was visibly trying to keep his expression blank, it wasn't working.

"Yeah, Ty," Vanessa said with a smile. "Let's drop it, okay, babe?

Before Will explodes."

Will shot a glare in Vanessa's direction. "Shut up, Vanessa. God." "Adding 'god' for emphasis isn't gonna make me any more likely to shut up," Vanessa pointed out. "But I will because I'm a nice person."

I pursed my lips. If she hadn't brought this up in the first place, we wouldn't be in this situation right now. I opened my mouth to say something, anything.

And then Henry's whistle cut me off before I could. "All right, guys! It's crunch time."

Vanessa rolled her eyes. "Yay," she muttered. And then she stuffed the rest of the popsicle into her mouth. "Let's go, guys," she said through a mouth full of popsicle. "It's crunch time."

Will and Ty arrived at our cabin about an hour and a half after lights-out. Upon arrival, they informed us that everyone who needed to be sleeping was asleep, and that we were good to go if Vanessa was sure she could pull this off. Vanessa rolled her eyes at the implication before telling them that, for the thousandth time, yes, she'd be able to pull this off.

As Vanessa defended her thieving skills, I glanced Will's way. His irritation from earlier seemed to have disappeared completely. Thank God. It would suck to have Will in a sour mood for the second prank in a row.

"So you know what to do, right?" Will asked. Again.

Vanessa let out an exasperated sigh. "Yes, Will, I know what to do. Now, can you let me go get the freaking razor? Please?"

Will rolled his eyes but nodded. "Go ahead," he said.

Vanessa grinned, edging toward the door like she thought Will would change his mind at any second. He didn't, and soon she had her hand on the door handle. "I'll see you guys in five-ish minutes," she told us with a confident grin.

And then she was gone, the cabin door shutting softly behind her.

PHASE 24

"Razor ready?"

I gripped the razor, unable to help the mischievous grin forming on my face. In the back of my mind, I wondered if this was how Arabelle felt before she shaved off our dad's hair. But for the most part the words "This is it!" just played on repeat in my head. "Hell yeah!" I paused. "You plugged it in, right?"

Vanessa gave me a look that said I was incredibly stupid for asking such a question. "Falarabelle, seriously?"

"Well, I was just making sure." "Dude, you watched me plug it in." Oh, yeah.

"Ladies, ladies!" Ty threw his arms over our shoulders and tugged us toward him. I didn't have to look at him to know he was grinning. "As amusing as you two are, which is incredibly so, might I say, I'm pretty sure this process includes you actually shaving the ass' hair off. So let's get a move on, shall we?"

"Babe, you're turning into Will," Vanessa said, shrugging away from her boyfriend and taking a step toward Tiffany's bed. She sent a wink his way. "Bossy, bossy."

From the corner of my eye, I watched as Will stood with his hands shoved into his pockets. He had an impassive expression on his face. He didn't reply to Vanessa's jab, not that I really expected him to. When he caught me staring, his lips twitched. I smiled back.

"Okay, I've got it," I said, turning to face Vanessa and Ty. I flicked on the razor and then winced. Damn, that was too loud for comfort. "This isn't going to wake them up, is it?"

"You ask that now?"

I scowled playfully at Vanessa and then shot a cursory glance around the room. Neither Tiffany nor her minions moved an inch, which made me feel both relieved and flabbergasted at the same time. I think it was safe to say they wouldn't do well in midnight catastrophes.

Razor tight in my grasp, I edged towards Tiffany, suddenly nervous. I'd put so much energy into being excited that I didn't even think about what could happen if this went wrong. What if she woke up when I brought the razor too close to her ear? Well, I wouldn't live to tell everyone about it. That's for sure.

Before I could chicken out, I brought the razor to Tiffany's head and shaved off a strip of hair.

Well. There was no going back now.

"Okay, my turn!" Vanessa grabbed the razor from my hand and removed a chunk of hair. I felt my stomach loosen as she shook with laughter. Why was I worrying about this? Tiffany was a deep sleeper. She proved that much already. Everything would be fine. Well, until tomorrow when Tiffany woke up with no hair. But now wasn't the time to concentrate on that.

"You want a turn, sweet cheeks?" Vanessa asked, waggling the razor in Ty's direction.

"Why thank you, darlin'." Ty winked, accepting the razor from Vanessa's outstretched hand and taking his place next to Tiffany's bed. I could tell it took all the control he had not to laugh when more hair fell onto Tiffany's pillow. "This is so awesome!" He straightened and held the razor to Will. "Will?"

For a moment, all Will did was stare, his eyes flicking between Ty and the razor, like he wasn't sure he was in the mood to participate in this prank. But then he nodded and switched places with Ty, sending me a shadow of a smile before following our lead.

We swapped off like that for the most part, but instead of doing one strand at a time, we did a few and then passed the razor on. Slowly, but surely, more hair began surrounding Tiffany's frame.

"You know, we should work at a salon," Ty joked as I worked on Tiffany's hair. "We'd be fantastic."

I tossed a glance Ty's way, unable to help but smile when I saw he had his thumb and pointer finger to his chin, like he was brooding about our possible future as hair-care workers. "We'd have to give refunds," I told him. As I pulled a clump off and tossed it to the side, I said, "We would suck and you know it."

"True." Ty said.

"What if we left just one strand there?" Vanessa suggested. "That would be so hilarious."

Though the idea was tempting, I shook my head. "I promised her a shaved head," I reminded her. "So that's what she's gonna get."

Vanessa nodded, and I finished off the bit of hair left standing. "Done!" I squealed as I took a step back to examine our work. "Oh lord, she looks fabulous."

Ty and Vanessa snickered, while Will just nodded, his way of saying, "Job well done." My lips pricked upward as I picked up the trashcan from the floor and threw away Tiffany's hair. We did it!

"Aw, look at Jessica, cleaning up after herself," Ty teased. "You know, it would freak her out more if she woke up with a crap ton of hair all around her."

I shrugged. "Yeah, well, I already started cleaning up. And besides," I added as a thought occurred to me, "it'll take her longer to realize she's bald if her hair isn't in clumps around her face."

Ty nodded. "That is true," he said.

"Of course, it's true." I laughed and finished cleaning up. "Are we ready to go?"

Vanessa and Ty shared a glance and then shrugged. "Yeah," Vanessa said. "I'll meet you back at the cabin," she told me. "Need to get this bad boy back to Henry's office before he notices that it's missing." She held up the razor as though I needed clarification.

I nodded. "Okay."

We exited Tiffany's cabin and stepped outside into the warm night air. "Brace yourselves," I said, twirling around to face my friends. I walked backwards with my arms in the air. "We're probably going to wake up early to Tiffany's screams tomorrow."

Vanessa scoffed. "Can't wait."

"I can't either, but sleep deprivation is a nasty thing." Ty sighed dramatically. "If I die because I didn't get enough sleep, I'm blaming you, Jess."

I grinned. "Okay, whatever you say."

There was no sign of Tiffany all morning.

Not only did she not scream the whole camp awake, she also didn't attend any of the daily activities. When she didn't show up to our morning class, I thought one of the workers was going to drag her out of her cabin kicking and screaming, but no one did. Her minions showed up, though, and gave us the dirtiest looks they could muster before sitting down on their chairs, arms and legs crossed.

It was when Henry announced that there would be an emergency camp meeting right after lunch that I realized they gave her the day off. I couldn't say I was surprised. Tiffany could play the wounded puppy act well. But it still irritated the hell out of me.

"Of course, they gave Tiffany the day off," Vanessa said, eyeing Tiffany's vacant seat in the cafeteria with distaste. "She tried to drown Falarabelle in a friggin' toilet, and she gets the day off. Typical."

"Right," I replied, taking a huge bite of my less-than-delightful sloppy joe. I was only using one hand, due to the fact that my other was clasped with Will's. It had become a mealy occurrence for us— a perk to being in the farthest part of the cafeteria and out of direct view of everyone else.

"And we're about to get our asses whooped by Henry," Ty said as he wiped his mouth with the back of his hand. "You can tell he's pissed."

"Well, yeah." Vanessa shrugged. "He keeps handing out punishments, and the pranking isn't stopping. He's running out of things to take away from us. Not only that, but his razor was used to shave

Tiffany's head. If I were Henry, I'd be pretty pissed, too."

My lips twisted. While I didn't regret what I'd done to Tiffany throughout the summer, I felt awful for the workers here. It sucked that they got stuck in the crossfire.

"What do you think she's doing with her day off?" Ty asked. "She's obviously not brushing her hair."

"She's probably planning my demise," I said. And by probably, I meant definitely because there was no way she wasn't. Yeah, she may have pretended to agree to Will's terms earlier, but there was no way in hell she was going to let this go.

"Yeah," Vanessa agreed. "But I don't know what the hell else she's gonna do. There's not much to work with around here, and we've pretty much used every resource possible."

I took another bite of my sloppy joe as my thoughts shifted from my possible-but-totally-definite demise to this whole war in general. We were running out of things to work with, and honestly, I'd used nearly all of my pranking *oomph* with that last one. I didn't know how much more of this I could take.

"Just because she can't think of a prank doesn't mean she won't do something else," Will said. His hand tightened around mine, and when I glanced at him, I could see the concern in his eyes. I squeeze his hand comfortingly, but his expression didn't change.

"True." Vanessa sighed and took a huge bite of her sloppy joe. "We'll just have to be on the lookout," she said after swallowing.

We nodded.

If I found this at all funny, I probably would have laughed at the irony.

I mean, seriously. Throughout practically all of our lunch period, we discussed how important it was that we keep an eye out for Tiffany. And then, right after lunch, she grabbed me and hauled me behind the building we'd just exited from. I didn't even have time to register what was happening, so I couldn't struggle against her or call for the others.

She let me go almost immediately after we reached her selected destination. I wound my arms tightly over my chest and put on a brave face, trying to convey the fact that her vicious scowl didn't scare me— which it totally didn't. Nope. Not even a little. Nuh-uh.

Okay. So maybe it did. Just a little. Or a lot. Whatever.

"What do you want?" I asked when Tiffany didn't seem in the mood to talk.

"What do I want?" Tiffany hissed. She jabbed a finger toward her head. "You shaved my hair off!"

I raised my eyebrows. "I don't know what you're talking about." "You know exactly what the hell I'm talking about."

"Actually, I don't," I said, teetering back on my heels and casting a quick glance behind me. There was one possible escape route, but I wasn't sure if I'd be able to outrun Tiffany to the hill. What if she caught me before I could get away? Then what? Would she hurt me even more for trying to run? "But I thought you did something differently with your hair this morning. Looks good."

Tiffany slammed me into the wall, her nails digging painfully into my skin. All in all, it hurt like hell, but I refused to give her the satisfaction of seeing my pain. "Cut the shit," she spat. "You're going to pay for what you did, you bi—"

My expression turned cold, and I found myself shoving her away from me. Suddenly, I was so sick of this. Sick of Tiffany cornering me and getting me alone so that she could hurt me. Sick of her threatening to make me pay. I was sick of her. I was just so done with this.

"You know what, Tiffany?" I snapped. "Why don't you grow a pair and attack me with others around instead of waiting until I'm alone?" Tiffany scoffed. "What? So your boyfriend can come help you and threaten to end me if I touch one little hair on your precious head? Please.

You depend on him, don't you, Arabelle? You act as if you're this little badass, but in reality, you're not. You're a pathetic loser. And so is Will. He can threaten me all he wants, but he doesn't have it in him to hurt me. You know why? Because he's weak, and he's worthless. Just like you."

My hands clenched into fists at my sides.

"And you know what?" she continued, grabbing ahold of me again. Before she could get a good enough grip on me, I ducked under her arm and tried to make a run for it, but almost immediately after I started for the hill, her fingers curled around my arm and she yanked me back with so much force I almost toppled over. "Where the hell do you think you're going?" she seethed.

"I'm so done with this," I snapped, wriggling in her grip. But she was holding me too tightly now.

"You're not done until I say you're done." Her nails dug threateningly into my skin. "You started this. I'll be the one to finish it. Not you."

"I started this how? By standing in front of the gym with my friends?" I rolled my eyes. "Come on."

"You locked me in a locker room full of spiders!" she hissed.

"You tied my hair to my bed!" I tried to shake my arm free. When that failed, I attempted to pry her hand away with my fingers, but she refused to let go. "Let me go, Tiffany."

The next thing I knew, Tiffany lifted her free hand and whipped it across my cheek. "No," she said. "We're gonna stay here until you've paid for what you've done. And then, when I'm done with you, I'm gonna go ahead and teach Will a little lesson, too. How long do you think a little weakling like him would last in a fight with me? Certainly longer than you."

It wasn't the fear of being trapped here while she beat me that did it. It was the threat to Will, the idea that Tiffany would hurt him. That, combined with everything else that had happened, was enough to tip me over the edge.

Before I could even register what I was doing, I curled my hand into a fist and threw it at her, punching her in the face as hard as I could. She reeled back with a shocked cry, and as I lowered my arm, I watched her hover a hand over her cheek and stare at me with wide, stunned eyes. In the back of my mind, I was just as shocked as she was, but most of me was just pissed. Extremely pissed.

"Don't you dare," I spat. "Don't you dare threaten me. You can throw your little lame-ass attacks on me all you want. You can hit me; you can give me a friggin' swirly. But you do not threaten my friends. Do you understand me?"

Tiffany growled and slammed me against the wall, her eyes dark with rage. She stood there, fist poised at the side of my face, malicious grin sprouting on the tips of her lips. "Oh, look at the invertebrate growing a spine," she said. "It appears I've hit a soft spot."

When my only reply was to wriggle in her grip, she slapped me again. I'm sure it was meant to deter me, but it had the opposite effect. My struggling intensified. It was ridiculous, really, how strong her grip was. Honestly, was she even human? Or did I just need to work out more? Either way, I needed to free myself from her grip— and fast.

When wriggling and pulling at her unmovable hand proved futile, I decided it was time to try another tactic. "It's over, Tiffany," I said. "I'm done with you."

Tiffany lifted her hand to hit me again, whether by punch or slap I wasn't quite sure, but I hit her before she could. First with my fist, and when that didn't prove as effective as the first time, I kicked her in the leg— hard. And finally, Tiffany released me from her grasp, stumbling back and nearly falling onto the woodchips.

As Tiffany let out a string of curses, I rushed away from her and the cafeteria, putting as much distance between her and me as quickly as possible. Hopefully, my kick to her leg inflicted enough pain so that she couldn't run after me. I meant what I said. I was done. No more pranking. No more Tiffany. I was done.

If Tiffany had anything else to say, I didn't hear it. I was already gone, heading down the hill and toward the camp meeting.

PHASE 25

No one seemed to notice my absence as I joined in with the group of campers. I would have tried to find the others, but I didn't want to bring any attention to myself. Henry was already ticked. I didn't need him calling me out, too.

While Henry spoke, my eyes shot down to my right hand. It throbbed from the two punches I'd thrown at Tiffany. The pain was so worth it though. Whenever Arabelle came home claiming to have punched someone, I used to stare at her like she was nuts. How could she just punch someone? What possessed her to use physical violence instead of, I don't know, talking it out?

Well, now I knew.

"Someone broke into my office last night, stole my razor, and used it to shave the hair off of another camper," Henry said stiffly, the anger clear in his eyes and posture. I barely glanced his way. "Don't bother looking," he added when everyone's heads swiveled around in search of the newly-bald camper. "They're not here."

I felt triumphant about how things went down with Tiffany. I fought back. I didn't take her shit. And I actually made it out in one piece before she could do any real damage.

But still... I punched someone— more than once. That was totally different from pranking. It was physical violence. Slowly but surely, the sense of victory began to dissolve into guilt. Yeah, I just said it was worth it, but now I felt sick to my stomach. I'd resorted to physical violence.

Oh god. Now, I was confused.

Did I care that I punched someone or not? I mean, part of me didn't. It wasn't like I didn't have a good reason to plant one— or two— on her. Not only did she threaten Will, but she was also coming after me *again*. Yet another part of me hated the fact that I sank to Tiffany's level. At least before, I could say that I hadn't physically hurt her.

Confliction sucked. Majorly.

The more I thought about it, the more confused I got. How did this happen? One moment I was all, "Whatever, she deserved it," and now I was, "Oh god, I punched someone. I'm a terrible human being!"

Was it normal to second-guess like this? Did Arabelle go through this when she punched someone for the first time? Nah, probably not. Arabelle was always a hitter, even when we were little. I guess it made sense that I was so conflicted. Before I came here, the thought of punching someone seemed foolish to me.

Maybe it wasn't the punching that disturbed me. Maybe it was the fact that I feared I was becoming more like Tiffany by doing so.

The opposing thoughts threatened to overwhelm me as Henry continued to reprimand us for our actions. I felt my stomach thrash as my thoughts crashed around in my head. My mind replayed what happened with Tiffany on an endless loop. With each replay, my stomach hurt more and more.

What had I done?

"No more popsicles during exercises. For those of you who are innocent in all of this, I again apologize. For those of you who were a part of this misdemeanor, please do the responsible thing and turn yourselves in." He paused as he waited once again for someone to fess up to the crime. No one said a word. "You're dismissed."

We didn't have to be told twice. All at once, we all turned and headed back up the hill. I followed along slowly, searched for any sign of my friends. But no luck.

"Hey."

I winced and almost let out a whimper when someone tugged on my sore hand and spun me around. I couldn't help but let out a sigh of relief, however, when I saw it was Will who'd grabbed me.

"Where were you?" he demanded. "We thought…"

"You thought right," I said, shaking my hand out of his grip. Will's expression flashed with what I thought might have been hurt, but it faded away almost immediately. That didn't stop me from feeling terrible though. "It's not that I don't want to hold your hand, Will. My hand hurts."

Will nodded, and then we resumed our way up the hill. "So what happened?" Will asked as I fell into step with him.

"Got in a fight with Tiffany." I sighed. "I'll explain when we're alone. Bottom line: my hand is just really sore."

Will nodded for the second time. Then he flashed me a small smile. "I think I've got a solution for that."

"Ice?" My eyebrows shot upward. "How did you even manage that?"

I sat back on my bed and watched as Will shut the cabin door behind him and stepped further into the room. We had to leave for our various community service activities soon, but we had about fifteen minutes before we needed to gather in the main area.

"The kitchen," Will replied with a cheeky grin. He sauntered over to my bed and sat next to where I had flopped, my legs crossed my injured hand holding lightly onto my non-injured one.

"Here."

I winced as Will took my right hand gingerly within his own and placed the ice on top. At first, the coolness of the ice stung, and my wince turned into a grimace. But then I let out a sigh of relief as the pain eased. "Thank you, Will," I said softly.

Will nodded. "So, are you going to tell me what happened?"

I paused before answering. The guilt and satisfaction meshed together again, and I wanted to throw up. But I wasn't going to puke in front of Will. Not again. "I punched Tiffany," I admitted, eyes locking on the floor. "Twice."

Silence. My gaze shot up to Will. Why wasn't he answering? Was my having punched her that bad? Oh god, I *was* terrible for punching her, wasn't I?

Will blinked. "You did what?"

"I…" I swallowed. "I punched Tiffany."

Will went quiet again, like he was trying to comprehend my words. I didn't really blame him. We both knew I wasn't the type of person to throw punches for no reason.

"Why did you punch her?" he asked. "Did she come after you?" I sighed and nodded. "She did, but I'd be lying if I said that's why

I really did it."

"So why did you?"

I sighed again. "She said something I couldn't tolerate."

"What did she say?" Will's voice was soft, understanding as he asked his questions. I watched, lips folded together as he tilted his head to the side and waited patiently for my answer.

I was suddenly self-conscious. What would he say when he found out that he was the reason I punched Tiffany? Was he going to get angry with me for doing something so stupid in his name? Was he going to march out of the cabin and pull another silent treatment on me like he had when we first arrived to isolation? No, he wasn't going to do that. He'd changed since then, and just from the look on his face I knew deep down that he would understand.

"She, um…" I paused, shaking my head. "Well, uh, she pulled me behind the cafeteria, and she pushed me into the wall. I didn't help things by goading her."

I was rambling to avoid the subject. Just because I knew Will would understand didn't mean I was excited to divulge it.

Will's eyebrows creased as he listened to what I had to say. I went through the rest of the story quickly— so quickly that I wondered if he even understood what I was saying. But I didn't stop talking, and I didn't change the speed in which I spoke. Now that I started, I seemed unable to stop.

"So, basically, she cornered me, threatened you, and I got pissed enough to punch her in the face," I summed up and ran a hand through my hair. My eyes darted back toward the floor.

Will's response was a single word after a moment's pause.

"Wow."

"Yeah." I hesitated. "Does it make me a bad person?"

"What?"

I met his gaze, my eyes burning with guilt-ridden tears. "Does it make me a bad person— punching Tiffany?"

Will's hand went to my arm, and he gave it a comforting squeeze. "No," he said. Though his tone was stern, it was soothing as well. "No, it doesn't make you a bad person."

I bit my lip. "But I sank to her level, Will. And I'd be lying if I said I felt all that bad about what I did. The only reason I feel guilty is because of what it might mean for me. I just feel like me resorting to this—"

Will answered by pulling me into a hug. I leaned into him, arms like limp noodles in my lap. I wanted to wrap my arms around him, but I couldn't with the ice on my hands. "You're not a bad person, Falice," he told me. "Not even close. You stuck up for yourself and for me. That doesn't sound like a terrible person to me."

"But I…"

"Just because you punched her doesn't mean you're turning into her," Will assured me, his arms tight around me.

"Arabelle's punched people, hasn't she? You wouldn't compare her to Tiffany, would you?"

I shook my head into his chest. "No," I mumbled.

I didn't elaborate which question I was actually answering, but I didn't have to. He already knew.

"Exactly." Will shifted and held me out at a distance. His eyes searched my face. "Don't think for even a second that you're anything like Tiffany, okay? You're not."

I smiled. "Thank you. That means a lot."

Will smiled back. My breathing came to a stop as one of his hands slid up to my cheek. He'd held me like this before, but today, it felt different. Somehow, this was more intimate, like he actually planned on going somewhere this time.

And then his hand glided to the back of my neck, and he tugged me toward him. My heart pounded like a dysfunctional drum, and my eyes fluttered shut. Oh my god. This was happening. This was actually happening!

I was going to kiss Will Dyer.

For a few seconds, I was suspended in what felt like an eternity of anticipation. Then Will's lips were brushing mine, and—

"Oh, shit!"

Will and I pulled apart, and I shot a surprised expression toward the door where I found Vanessa leaning heavily against its frame. "Shit, I'm sorry!" she cried. "Dammit, I totally ruined your moment, and oh my god."

I resisted the urge to groan as I pursed my lips. I'd been so close to getting my first kiss. So close. "It's okay, Vanessa," I said. My gaze slid over to Will. He appeared to have been rendered speechless, frozen in place as he stared at Vanessa with a blank expression on his face.

"No, it's not okay," Vanessa wailed. "I just totally made it to the top of the 'Worst Friends in the Entire World' list. Oh my god, I'm a terrible human being. I'm just gonna go suffocate myself with my pillow now."

With that, she collapsed on her bed and threw her pillow over her face.

Will blinked and shook his head, forcing himself out of his reverie.

Then he gave me a soft smile. "To be continued," he murmured. He pulled me back to him, and for a moment, I thought he was going to kiss me anyway, but all he did was press his lips against my cheek. It didn't matter though. My heart was still set aflame. "I'll see you later."

And then he left.

I fell back on the bed and closed my eyes. "Hi, Vanessa," I said. "How was your visit to Ty's cabin?"

Vanessa groaned back in response. "I suck," she announced. "I suck so much. Ah, shit, I suck more than a black hole."

I couldn't help but laugh at that. "Oh, come on, you don't suck that much."

"How are you not mad at me right now?" Vanessa threw her pillow away and sat up, eyes wide. "You guys were this close to kissing— you were there— and then I just decided, 'Oh, hey, I should get back to the cabin before it's time to go!'" She groaned again. "I pulled exactly what people do in the movies. If we were in a movie, the audience would be booing me. Oh lord. I deserve it, too."

"You're so dramatic," I teased before I got up and flopped onto her bed. She refused to look at me as she glared at herself in the mirror. "Dude, chill! He said 'to be continued.'

So, obviously, you haven't rendered me kiss-less for the rest of my life. Okay?"

Vanessa pouted but nodded. Her eyes shot to my hand. "Damn, girl," she said, eyebrows shooting upward. "What the hell happened to your hand?"

PHASE 26

Thoughts of my almost-kiss with Will held my mind hostage for the rest of the day. I was in a daze through my afternoon activities, lost in my daydreams about what would have happened if Vanessa didn't arrive when she did. The idea of Will's lips on mine sent a rush of giddiness through me, and, to be honest, it was hard to even look at Will without fighting the urge to finish where we left off.

Hormones were crazy. Enough said.

However, our almost-kiss triggered another, less giddy-inducing thought: homesickness. In particular, how much I missed Arabelle. I had so much to tell her, and because I wasn't smart enough to bring my own decoy cellular device, I couldn't. Well, that's not exactly true. The others had offered, but their minutes were limited, and I didn't feel right hogging whatever minutes they had left. I'd used enough of Vanessa's, and after a call or two from Will's phone, I felt guilty about stealing his minutes, too. So I decided to just tough it out. I was a big girl. I could handle a couple weeks without my sister. It's not like we were going to the same college. This was good practice.

I had to use all my mind power to steer my thoughts away from my sister and home. And the almost-kiss helped with that— a lot.

"Dude, are you okay?" Vanessa asked as we wrapped our towels around ourselves and made our way toward the locker room. "You've been quiet like all afternoon. You promise you're not pissed?"

I smiled. "For the millionth time, I'm not mad at you. I'm just, you know, thinking about it."

The concern immediately disappeared from Vanessa's face as she grinned. I had no doubt that the holy-crap-I've-ticked-her-off-and-she's- been-lying-the-whole-time look would return in no time. It'd been like that all day. "When do you think he'll continue?"

I snorted out a laugh at the emphasis she put on the word "continue." "I dunno," I told her as I heaved the locker room's door open. "We don't have plans to practice the course at the moment, so it could be anytime."

Vanessa wriggled her eyebrows. "Ooh, maybe he's gonna be spontaneous." She sighed dreamily. "Man, I'm just so happy he finally did it. He freaking grew a pair."

"Yeah, but maybe you crushed it with the door you threw open," I teased.

We stepped into the locker room, which was thankfully empty, and hurried into the first two free stalls. At least, this way we could talk freely without having to worry about someone overhearing.

"Okay, so not funny!" Vanessa huffed and then paused, and even without looking at her I knew a worried frown was over her face. "Oh lord, you don't think I did, do you?"

"No, I don't think you did," I assured her. "Besides, if he doesn't continue, I will okay? I promise we'll have kissed by the end of next week."

"The end of next week isn't soon enough!" Vanessa complained with an exasperated sigh. "You know what? This would be a great time for Will to magically show up because he felt some random romantic tug. He could come in here and be all, 'Oh, Falarabelle, I just couldn't stand to be away from you any longer! Kiss me!'"

I tugged off my bathing suit and said, "He doesn't call me Falarabelle."

"Whatever," Vanessa said. "You know what I mean. Tell me right now that you wouldn't be totally happy if Will showed up in the locker room at this very moment so he could confess his love to you."

"I wouldn't be happy if Will decided to show up right now to confess his love to me because I happen to be indecent at the moment,"

I replied as I grabbed my bra and undies and threw them on. Then it was time for my shirt— which, safe to say, was a struggle. It kept pulling on my hair, and when I tried to tug my hair out from underneath, a few strands got caught on my bra. It wasn't fun.

Vanessa scoffed. "Whatever, smartass. You know I'm right. If Will came in here right now, you'd be so happy that you'd probably pee yourself."

"Well, that would certainly ruin the mood," I joked. "You're impossible!"

I snickered. "But you love me anyway."

As I tugged my shorts over my thighs, I heard Vanessa sigh. "That I do, Falarabelle. That I do."

Missing Arabelle finally overpowered everything else after lights-out.

After lights-out, all the almost-kiss thought enablers were gone. Vanessa was asleep, so she wasn't obsessing over how she ruined our moment, and Will wasn't around to stare at. Sure, the thoughts were still there, but now, I couldn't stop thinking about how much I wanted Arabelle to know that Will and I had a moment. I wanted to tell her everything.

Not only that, but I wanted to know how her summer was going. How was she? Was she having fun? How was Danny treating her? Poorly, no doubt. Had she realized what a huge jackass he was yet? If she had… oh god, she'd be miserable.

Was she miserable right now?

I folded my lips as my eyes burned. The homesickness was twisting into something that felt so much worse. It was the same thing but more intense, and suddenly, I wanted to bawl my eyes out. Big girl be damned— I needed my sister. Yeah, I missed my dad, Beth, and Caroline, but Arabelle and I had been inseparable since birth. We'd never been apart this long. And it kind of sort of really sucked.

One tear dribbled down my cheek, and then another. I cried as softly as I could manage, and next to Vanessa's snoring, I couldn't hear my sniffles at all. I was being ridiculous, I thought as the tears continued to slide down my cheeks. I shouldn't be crying right now. I should be giggling and anticipating when Will would pick things up where we'd left off. But thinking about that somehow only made me cry harder because now, I was thinking about how Arabelle was always the first person I went to, even before Beth and Caroline. And I was the first one she went to. It was pretty much an unspoken rule: tell the sister first and the friends after.

I shook my head. *Get a grip, Falice!* I'd be able to tell her soon enough. Summer was almost over. This wasn't the time for tears. My crush actually liked me back. That was great! Also, my fight with Tiffany was officially over. Yeah, she'd probably enact some form of revenge, but I'd made up my mind: I wouldn't react. I was done with her, which felt great, but…

The tears still came. Harder now, too.

Dammit, Falice, my mind cursed. *The summer is almost over and you're breaking down* now?

Uh, I guess so.

My mind was about to snap at me some more when there came a light knock on the door. I felt my heart contract, and I almost forgot about how flushed I probably was and that I couldn't breathe through my nose. Of course, when I realized this, I hurried to blow my nose and feverishly wipe my face with the back of my hand. There was no point in doing any of this. He'd notice anyway. But I still tried.

"Will," I said, a smile on my face as I pulled open the door. "Damn, I'm so happy to see you."

Will smiled back, but faltered when he saw the drying tears on my cheeks. "Homesick?"

I nodded.

Will nodded too. Then his smile returned full-force, and he grabbed onto my hand. "Come with me," he said softly.

I didn't have to be told twice. Without hesitating for even a second, I tugged on my shoes and followed Will out of the cabin, the door shutting quietly behind me. As we walked, our hands slid together automatically, and I wasn't even sure who initiated the hand-holding this time. It didn't really matter though. All I knew was that my homesickness was slipping away, sent packing by the thought of Will's hand in mine.

"We're not practicing tonight?" I asked as we started down the hill. This was new.

"No." Will shook his head.

My eyebrows rose. "So what are we doing?" "Going down by the lake."

"Why?"

"Because I feel like it." "Why?"

"Because." "Why?"

Will tossed me a pointed look. "Geezum crow, Falice. The 'Why' game, really?"

"Sorry, couldn't resist," I apologized with a grin.

"Didn't want to resist, more like." Will rolled his eyes, but I knew he wasn't actually irritated with me.

We continued down the rest of the hill in silence. I swayed our hands back and forth, thinking about how this had to be it. I was going to receive my first kiss tonight. From the corner of my eye, I could see Will smiling and felt my lips tug even higher. Something about Will smiling was just, well, perfect. It lit up his entire face in a way that didn't light up any others. I could be a little bias though. I did have feelings for the guy after all.

Nah, he just had a great smile.

After settling on the sand a few feet away from the lake, I let my head fall onto his shoulder, while he rested his head on mine. I glanced down at our hands, which were still entwined, and beamed. It felt so natural, sitting here like this with him.

"Do you want to talk about it?" Will asked. He didn't elaborate, but I didn't need him to.

"Not right now," I replied.

For a moment, it was quiet. We both stared out at the water, just enjoying each other's company. It was the peaceful kind of silence, and even though I really wanted to speak with Will and figure out what was going on inside his head, I couldn't bring myself to break it.

But apparently he could. "I want to kiss you" he said softly.

I folded my lips together to keep from smiling a ridiculously large smile that would probably make me look like Arabelle that morning she let me in on her plan. It was hard. I mean, Will just admitted he wanted to kiss me. It was damn near impossible to contain my excitement. Actually, I think it's pretty impressive that I was able to at all. "So why don't you?" I asked.

A moment of silence. And then, "I need to tell you something first."

Will lifted his head from mine, and I removed my head from his shoulder. I watched without a word as he stared at me intently. What was he looking for, exactly? And what exactly did he need to tell me?

"You asked me why I was sent here," he said finally. "And I've decided to tell you."

My eyebrows shot upward before I could stop them. "Are you sure?" I asked, despite my curiosity. This was clearly a difficult topic for him, and I didn't want him to feel like he had to tell me when he wasn't ready. "Because you don't have—"

"Yes, I do," he said, giving me a small, reassuring smile. "And I want to. Because kissing you and asking you to be my girlfriend would be wrong if you don't know."

Girlfriend, he said. I think he was secretly trying to give me a heart attack. Yep. That was definitely what was going on here. I would have said just that, maybe make a joke to conjure the blush that was undoubtedly hiding just beneath the surface, but his expression was too serious and I knew now wasn't the time. So I just sat a little straighter and waited patiently for him to say what he had to say.

Digging his teeth into his lip, Will looked away from me and towards the lake. My eyebrows creased. What could he have possibly done that he couldn't even look at me when he told me? I wasn't going to judge him. We all made mistakes. He had nothing to worry about, not with me.

"I didn't do anything to get sent here," Will confessed, catching me completely off guard. He let out a deep sigh, like he'd just removed a huge weight from his chest, and edged his gaze back toward me.

I blinked. "What?"

He pursed his lips. "I'm just like you, Falice. I don't belong here."

My moth dropped. "What?"

I couldn't believe it. I just couldn't believe it. The Will I met was the definition of a guy with a serious need for an attitude adjustment. How could he have been faking that this entire time?

But... it explained everything — why his happy and sweet side seemed so much more genuine than his angry, bitter façade or why nowadays he always seemed to be fighting a smile. Why, even when he was acting irritable, he was gentle.

"It's a really long story," he said.

I reached for his hands and held them reassuringly in mine. "I've got time."

"You're sure?"

I nodded. "Please."

Will returned my nod and then let our hands fall. He fell back in the sand and stared up at the night sky. I shifted my position so I could properly see his face and then sat there, waiting. It wasn't long before he spoke. "My dad died when I was six," he began.

He glanced up at me, and I felt my heart break a little for him. "I'm so sorry," I said. "My mom died when I was little too." I fell into the sand beside him and rested my head on his outstretched arm. As I grabbed onto his hand and began toying absently with his fingers, I asked, "Were you and your dad close?"

He nodded. "Yeah, we were. But it was a long time ago. I miss him, but my mom didn't handle his death well. They'd been friends forever, and when he died, she just kind of... I don't know. She started dating all these losers, and the next thing I knew, she sat me down on the couch and told me that she was getting married again."

My gaze fell to Will's hand while my fingers grazed over his scar. "Oh my god," I whispered as realization struck. "Rick."

Will's jaw was tight as he nodded. "Rick," he said. He paused, anger momentarily moving him to silence. "I hated him more than any of her other boyfriends because while some of them were verbally abusive, they never hit her. But he did." Another pause. "I tried to convince my mom that he wasn't good for her, but she wouldn't listen to me. I was a kid— I didn't know any better. And then one weekend, she came home and told me they decided to elope in Vegas. She showed me this cheap-ass ring and smiled as though I was supposed to be happy about it."

"That's terrible." And it was. I couldn't imagine what it must have been like to go through this. I tried picturing my dad in one bad relationship after the next, but I couldn't do it. To be honest, I couldn't imagine him with anyone at all. "How old were you when it happened?"

"Nine."

I gaped at him. "He's been in your house for seven years? What the hell?"

Will chuckled, but there was no humor in his laughter. "Yep. Their anniversary is coming up too. Great, right?"

"No." My eyes shot down to his hand. "Oh god," I whispered, horrified. "He did that to you, didn't he?"

He nodded, and I felt my heart shatter. The thought of this man putting his hands on Will made me want to rip things apart. Or, rather, Rick apart.

"He and my mom were arguing," Will explained, his voice just a notch over a whisper. "Which isn't an odd occurrence. Rick is an alcoholic, and he drank a lot which obviously didn't help the situation. They were both screaming at each other, and when he shoved my mom, I intervened. He broke the beer bottle he was holding and tried to hit me with it. I lifted my hand to protect myself."

I couldn't begin to explain the emotions that crashed through me while Will described what happened. I could see it clearly in my mind— watched as this ass of a man cut Will with the jagged end of a broken beer bottle. The fear Will must have felt that night… To have a man come at you with broken glass…

Without pausing to think about what I was doing, I pulled Will's hand toward me and pressed my lips against his scar, like that could actually make everything better. It wouldn't, I knew that, but it wasn't like there was anything else I could do. "I'm so sorry," I said. "No one should have to go through that. No one."

When Will didn't answer, I looked over to find him staring at his scarred hand with a vaguely dazed expression on his face. The moment he shook his head, however, his gaze was clear. "It's not your fault," he said. "Anyway, now my mom knows how dangerous Rick is. She wants to leave him, but, at this point, she's too scared to try. She's afraid he'll kill us if we do, you know?"

I nodded.

"But at the same time she wants me away from that environment as often as possible. So she devised a plan to send me away to camp during the summer so I'd have at least two months away from him. But Rick caught her looking up summer camps online, and he said that if it wasn't a camp to smarten me up, then I wasn't going to a camp at all. She was too afraid to argue with him. So now she sends me here."

There were no words for what he'd just told me. No damned words at all.

"I don't know what to say," I admitted. I turned to Will. "You're so damn brave, Will. I can't imagine what it must be like for you."

"Mmm," Will replied. His eyes searched my face. What he was looking for, I wasn't sure, but I didn't ask him. Just met his gaze and tried to convey just how sorry I was that this happened to him. "I almost didn't come this year. Rick's been getting more unstable, and I was afraid he'd do something while I was gone. But my mom insisted."

The thought that I almost didn't have the chance to meet Will this summer sent my stomach rolling— and not in a good way. What would this summer have been like without him? It would have been completely different. Too different. "I'm glad you came," I said.

Will smiled at me. His free hand went to my cheek, and for a moment, I thought my heart was going to come to a complete stop. "I'm glad I came, too. As worried as I am about my mom, I don't regret coming this year."

I swallowed. "You don't?" "I don't."

I was in the middle of fumbling for a reply when Will's hand slid from my cheek and to the back of my neck, pulling me to him. I barely had time to register what was happening before our lips came together. It didn't take long for me to catch on, however. My eyes slipped shut, and I kissed him back, the whole world slipping away as Will's lips moved on mine. Nothing mattered but us. Nothing at all.

His lips were so soft. So, so soft.

Will pulled away soon after— too soon, if you asked me— with a smile at the ready. "Hmm."

"Hmm?" My eyebrows rose. It was all I could manage. I was too consumed by the fact that my heart was beating rapidly in my chest. I had the urge to grab him by his shirt and close the distance between us again. I was wrong when I said holding Will's hand was the best thing ever. Kissing Will was the best thing ever.

"I've wanted to do that for a while," Will said.

"Well, you should have!" I teased. "Do you know how long I've been waiting for that, Dyer?"

"Sorry," Will said, not sounding very sorry at all. "But, on that note, I have something else you've been waiting for."

I watched as Will's hands slipped into his pants pocket. What was I waiting for besides a kiss exactly? I mean, there was that pony I begged my dad for when I was younger, but I only asked for one because everyone else wanted one, and I thought we were supposed to want one or something.

"Oh… my… gosh."

My jaw dropped as Will took one of my hands and set a bracelet onto my outstretched palm. It was a threaded, pink bracelet with my name spelled out in small wooden blocks along the front. I glanced between Will and the bracelet, unable to believe my eyes. Will was just full of surprises tonight, wasn't he?

"What are you gaping for?" Will asked jokingly. "You're the one who demanded a friendship bracelet."

"I didn't think you'd actually do it!" I exclaimed, staring down at the bracelet in awe. No one had ever given me a friendship bracelet before. Arabelle and I used to make them when we were younger, but we considered them sibling bracelets, not friendship bracelets. Beth and Caroline never went through that phase, so we never invested in the "best friends forever" bracelets you could find in a few stores at the mall. "Holy crap, Will, how did you even make this?"

"Ty's brother sends him with an arts-and-crafts kit every year as a joke." Will shrugged. "It's not that big of a deal."

I slipped on the bracelet, beaming. "You are so amazing," I squealed. "Thank you so much!"

Will seemed about ready to reply, but I didn't give him the chance. I grabbed him by his cheeks and pressed my lips to his. I smiled against his lips as his hands traveled to my hair. He pulled off my hair band, and my hair fell down my shoulders, but I didn't have time to concentrate on that because then Will's hands were in my hair, and my mind went haywire.

"Are you aware how long it took to perfect that messy bun?" I asked with a breathless smile as I pulled away.

"No," Will said. He held out my hair tie. "You can redo it if you'd like."

"What, so you can just pull it out again later? I don't think so." I placed the hair tie on my wrist, letting it sit behind my newly acquired friendship bracelet. "I'm so making you a friendship bracelet now," I said.

"With what?" Will asked. "Are you saying you have an arts-and-crafts kit? You know what, I wouldn't be surprised."

I slapped him playfully on the chest. "No, I'm going to make Ty share unless you used it all."

"Nah, I'm sure there's enough left." He paused. "Unless Ty lied, and he packs the crafts for himself. Then it might be all gone."

I sputtered out a laugh, hiding my face in his shoulder. If someone told me Ty packed himself an arts-and-crafts kit to amuse himself throughout the summer, I wouldn't find it hard to believe. "What would Vanessa say to that?"

"She'd demand to know why he wasn't making her jewelry all this time," Will said. "And then she'd force him to make her something."

I could totally see her doing that.

After that, we were quiet for a while. I played with Will's fingers while I laid my head on his shoulder, loving the fact that he wasn't pulling away. Will stared up at the sky with a thoughtful look on his face. And every so often, from the corner of my eye, I'd see him glance over at me.

I was the one to break the silence this time after Will rested his head against mine again. "Hey, Will?" I asked.

"Yeah?"

I shifted to face him, trying very hard to ignore the fact that his face was just an inch away from mine. "What are we going to do when the summer's over?" I hoped my nervousness didn't show— at least, not too much. I'm not going to lie, a part of me was terrified he'd say that we'd enjoy the time we had left and that'd be that. That's how summer flings went, right?

I didn't want this to just be a summer fling.

Apparently, neither did Will. "We'll figure something out," he assured me, stroking my cheek with the back of his hand. "Maybe I could hitchhike."

I let out a small laugh. "Ha-ha." I paused. "You know, I was talking to Vanessa a little while ago about holding a fake delinquent camp at my house during the summer so we could all see each other without being stuck here. Even if Vanessa and Ty can't, the option is still open for you."

Will's lips twitched. "That sounds like an evil genius sort of idea.

You sure you thought of it?"

"I'm going to kindly ignore that comment," I told him. "Do you think though? Your mom could tell Rick she's sending you here when in reality you're coming to my house for the summer. You could just be yourself."

"Would your dad let you?" Will asked, his voice low, thoughtful. "How would you even explain this without him finding out that you pretended to be Arabelle for the entire summer?"

He had a point. "I'll figure something out." I paused. "Oh! Maybe I could just say a friend from school is having problems at home and needs a place to stay for the summer. I mean, it's half-true."

Will chuckled. "You've turned so devious. I think I might have created a monster."

I looked him in the eye, letting him know just how serious about this I was. "I'm going to get you out of there, Will," I promised. "Even if it's just for the summer. If I have to lie to my dad, then whatever. It's better than you suffering, isn't it?"

Will stared at me for a long time. "You're serious about this?" he whispered. His expression was filled with disbelief, like he couldn't believe I'd go through such lengths for him.

"Of course, I am!" I smiled. "What are girlfriends for, right?"

Will's lips formed into a half-smile. "Like how you just slipped that in there."

"Saw the opportunity and went for it." I hesitated. "I'm not wrong, am I? I mean, you said something about asking to be my boyfriend earlier, and—"

"If you want to be my girlfriend, I'm all in," Will said, effectively cutting me off before I could nervously babble his ear off.

"Of course." My smile returned. "If you want to be my boyfriend, that is."

Will gave me a look that said this shouldn't even be a question.

Which technically it wasn't. Do you see any question marks in that sentence?

"Duh, Falice."

"You did not just 'duh' me." "But I did."

"You suck."

"You suck more."

"You wound me, Dyer," I gasped, raising a hand to my heart. "However will I survive that burn?"

"I'll get you some more ice," Will said.

"Well, it's the least you could do— burning me and all."

Will smiled, and I laughed. I sat up just long enough to adjust my position, and then I fell backward again, this time with my head on Will's stomach. I'd always wondered what it was like to lay like this. Now seemed like a perfectly good opportunity. "Did I ever tell you how comfortable you are?" I asked.

"No, but you've never laid on me before," Will replied.

"That's true." I rolled over slightly. The goal was to see Will's face, but all I got was his chin. "You wanna know what's hilarious?"

"What?"

"When you first blackmailed me, Arabelle told me to kick you in the balls if you made a move on me."

"That's not funny," Will said, but you could hear the humor in his voice. "Sounds rather painful, actually."

"Well, I didn't kick you," I felt the need to point out. I pushed myself up on my elbows and looked down at him, eyebrows raised. "Question for you, Dyer: Why'd you have me make Tiffany's life a living hell in the first place?"

Will bit his lip as his eyes raked my confused expression. It was a perfectly legitimate question, one that I'd asked myself multiple times throughout the whole summer. What brought this on? Did he have a past with Tiffany? I internally grimaced at the thought. If he dated Tiffany, I was going to vomit. Like, legitimately vomit.

"Well, I wasn't actually planning on following through with the blackmail," Will admitted after a few moments of silence. I gaped at him, appalled. "What? It was just a way to let you know that I knew you were faking it so I wouldn't have to spend the whole summer calling you by a name I knew wasn't yours."

"You had me panicking all week!" I chided with a glare. "Seriously, man. That's just mean."

Will's expression turned impish. Obviously he wasn't as sorry as I thought he should have been. Okay then. "I could tell. I was trying to figure out a way to let you know that I wasn't going to make you do anything without seeming suspicious, but then Tiffany shoved you on the way into the gym, and then there was all that talk about being on her bad side. I decided I wasn't going to tolerate her being a jerk to you."

"Holy crap," I said. "I can't believe this."

"Can't believe what?"

"Arabelle was right." I collapsed on his stomach, resisting the urge to laugh as Will let out a soft *oomph!* "She said that you were only doing it because Tiffany was a jerk to me, but I didn't believe her. I didn't think you liked me enough to do that for me." I grinned. "Guess I was wrong, huh?"

"Guess so."

"I'm done pranking Tiffany, though," I told him, closing my eyes for a moment before reopening them. I was beginning to feel tired. "That last confrontation with her made me realize just how done I am with all of it."

Will reached over and took one of my hands in his. It was hard to comprehend that we'd be doing this all the time now— except, you know, when we were around everyone else. Will being my boyfriend had been a wonderful daydream for what felt like forever, and now, he actually was my boyfriend. It was just so hard to take in.

"That's understandable," Will said. "And a good idea."

"If I punch anyone again, it'll be too soon," I said. "Unless Rick decides to show his dipshit face. Then I'll have no problem."

Will's thumb drew circles on my skin. "That'll never happen. I won't let it."

"You should call the police on him," I advised with a yawn. "Get him off the streets and into a cell where he belongs."

"Mmm," Will murmured absently. I could hear the tiredness in his voice, and I knew that he was getting ready to fall asleep, too. With a small sigh, I rolled off his chest and settled in the crook of his neck. His stomach was comfortable, but I enjoyed this spot so much more.

"We should probably head back up," I told him halfheartedly. I was quite content where I was, but felt obligated to try to do the responsible thing. "You know, head to bed."

"Mmm."

"Mmm? Is that all you say now?" "Mmm."

I let out a pretend exasperated sigh before snuggling into his shoulder and closing my eyes. Will's hand curled upward and stroked my hair and the side of my face, like my dad used to when Arabelle and I were younger. It was his way of getting us to fall asleep when we were wound up. I wasn't sure why, but something about the motion through my hair and the softness of his touch always lulled me to sleep. And with Will, it was no different. Soon, my acknowledgment of our need to get back to our cabins was forgotten, and I fell asleep.

I awoke to the feeling of someone breathing on the back of my neck.

At first, I was confused and quite alarmed, but when I rolled over and was met with Will's face, I felt myself relax. And then I was smiling so largely that my mouth hurt. It wasn't a dream. I'd actually kissed Will last night, and he was really my boyfriend.

But then of course, my happiness slipped away when I looked up at the morning sky. The sun shined brightly down on us. "Will," I said, sitting up abruptly and giving him a slight shake. "Will, you need to get up!"

Will groaned and swatted at me, his eyes still closed. "Five more minutes," he grumbled.

I gave him a flat look. "Will, it could be time to get up any minute! We have to get back up there before someone sees us and gets us in trouble."

That seemed to get his attention, but not by much. He sat up, his eyes covered with his hands. "Who cares about people?" he muttered. He teetered, like he was getting ready to fall back in the sand, sleeping those five extra minutes whether I liked it or not. "I hate people."

"Yeah, well, suck it up," I said. I stood up and wiped at my shirt and shorts. I probably had so much sand in my hair right now. Bringing myself to care, however, was an impossible task. "Come on, Will. We have to go. Wakey, wakey!"

Will let his hand fall with a scowl. "'Wakey, wakey'? Seriously?" I grinned and held out my hand for him to take. "Just get up, Dyer.

Be a man and embrace the day. The sun is shining, the water looks positively clear instead of brown, and the hill isn't that steep! Tell me that isn't amazing."

"That isn't amazing," Will said, grabbing a hold of my hand and getting to his feet, his fingers immediately entwining with mine. I could tell that he'd accepted my hand because he wanted to, not because he needed any help. "But I appreciate the optimism."

"Thank you." I laughed. "Because, to be honest, you know how steep the hill is."

"That is true."

We ventured up the hill, enjoying these last moments before we had to spend the day pretending we weren't a couple. It would be hard, but hey, Vanessa and Ty had been doing it for years. I had no doubt we'd be able to pull it off, too. At least, I had meals and course practices to look forward to.

"Guess this is where we part ways," I said as Will and I paused in front of the obstacle course. Henry's office glared at us from the distance, daring us to show any notion that we were now a couple.

Well, challenge accepted.

"Mm-hm." Will let go of my hand and wrapped his arms around my waist, tugging me toward him. "I'm gonna kiss you first, though."

"Ah, but what if I don't want to kiss you?" I teased. "You know, what if I'm not in the mood? Morning breath—blech."

"Then screw you," Will said simply, a playful smile on his face. He didn't seem at all worried about morning breath, which was quite a relief. Actually, he seemed more carefree than usual, and had since we went to the lake last night. It was amazing.

"Uh, uh, uh." I waggled my finger at him. "No sex in the cell!"

His expression flattened. "I'm going to ignore the fact that you just said that."

"But, Will!" I gasped. "We can't just disregard the rules!

Remember, camp rules still—"

Will rolled his eyes before catching my lips within his own. I'm pretty sure this was half to kiss me and half to shut me up, but I didn't really care. My arms still went around his neck and pulled him closer to me. You know how some people said that they felt like they were flying while they were kissing someone? Well, I kind of felt like that. I felt like I was so high up that no one could touch me. Nothing could destroy this moment. Nothing.

"Miss McAtee, would you kindly disentangle yourself from Mr. Dyer and report to Henry's office?" Okay, well, maybe that could.

Will and I pulled apart, and I shot him a wide-eyed look before turning in the direction of the voice that had interrupted our moment. Gilbert stood in front of the cafeteria, his hands folded over his chest and a triumphant expression perched on his face. I had no doubt he was saying something along the lines of "Got you!" in his mind.

"I'll be right back," I whispered. I was in trouble. The look on Gilbert's face proved that. But I had a feeling it had nothing to do with getting caught having romantic relations. Otherwise, Will would've been called in too, right?

Will nodded, and I headed over to Gilbert, crossing my arms uncomfortably over my chest. When I reached him, Gilbert put a hand on my shoulder and steered me toward Henry's office. "You've really done it this time," he told me, way too happy about the fact that I'd screwed up. "You've really done it."

Well, shit.

Gilbert opened the office's door and ushered me inside, releasing his grip on my shoulder. "Sit," he said, and then left, disappearing outside. I eyed the two uncomfortable-looking chairs with distaste. Hmm, which to choose, which to choose?

After pretending to think about it for a second, I settled into the seat on the left, glancing around at my surroundings. The office wasn't much really. It was literally just the space taken between an indent in two walls. It was no bigger than my house's bathroom, crammed with Henry's desk and filing cabinet. On the back wall was a window, but it was so small that it brought in only a smidgen of natural light.

And sitting behind the desk was Bruce Willis, typing on his laptop.

Okay, maybe it wasn't Bruce Willis. But that would have made this situation so much cooler.

"Thank you for coming, Miss McAtee," Henry said as he closed his laptop and folded his hands together. I tensed. All summer, he'd referred to me as Arabelle. Why the sudden change? "Do you know why you're here?"

I shook my head. "No, sir."

Henry gave me a hard stare. I forced myself not to squirm under his gaze. "Well," he said finally, "I can tell you that it has nothing to do with your relations with Will."

I nodded. I'd already suspected that, but it was still a relief. "May I ask why I'm here?"

A thought occurred to me as Henry's lips dragged into a disapproving frown. Had Tiffany told him what I'd done? Was that why she didn't antagonize me after what happened yesterday? It made sense.

Oh god, he knew.

Henry was just about to tell me if my hypothesis was correct when someone cut him off. "Let me go out there, dammit!" a girl yelled. "You can't hold me in here!"

I froze. I knew that voice.

Suddenly she stormed down the hall, and she was in my line of sight. She looked flabbergasted and all-around pissed as she stomped toward me. I gaped, and I forgot Henry was there and that he would hear me as I gasped, "Arabelle."

Arabelle came to a stop in front of me, her hands on her hips. "Hey, Falice."

PHASE 27

"Did you know they have a jail cell back there?" Arabelle asked, casting a glance behind her. "They don't actually put kids in that, do they?"

I barely heard her. I was too overwhelmed by the fact that Arabelle was here. Then I was out of my seat and flinging myself at her, almost knocking her over in my excitement. She didn't hesitate to hug me back, laughing softly as she wrapped her arms around me. And for a moment, it didn't matter that Arabelle was supposed to be in London right now and that we were probably— no definitely— so screwed.

"I've missed you so much!" I whispered into Arabelle's ear as I gave her a final squeeze. Then I pulled away, wide-eyed. "What are you doing here?"

The elation of being reunited with my sister faded away as reality set in. Henry didn't seem at all surprised to have two identical people in the room or that we'd called each other by our actual names. This was why I'd been called for. Oh, shit.

"My trip to London got cut short," Arabelle said softly, biting her lip. I could see that she wasn't telling me the whole story, but I didn't comment on it. We'd talk about it later, when Henry wasn't staring at us.

Before I could even think of a reply, Arabelle grabbed ahold of my wrist and held it up for inspection. "What is this?" she asked even though she clearly knew what it was. She wriggled her eyebrows and grinned, like she knew full well who created this masterpiece on my wrist even though I wasn't able to update her on anything. "Damn, whoever made this is skilled. The ones I gave you always sucked. Not that yours were pretty either."

I rolled my eyes at her jab at my friendship-bracelet-making skills, despite the fact that it was totally true. "Will made it," I replied.

Arabelle did not look surprised. "Ooh, he's quite the craftsman.

How are you two do—?"

"Ladies," Henry interjected. An irrational part of me wanted to inform him that he'd broken one of his own rules—don't interrupt when someone else is speaking. I didn't tell him that though, for obvious reasons. "Please take a seat."

I immediately complied and gestured with my eyes for Arabelle to do the same. She met my gaze and held it before rolling her eyes and collapsing into the seat next to mine.

"So," Henry began. "Care to explain what's going on here?"

"I can explain."

Arabelle and I spun around in our seats as our dad appeared out of what felt like nowhere, the fury clear on his face. My stomach and mouth dropped. What was the level after screwed? Because I'm pretty sure we were there. I really shouldn't have been surprised. Arabelle had to get here somehow, and I seriously doubted Danny would've been willing to drive her to New Hampshire just to pick up the sister that hated him. Even if I didn't hate him, he wouldn't have been willing.

"Oh, yeah," Arabelle mumbled. She tossed me an apologetic glance. "Dad's here, too."

My dad glared at her before directing his gaze at me. His expression was the definition of shame-inducing. "My daughters decided it would be funny to switch places," he said. His eyes didn't stray from me as he spoke. "Like I told you earlier, my daughter, Falice, has been here this whole time."

"I know what you said, Mr. McAtee," Henry said, not at all fazed by my dad's hostility. That made sense. He was the head of Camp Sunshine Brooks after all. "But I was hoping that your daughters would explain what happened themselves."

I continued to gape. This was all happening too fast. One moment, I was enjoying my morning with Will, and the next, I was being called into Henry's office to find out that the jig was up.

"Well?" Henry prodded when neither Arabelle nor I moved to give an explanation. "Which one of you is going to tell me what happened?"

When it appeared that I wasn't going to talk, Arabelle took initiative. She let out a deep sigh as she slouched back in her chair. It was her way of saying, "Fine, I'll tell you, but I'm not going to be happy about it."

"I asked Falice to come here," she confessed. "I really wanted to go to London, and when I asked her to come here for me, she agreed."

"Well, I hope you're proud of yourselves," my dad snapped, "because now, you're both in trouble." His glower, which had traveled to Arabelle, found its way back to me. I couldn't say I missed it for the few seconds it had strayed away. "Go pack your things. We're leaving."

I sat straight up in my chair, eyes wide.

No!" I cried. "Please, Dad—"

"Are you saying you want to stay here?" my dad demanded. "Yes!" I couldn't go. Not now. I wasn't ready to leave Will and the others. On top of that, Will and I just started our relationship. We hadn't even been dating for twenty-four hours yet, and my dad expected me to just leave? "Dad, please let me stay until the end of the summer. Please."

"No."

I stood up, arms crossed over my chest. "Why not? There are only a couple weeks left anyway!"

"Because you don't belong here, Falice."

I glared. I've never really been angry with my dad before— at least, not to this extent. Sure, there were times when he frustrated me, and I wanted to yell at him, but for the most part, we got along. But now, I wanted to scream at him until my throat was raw, and then I didn't want to see his face for at least a week— or two, just to be safe.

"I'm not leaving," I said.

My dad's scowl met my own. "Yes, you are. It's game over, Falice. Now go pack."

Arabelle shot me a sympathetic look before twisting around in her seat to face our father. "Dad—"

"Not a word, Arabelle." My dad's hand shot up in warning. "We've already discussed this in the car."

The expression on Arabelle's face said that she wanted to argue more on the subject, but she didn't. My eyebrows almost rose in surprise. Arabelle, not fighting back? Was this because of the deal we made back before I agreed to come here, or because she didn't have the energy after whatever happened in London? "I'm sorry," she said, returning her gaze to me. "I know how close you are to some people here."

"That's what this is about?" my dad exclaimed, like he couldn't believe I actually made friends here. My nails dug into my palms. "You have friends at home, Falice— friends that you were apparently willing to ditch for an entire summer because of this ridiculous plan."

But you fell for it, didn't you? "Yeah, I have friends at home," I said, making sure to keep my voice at an appropriate decibel. "But that doesn't mean that I don't care about people here. Please, Dad. Please don't make me leave."

"Even if I wanted to let you stay— which I don't— I can't. You're not Arabelle. You're lucky I didn't get in trouble for sending you here instead of her." His gaze was like ice, and I knew that fighting with him would be pointless. "Now, go pack your things. I won't ask you again."

My eyes burned. "Whatever," I muttered.

Without another word, I twisted on my heel and stormed out of the office, slamming the door behind me. My feet pounded against the woodchips as I rushed back to my cabin. I couldn't believe this. I could not believe this was happening.

I took a moment outside of Vanessa's and my cabin to attempt to mentally prepare myself. The infuriated tears screamed to be released, but I refused to shed them. I didn't want to give my dad the satisfaction.

I was expecting to find a sleeping Vanessa when I entered, or maybe an oblivious Vanessa getting ready for the day. Instead, I found her and the boys crowded on her bed, eyes glued on the door while I pulled it open. As I stepped inside, Will got to his feet, and Ty's hand tightened around Vanessa's. The concern was clear on all of their faces.

"Falice…"

I shook my head. "It's over," I said.

Will closed the distance between us and wrapped his arms around me, and I immediately hugged him back, pressing my face against his chest. "What's all over?" he asked softly. "What happened?"

"Hey."

We all glanced toward the doorway as Arabelle entered, looking as pissed as I felt. Will's arms tightened around mine, and I knew he understood what I meant now.

"I'm Arabelle, in case you were wondering," Arabelle said, hands going straight for her hips. She eyed Will and I with a knowing expression as she fell back on my bed and crossed her legs. Despite our situation, she managed to crack a small grin. I guess she officially had the answer to her question.

"Holy shit," Vanessa breathed.

I forced myself out of Will's embrace and faced my friends. "My dad somehow found out that I was pretending to be Arabelle," I told them. "I have to go."

I held my tears back. Even as my friends' expressions crumbled into devastated shock. Even as Will dragged a hand down the bottom half of his face in a blatant attempt to keep his cool. It was incredibly difficult, but my efforts paid off when my cheeks remained dry.

"If it makes you guys feel any better," Arabelle said, "she tried to convince him to let her stay."

"It doesn't!" Vanessa exclaimed. She detached herself from Ty and scurried over to me, planting herself a foot from where I was standing. "So, that's it? You're just leaving?"

"I don't have a choice."

Will took one of my hands in his and gave it a comforting squeeze. It was clear from the look he gave me that he understood how hard I was trying to keep myself together. "What time do you have to leave?" he asked.

"Well, in about fifteen minutes our dad will probably come and pack the rest of her things himself if we're not done," Arabelle answered for me. "He sucks like that."

Will's eyes settled briefly on Arabelle, and he nodded. "Okay."

I don't know if I'm the only one who caught it, but I could tell from the tone in his voice that he didn't think this was okay at all. I squeezed his hand before letting go and crossing my arms irritably over my chest. "Well," I said. "This sucks."

Vanessa threw her arms around me then. "It sucks so much," she agreed as I wrapped my arms around her. "You'd better keep in touch, you got it? And Camp Falarabelle better become a thing."

I let out a soft laugh. "I doubt I'll be able to convince my dad of that now, but I'll try my best."

Vanessa pulled away, and then it was Ty's turn. "I'm going to miss you, Jessica," he told me, swaying us back and forth. "So much."

"I'm going to miss you, too," I said, hoping that they all realized just how much so. This day was coming eventually,

I knew, but it was painful knowing that it was here early and unexpected.

After Ty and I parted ways, I went back to Will, hugging him briefly but tightly. I could have stayed in his arms forever, honestly, but Arabelle was right: If we didn't finish packing by a certain time, my dad would come and finish packing for me. And I really didn't want to deal with that right now.

"Let's get this over with," I muttered as I hauled my duffel bag out from underneath my bed. From the corner of my eye, I saw Arabelle frown. Neither of us were prepared for this; not for getting caught, and definitely not for me caring so much about being sent home.

Arabelle hopped off the bed and helped me unload all my clothes from my bureau. She was about to haphazardly dump a bunch into the duffel bag when she noticed the condition of her beloved Converse. "What the hell happened to my babies?" she demanded, holding her shoes in the air and giving us all an accusatory glance. "It looks like someone got sick all over them— from both ends."

"We were at war, and they were caught in the crossfire," Vanessa kinda-but-not-really explained.

"Tiffany dumped a bunch of oatmeal in the bag, and your shoes were in there," I elaborated. "We tried to clean them, but…"

Arabelle groaned. "She so owes me a new pair of shoes." "Good luck with that," Vanessa said.

As Arabelle dropped her Converse back into the duffel bag and began stuffing my clothes inside as well, I grabbed my peanut butter jar and unscrewed the cap. Dammit. Of course, the moment when I actually needed peanut butter, the jar was empty. Though, I had to pat myself on the back— the jar lasted a lot longer than I thought it would.

"This is so unfair," Vanessa said. "Especially for Will. He was finally happy, and—"

"I'm right here," Will snapped. "You don't need to talk about me like I'm not in the room."

"Fine." I didn't have to look to know that Vanessa was rolling her eyes at him. "This is so unfair for you because you were finally happy. Better?"

"I'm sorry," Arabelle whispered, taking my attention away from Will and Vanessa's conversation. "I didn't mean for this to happen."

I sent her the largest smile I could muster, which wasn't that big, to be honest, and shrugged. I wasn't mad at Arabelle. Why would I be? No matter how hard she tried to hide it, I could tell that she was upset about something other than getting caught by our dad. I wanted to ask her about it, but I knew she wouldn't tell me with anyone else in the room.

"Why does that Ty guy call you Jessica?" Arabelle asked suddenly, expression changing from upset to amused in an instant. "Just out of curiosity."

I shrugged again. "He's just always called me Jessica. Vanessa calls me Falarabelle."

Arabelle snorted before chucking the last shirt into my bag. "You've made some interesting friends." She sighed and gave me another remorseful look. "I really am sorry."

"You have nothing to be sorry for," I replied.

Arabelle frowned like she didn't believe me, but didn't say anything as we finished packing. She hoisted my duffel bag over her shoulder after we'd zipped it and double-checked that I hadn't forgotten anything. I tried to tell her that I could carry it myself, but she was feeling guilty about this situation and was attempting to make up for it in any way that she could. So I let out a resigned sigh and let her do what she wanted. If she thought carrying my duffel bag to the car would make me feel at least a little better, then so be it. I wasn't going to argue with her.

As Arabelle started for the door, I turned to my friends again. With a small, nearly miniscule smile, I said, "Well, I think another round of hugs are in order, don't you?"

Vanessa and Ty laughed before each giving me another quick hug. And then I returned to Will's arms, letting out an almost-content sigh as he enveloped me in his embrace. The hug lasted longer than time allowed, but I didn't care. My dad could wait.

"I'll convince my dad to let you come over next summer, okay?" I assured him, turning my head so my voice wouldn't be muffled by the fabric of his sweatshirt. "I meant what I said last night."

Will pulled away ever so slightly so he could see my face, and he smiled a small smile. Then he kissed me, sweet and slow. I wanted the kiss to last forever. Sadly, no matter how slow the kiss was, it wasn't slow enough. All too quickly our lips parted ways, and I said goodbye.

"You guys are so cute," Arabelle told me with a good-natured nudge as we made our way back to Henry's office. I had no doubt in my mind that, at this very moment, my dad was apologizing for our indecency and probably annoying Henry in the process.

"Thanks." I sighed. "And now I have to go."

Arabelle threw an arm over my shoulders and gave me a comforting squeeze. "I wish I could fix this," she said softly.

"But I think if Dad were to let me stay for the rest of the summer— which he wouldn't, obviously— he'd immediately know we'd switch places again."

"That's probably why he won't even think about making you stay," I said. "That, and Henry is probably blacklisting him."

"Huh." Arabelle removed her arm from my shoulders and adjusted the duffel bag. "Well, he looks like a Bruce Willis if you ask me."

"Right?" I couldn't help but laugh. "I've always thought so."

We reached Henry's office and trudged inside. Like I predicted, my dad hadn't moved an inch in the time we were gone, and he was repeatedly telling Henry that he was so, so sorry for our behavior. I came to a stop near the doorway, and Arabelle did the same, crossing her arms defiantly over her chest. "I'm here," I said stiffly.

Henry nodded, and my dad just stared at me as if he didn't know who I was anymore. I'd be lying if I said that didn't hurt because it kinda-sorta really did.

"Joel is retrieving your cell phone," Henry said. "After that, you're free to go."

Oh, yeah, Arabelle's cell phone. Now that I thought about it, I should have asked Vanessa to nab it while she was stealing Henry's razor.

Henry's razor. "Um…" I hesitated, fidgeting uncomfortably. I knew I had to do this, but that didn't make getting the words out any easier. Henry raised his eyebrows, but didn't say anything as he waited patiently for me to say what I wanted to say. "You can stop punishing the campers," I said finally. "I'm the one who put the spiders in the locker room."

He blinked. I don't think that's what he was expecting me to say. "What?"

"I'm the one who's been messing with Tiffany all summer. And, just so you know, she's done a great deal to me, too. I just didn't take advantage of what she was doing to me."

I probably sounded like a brat right now— no, definitely. But I didn't care. I was too upset and suddenly ranting about Tiffany seemed like a nice outlet.

"You did what?" my dad seethed. "Falice Alison McAtee…" "She started it."

I could feel more than see my dad's disbelief, though he definitely didn't try to hide it on his face. "That's how you're going to defend yourself? 'She started it'?"

I nodded once. "Yeah."

Henry stared at me intently, as though he, like my dad, was trying to figure out who I was. I know it's weird, but that fact hurt me too. I was so used to his kind smiles and words of encouragement that being under his scrutinizing gaze was painful. I avoided it completely, eyes latching onto the far wall. "I'm just trying to understand," he said eventually, "why an apparently well-behaved child would do all these terrible things to someone else."

I folded my lips together before answering. I'm hoping he took my moment of silence as anger, not scrambling for an excuse. "I was just trying to fit into my role," I lied. "Anyway, you know who's behind it now, so you don't have to keep punishing everyone else for my actions."

I don't know if Henry believed me, but I did know that he was angry with me. He hid it well, but it was there, just beneath the surface. But what could he do? I was leaving and was no longer a part of his camp. However, if I was being honest, I think I would have preferred his punishment to my dad's. At least, Henry's punishment would only last until the end of the summer. My dad's could go on forever.

"Thank you," Henry said, "for coming clean. I'll make sure to set things right. And you worked alone?"

"Yes," I said. "This was between me and Tiffany." I paused and then gave him a small, apologetic smile. "I'm sorry for all the trouble I've caused you."

Henry nodded and said a soft, "You are forgiven." Then he glanced to the left. I followed his gaze and grinned when I spotted Joel approaching us, Arabelle's cell phone in hand. When he reached me, he held it out and returned my smile. "I suppose you'll be needing this," he said.

I accepted the phone from his outstretched hand. "Thanks, Joel." "No problem." His smile grew.

"I'd like to apologize one last time for all the trouble," my dad said louder than necessary. "Is it all right if I take my girls home?"

"Oh, please," Henry replied. I almost laughed at his tone and expression. He didn't say it in a way that conveyed he wanted me out of there pronto, but I got the message. Apparently, Henry O'Brien didn't appreciate the drama. "Have a nice day, Mr. McAtee." He peered over at me. "I hope you learn from this experience, Falice. There are consequences to actions like these."

I nodded. "It was nice meeting you."

With that, my dad practically pushed Arabelle and me out the door.

While my dad stormed over to the car, muttering angrily under his breath, Arabelle and I took our time. My eyes locked on the course, and I grimaced. I never got to prove that I could complete it in five minutes… But, then again, that's not why I was upset. Will and I had just made plans to practice the course a few nights this week. Tonight was practice night too. Guess that wasn't happening anymore.

"I still can't believe you did all that to that Tiffany girl. Not gonna lie. I didn't think you had it in you."

I gave her a wan smile. "I didn't either."

Arabelle glanced at me from the corner of her eye, and I knew she wanted to press more on the subject, but I was glad she didn't. The closer we got to the car, the less I wanted to talk. I just wanted to sulk and feel sorry for myself, which was exactly what I planned on doing once my dragging feet inevitably reached the car.

"Hurry up, girls!" my dad called. "Walking as slowly as you can isn't going to change the fact that we're going home."

I watched without interest as my dad sat himself in the driver's seat and slammed the door behind him. I think it was safe to say that this was going to be a very, very long car ride.

"Don't worry," Arabelle said. "He's angrier at me than he is at you."

"I doubt it."

"Well, don't." Arabelle shrugged. "I'm the one who came up with this whole charade. And, on top of that, I actually left the country. So, while you might be grounded till Christmas, I'll probably be grounded until the end of senior year."

My eyebrows rose. That was a long time. "Doesn't make much a difference to me," I admitted with a shrug, casting a longing glance behind me. "How long I'm grounded, I mean."

Arabelle pursed her lips. "I'll find a way for you guys to see each other again," she promised.

Despite the fact that there was no way for her to be sure of her words, I found myself smiling. "Thank you, Belle."

Arabelle grinned. "No problem, babe."

My lips fell as we reached the back of the car. I opened the trunk, and Arabelle carelessly tossed the duffel bag inside. As I got ready to close the trunk, my eyes strayed to my wrist. It was really a great bracelet, I thought. *Dammit, Dyer, you're amazing.* I let out a small sigh and slammed the trunk shut. "Let's go," I said.

I never thought I'd feel uncomfortable in my dad's car, seeing how he'd had the thing since before I was born. But now, as I pressed myself close to the window and rested my head against the glass, I felt it. Was this how Arabelle felt every time she and our dad were stuck together in close quarters after a major blowout?

"Falice," Arabelle said. She unbuckled her seat and scooted to the middle, pointing to something outside our window. "Look."

Eyebrows creased, I did as she instructed. I forced my head off the window and twisted around to see what she was talking about. It was Will. My heart contracted when I spotted him standing in the middle of the main area with his hands shoved into his pockets, watching us with a dejected expression on his face. Will...

Those stupid tears burning again, I lifted my hand and waved. "Bye, Will," I whispered.

He waved back, and I swallowed down the lump in my throat.

The car lurched as my dad began pulling out of the parking lot. I spun around and stared out the back window, not wanting to waste these few seconds I had left. I kept my eyes trained on Will, wishing that he'd somehow get me the hell out of this car and back into his arms, no consequences.

But he never did. Instead, he stared right back at me until the car reached the wooded area and we couldn't see each other anymore.

PHASE 28

"Why was that boy staring at our car?" my dad demanded, his grip tight on the steering wheel. After a moment's thought, he muttered, "He probably wants to steal it. Gives me the creeps."

"Yeah, because everyone is trying to figure out the most efficient way to steal your shitty car," Arabelle snapped. I would have nudged her warningly, reminding her of the deal we made before summer began, but right now, I was too pissed at my dad to care. I wanted to high-five her more than anything, and I glared at the back of his head along with her. In the back of my mind, I observed that his hair was growing back nicely, but who the hell cared? I, for one, hoped Arabelle would shave it all off again.

"Arabelle—"

"Well, what you said was rude," I cut in before he could finish his sentence. "Assuming that he's planning on stealing your car? That's so judgmental." After pausing for a second, I added, hoping my tone conveyed just how unimpressed I was with him, "And, by the way, he wasn't figuring out how to get his hands on your car. He was saying goodbye to me."

My dad's eyes found me through the rearview mirror, wide and irritated. "I don't like this new attitude of yours, Falice," he said. "This camp is supposed to straighten out attitudes, not create them."

"She wouldn't have an attitude if you didn't just waltz in there, start yelling, refuse to listen to her, and then act all judgmental," Arabelle pointed out. "You are aware that you just called her boyfriend a creep, right?"

For a moment, our dad didn't reply. I sighed and hid my face in Arabelle's shoulder. Maybe I should've been annoyed that she just outed me without asking me first, but I wasn't. And I'm pretty sure that's why she said it. She knew that I'd be weirdly okay with it, and that it would shut up my dad and maybe force him to think about the ass he was being.

"You're dating a delinquent boy?" my dad asked finally. The expression on his face stated that he was so not okay with this.

Okay, so maybe this wouldn't force him to think about the ass he was being.

"He's not a delinquent!" I snapped. Maybe I could have said that a little more civilly, but his tone and expression were pissing me off to the max.

Arabelle grabbed onto my hand and squeezed. I glanced at her and struggled to smile. It didn't work out very well, being ticked off and all.

"Oh, yeah?" my dad challenged.

"Oh, yeah." I glared. "What, you see him watching our car leave, and you assume you know everything about him?

You don't know Will at all, Dad, and you're just making yourself look like a jerk for pretending that you do."

I was tempted to tell him just how much he'd misjudged Will, but that wasn't my story to tell. The last thing I wanted to do was betray Will's trust just because I was angry with my dad. I didn't even plan on telling Arabelle until he gave me the okay. If it were something smaller, maybe I wouldn't have been so hesitant, but I knew it took a lot for Will to even tell me what happened to him.

"What is going on with you?" my dad demanded. "I'm your father, Falice, and you will treat me with respect. You used to understand that."

"It's a two-way street, Dad," I said. "How do you expect me to treat you with respect if you don't give me or the people I care about the same courtesy?"

He didn't answer. He just turned his attention to the road and gripped the steering wheel like he was trying to squeeze the non-existent life out of it. I stared at him for a little while, waiting for the retort that obviously wasn't coming, and then finally relented, settling my head on Arabelle's shoulder. She wrapped an arm around my shoulders and held me to her.

The burning sensation returned, and I closed my eyes to prevent myself from shedding any tears. *It'll be okay,* I tried to reassure myself. *You have their numbers in your phone. Of course, you don't actually know whose number is whose, but still.*

In hindsight, I probably should have asked Arabelle to add their numbers to my contacts instead of letting them sit there in the call log unnamed and disorganized. But I was too lazy. And seeing how Arabelle didn't know whose number was whose, I highly doubted she made an effort to add them to my contacts. Not that I blamed her. I wouldn't have either.

My eyes opened, and I shifted to face Arabelle, hand outstretched. "Hey, can I see my phone?" I asked.

Arabelle nodded and tugged my phone out of her pocket. "Trade ya?"

We switched phones, and I hurried to pull up one of the numbers

I'd been calling from all summer long. I didn't know who I was about to text, but I didn't doubt that my dad would take away our cell phones the second we stepped through the front door, so I wanted to at least warn one of them that I wouldn't be able to text or call for a while.

"So what's my punishment, Dad?" I asked after hitting send, speaking calmly as I looked up at the rearview mirror. This way, if he screamed at me, he'd look like a huge ass.

"Grounded," my dad said. He paused, let out a sigh, and then decided to elaborate. "No phone, no electronics, no friends over, no going out, and no reading for pleasure. Bed by eight o'clock."

I gaped. "No reading?"

I think it's safe to say that my dad was trying to kill me.

"You like reading." My dad shrugged. "It seems like a perfectly good punishment to me."

Well, okay, he had a point there. But seriously— no reading?

After that, our conversation died, and the suffocating, awkward atmosphere returned. I returned my head to Arabelle's shoulder and closed my eyes. It wasn't long before I fell asleep.

My eyes opened just as my dad pulled into our driveway.

I blinked blearily and sat up, staring blankly at our house. Beside me, Arabelle, who fell asleep sometime after I did, groaned and stretched out her arms. She let them fall carelessly into her lap as she muttered, "We're home."

"Nah, I'm pretty sure we're in Candy Land," I said.

Arabelle rolled her eyes at me, and I smiled a small smile. I could really go for a trip to Candy Land right now.

But obviously that wasn't possible, so I nodded, and after letting out a small sigh, I unbuckled and slid out of the car. Arabelle wasn't far behind, and together we went to retrieve our baggage from the trunk. We shared a glance as we made our way towards the porch, where my dad stood unlocking the front door. I was pretty certain that she wished that we could be anywhere but there at that moment in time, like me.

After getting inside, I went straight for my bedroom. At that moment, I wanted nothing more than to fall onto my bed and sleep for ten years. Well, okay, maybe that was a lie. I actually wanted to talk to Arabelle and see how the plan fell to pieces more than I wanted to sleep for a decade— but not by much.

Arabelle followed after me, and she opened my door right as I threw my duffel bag onto my bed. I turned as she entered and crossed my arms lightly over my chest, waiting patiently for her to explain what happened.

For a second, Arabelle just fidgeted uncomfortably, like she was nervous. I didn't understand why she was acting this way. I mean, it was me she was talking to. But then she let out a sigh, looked me in the eye, and said, "I called Dad."

I blinked. "What?"

That was the last thing I expected to hear. Arabelle wouldn't have ruined everything on purpose, so for her to call him…

Arabelle bit her lip, and her face reddened. My stomach dropped. "I'm sorry," she said. "I didn't have a choice."

I pursed my lips and sat down on my bed, gesturing for Arabelle to take the spot next to me. "Why?" I asked as she shuffled over to my bed and settled down beside me. "What happened?"

Arabelle grabbed one of my pillows and twirled it in her hands. She kept her face down, but I still noticed when a tear rolled down her cheek. "Danny happened," she said thickly.

I didn't even think before looping an arm around her and pulling her to me. She leaned into me, her arms wrapped tightly around my pillow. "Did you guys get in a fight?" I asked.

"You could say that." Arabelle let out a bitter laugh and wiped at her eyes. "Dammit, I hate crying." She sighed shakily. "We broke up."

Wow. When I said that I hoped she'd realize what a crappy boyfriend he was, I didn't think it would actually happen. And now that it had, all I could do was sit there and stare blankly at the wall, too shocked to really do or say anything.

"I know you didn't like him," Arabelle continued when I didn't speak. "I should have listened to you. You were right about him. He's a jerk."

"What happened?" I asked. "What did he do to you? Do I need to go beat him up?"

Arabelle let out a small laugh. "Yeah, like you'd beat someone up." She paused when I didn't reply, and then pulled away so she could see the expression on my face. "Holy shit, Falice. Did you beat someone up at camp?"

"No," I said truthfully. I folded my lips together. "I just... punched her."

Arabelle's mouth dropped. "What—?"

"This isn't about me!" I exclaimed, waving her questions away.

"I'll explain later. Right now, we're talking about you, okay?"

Arabelle deflated, and I felt a stab of guilt as she dragged a hand down her face. This was for the best though. She needed to talk about it— I knew she did. "He was cheating on me," she told me.

I wasn't surprised, but I sprang from my bed anyway. "I'm going to kill him, " I hissed, hands curling into tight fists by my sides.

"Don't tell me you killed a camper, too." Arabelle grinned lamely at her own joke before shaking her head. "I've already kicked him where he needed to be kicked. Not before slapping him across the face, of course."

I smiled. "Good job."

"Thank you." She returned my smile, but it faltered almost immediately as she involuntarily sniffled.

"How did you find out?" I asked.

"I'd just gotten out of the shower," Arabelle said, wiping at her eyes again. "And after I finished changing, I went out to ask where he put the hairbrush, and I heard him on the phone with his other girlfriend— who, by the way, is Sadie Valle. I found out when I stole the phone from him and told her to go screw herself."

"What did you do after that?" I asked, stomach aching. I couldn't imagine what it must feel like to go through what she's been through.

"Well, after I hung up with Sadie," she explained. My eyes widened when she didn't say Sadie's full name, "Danny and I got into a huge fight. When he started screaming at me like I had no right to be pissed at him, I slapped him, just like I told you. I told him he had to get me a plane ticket because I wasn't going to stay in that house another minute. He told me to find my own way home because he wasn't wasting any more money on me." She frowned. "So, after kicking him in the balls, I left and called Dad. I had to tell him everything. Otherwise, I would have been stranded in London with nowhere to go."

I nibbled on my cheek as I took a moment to absorb her words. A moment wasn't enough. "I can't even…" I sucked in a breath. "I'm so sorry he did that to you."

Arabelle stood and nodded. "Yeah, well, I'm sorry I basically ruined your relationship. You guys didn't even get a full day together, did you?" When I shook my head, she let out a grumbled sigh. "I was such an idiot."

Without another word, I hugged her. I could feel Arabelle shaking with silent tears as she returned my embrace. She'd had many boyfriends over the years, but this was the first time she'd ever cried over a breakup. No matter how much I hated the guy, she liked him. Really, really liked him. And he broke her heart.

I didn't think it was possible for me to hate Danny even more than I already did, but, apparently, it was.

"I'm sorry," Arabelle muttered, pulling away to wipe the tears from her eyes. She sniffled. "For crying and for ruining your summer. The whole summer, not just the end. I know you didn't want to go in the first place, and I made you because I thought I was in love. Dammit."

"I'm glad I went for you," I told her. "It's probably the best thing I've ever done, Belle. So please don't apologize for that."

Arabelle gave me a shaky smile before wrapping her arms around me again. "Ugh, I love you." Her arms tightened their hold on me. "I love you so much."

"I love you, too," I replied. I hugged her back for a little while before pulling away and reaching for her shoulders. "Now, what do you say to going downstairs and binging away our sorrows on some peanut butter?"

Arabelle grinned. "Hell, yes!"

PHASE 29

Over the course of the next few days, Arabelle and I avoided our dad as much as possible. When we weren't sharing our boredom, we were hiding in our rooms doing basically nothing— you know, because we were grounded, and therefore, had no interesting way to live our lives. It was still summer vacation, so it wasn't like we had any homework to do. Most of my time was spent staring blankly at the ceiling and imagining what would've happened if my dad and Arabelle hadn't shown up when they did.

There were two main scenarios that I came up with. One, I would've spent my days with Will, Ty, and Vanessa, enjoying my time until the end of camp, and two, I would've ended up dead because Tiffany didn't quite agree that the war was over and took one of her attacks too far. *Tiffany corners me in the bathroom again,* my mind drawled as I sprawled on my bed, eyes on the ceiling. *And then, after a few choice words, she kills me. How? She bores me to death.* Oh, wait no. That's Dad.

As you can see, I was running out of the more interesting scenarios.

I looked to the right as the door opened, surprised to find my dad in the doorway. I was under the impression that he was avoiding us as much as we were avoiding him. Since we got home, he'd made three attempts to speak to Arabelle and me. All of which had been ultimately thwarted by our silence. I wasn't pulling a silent treatment or anything, but I wasn't in the mood to have a normal conversation with him either. So he and I would suffer through a few seconds of half-assed conversation, and then he would give up and leave the room. Arabelle didn't bother speaking to him at all.

"Hey," I said as he continued to stand there, looking as awkward as I felt.

"Hi," he replied. He gave me brief smile. "Can we talk?"

I hesitated and then nodded. I sat up to give him room as he stepped further inside. He perched on the edge of the bed, folded his hands in his lap, and turned to me, his expression filled with remorse. The apprehension inside of me died a little. "What's up?" I asked.

"I wanted to say that I'm sorry." My dad sighed. "For what I said about that boy, Will, was it?" I nodded, and he returned the gesture, letting out another long breath of air. "I know I handled the situation poorly. More than poorly really."

"It's okay," I mumbled even though it wasn't okay. I just didn't know what else to say. I hadn't expected him to apologize for his actions, and now that he had, it was difficult to hold on to the remnants of anger I still had left.

"No, it's not." My dad paused. "And what you did wasn't okay either."

"Yeah, I know," I said. "I'm sorry for deceiving you. And for yelling at you."

"I forgive you." He reached over and put his hand on my shoulder, giving it a small squeeze. "I just want an explanation. Can you tell me what happened? Why you did what you did?"

I folded my lips together and picked at a hangnail so I could avoid looking at him. The weight of his gaze was too much. "I, um…" I cleared my throat. "Well, when Arabelle asked me to go for her, I didn't agree right away. But after hearing her out, I decided that I would. I am going to pay you back for that camp in California. That was always part of the plan." I looked up then, just in time to see my dad nod. "Arabelle was supposed to give you back the money you gave her for a plane ticket," I added.

"She did," my dad replied. "She handed it to me when she gave me your guys' cell phones."

I nodded, proud of Arabelle. "Good. Anyway, I agreed to go, and so I did."

At first, my dad didn't say anything. He just fiddled with his hands and stared at my bookcase. I could tell that he was trying to figure out how to word his next question, and I waited patiently for him to do so. I continued to pick at the hangnail. It was painful, but a pretty good distraction from the uncomfortable atmosphere.

"And what about that girl— Tiffany?" my dad asked, his voice soft. "Why did you do all those things to her?"

I didn't want to answer him. Like, really didn't want to. But if there was any hope of moving past this, I didn't really have a choice in the matter. "She's a Class-A bully," I said, not removing my gaze from my fingernails. "If there was a higher level, actually, I'd put her there." I sighed and then went on to explain about the prank war and how it ensued. I tried to make Will's blackmail seem less, you know, blackmail-y, but it was hard to sugarcoat "he told me to make her life a living hell." From the lack of an are-you-friggin'-kidding-me expression on my dad's face, however, I think I did pretty well.

When I finished my story, my dad looked like he wanted to demand why I didn't put a stop to it before it got that bad, but he didn't. He just nodded, thanked me for my honesty, and then fell silent again.

As I glanced between my dad and my fingernails, a few questions popped into my head almost simultaneously. Was I in more trouble now that my dad knew the extent of what I did? Would our silences ever stop being awkward? And would he even consider letting the others come now that he knew what we'd been doing all summer long? It would've already been difficult convincing him to let three people stay with us for the summer, but now? It felt like it would be impossible.

Finally, after what seemed like forever, my dad spoke. "Beth and Caroline called," he said. "And they asked if they could see you before school starts."

I perked up at the sound of my friends' names. "And?"

"And, I've decided that you can. Arabelle will have the chance to have a couple friends over too, so that it's fair. But as soon as school starts, no friends over, got it?"

For the first time since coming home, I smiled a big, wide smile. "Thank you!" I squealed. And then, because it was necessary, I pulled him into a hug. He chuckled before hugging me back. After a few seconds, he patted me lightly on the back and let me go.

"You're welcome," he said. "But remember that even though you can see your friends, it doesn't mean you're not still grounded. All other consequences are still in place."

I nodded in understanding. "I know."

My dad stood up then. Apparently, he'd gotten whatever he needed to say out of his system. I watched as he prepared to leave, feeling a lot lighter now that this problem— at least, where he was concerned— was somewhat resolved. Yeah, I was still stuck without any way of contacting Will and the others, but my dad had apologized and I was now able to see Beth and Caroline. It was something, at least.

"Also, I'm going to give you the *talk* later," my dad warned as he started for the door. "Like I did with Arabelle when she first started dating."

"I promise I won't try to run out the room," I joked. Arabelle started dating her first boyfriend, Todd, when she was, like twelve, and when our dad found out, he tried to sit her down and tell her about the do's and don'ts. Needless to say, she didn't appreciate it. I could remember hearing her scream for me to save her from the terribly awkward situation while I was upstairs and laughing my butt off. Just the thought of it made me want to laugh again.

"I appreciate that." My dad sighed. "Now, I need to go talk to your sister."

"Okay." I pursed my lips as I tried to imagine him and Arabelle sitting down and talking like we just did. I couldn't do it. "Thank you again, Dad."

My dad nodded, and then he was gone, shutting the door softly behind him. After he left, I fell back on my bed and resumed my aimless staring at my bedroom ceiling. It was hard to explain how I was feeling right now. I mean, I was happy.

My dad and I were on okay terms again, and now, I could look forward to seeing Beth and Caroline. But I was also dejected. How could I ask my dad to let Will, Ty, and Vanessa stay next summer right after he just cut me some slack? It would seem like I was trying to take advantage of him, and that would be like begging him to say no.

It's not like I'd be able to ask him now and have him say yes anyway. The smart thing to do would be to wait until later when all this drama blew over. Maybe wait until I wasn't grounded. For now, until Beth and Caroline came over, I'd have to settle for boredom-induced scenario creation and occasional card games with Arabelle.

And so I did. *Gilbert oh-so-rudely interrupts my moment with Will...*

I was in the middle of a rather crazy scenario about Gilbert turning into a fanged beast and killing us all when Arabelle knocked softly on the door and stepped inside without waiting for me to tell her that I was decent. "I could have been naked," I informed her as she entered, raising my eyebrows at my sister's upside down figure. "You could have been traumatized right there— just saying."

"Yeah, okay." Arabelle scoffed. She held up a pack of cards. "Go Fish?"

I smiled. "Sounds good."

As Arabelle approached, I sat up and crossed my legs to prepare for our game. Arabelle, unlike Will, was hard to beat at Go Fish. Actually, most of our games ended in a tie. We played Go Fish over a dozen times since being grounded and only two of those games ended with a winner. Me, one. Arabelle, one. Even our winning records were tied.

"I'm going to beat you this time," Arabelle informed me. The look on her face told me that she, like I, had accepted tying as an inevitability and didn't care one bit. "It's my life's mission."

"I support your mission." I grinned and grabbed the card deck— which was Disney princess themed, a glorious purchase during our trip to Disney World when we were seven— from Arabelle's outstretched hand. I was about to start shuffling when my door opened again, and my dad appeared, holding the wireless home phone.

"Caroline's on the phone," he said.

Yesterday, Arabelle, my dad, and I made a deal: we could coordinate our newly allowed hangouts with our friends on the phone, and that was it. We had five minutes to discuss details with our friends, and then we were to hang up the phone, whether we were finished or not. These rules were pretty much just for me, seeing how none of Arabelle's friends could hang out before the end of summer. That sucked, but Arabelle didn't seem to care.

"Great!" I tossed the cards to Arabelle, hopped from the bed, and took the phone from my dad's hand. I brought the phone to my ear and said, "Hey, Betty Crocker."

"Hey!" Caroline said. "I'm heading out with Beth to get the friendship bracelet kit you wanted. Is there any specific kind you want?"

"No, not really," I replied. I paused. "Wait! Can you get me one with block letters?"

Arabelle snorted from her spot on my bed where she was currently dealing out cards. She was very interested in seeing how this whole friendship-bracelet-for-Will thing was going to work out. I think she had about as much faith in the end product as I did, which was pretty much none.

"Yeah, sure! If there aren't any, we'll just get you some little letter beads. Wal-Mart has those, don't they?"

"Yeah, I think so." I shrugged even though she wouldn't be able to see. "Let me know how much it comes to, alright?"

"'Kay." From the tone of Caroline's voice, I could tell she had no intention of letting me know how much it cost. Paying her back was always a battle. Usually, hiding money was involved. "Beth and I should be at your house in about a half-hour. Maybe longer, depending on how long it takes to choose a kit. Beth will probably sit there for a while because she's so indecisive."

"Hey!" I heard Beth shout. "I so will not!"

She so would, but I didn't say so, just laughed and said, "Okay, I'll see you then. Now, if you'll excuse me, I have a very intense game of Go Fish to play."

"Oh god." Caroline snickered. "Please don't kill your sister. I don't need you grounded until college."

"Not kill." I sent a wink Arabelle's way. "Just maim." Arabelle rolled her eyes, but smiled.

"Okay. Well, we'll see you in a bit. Ta-ta for now!" And then she hung up on me.

After handing the phone back to my dad, I thanked him and went back to my bed, careful not to move any of the cards as I sat down. "You ready to go fishing?" I asked as my dad left the room.

Arabelle grinned. "I've never been more ready for anything in my entire life."

"Good." I set down the one pair of cards I had and then scanned the rest of the cards in my hand. "Do you have a four?"

PHASE 30

The first thing Caroline and Beth did when they walked through the front door was attack me with a group hug. Their grip on me was so secure that I couldn't get out of the embrace even if I wanted to. I laughed and hugged them back— or tried to anyway. It was kind of impossible to move my arms, so I couldn't actually hug them. Oh, well. It's the thought that counts.

"It's good to see you!" I squealed.

"We missed you so much!" Beth said, tightening her grip. I didn't think that was possible, but there you go.

"With you gone, there was no one for Beth to agree with," Caroline complained. "She was so lost without you."

"Hey!"

I grinned.

After another moment of trying to squeeze me to death, they released me and took a step back. They looked like they were practically bursting with questions, but I spoke before they could ask me anything. "Were you able to get a kit?"

Caroline twisted around and plucked the Wal-Mart bag I'd failed to notice from the floor. "Yup! It came with block letters, so that's a plus."

"Awesome!" I took the bag from Caroline's hand and pulled it open. A friendship bracelet kit greeted me from inside. "Thank you so much."

"What do you need that for anyway?" Caroline asked. "You and Arabelle aren't back into that whole let's-make-each-other-sibling- bracelets-even-though-we-suck-at-it phase, are you?"

"I'm going to kindly ignore the fact that you just insulted my friendship-bracelet-making skills," I said. Her words were true, of course, but she didn't need me to tell her that. "And no, it's not for Arabelle. I'll tell you when we get upstairs. Now come on!"

Beth and Caroline followed without question. I felt my lips tug upward as we headed up to my bedroom. It felt so good to see them again. Yes, I wished I could have spent the rest of my summer at Camp Sunshine Brooks like planned, but I'd missed Beth and Caroline.

We piled into my room to find Arabelle lying on my bed and filing her nails. She wasn't there when I went downstairs to greet my friends, but I wasn't surprised to see her. "Move over," I said. Weren't my greetings beautiful?

Arabelle snorted, but complied, sitting up and leaning against my headboard. "Hello to you too," she replied. She nodded at the bag in my hand. "I see they found what you were looking for."

"Yes, yes, they did." I fell back beside her and tugged the kit out of the bag. I turned the box over in my hands as Beth and Caroline sat in the last available spots on the bed, legs crossed. They leaned forward with their chins resting in their hands. "Let's see if I somehow stopped sucking since I last made one of these."

Beth leaned back on her hands now and lifted her eyebrows. "Who are you making this for?"

"She didn't tell you?" Arabelle asked. Beth and Caroline shook their heads.

"Well, I couldn't exactly tell them without explaining everything, and that would take more than the permitted five minutes," I said with a shrug.

Arabelle rolled her eyes good-naturedly. "Yeah, okay." She tossed the nail filer onto the floor and crossed one leg over the other, sending Beth and Caroline a mischievous smile. "She's making the bracelet for Will," she told them. "You know, her boyfriend."

Is it strange that the *dun-dun-dun-dun* music theme played in my head when Arabelle revealed my not-really secret? Probably.

"What?" Caroline asked as Beth's mouth dropped.

I shoved Arabelle playfully and then let out a sigh. "Yeah, um, I have a boyfriend."

"Will," Arabelle elaborated even though there was no need because, you know, she just told them that; not that I was one to talk.

"Okay." Beth sat up and held up her hands. "Spill. Now."

I nodded, and they all adjusted their positions so they'd be more comfortable. As Beth snatched one of my pillows and nestled onto Caroline's lap, I was reminded of the times my dad would read stories to Arabelle and I before bed, and we'd curl up in my— or her— bed, preparing for the awesomeness that was my dad's narration. "Okay, well, when we got to the camp, there was this guy that gave me this death glare, and I thought he was going to eat or murder me. Literally, I wouldn't have been surprised if he resorted to cannibalism."

"Ooh, was it Will?" Beth looked over at Arabelle even though I was the one telling the story. "It was Will, right?"

"Yes," Arabelle said. "And he was so hot."

Was? I wanted to counter, but I didn't. Instead, I just rolled my eyes and continued on with my story. They all listened attentively as I told them about Vanessa and Ty and how they attended every year just to see each other. Arabelle listened intently too despite the fact that I told her everything— except for Will's home life— the day we got home. While I talked, I started working on my friendship bracelet for Will. I could honestly say it was going to be nowhere near as nice as the one he made for me.

"What a lovely start to a romance," Beth mused after I finished telling them about Will's blackmail. Unlike with my dad, I didn't make any attempt to sugarcoat anything with Beth and Caroline. I had no reason to.

"Right?" I grinned. "Anyway, he took his sweet time telling me what the heck he wanted me to do, which freaked me out. I thought he was going to make me murder someone or something."

"You appear to have associated him a lot with murder," Caroline said with an amused smile.

"Yep," I agreed. "So one morning when the others and I were talking in front of the gym, Tiffany, the girl I had to do the course with, shoved me. And that kinda sparked everything. My being in her way got me on her bad side, and that night, Will told me that I had to make her life a living hell."

I paused to fight with the strings of the friendship bracelet. I was swiftly remembering why I quit making these in the first place. They were so freaking frustrating. On top of that, this bracelet was coming out just as crappy as the many others. *Yay.* "I later found out," I continued after a minute or two of war with this caring gesture, "that he never actually planned on going through with the blackmail. Apparently, it was just a way that he could call me Falice instead of Arabelle."

"He couldn't have just said he knew who you were and that your secret was safe with him?" Caroline asked. "Why make it so complicated?"

"He was kind of in the same situation as Vanessa and Ty," I explained. "He doesn't really need to attend the camp but does anyway for… personal reasons. But, basically, he had to act like he hated everything and everyone and that he only wanted to see me squirm." I shrugged. "Either way, I ended up in this prank war with Tiffany. It was crazy."

And thus, commenced the list of pranks that Tiffany and her minions pulled, and the pranks we retaliated with—with other details in-between. Arabelle was shaking with laughter as I went through them all, only pausing when I mentioned her Converse. "I'm seriously sending her a bill," she muttered, squinting at my bookcase like Tiffany was going to materialize there. How much would it suck if she actually did appear out of nowhere? Where was Will to pick a point on the scale when I needed him?

"So yeah, that's pretty much what happened," I concluded. "That was a lot of pranks," Caroline said.

Beth laughed. "Yes, but the puking in front of Will though." "I'd rather not be reminded of that. Thanks."

"You puked in front of your crush!" Beth sang.

I would have slapped her if it weren't for this dreaded bracelet in my hands. It was coming out really… lumpy. "Yeah, well, I'm dating him no, so ha!" I retorted, scrunching my nose at her. "Maybe you should puke in front of Cam."

Beth nodded her head from side to side. "Maybe I should."

"I still can't believe you shaved her head." Arabelle snickered. "Holy shit! That is the best thing ever."

"I learned from the best," I said, nudging her with my elbow. "I wonder what she's doing now though. I mean, I'm not there for her to torture anymore, so…"

"She's probably rubbing the fact that you had to leave early in their faces," Arabelle replied. She glanced down at my bracelet. "Babe, there's a reason we quit making those."

I stuck my tongue out at her because I was mature like that. "Yeah, well, whatever." I sighed and held out the wrist with the bracelet Will made for me. "He's gonna have to tell me how the hell he made this. He's more artsy than me, and it's depressing."

"Art is the place where your ego goes to die," Beth quoted. I held out my hand, and she slapped it.

We all laughed as I continued my battle with the bracelet. Seriously, how did Will make his look so professional? That was the first thing I was going to ask him when I was finally able to call him. Okay, well, maybe not the first. Perhaps, the second.

"Hey, do you think you'll be able to go to the back-to-school swim party now?" Caroline asked. "Or will you still be grounded by then?"

"I'm pretty sure I'll still be grounded," I said. "Seeing how it's like three days away. We're basically grounded until he feels like un-grounding us."

"Yep," Arabelle agreed. "Last night, I asked Dad how long we're grounded for, and he says he's not sure yet."

I glanced at her curiously from the corner of my eye. They'd gotten along freakishly well since he apologized to us both. Despite her promise, I'd expected... I don't know, more yelling? I definitely wasn't complaining though.

"Well, ask if you can come to the party!" Beth said. "By then, it will have been like a week and a half. That's long enough, isn't it?"

"Have you ever been grounded before?" Arabelle asked incredulously, her eyebrows shooting upward. "Like, ever?"

"No," Beth admitted. "But isn't the standard time like a week?"

"Yeah, if you don't do the dishes or come home late or something." Arabelle scoffed. "Falice and I switched places and deceived him for, like, two months. I'm probably grounded until next year." She waved the topic away with her hand. "Either way, she doesn't need to ask. We're going to the party."

I blinked, hands freezing. "What?"

Arabelle beamed and winked at me. My eyes narrowed. "Don't worry, Falice. We have permission from Dad."

"But..."

"Shhh." Arabelle pressed her pointer finger to my lips. "No questions. You have a crappy friendship bracelet to make."

I licked her finger, and she pulled away with a laugh. I rolled my eyes and resumed working on Will's bracelet, unable to resist returning her smile. As I toyed with the strings though, I couldn't help but wonder. Why would my dad give us permission to go to the back-to-school party when he made it clear that we were under house arrest?

What was going on?

Sure enough, a week later I was sitting with my feet in the water of Caroline's in-ground pool, eating some peanut butter as teenagers splashed and laughed around me.

I was still grounded, and would be until October, but apparently, my dad and Arabelle made some sort of deal that gave us the day off. Maybe this was because she wasn't able to have any friends over? I wasn't sure, but I never really got a straight answer when I asked. She was up to something, and this time my dad was in on it too, which was weird.

I thought about the way Arabelle stealthily avoided answering my question this morning at breakfast while I took my second scoop of peanut butter and stuffed it into my mouth. I wasn't really upset— except for the fact that I was going through major Will, Vanessa, and Ty withdrawals— but I spotted it on the island before leaving the house, and who was I to deny the peanut butter the privilege of being eaten?

"Hey, Falice!" Caroline called from the deep-end of the pool. "Come swim!"

I glanced down at myself. Even though I was dressed for the occasion— in my polka-dotted bikini— I wasn't really feeling the whole "swimming" thing. I was content where I was.

"I'm good!" I shouted back to her. "Quite comfortable, actually."

Caroline shook her head and laughed. "You're such a party pooper!"

"Yeah, Falice!" Beth exclaimed from her spot next to Caroline. "Come on! Everyone else is swimming!"

"Arabelle isn't swimming," I pointed out.

It was true. Arabelle was participating in the more social part of the party. She was currently lounging on one of the lawn chairs with a group of school friends and laughing as she sipped at some lemonade. None of her close friends were here, but she didn't seem to mind.

"Yeah, yeah, whatever!" Beth shook her head disapprovingly, but she was smiling. "Suit yourself!"

I gave her a thumbs-up and swallowed some more peanut butter as my friends went back to swimming. I was probably going to run out soon and then I'd actually have to swim, just to work off all the peanut butter I ate. I mean, I wasn't a health buff or anything, but eating half a jar in one go was probably unhealthy.

My thoughts of the unhealthiness of eating all this peanut butter were disrupted when someone sat down beside me and snatched my spoon from my hand. I stared blankly at my now-empty hand... and then at my other empty hand when this mystery person robbed me of my peanut butter jar. *What the hell?*

I scowled down at the person's legs, trying to calm myself before facing them head-on. The legs were muscular and masculine. So, some guy thought it would be funny to ruin a perfectly fine day by stealing a girl's peanut butter, huh? Well, okay.

I was doing a great job of containing my irritation, obviously. "Mmm," the guy murmured. "You know, I was never a huge fan of peanut butter, but now I can see why you're obsessed with the stuff." *No way.*

My head snapped over to face the boy beside me. My mouth dropped, and my eyes widened when I saw who was sitting next to me. He was as attractive as ever with his tan skin and dusty brown hair. A mischievous smile played on his lips, and amusement danced in his eyes.

I couldn't believe it. I could not believe it. "Oh my god," I breathed. "Will."

PHASE 31

For a second, all I did was stare. I just… What? How was Will here? How was he sitting here smirking at me and eating my peanut butter? How? What? How?

And then I started bouncing up and down and flailing my arms around like a lunatic.

"Will!" I shrieked so loudly that most of the people in the pool stopped what they were doing and looked over at us. "Oh my god! How are you— what are you— holy—!"

If I were in my right mind, I might have noticed that I was shifting my body closer to the edge of the pool. However, I was too wrapped up in the fact that my boyfriend was sitting right beside me instead of on a plane to Washington. It was cause for, you know, shock.

So I guess it shouldn't be surprising that my flailing around led to me falling in the pool.

Yes. I, being the genius that I am, managed to accidentally throw myself into the pool. *Nice one, Falice.*

I let out a small gasp as I fell in, which only led to me swallowing a bunch of water and that obviously didn't help the situation. By the time I returned to the surface, I was a coughing and sputtering mess. *Another nice one, Falice.*

My eyes shot upward when someone started slow-clapping, and I couldn't help but smile as Will shook his head and chuckled at me. He let his hands fall to his sides now that he was done applauding my performance. "That was good, Falice," he told me. "You're more talented than I thought."

"Jerk!" I retorted with a grin. "A girl falls in a pool, and you laugh at her? I can't wait to see how you treat your girlfriend."

Will smiled and crouched down so that we were closer to eye level. "God, I've missed you," he murmured.

My heart thrashed around in my chest as I smiled broadly. "Aw, that's comforting," I teased. How I managed to banter normally was beyond me. I should get an award. What for? I didn't know. Maybe a "Speaking in a Normal Voice When All She Wanted to do was Squeal and Smile like an Idiot" award? "Care to give me a hand, Dyer?"

"Hmm, I dunno." Will stood up and folded his arms over his chest. "I think there's a very nice set of stairs over there for you."

"Yeah, but you made me fall," I said. "So it's the least you could do."

"I didn't make you fall," Will said. "You did that by yourself."

I paused as my memory traveled back to the night I fell off the rock wall. It felt like forever ago and like yesterday at the same time. "Nope, you most definitely made me fall." I grinned. "If you don't help me up," I continued, "then I'm going to pull you in."

"Yeah, like you have the upper-body strength." Will rolled his eyes good-naturedly. "You may have gotten good at those push-ups but not that good."

"I'm going to kindly ignore what you just said," I said. "Now, are you going to help me up or what?"

Will let out a long, dramatic sigh before holding out his hand. I stared at it for a moment, making no move to grab it with my own. I still couldn't believe he was here right now. How did he get here? I just didn't understand. His mom obviously didn't drive him, and I doubt the plane would reroute itself to Massachusetts for his convenience. So how?

"Are you going to grab my hand or what?" Will asked, pulling me out of my reverie. "Geezum crow, Falice."

With a short laugh, I reached for his hand. Will held out his other one, and I grasped onto it. I resisted the urge to giggle as he pulled me out of the pool. I hadn't been lifted out of the pool this way since I was a kid, when my dad or uncle would tug me out of the deep end when it was time to eat or go home.

"Hey, Will," I said cheerfully after my feet came into contact with solid ground. My eyes scanned him up and down, not unlike the way Ty looked at Vanessa the morning we were all standing outside our cabins in our pajamas. He was in bathing suit trunks, and that was it. Did I ever tell you that a shirtless Will would be so unhealthy for me? Well, if not, I'm telling you now.

Let's just say that the daily exercises did him no harm. "Hey," Will replied.

For a short moment, we just stood there and took each other in. And then Will let his hands fall from mine. He grabbed me lightly by the cheeks, tugged me to him, and brought our lips together. I immediately kissed him back, a smile spreading across my mouth as I did. I knew that I missed Will a lot, and I mean a lot, but I hadn't really realized how much I missed this.

My arms wound around his neck, and I drew him closer to me while one of Will's hands slid through my hair. I was suddenly glad that I'd decided to keep it down today. If he tried to get the hair tie out of my wet hair, it wouldn't have gone very well.

It was only when Will and I pulled away that I remembered that we were at a party full of people. A group of boys whooped obnoxiously, and from the corner of my eye, I could see Beth squeal and whack Caroline on the arm. Caroline winced with each slap and eventually dunked Beth headfirst into the water.

"Hell yeah, baby!" Arabelle hollered.

I twisted around and laughed as Arabelle jogged over to us with a huge smile plastered on her face and her lemonade in her hand. "I see you got here safely," she said to Will as she planted herself in front of us, her free hand on her hip. She sipped her lemonade. "Glad you didn't mistake me for her. That would've been awkward."

Will scoffed as though the suggestion of mistaking Arabelle for me was preposterous. He shifted out of our embrace and then brought his arm around my back, tugging me to his side. I did the same, looking between Will and my sister with blatant confusion. "Yes, I got here fine,"

Will said. "But I have to say, the conversation with your dad on the way here was… unpleasant."

I blinked. Arabelle knew Will was coming… my dad was involved? "What's going on here?" I demanded.

"What's going on here is that your dad gave me the *talk*," Will explained— rather poorly, in my opinion. "Falice, are you aware how uncomfortable the *talk* is?"

"Yeah," I said. "Wait are you talking about the one for puberty or dating?"

"Dating."

"Oh." I laughed. "He just gave me that one actually. Arabelle had the pleasure of receiving it when she was twelve."

Arabelle scrunched her nose at me. "Please, do not remind me." "Yeah, but he's your parent," Will said. "He's not mine."

I grinned. "Did he tell you not to have sex in the cell?"

Will rolled his eyes at that. "I think if he had, the conversation would've been so much simpler."

"Wait a second." I held up a hand, suddenly remembering that I'd yet to receive a proper explanation. "Why were you in the car with my dad? Can someone please tell me what's going on here?"

Will and Arabelle shared a glance before Arabelle raised her lemonade to her lips. "Well," she said after she'd swallowed. "You know how Dad came to talk to me?"

I nodded. "Yeah."

"First, he apologized for making an ass out of himself and asked if I was okay with the whole Danny thing." She grimaced at the mention of her ex's name. "He also asked me what places I went to and stuff like that."

"What happened after that?" I asked as Arabelle took another sip of her lemonade.

"Well, Dad told me about how he was letting us have friends over until school started," Arabelle continued. "And that gave me an idea."

I glanced at Will. He met my gaze and gave me a small smile. "What idea was that?" I inquired, forcing my eyes away from Will and back to Arabelle. It took a lot of effort.

"To get Will here for the last week before school starts obviously." Arabelle laughed. "I made you a promise, and I intended to keep it. I honestly didn't know if Dad would agree, but I knew he felt shitty about what he said in the car, so I went for it. I told him I wanted Will to count as my friend. Because we're besties, am I right?" She sent a wink Will's way.

"Anyway, he didn't know if it was possible, but I told him that if we got Will's number, then we'd be able to call him and coordinate it.

"So Dad gave me your phone, and I chose one at random. It was Ty. He says 'Hi, Jessica!' by the way. In all caps." Arabelle grinned.

I couldn't help but do the same. I missed Ty so much.

"I got Will's number on the second try, called him, told him my plan, and then asked for him to call his mom and see what she thought about it. After she gave him the okay, he gave me her cell phone number so the 'rents could talk. You know, so they could figure out how to get Will here and then back home. They ended up agreeing to have Dad pick Will up from camp and bring him to the airport when it's time to go. They talked for a while, and somehow they ended up discussing Will coming here every summer instead of going to Camp Sunshine Brooks."

My mouth dropped. "And?"

The look on Arabelle's face gave me the answer I needed even before she replied. "Dad said yes. Don't ask me why because I have no freaking idea. But he said yes."

The next thing I knew, I was jumping— quite literally— for joy. "Oh my... oh my... oh my..." I gave up trying to finish my sentence. Not only did Arabelle and my dad do something incredible for me, but also now I was able to see Will every summer. "This is amazing! I can't... I can't!"

Will and Arabelle watched my reaction with matching smiles on their faces. It was pretty incredible that Will didn't even hesitate before letting his lips tug upward. That fact only made me giddier, and my enthusiasm grew. Holy crap!

Eventually, I was too tired to hop up and down, and my feet went still. "So my dad drove to New Hampshire to pick you up," I said, forcing myself to speak at an appropriate tone.

"Yeah."

"And he gave you the *talk*."

"Yeah."

"What point in the car ride did he give it to you?" I asked curiously. There was no perfect time to receive the *talk* obviously, but how much would it suck if that's how his ride to Massachusetts began?

"Somewhere near the end," Will replied with a shrug. "But my mom gave me her version of the *talk* right as I was getting in the car. So I got hit twice in one day."

"That must have been painful," I mused.

Will opened his mouth to reply, but Arabelle cut him off before he could. "Well, I'm going to give you two some alone time," she said, backing away and drinking some more of her lemonade. "Keep it PG, all right? No need to gross out the other partiers— and by other partiers, I mean me."

With that, Arabelle twisted around and sauntered back to her friends. I bit my lip and watched as she made her way to her chair. Someone had stolen her seat while she was gone, and even from this distance I could hear her demanding for the kid to move his ass out of her seat. When he refused, she dumped the rest of her lemonade on his head.

As the boy flew out of her seat with some choice words, I snorted and turned to face Will again. "So," I said, taking a small step toward him. "I guess Camp Falarabelle is happening, huh? All we need is Vanessa and Ty."

"Mm-hm," Will murmured. He followed my lead and closed the distance between us, enfolding me in his arms. I almost let out a content sigh as he pulled me close and rested his chin on my head. Damn, it felt so good to hug him again.

I closed my eyes and let my head fall on his bare chest. The only thing that could ruin this perfect moment was Gilbert and his *"Miss McAtee, kindly please detach yourself from Mr. Dyer, blah, blah, blah."* Yes, he would say "blah, blah, blah." He was articulate like that.

"How have you guys been?" I asked softly. "Tiffany didn't do anything, did she?"

"We've been okay," Will replied. "And as for Tiffany, well, she didn't prank again because you weren't there to get pranked on. But she didn't let us forget that you weren't there anymore either. Ty had to restrain Vanessa a couple times to keep her from punching her."

I sighed. "Ugh, Tiffany is so annoying." "Yeah, but we never have to see her again."

I lifted my head from his chest and grinned. "On a scale of one to ten, how happy are you about that?"

Will pursed his lips with mock thought. "Maybe a seven-point- eight," he said.

"Only a seven-point-eight?" I cocked an eyebrow. "I'd give it at least a seven-point-nine."

Will looked to the sky. "Whatever," he said.

"Hey," I said, the teasing tone in my voice fading away as I switched to a more serious topic. "Arabelle said your mom and my dad talked, and that led to plans for you to come over every summer... Did she tell him about...?"

"Rick?" Will frowned as Rick's name slide from his tongue. "Yeah, she did."

I pressed my lips together. "Would it be okay if I told Arabelle?" I asked. Now seemed like as good a time as any.

Will's eyebrows rose, and he gave me a look of surprise. "You haven't yet?"

"Well, I didn't want to betray your trust." I made a face when he started to laugh. "What?"

"Nothing." Will cleared his throat before pressing his lips to my forehead. "Thank you for not wanting to betray my trust. But, of course, you can tell Arabelle."

I smiled. "Thanks."

Will nodded. "Now," he said, pulling away and gesturing to the pool. "Let's go swim."

I blinked. "But I was eating peanut butter."

"Yeah, well, now you're not," Will countered. "You made me drop the peanut butter when you fell in the pool. I'm pretty sure it's soaked by now."

My gaze flew over to where I took an unexpected dive in the pool. It was there that I found my jar of peanut butter tipped over, and I immediately knew that chlorinated water had gotten inside. "Dammit, Dyer!" I said. "First, you steal my peanut butter, and now, you ruin it? Are you trying to kill me?"

"I'll buy you another jar," he assured me, not as concerned about the fact that he'd murdered perfectly good peanut butter as I thought he should have been. "Now let's go."

Before I had a chance to argue, Will grabbed me by the hand and dragged me toward the pool. I could see Beth and Caroline staring at us as we approached the water. They were trying to be discreet about it, but they were doing a terrible job.

When we reached the edge, Will didn't hesitate for even a second before jumping into the water. I watched as he sank to the bottom and recoiled when droplets splattered on me. Honestly, it was really stupid that I shied away, seeing how I was going to jump into the water in a moment... or two... but whatever.

Will reappeared soon enough, his hair matted on his face. "What are you doing?" he demanded when he saw that I wasn't yet in the pool. "Get in the water!"

"Well, sorry for respecting your space." I stuck my tongue out at him. "Knowing me, I could have fallen on your head or something."

"Yeah, okay." He scoffed. "Come on."

I twisted my lips to one side. "Yeah, uh, I'm not really feeling the whole 'jumping' thing."

"You did perfectly fine on the rock wall." "That was falling, Will. Complete difference."

"Well, didn't you just fall into the pool? You're very good at falling. Why don't you try that?"

My gaze flattened. "Why am I dating you again?"

He chuckled, waded over to me, and rested his arms on the tiles. "What are you, scared?" he teased. "Come on, Falice. I promise you'll be fine."

I tilted my head to the side. "Pinky promise?" "Pinky promise."

It struck me how different Will was. Of course, he smiled and bantered with me when we were by ourselves, but at camp, there was still this aura around him that said he wasn't completely happy. But here? He was all laughs and smiles, and I realized that this was the real Will.

I liked it.

With that in mind, I braced myself before hopping into the pool, landing heavily in the water. A moment later, I was up again, snickering as he wiped at his eyes. Apparently, I splashed him. *Oops.* "I'd apologize for that," I said, "but I'm so not sorry."

Will raised his eyebrows before splashing me right back. "Don't worry," he said. "I'm not sorry for that either."

I waded over to him. We were in the deep end, just out of the way of the diving board. All around us, teens goofed off, splashing and playing various pool games. I looked over at Caroline and Beth and waved. They waved back. "So," I said as I came to a stop right in front of him. "Is this what you're like when not pretending to be a delinquent?"

"For the most part, yeah." He smiled as though to prove his point. "Though, it helps that I'm in a pretty good mood."

I gasped playfully. "Are you saying that you're a people person, Will Dyer?"

Cue the snorting. "Of course not," he replied. "People are annoying. I'm just not miserable."

"Ah, good to know." I smiled. "Now, let's go see Beth and Caroline!"

Will pursed his lips. "Didn't I just say that I'm not a people person?"

"They're not people!" Not the typical way to go about defending my friends, but there you go.

"So those from Massachusetts aren't people? Good to know." "Shut up," I retorted oh-so-greatly before grabbing onto his arm.

"Come on, Dyer. I got in the pool. You can come meet my friends."

Will's eyes latched onto my wrist. "You're still wearing the bracelet," he said blankly.

"Well, yeah," I replied. "Why wouldn't I be?"

His lips pricked upward ever-so-slightly. "No reason."

I tugged on his arm again. "No distractions, Dyer! You're meeting my friends whether you like it or not."

After sighing and pretending that my request— rather, demand— was so much worse than it really was, Will nodded and followed me over toward Beth and Caroline. When we reached them, I proceeded to introduce them and watch, with more than a little amusement, as Caroline and Beth grilled him mercilessly. He took it in stride, not at all intimidated by their questions or threats to hang him if he broke my heart. I wouldn't really expect him to be intimidated, because, you know, he was Will.

As I sat back and observed my friends, I thought about how perfect this was. Not only was Will here, but he was acting like himself. If Ty and Vanessa were here right now, their jaws would be dropping to the floor. Will was relaxed, not tense and acting like he had a stick up his butt, as Vanessa once said while planning a prank. What he was projecting now was the Will I'd met in isolation, except more real.

It was freaking fantastic.

"You know what we need?" Arabelle asked as she collapsed on the couch. "Popcorn. We can't watch a movie without popcorn."

I twisted around in my spot in front of the couch. "That sounds like a great idea," I told her with a grin. "Care to go make some?"

"I'll do it!" Beth immediately volunteered and hopped up from her spot on the floor. "Come with me, Care!"

Caroline, who'd been sprawled next to Beth on the floor with her blank gaze veered toward the ceiling, sighed, nodded, and struggled to get up before following Beth out of the room. I watched as they left, a smile at the ready. They'd made it quite clear that they approved of Will and that they were happy for me. Even my dad liked him now. I got to say, it really meant a lot that everyone was so supportive.

Will himself was seated behind me, his arms wrapped around my torso and his back pressed against the couch. My dad walked into the living room a little while ago and raised his eyebrows at our seating position, but didn't pull the stay-three-feet-away-from-my-daughter thing that some parents did. Since we got home, I already thanked him a thousand times for what he did for me, but I was certain that I could never thank him enough.

"You know, I think you squeaked a little when you touched the snake," Will drawled. "Which technically counts as screaming. So obviously, I shouldn't have to watch this."

I dropped my head on his shoulder and looked up at him, a triumphant smile at the ready. "I so didn't. Get over it, Dyer. A deal's a deal. Pinky promises are legit, remember? Are you doubting the power of my pinky?"

"Oh, damn, don't do that," Arabelle said. "I broke a pinky promise once. It wasn't pretty."

"Precisely." I laughed. "You're watching *The Lion King* whether you like it or not."

Will wasn't impressed. "Fine," he said. "But I'm not going to be happy about it."

"Yeah, you will. And you'll just love when we break into song during '*Hakuna Matata*'."

"Looking forward to it." "Yeah-huh."

For a few minutes, we debated about *The Lion King* and how much Simba did or did not suck, and then Caroline and Beth returned with a huge bowl of popcorn. Arabelle made a noise in the back of her throat and jumped to pry the bowl from Beth's hands. It appeared that none of us would be getting popcorn. Okay then.

"Okay, let's do this!" Beth said, not at all upset that Arabelle had taken the popcorn away from her. She claimed the free spot in the recliner. "Be prepared, Will. We get pretty emotional over this movie."

"I think we should be more worried about his reaction." I patted Will's arm. "Speaking of which, make sure he's nowhere near the remote. We don't need the TV broken."

"Well, it's not my fault the movie is rage-inducing," Will defended himself. "If Scar wasn't such an asshole, we wouldn't have this problem."

We all laughed. "He's so passionate," Arabelle mused. "I like you, Will. Even if you looked like you were going to eat my sister when we first got to camp."

"Eat her?" His eyebrows shot upward as he turned around. "What?"

"Falice said you'd eat her in her sleep and enjoy it." Arabelle grinned. "You had one mad glare there. You should totally get into Hollywood. Right, Falice?"

I nodded. "You're a really good actor, dude."

I felt Will laugh more than I heard him. My eyes shot down to his arms around me, and I felt myself smile yet again. My excuse of a friendship bracelet decorated his wrist. I tried to tell him that he didn't have to wear it— because, you know, it sucked— but he insisted. The only parts that didn't suck about it were the wooden blocks that spelled out his name. Sadly, his name only had four letters, so it didn't take up that much space.

"Let's get this party started," Caroline said, pressing play on the DVD player and plopping down next to Will and I. "We should totally have a Disney marathon."

"Ooh, that sounds fun!" I clapped my hands. "We should totally do that. You up for that, Will?"

My stomach fluttered when he pressed his lips against my temple. "As long as there are no repeats of *The Lion King*, sure."

"Um, hate to break it to you, but there are three movies for *The Lion King*."

"Dammit!"

We all laughed, but then hushed as the movie began. Will made irritated comments about Scar and Simba throughout the whole thing, but he managed to make it through to the end. He even kept his eyes open during Mufasa's death, which was more than I could say for myself. I couldn't bear the thought of seeing Simba find his father's body, so I covered my eyes and cried about how tragic this was and how I couldn't deal with it. Will then told me that it was demented and he had no sympathy for me because this was my idea in the first place.

How loving, really.

As the rest of the movie went on, I leaned against Will and enjoyed my time with my friends. It occurred to me how different things would've been if I'd refused to take part in Arabelle's plan. What would I have done this summer? Anything noteworthy? No. I would have chilled around all summer, reading, and hanging out with Beth and Caroline like I always did. I wouldn't have met Will, Ty, or Vanessa, and I wouldn't have learned to take a risk every once in a while.

At the beginning of this plan, I thought I was going to hate every second of it. I'd never been more wrong about anything in my entire life.

"So what did you think of the movie?" I joked as the ending credits scrolled their way up the screen. "Still think it sucks?" Will sighed. "It wasn't as bad as I thought."

"I told you—"

"But Simba is still a dipshit."

I shook my head and laughed. "Way to kill the mood, Dyer!" I paused to let my giggles subside. Then I smiled brightly at him whilst saying, "Ready for the second one?"

Will didn't answer at first, and for a second I thought he was going to refuse. But then he nodded. "Bring it on."

Mission Accomplished

"Jessica, how much longer until the fireworks start?"

This was the thousandth time in the last ten minutes that Ty asked that question. The ten millionth if you counted all the times he'd asked since this morning. I was exaggerating obviously, but seriously. He'd been repeating the question basically non-stop all day. Even now, as we made our way through the steadily growing crowd at Riverfront Park, he continued to demand an answer. It was impossible to get annoyed though. At least, for me.

I'd been in what felt like a permanent good mood since June when Will, Vanessa, and Ty arrived for their summer-long sleepover at my house. Actually, I might have been in a good mood since April, when my dad agreed to let Ty and Vanessa stay with us in the first place. It took a while to convince him to let Vanessa stay, seeing how he would be helping us deceive her mom, but once he understood the situation, he said yes.

I had the greatest dad ever.

"Dude, calm yourself," Arabelle said, shooting him an exasperated look. I wondered distantly how many more times Ty could get away with repeating himself without getting slapped upside the head. Arabelle wasn't the most patient of people. "You know they start at nine. Check your phone for the time and do the math yourself."

"Too bad he sucks at math," Vanessa said with a snort.

Ty gasped as though Vanessa had wounded him. "That hurts, Vanessa! You're so mean to me."

"Sorry, babe," Vanessa apologized, not sounding very sorry at all. "Not my fault you make it so easy."

A bright smile sprang to my lips as my eyes shot down to their hands. Like mine and Will's, they were clasped together. Throughout the summer, Vanessa had told me how strange it was to be able to publically be a couple without breaking any rules. We still had to keep our PDA to a minimum— meaning basically nonexistent— when my dad was around, but other than that? We were allowed to hold hands, hug, and kiss around other people. It was pretty fantastic.

"I bet you five bucks that Ty's going to realize you didn't answer his question and ask you again in two minutes tops," Will said, his lips brushing against my ear as he spoke.

I pulled out my cell phone to check the time— 8:03pm— and grinned. "It's on."

"Dude, Will smiling is still so weird," Vanessa said, her eyes wide when she spotted the small smile on Will's face. "Will, if I hug you, are you going to kill me? I mean, since you're actually a nice guy and all..."

"Touch me and die."

"How come Falarabelle gets to hug you and not die?" Vanessa whined. "That's hardly fair."

"She's my girlfriend. She has rights."

"So? Falarabelle hugs Ty, and you don't see him threatening to kill her."

I pressed myself closer to Will as we squirmed through a particularly tight section of the crowd, laughing along with (almost) everyone else at Vanessa's retort. When Caroline made a comment about comparing apples and oranges, I glanced back at her and Beth, grinning wider now. She had a point.

It didn't take long for her and Beth to warm up to Vanessa and Ty. Of course, at first, they were weirded out when Ty proclaimed them forever more, Madison and Alyssa, but they got used to it. Caroline turned around whenever anyone called out for a Madison now. It was pretty funny.

"Madison, honey," a woman called, proving my point when Caroline craned her neck to see who'd called "her" name, "don't walk too far ahead!"

Caroline sighed. "Darn it, I've got to stop doing that."

"Aw, why?" Beth asked. "It's amusing."

"Jessica!" Ty exclaimed, prying my attention away from Caroline and Beth as they began bantering about what was and wasn't amusing. "You never answered my question. When are the fireworks?"

"Time!" I called out in response. "How many minutes was that, Dyer?"

Will took his phone out of his pocket and checked. "Damn. Three minutes."

"You so owe me five bucks."

Ty twisted around, walking backwards while he scrunched his face at us. "I'm confused," he said.

"Not surprised," Arabelle drawled with a snicker.

"Shut up, Jessica II." Ty huffed. "Now, Jessica, could you please tell me how long it is until the fireworks start?"

"You have about an hour," I replied. "Now, why don't we see how long you can go without asking? If you go until the fireworks start, I'll let you eat some of my peanut butter."

"Shit just got real." Arabelle breathed. "And, once again, why the hell am I Jessica II? You couldn't have just thought of another name?"

"Why would I think of another name?" Ty asked as though the thought was foolish. "Jessica looks like a Jessica. You look exactly like her. So obviously you're Jessica II."

I was tempted to remind him of his response when I first told him Arabelle's name, but he and Arabelle were in a heated debate about his name selection, and I didn't feel like interrupting. So I listened silently and swayed Will's and my hands back and forth as we approached a free spot on the rocks that overlooked the river. Thank God, the spot was free. It was our favorite spot to sit and watch the Fourth of July fireworks.

"This is going to be the first set of fireworks I see in, like, three years," Vanessa told us, excitement laced in her tone as she settled onto one of the rocks. We all followed her lead and dropped to the ground, getting comfortable. I leaned my head on Will's shoulder and watched from the corner of my eye as Arabelle claimed the spot on my other side and Caroline and Beth snagged the next two spaces after her. "Can you believe that?" Vanessa asked. "Three years."

I looked up to find she and Ty on Will's other side, Ty's arm wrapped around Vanessa's waist.

"Me, too, babe!" Ty grinned. "How long has it been since you've seen the fireworks, Will?"

I glanced at Will, truly curious. I had a feeling it'd been longer than three years.

"A long time," he said softly. He frowned. "I think I haven't seen any since I was nine? Maybe younger?"

Everyone, besides Arabelle and me, simultaneously gasped. That wasn't exactly surprising, seeing how she and I were the only ones in our group that knew all the details of his home life. The others had the basic gist, but they didn't know everything.

"What?" Caroline exclaimed, leaning forward so she could see Will's face. "Since you were nine?"

Will shrugged. "Yeah." He glanced at me and smiled. "So I'm looking forward to this."

I squeezed his hand and returned my head to his shoulder. "They're going to be great," I told him. "Right, Care?"

"Definitely," Caroline said. "I freaking love fireworks."

"That's hilarious coming from someone who cried the first time her mom brought her to see them," Beth teased.

"If I recall correctly," Caroline said, "you peed your pants."

Beth gasped. "I did no such thing!"

"You so did," Arabelle replied, backing up Caroline without hesitation. "I remember. You told me while thinking I was Falice."

"What?" Beth cried. "I don't remember…"

"Of course, you don't." Even though I wasn't looking directly at her, I knew Arabelle had a smirk spread across her lips. "I never told you it was really me. The perks of being an identical twin. We were in fourth grade, by the way."

I snorted. "It looks like you were pretending to be me a lot longer than I was pretending to be you."

"Of course!" She paused as someone behind us yelled for their child to slow down. "Dude, you know what we should do?" she asked.

"We should try switching places during classes for a day and see if anyone notices. I've always wanted to do that, but I knew you wouldn't go for it. But now…"

"You think I'd agree?" I finished for her. "Whatever gave you that idea?"

"Oh, I don't know. Maybe agreeing to pretend to be me for the whole summer?"

"Yeah, but we got grounded big time for that, remember?" I countered even though the idea was enticing. I'd be lying if I said it had never occurred to me. It had, but the thought of getting in trouble had always been enough to squash any temptation. But now, I had to say, I was kind of, sort of willing to try— someday anyway. "I think I'm all set for now. You'll have to wait and see."

Arabelle sighed deeply. "Fine. But it has to be a day when I have tests every block."

"Fine. I'll fail them on purpose." "You wouldn't."

"Oh, but I so would."

"No you wouldn't," Ty supplied unhelpfully. "You're too nice." "Come on!" I threw my free hand helplessly into the air. "Will, do you think I'm too nice?"

"Is this a trick question?" Will asked.

I gave him an unimpressed look. "Thank you so much for your help."

"No problem."

I punched him playfully on the shoulder, but otherwise dropped the subject. It was almost immediately forgotten as we moved on to other topics, laughing and joking around while we waited for the fireworks to begin. As time jogged on, I decided that this, as of right now, was the best summer of my life. I had Will, Ty, and Vanessa here with me without the threat of Tiffany punching me in the face or giving me swirlies.

The thought of Tiffany made me realize something. Arabelle's plan changed all of our lives— and for the better.

Wow. If I hadn't gone to Camp Sunshine Brooks for Arabelle, I wouldn't have met three of my best friends. Ty, Will, and Vanessa would be stuck at a camp that none of them belonged in. Arabelle would probably still be in a relationship with an asshole. My dad and Arabelle wouldn't get along the way they did now. It wasn't perfect, but it was a lot better than a year ago.

My corny thoughts were cut off as the fireworks finally began. Ty whooped and hollered, pure elation on his face. His enthusiasm must have been contagious because suddenly we were all cheering as each firework boomed in the sky. Different shapes, different colors. Absolutely beautiful.

"Oh my god, these are amazing!" Ty shouted. "Vanessa, look at that one!"

"I have eyes," Vanessa said. She paused to watch another firework burst. "Holy shit, I forgot how much I love these."

I found myself smiling this ridiculously huge smile and unable to stop for the rest of the show. I'd always loved the fireworks, but this year felt different. More exciting, I guess? I don't know how to describe it.

"Get ready for it!" Beth called. She didn't say so, but I knew she was speaking to Ty. "The finale is coming up."

"Yes!" Ty threw his fists in the air. "Vanessa, babe, I can't possibly sit here while this is going on. Stand and jump with me!"

And then Vanessa and Ty were standing up, jumping, and shouting with glee. The finale hadn't even started yet, but that didn't seem to matter to them. I watched as Vanessa twirled around and pumped her fists as if she was at a rock concert, and then spared a glance behind us, to where the horde of people was located. Some of the people closest to us eyed Vanessa and Ty with amusement, but for the most part everyone was too entrapped by the fireworks to pay us any attention.

"Falarabelle, jump with us!" Vanessa beamed down at me. "You too, guys. Everyone, up off your asses! We're jumpin' for joy!"

Beth and Caroline immediately complied. They hoisted themselves to their feet and joined Vanessa and Ty as the couple bounced and danced like they didn't have a care in the world. Arabelle hesitated only for a moment before muttering something along the lines of "Screw it!" and getting up.

And just like that, Will and I were the only ones left with our butts on the ground. "You wanna get up?" I asked.

For a moment, Will just stared out at the view around us. Then he grinned, stood up, grabbed onto my hands, and lifted me from the ground. "Let's do it," he said.

"Time for sparklers!" Beth squealed as we approached my front porch. It was a little after ten, which was pretty good considering the density of the crowd and the twenty-minute drive required to get from Gardner to Fitchburg. Caroline said it was the stealth in which she drove, but I'm pretty sure she just got lucky. "So excited!"

Beth had always loved sparklers. I liked them too, but my enthusiasm was kind of dampened by the fact that I always managed to burn myself.

"Where are the sparklers anyway?" Caroline asked. "Did your dad leave them out?"

Arabelle nodded. "Yeah, I think he left them on the island. But he's probably holding the matches hostage and won't let us have them until he talks to us about the hazard of playing with fire. So be prepared to get a speech about not setting the lawn on fire."

Beth and Caroline groaned while Vanessa and Ty snickered.

Will and I were at the very back of our group of friends, so no one noticed when he tugged me to a stop. I gave him an inquisitive look but said nothing as the others went inside. "Will?" I asked after the door shut behind them. "Why aren't we going inside?"

My eyes met his, widening slightly when he let go of my hand to rake his fingers through his hair. He let out a long breath of air. "I need to tell you something," he replied.

I stared at him for a long time, analyzing his tone and expression in an attempt to figure out which direction this conversation was heading. However, he made it impossible. His face was blank.

"Is it good news or bad news?" I asked finally, deciding that that would be the most efficient way of getting the answers I wanted.

Will suddenly broke into a huge smile. "It's great news."

For a moment, all I could do was ogle at him. Damn, that smile was gorgeous. And the way it sprang forward, like he couldn't help himself, was just so… remarkable. And then I remembered that I was having a conversation, and I beamed right back at him. "So what's the great news?" I asked.

Will bit his lip, trying to contain himself, but he didn't succeed. Wow, this must have been spectacular news if even Will Dyer couldn't keep a straight face. My mind made some guesses as to what he was about to say, but then his hands were cupping my cheeks and he had my full attention. "My mom called earlier today," he said softly.

Hope poured over me. Could this finally be it? Had she…?

"And?"

"She left Rick." Will paused, like he couldn't quite believe his words. "They had this huge fight, and she finally called the police and is in the process of getting a restraining order. He's in jail, Falice. He can't come anywhere near us again."

Will's hands fell from my cheeks as I leaped up and down, a hand over my mouth to block my ecstatic squeals. "Are you serious?" I shrieked through the block over my mouth. "He's gone? Oh my… oh my god!"

Will nodded.

His confirmation only added to my excitement, making me jump higher and squeal louder. He waited patiently for my energy to run out, not bothering to hide just how exultant this information made him. Eventually my pace slowed, and then I came to a complete stop, a breathless smile perched on my lips. Will returned my grin before he kissed me. When we pulled apart, he rested his forehead against mine. "He's gone," he breathed. "I never have to worry about him killing my mom in her sleep again."

I pulled my head away and brought my hand to his cheek. As I stroked his cheek with my thumb, I murmured, "I can't imagine how happy you are right now."

And I couldn't. Whatever elation I was experiencing could have nowhere reached what Will was feeling right now. This was just so freaking amazing!

"Pretty damn happy to say the least. But I think I'm still in shock," he admitted. "After so many years of his shit... he's gone. It's just hard to comprehend."

Without another word, I brought him into a tight embrace. Will hugged me back with one arm wrapping securely around my back and one hand sifting through my hair. I squeezed him with all the strength I had, even after my arms started to hurt. Rick was out of Will's life for good. The constant worry could end. They were safe. Do you know how hard it was during the school year? Missing Will was only part of it. Knowing he was in the same house with Rick was excruciating; even more so when Rick went on rampages while Will and I were either on the phone or on Skype. And now, I could watch him go back home with the peace of mind that he was returning to a better home life.

"I'm so happy for you," I whispered in his ear. "So damn happy."

"Me, too." Will laughed softly. "I feel like I'm going to wake up any second with him standing over me, drunk as hell."

My grip loosened as I held him out at arm's length and gave him a stern look. "This is not a dream, and he's not coming back. Ever." I paused as my firm gaze fell and my smile returned. "I'm so proud of your mom!"

Will brought a hand through my hair again and gave me another quick kiss on the lips. "I'm proud of her too. I'd given up on the hope that she'd turn him in a long time ago."

"That teaches you," I teased. "Yeah." He nodded. "I guess so."

"Hmm, maybe now, I can actually come visit you," I mused. "Yeah," Will agreed. "Maybe during vacation or something."

My mind was already trying to figure out how to save up money to buy a ticket to Seattle. A job would obviously be required. My allowance would hardly get me the amount of money I needed by the time I wanted to go. At this moment, actually, I had no money, seeing how Arabelle and I were using our allowances to pay for the camp in California. "Sounds like a plan," I said.

We shared another swift kiss before letting our arms fall to our sides. Fingers entwined, we resumed our journey to the house. There was a new bounce in my step as we traveled up the porch steps. Rick was gone. He couldn't hurt Will anymore, couldn't give him anymore scars. There were no words for how amazing those facts were.

Hands down, this was the best news I'd ever received. I was pretty sure nothing would ever top this.

"You're still coming to Camp Falarabelle, right?" I asked even though I knew what his answer would be. Just, you know, had to check and make sure.

Will shot me a look that told me I was stupid for asking him such a ridiculous question. "Duh, Falice."

"You did not just 'duh' me." "I so did."

"You know what? I think maybe you're going to have to sleep outside tonight."

"Sounds fine to me."

I stuck my tongue out at him. "Whatever, Dyer. Let's go do sparklers."

Will chuckled. "Alright."

Together, we walked inside and into the kitchen. It was there that we found the others gathered around the island, sparklers in their hands as they "listened" to my dad drone on and on about fire safety. He probably could have saved himself a lot of trouble by going outside with us, but I wasn't about to question him. So I just "listened" along with everyone else, one hand gripping Will's, and the other twirling a stick of fiery death. No one had noticed that Will and I were late to the speech, and I was quite all right with that. If my dad had noticed, he would've started all over again. Which, for obvious reasons, was something none of us wanted.

Eventually he released us, and we hurried back outside. Arabelle went around lighting up all the sparklers once we were all in the yard, joking around about fire hazards as she did so.

For the first time in years, I wasn't worried at all about being burned as I waved my sparkler around with everyone else. I was in too great a mood to concentrate on that, and besides, it was only a matter of time before the sparkler singed my fingertips.

"Hey, Jess," Ty called.

I turned to him, a grin at the ready. "Hey, Ty."

Ty flashed me a broad smile. "I get some of your peanut butter."

My face fell, and I pouted. "Crap," I said. "I completely forgot about that."

I glanced at Will to find an amused expression on his face. Well, there goes the hope of him helping me get out of this treacherous deal I made. "It's your fault for offering it," he pointed out, obviously having no sympathy for me whatsoever. The traitor.

"I didn't think he'd actually make it!"

"She has a point," Vanessa said, sticking up for me like the amazing friend she was. "I was surprised he made it too."

I huffed, waving my sparkler around with a grimace on my face. "Ugh," I said. "This is depressing."

"You know, sometimes, I wonder if you love your peanut butter more than me," Will joked.

I let out a playful gasp. "How could you ever think that? Of course, I love you more than peanut butter."

"Oh, yeah? Let's play a game of either-or. Me or peanut butter."

I pretended to deliberate on that for a second. "You know, if you loved me, you would never ask me that," I told him, pretending that the faux ultimatum cut me deep. I laughed and shook my head. "Obviously, I would choose peanut butter."

"You totally just contradicted yourself."

"See, this is why I would choose peanut butter. It doesn't talk back. It just lets me eat it."

Will rolled his eyes. "Great. So you want to eat me."

"Says the guy who looked ready to resort to cannibalism on the first day of camp."

"I was practicing my glare. There's a difference."

I gave him a flat look. "And you practiced on me why?"

He shrugged. "You looked nervous."

"You're so mean!" I accused good-humoredly.

From their spots a few feet away, Caroline, Beth, and Arabelle laughed at us like we were the funniest things they'd ever come across. According to them, we were hilarious. Vanessa and Ty joined in too, even giving examples of how comical we were at camp (usually surrounding our "sexual tension"). Of course, that only made the three girls laugh even harder. So hard, in fact, that I actually feared they were going to drop their sparklers and set the lawn on fire.

"They're totally making fun of us right now," I observed blankly. Will nodded. "Yup."

As the laughter faded, Ty tossed me an impish smile. "Hey, Jessica?"

I let out a light sigh, mentally preparing myself for what he had to say. What else had I promised him? I hadn't offered him my soul, had I? "Yeah?"

"How much longer until the fireworks start?"

"Three-hundred-sixty-four days and twenty-three hours," I said without missing a beat. "Think you can make it that long without asking again?"

Ty laughed. "I don't know. I guess we'll have to wait and see."

Will leaned into my side a murmured, "I bet you five bucks he doesn't make it."

"Oh, it's on, Dyer," I said. "It'll be my pleasure to win five more bucks from you."

Not two minutes after the bet began, I lost. "How much longer until the fireworks start?" Ty asked, waving his sparkler around like a maniac.

Well, that bet didn't last long.

"You so owe me five bucks," Will said. I sighed. "I suppose I do."

"Don't worry," Will assured me. "You always have next summer to win it back."

I shoved him playfully, and even though we were now even and owed each other no money at all, I wriggled my eyebrows and said, "It's on, Dyer. On like Donkey Kong."

"Pinky promise?" Will asked jokingly, holding out his pinky. Over the course of our time together, he'd become more comfortable with initiating these legit promises. It was awesome.

I smiled, hooked our fingers together, and shook them. "Pinky promise."

The end.

Can't get enough of Falice? Make sure you sign up for the author's blog to find out more about them!

Get these two bonus chapters and more freebies when you sign up at ashley-winters.awesomeauthors.org!

Here is a sample from another story you may enjoy:

Faking Delinquency 402

Faking Delinquency 404

TWO YEARS LATER

I remember the first time I fell off a swing at a children's play park. While my father had asked if I was okay, my mother had asked what I would do if the situation had been such that I couldn't get up on my own, and they weren't there to help me.

I almost started crying at the thought, but my mother cradled me in her arms and said something I didn't think I'd ever understand.

But now it's a memory I don't think I'll ever forget.

"Sometimes, little people with little personalities in a little world like this one, just like you, trip and fall down, and sometimes, they're too hurt to get up by themselves, but that's okay. You're not weak if you lean on someone else. You're just learning. You know, you need to get up again even if it's not on your own."

Even if it's not on my own.

When Danny and Arabelle broke up, I had to see my sister in a state of uncharacteristic distress, and it was *horrible*, but she knew that she had me.

She had *me*.

"College will be *great*, I'm sure," Will smirked and took my hands in his before placing a soft kiss on my knuckles.

I rolled my eyes and pulled my hands away from his, crossing them over my chest instead. "Just because you don't have to go for two more months, it doesn't mean that you have to make me anxious that I'm leaving *tomorrow*!" I exclaimed, frustrated. The fact that I was leaving for college tomorrow was absolutely nerve-wracking and admittedly, maybe slightly exciting, but Will's stupid comments most certainly weren't helping ease my nerves. I wanted to forget about it for my last night at home, yet all I seemed to be doing was worry!

The idea of leaving my family and friends to start a new life all on my own surfaced my thoughts again, and I couldn't seem to picture anything else. We were all going to different colleges but within the same country except for Caroline, but I doubt we'd be able to meet any time other than summer and winter break, especially with *family*.

"Hey, hey, hey." my boyfriend's voice brought me back to reality as he wiped away the tears I didn't even know were dripping down my cheeks. "Are you okay?"

Stumbling back a bit, I fell onto the little swing in the corner of the park, jumping when it creaked. Since it had been after midnight when Will called and suggested that we meet here, everything was silent and slightly spooky, so the slightest of sound or movement made me uncomfortable.

I placed my head in my hands and felt Will crouch down beside me, rubbing my back with his knuckles.

"Y-yeah, I'm fine," I mumbled, lifting my head and wiping my eyes.

"No, you're not. What's wrong?"

"N-nothing," I tried to say, but it came out as more of a sob as Will pulled me off of the swing and into his arms, both of us now sitting on the damp soil.

"Tell me what's wrong," he said, placing a chaste kiss on my lips to calm me down. "It's okay."

Choking back a sob, I said, "I-I don't think I'm ready."

"For college? Falice, hey," he said softly. Using his fingertips, he lifted my chin, so I was looking straight into his eyes. "You'll be okay. We can always postpone your flight or—."

"No, *no*, it's not college. I'm not ready to— to leave *you*."

When he didn't say a word, I closed my eyes and sighed. I knew that he couldn't do anything about it. We'd both just have to figure it out. We'd have to *deal*.

My eyes snapped open when I felt his arms unwrap themselves around me when I heard slow music playing. I looked up to find Will standing in front of me, the music coming from his phone. He placed it on a park bench near the swing set and increased the volume.

He bent down in front of me, and took my hand, smiling, "May I have this dance?"

Giggling, I wiped my eyes figuring I probably looked like a mess although Will certainly didn't seem to care. Taking his hand, I stood up and wrapped my arms around his neck, leaning my head against his chest.

At that moment, I hoped for one thing… that no matter what, *we'd* be okay.

"Try calling his cellphone."

"It's switched off!"

"Are you fucking kidding me?"

Caroline shoved her phone back into her pocket, no doubt extremely angry. Beth sighed and looked around one more time to see if he had finally shown up.

"He promised to be here almost an *hour* ago," Vanessa growled, her anger obviously being pushed to its limits. Her fists were clenched tightly, and sweat was beading on her forehead as she cursed under her breath. Tyler and Arabelle were trying to calm her down, but clearly, it wasn't working.

And I was standing in the midst of this mess, panicked, not about the fact that my friends and family were agitated, but about the fact that if Will didn't arrive within the next ten minutes, I might not get to say goodbye. And I won't like that.

I won't like it at all.

"Alright, everyone, calm down. He'll be here. He promised. He has to be here," my dad said, almost as if he were trying to reassure himself.

Will and I were doing just fine, I didn't see why he wouldn't come to see me off to college.

"FLIGHT NUMBER 445 TO L.A.X. IS NOW BOARDING," a lady announced, and immediately, passengers started forming a line. I began to hyperventilate, almost sure of the fact that I wouldn't get to see him one last time before I left.

"FLIGHT NUMBER 445 TO L.A.X. IS NOW BOARDING," the lady repeated, waving in my direction. "I REPEAT. FLIGHT NUMBER 445 TO L.A.X. IS NOW BOARDING."

I turned back to my friends and family, frantically searching for some form of assurance. They all looked around, clearly just as panicked as I was, and I turned back, slightly relieved when I noticed that the line of people who were boarding this plane was very long.

Five minutes later and we were still waiting, and I was starting to *really* worry now. Arabelle and dad had left, not before apologizing profusely to me, but I had assured them that it was okay. He had to drive Arabelle to her university campus, and I completely understood. What I didn't understand was why Will wasn't here yet.

"LAST CALL FOR FLIGHT NUMBER 445, DESTINATION L.A.X.," the lady called. My vision was starting to get blurry with tears, and I ignored my friend's calls as I went to stand in the line behind a large family, who were already handing the flight attendant their boarding passes.

"Wait!" An all too familiar male voice called, and I whirled around, the flight attendant asking for my boarding pass.

I can't say how relieved I was to see my boyfriend, albeit soaked due to rain, standing there with a frail rose in hand. In absolutely no time, I was in his arms as he spun me around and held me tight by the waist.

"I'm so sorry," he whispered and kissed my forehead before handing me the rose. "I really wanted to make today special for you, and I was supposed to bring you breakfast and everything, but then I woke up late and started puking, and I'm—."

"It's okay," I reply, smiling at him through tears. "You're here now."

"Ma'am, please—."

I spun around. My attention was drawn to the seemingly impatient flight attendant whose hand was extended out to take my boarding pass from me.

"Just give me one second," I pleaded, and she nodded although reluctantly. Turning back around, I wrapped my arms tightly around Will's figure and placed a feathery kiss on his neck. Looking over his shoulder, I saw all our friends smiling and looking relieved, which made me smile even wider. But then I realized it was time to go.

"I-I've gotta say goodbye now." I bit my lip. *But he had just gotten here*, I told myself. *Why did I have to go?*

"No, not yet," he grinned, and I raised an eyebrow in confusion.

And then I saw his boarding pass and his suitcase.

In a state of utter elation, I threw my arms around his waist. Our friends cheered in the background, and I figured that they were into Will's surprise all along.

But who cares?

So long as we were happy.

I would tell you that all endings are like this, but then I'd be lying.

More often than not, they aren't.

But whatever it is, make the most out of it.
Make it okay.
Even if people tell you, it won't be; and,
Even if you have to do it on your own.

Acknowledgements

First off, a huge thank you to God, who has made all of this possible.

Thank you, Mom, Kayla, Mimi, Tasha, Chip, Cameron, Shannon, Grandpa Libby and Grandma Libby for all of your love and support. I love you all lots! And, Mimi, it's all because of the flashcards!

Thank you, Glenn Ellison, for answering my questions about your summer behavioral camp program and consequently helping me shape the world around my characters. Your answers really helped me, so thank you!

A thank you to my agents throughout the process, Lean and Anna! You two are so sweet and helpful, and thank you so much for your help making this process seem a little easier.

Thank you, Ven, Anfie, and AJ for your hands in editing the manuscript! Without you, this probably would've been published with a bunch of typos (which is pretty much my worst nightmare). So, thank you!

A round of "thank you" to all of my friends, who have stuck with me all these years and supported me.

Thank you, Amber, Brooklyn, and Lex-C for always being there for me! Thank you, Ray, Trish, Valarie, Noelle, Jeni, and Marije for supporting and helping me with my writing! All of you are amazing, and I honestly don't know what I'd do without any of you.

Another thank you to Amber and Lex-C for helping me with the cover! Amber, you were a great model, and Lex-C, you took amazing pictures! I had a lot of fun, and I really appreciate you guys giving me a hand (and some great, meme-worthy pictures).

Finally, thank you to everyone who decides this book is worth reading! Your support means the world to me, and I seriously appreciate you taking the time out of your days to read my work.

Thank you all so much!

Love it or hate it, let me know!

Leave a review on Amazon or Goodreads!

About the Author

Ashley Winters, eighteen, is currently attending the University of Maine at Farmington and majoring in creative writing. Most of her time is spent writing or thinking about writing, and the rest is spent reading or fangirl-ing about people who don't actually exist. She loves God, her family, her friends, many, many fictional people, and pretty much anyone who makes a pun.

Printed in Great Britain
by Amazon